Goat Song

THOMAS DRAGO

All characters in this story are fictitious. Any resemblance to actual persons, living or dead, is unintentional, except where noted.

GOAT SONG

Cover design by Kanaxa, photo by Shutterstock

ISBN: 978-0578637969
Library of Congress Control Number: 2020901232
Published by Gold Avenue Press
Chapel Hill, North Carolina

This is for my mom, Linda Drago, my first editor and fan since I was thirteen and all I wanted to do was write like Stephen King.

"My mother was of the sky. My father was of the earth. But I am of the universe, and you know what it's worth."

—John Lennon, "Yer Blues"

"What we do is beautiful but fleeting. It doesn't grow old in museums and churches. It lives for *now*. For this moment only. And *this* is your moment."

—Thomas Leroy, *Black Swan*

"*You're* the one who doesn't exist. You're doing this because you're scared to death, like the rest of us, that you don't matter. And you know what? You're right. *You* don't. You're not important. Get used to it."

—Sam Thomson, *Birdman or (The Unexpected Virtue of Ignorance)*

"Leave me outside my address far away from this masquerade."

—Leo Sayer, "The Show Must Go On"

Setting

Crow Creek, modern day, with short excursions to Queensboro.

The Players

Brad Gleason, Sheriff of Crow Creek
Curly, deputy
Katie, deputy
Austin, deputy
Fire Chief Riddle
Becky Stokes, *Sentinel* editor
Her camera operator
Wanda Butler, librarian
Helms, her son
Clark Gufney, Food Castle cashier
Dante Rose, rock star
Pastor Aken of First Baptist
His receptionist
Waylon Osbourne, Sheriff of Queensboro
Deborah DeVito, bakery owner
Darrell Mebane, truck driver
Frank Edwards, linehaul driver from Winter
Miriam, Entech laboratory assistant
An Entech receptionist
Dr. Bob Cody, medical examiner

Orpheum Production Staff

James Patterson, producer
Ellie Miles, artistic director
Lynn Mayfield, production manager
Deidre Worth, finance officer
Meribel Sanchez, house manager
Gabriela Rossi, stage manager
Tommy Nolan, assistant stage manager
Joe Cox, technical director
Doug Cousins, head carpenter
Travis “King” Boggs, master electrician
Deanna Flowers, props mistress
Sara Cooper, props assistant
Terese Weber, costumer
Anika Vanhook, wardrobe assistant
Sania Cortez, lightboard operator
Cherlynne Lawrence, soundboard operator
Connor Simmons, run crew
Amanda, his sister
Anna Hernandez, box office volunteer
Heather Danby, former stage manager
Ralph Delacourt, late house manager
Peggy, his sister

Bury Me in Autumn Cast

Matt Leath, director
Paula Bradley, assistant director
Tariq Lucas, performer
Cedric Young, performer
Courtney Williams, performer
Ed Brown, performer
Bianca Whitt, performer

Act I

Deep Calls to Deep

scene 1.

We all have our own demons.

"The fuck you know about stage managing?"

Sara Cooper, for instance.

Gabriela purses her lips, remembering what *Mamma* taught her in Italian. *Sometimes people speak because they have tongues in their mouths.*

"I've been here for eight months," she says.

"Yeah, as a fucking ASM." Sara tugs her nose stud. A worn leather belt divides the space where a black crew shirt untucks from her jeans. "I've been here almost two years."

The demon Gabriela sketches on the last page of her promptbook looks like a goat. Black horns curl behind the ears, shaded light gray. The soulless eyes reflect dying embers of hellfire. Thick fur sweeps in tangled lines across the white page.

"In props."

"So?"

Gabriela remembers something else *Mamma* taught her that translates a little easier. *Kill them with kindness.* "And you do an amazing job with that."

"Fuck you, Gabriela."

"Please." Gabriela removes her headset and places it beside the open promptbook on the stage manager's desk.

"*Please* what?" Sara arches her unibrow. "Where did you even fucking come from?"

Gabriela rolls her eyes. "You have no reason to be upset."

"Are you serious?"

"What do you mean?" Gabriela adds gray ears to her sketch. The points form hollow tubes like a Madonna lily about to flower.

"They look over me for a second time in as many months, and you wanna know why I'm upset?"

Gabriela flicks her pencil against the railing above the steps to the orchestra pit. "But at least the last time it was in props."

"The fuck does that matter?"

"I'm not the props mistress."

"And?"

"You're not an ASM."

Gabriela can't spell this out any clearer. It's not unheard of for regional theatres to shift crew positions during a run but only when there aren't any direct subordinates. If anyone should be pissed, it's Tommy Nolan. Tommy's been with the Holt Players working ASM at the Orpheum for longer than Gabriela's been in Crow Creek.

Some people are born to be assistants.

Did Mamma *tell me that?*

"Fine." Sara squeezes a pack of cigarettes in her fist and grits her teeth. "I'm going on break. Be back in ten."

"Take your time," Gabriela says. "Props aren't called till seven."

"Thank you seven."

Sara doesn't look over her shoulder when she storms out the backdoor. Gabriela scoots under her desk and examines the sketch. The demon wears Sara's face and grins. Gabriela twists the *cornicello* dangling below her neck. The one *Mamma* gave her the last Christmas they spent together. Her eyes glisten. She flips the page so the sketch disappears. She tries to focus on the script but can't. The cues blur.

"Can't read her handwriting?"

Gabriela shakes her head. *"Eh?"*

James Patterson stands in front of the flyrail, his bald head reflecting worklights. His satin dress shirt a little too tight, especially around the collar where the button pinches his papery skin. He straightens his necktie and half-grins as if noticing where Gabriela stares. It's rare for the producer to make a backstage appearance, so Gabriela stands.

"No, please," Mr. Patterson says. "I don't mean to interrupt. I know it's a big day for you."

Gabriela manages a smile. "Kind of."

Mr. Patterson waves her off and steps to her desk in long strides. His open sports coat ripples as the air conditioner hums to life.

"You'll do fine," he says. "We don't open for three nights. I wouldn't have asked you to step in on such short notice if I didn't have confidence in you."

"Grazie," Gabriela says and realizes she's been clasping the tiny red horn in her fingers the entire time. She relaxes her hand and lets the charm settle on her chest where it belongs.

"Besides, I'm not here tonight because Heather left."

"Oh?"

"No, of course not. Not at all. You know her job as well as anybody else. As well as she did, really. We all knew it wouldn't take her long to get that job she's been chasing up in Boston."

Gabriela swallows. "True."

"I always believed she settled for this place, to be honest."

"Yeah?"

"Yeah." Mr. Patterson clears his throat. "That's one of the many things I admire about you, Gabriela. You don't settle."

"Don't I?"

"Not at all. You conquer." Mr. Patterson chuckles. "There's a huge difference."

"That's very kind." Gabriela bites her lip. The hidden demon sketch bleats with laughter that bounces off the backstage walls. "I think."

"Anyhow, don't let me keep you." Mr. Patterson strokes his pointy chin. "You seen Meribel?"

"Meribel?"

"Mmm."

"Did you check the front of house?"

"Yeah, just came from there. I need to drop off the comps we're expecting for Friday. Some friends from Raleigh Regional. Possible donors more like it."

"Buono."

"There's even talk of a partnership with a few smaller venues like ours. Might be worth entertaining." Mr. Patterson checks the time on his mobile. "I'll give Meribel another minute. The house doesn't open for an hour."

"Sounds good," Gabriela says.

"I can't believe how fast advance tickets have been selling for this show. And I don't mean just online. The walk-ups have been crazy. Unusual for this day and age."

"Glad we got the license."

Local editor Becky Stokes arranged for a press conference when the Holt Players announced *Bury Me in Autumn* as part of their upcoming season last spring and followed with a feature article in the *Sentinel*. She always seems to be around the Orpheum whether or not there's breaking news. Funny how the media in America takes itself so seriously, even in meaningless towns like Crow Creek.

"Got that right," Mr. Patterson says. "Especially so soon after the Lucille Lortels."

At the cast party at Heather's house during the awards program in May, Gabriela sipped ice water with a slice of orange. Heather drank Manhattans and raved about the inside tip she'd gotten that the Huntington Theatre in Boston expects to have an opening for a managing director later this year. Later is now.

"What was it, outstanding play and outstanding director?" Gabriela says.

"And don't forget outstanding lead actor."

"Oh, right."

Mr. Patterson checks his mobile again. "Odd their producer shut down so soon after, but regionals were where this baby was born and regionals are where it will die."

Gabriela slides the promptbook closer. More demon laughs within. "Let's hope not, sir."

"Well, don't let me hold you." Mr. Patterson exhales. "You tell me if you need anything, you hear? Otherwise, break a leg."

"I will." Gabriela smiles. *"Grazie."*

Mr. Patterson takes a few steps toward the proscenium and halts abruptly behind a drape. "You know where that expression comes from?"

"How's that?"

"Break a leg." Mr. Patterson glances up at the gridiron where stage lights dangle on iron clamps. "They say that in Italian theatre?"

"Something close, yes."

In bocca al lupo. Into the wolf's mouth. At least we don't say *merde* like the French.

"So, you do know then?"

Gabriela shrugs. "Tell me."

"During vaudeville, the performers only got paid if they made an entrance." Mr. Patterson shakes the nearest curtain. It's narrow and black. "If they stayed in the wings, they didn't break the legs, so they didn't get paid."

"Makes sense," Gabriela says. "But that doesn't matter to me."

"No?"

"Nope." Gabriela's face warms. "I never break the legs, sir, and I always get paid."

Mr. Patterson claps his hands. "Good answer, Miss Rossi. How do you say? *Molto bene?*"

"That's right."

"*Molto bene* and *bravo.*"

Mr. Patterson disappears in front of the drapes. His footsteps rattle as he trots across the fourth wall and into the house. Gabriela flips the promptbook to the first page (avoids her taunting demon) and traces her finger along Heather's scrawl. All very basic to start: house lights full, stage warmers half, house to half, stage warmers out, pre-show address go, house out, curtain out, warn first lights, first lights go.

The air conditioner clicks as it shuts off. Gabriela lifts her face. A hunched shadow crosses upstage, crooked neck extending so the ears look like horns.

"Hello?" she says.

The shadow pauses, rearing its skull, before moving off the far side.

Gabriela stands. "Somebody back there?"

A door creaks stage right. Possibly on set. Maybe the props closet. Backstage is dark. Not because the worklights aren't on. They are. Not because Gabriela can't see the call posts tacked on the backdoor or the graffiti scrawled on the walls beside the audio cabinet. She can. It's dark because it wants to be. How an old man always snores on the *Frecciarossa* from Turin to Milan. He doesn't know how not to. Neither does backstage.

"Sara?"

Floorboards moan. More footsteps. A chair drags. Maybe something heavier.

"Fanculo."

Gabriela shakes her head and crosses to the flyrail. She heaves the first lineset to clear the master curtain and moves slowly up the arbors, pulling each rope until the rags and lights sway above the scenery. A source four lighting instrument flickers to life in the catwalks, casting a bright narrow beam right of center.

"Hello?" Gabriela cups her palm across her forehead and squints as she looks toward the light. "Anybody up there?"

The lamp goes out. A flutter of wings fills the empty space.

"The fuck?" Gabriela sighs. "We need some fucking LEDs in this shithole."

Another lesson from *Mamma* stings Gabriela in the dimness backstage. *Ogni uccello il proprio nido è bello.* Roughly: Every bird loves her nest.

A door slams stage right. Not offstage. Onstage. The front door to the living room. Gabriela crosses the box set, avoiding the sofa and two armchairs spiked with yellow tape.

"Who's back there?"

The air conditioner switches to life in the rafters, carrying the stench of rotten fruit that Gabriela has smelled only once before.

Papà.

A shadow hovers in the wings beyond the half lite. More than a shadow now. A silhouette.

"*Scusi.* May I help you?"

Gabriela reaches for the doorknob, fingers trembling. She turns. The metal is cold to the touch. The door creaks on painted hinges as she opens and crosses the threshold.

"Sara?" Gabriela's heart pounds. "That you?"

The wings are quiet. Backstage remains untouched. No props out of place. No furniture moved. No shadows rippling.

"The fuck?"

Gabriela pivots upstage and faces the back wall. An elderly man stands in the darkness beside the disabled buffet the run crew set aside for repairs before tonight's rehearsal. Only he's not elderly. He's bent and shriveled but not old. Spoiled flesh sags on his face in tinted wrinkles. His frail body swims in a black suit, dusty and torn. A thick scar as wide and braided as a flyrail rope circles his neck.

"Beware the wolf's mouth," the apparition says. A maggot wriggles under his bloated cheek.

Gabriela fights the surge of vomit creeping into her throat and pinches the bridge of her nose. *"Eh?"*

"He rises in the wolf's mouth."

A scream from the house startles Gabriela. She whips toward the front of the stage, head swimming. Meribel flails her flabby arms by the auditorium doors.

"Help!"

"Meribel?"

"Miss Rossi, *please*."

Gabriela trots to the stage apron.

"Meribel, what's wrong?"

Meribel screams again. Her words form incoherent sobs as she collapses behind a row of seats. Gabriela glances upstage, but the ghastly visitor has vanished. Deep calls to deep, *Mamma* would tell her. But in Italian. *Da colpa nasce colpa.* Deep calls to deep. So many thoughts of *Mamma* this afternoon. Too many.

And he's not old. The rotting man's not old.

That, as she leaps off the pit cover and into the auditorium.

(the dead man's not old)

The fuck?

(the dead man the dead man the dead man)

Gabriela races up the house stairs and finds Meribel crouched over a lifeless James Patterson. A gaping hole gushes blood in the center of his chest. Vomit claws at Gabriela's throat again, but this time lurches into her mouth as Meribel heaves over the back of a chair, bathing the midhouse console with steaming cheese.

Gabriela swallows and wraps her arm around the rhinestone studs lining Meribel's shoulders.

"Here," she says. "Let's get you into the lobby."

"Thank you, Miss Rossi."

A light flickers in the catwalk, strikes the stage with a sharp beam, and puffs out.

Gabriela rubs her *cornicello*.

scene 2.

Sheriff Brad Gleason looks like a Hollywood movie star. Or like he plays the one in that hit Netflix series about ancient deities and mindflayers. The one that's been all the rage these past few years, making celebrities out of kids forced to skip their childhoods long before they're old enough to know how to live their lives. Wearing his tan uniform (gunbelt loose off a cocked hip), the sheriff's probably the nicest and kindest-looking man in Crow Creek. At least of all the men Gabriela's seen. And she's seen plenty. Crow Creek's small. A lot smaller than Pittsburgh, where she first found work after moving to America. More like *Châtillon* in Northern Italy where she grew up. The small town that the sheriff asks her about as Gabriela gets lost in his bright eyes and forgets laughing demons and the dead body in the theatre. The dead body and the dead man. The dead man with the rotting flesh and twisted scar around his neck.

Beware the wolf's mouth.

(he rises in the wolf's mouth)

"The Alps?" Brad says. "I didn't even know the Alps were in Italy. Always makes me think of the Swiss. But I ain't really that dumb."

Gabriela's legs stick to the faux leather cushions of the lobby bench where she sits beside Sara. Sara reeks of cigarettes. The snake tattoo on her forearm glistens as she flexes the pack in her grip.

"Of course not," Gabriela says. "It's a common mistake."

Brad sweeps blonde hair off his forehead with thick fingers. "Which town did you say?"

"You heard of the Matterhorn?"

"The ride at DisneyWorld?"

Gabriela chuckles. "Not quite."

Sara coughs. "She means the real mountain, Sheriff. The one in Italy."

"*Sì,* there," Gabriela says as she unfolds both palms.

"Oh." Brad dabs the tip of a pencil against his tongue, wriggling his bushy mustache, before jotting down a few notes on a yellow pad.

"And Disney World doesn't have the Matterhorn," Sara says. "Disney*land* does. The ride's more like Everest at Disney World."

"Oh, right." Brad scratches with his pencil again. "Sorry."

"No problem," Gabriela says.

"And you've been working here how long?"

Gabriela glances at Sara, who scoots away. "Eight months."

"You said Mr. Patterson talked with you backstage before Meribel found him?"

"Yessir."

"About?"

"Not much, really."

"Can you try and remember? Anything he said that might seem important?"

"Not really, no." Gabriela bites her lip. "He said he wanted to tell Meribel about some comps he had for Friday night."

"Comps?"

"Free tickets for guests he was expecting."

"No, I know what comps are." Brad chuckles and glances at Sara. "See? Told you I wasn't so dumb."

Sara rolls her eyes. "Yeah."

"I meant, who were the comps for? Did he say?"

"Not exactly."

"How do you mean?"

"Only that he'd invited sponsors from Raleigh Regional. It didn't seem like a big deal."

"No." Brad flips through his pad. "No, it doesn't."

"Potential investors, probably."

"Probably so."

"Maybe a merger or something. I'm not sure."

Brad twirls his sheriff's hat. "Yeah."

"How much longer is this gonna take, Sheriff?" Sara nibbles a fingernail already gnawed to the quick. "I got a seven o'clock call."

"We can take a break now," Brad says. "If you need to take a call."

"No," Sara says. "That's backstage talk for when my job starts. I have to be on the clock by seven. The cast will be here by seven-thirty. We're doing a full dress tonight."

"Oh." Brad leans back in the lobby chair and stretches, rippling his muscular arms and chest. "I don't think you'll be making any calls tonight then. We'll need to shut down the theatre while we continue our investigation."

Sara's eyes widen. "But we open in three nights."

"Should be good to go by tomorrow."

On cue, a chubby medical examiner, peeling off vinyl gloves, enters from the auditorium. He adjusts thick glasses on the bridge of his nose. "About wrapped up, Sheriff. Gonna send in for removal. They'll have the whole place cleaned up before long."

Removal. That's what they do with dead bodies. They remove them.

"Appreciate it."

"Damn shame, though."

"Tell you what." Brad stands. "About the nicest guy you'll ever meet. Give his last slice of bread to anyone with two loaves under their arm."

"And how."

Brad puts on his hat and tips it. "I'll catch up with you."

"Expect so." The medical examiner hustles across the lobby and exits the theatre while nodding to a nearby paramedic.

Gabriela's stomach tightens as Brad sits on the edge of his seat across from her.

"Where were we?" he says.

"You were about to ask Gabriela out on a date," Sara says.

Gabriela drops her jaw. "Sara!"

"Just saying. Shana ain't been in the ground, what is it, six months?"

Brad clears his throat. "Almost two years now."

"Still, she's about half your age. Ain't that right, Gabriela?"

(the dead man's not old)

Gabriela clenches her teeth and puffs her chest. *"Porca puttana."*

Fucking whore.

Sara ignores her. "You two talking up like you're courting. Meanwhile, we got a dead body in our theatre. A dead fucking body that happens to be our producer. James fucking Patterson, can you believe it? Maybe he skipped over me a time or two, but that's some serious shit, ain't it? You two going at it like you're getting coffee at Starbucks."

Brad narrows his eyes. "Skipped over you?"

"Yeah, you know?" Sara crosses one thick leg over another.

"Not exactly."

"For a promotion."

"Promotion?" Brad says.

"Yeah, a promotion." Sara paints Gabriela with shifting eyes. "You heard me."

Brad eases back. "Tell me."

"Look, we don't need to go down that path, okay?"

"I'm thinking maybe we do."

"What?" Sara stands, lifting to the toes of her steel boots and crumpling her cigarettes in her fist. "You think I'm some kinda murderer or something? Is that what you're thinking? Are you really that dumb, Sheriff, or are you still fucking with me?"

"Now, Sara, there's no reason to get upset." Brad tucks away his pad and pencil. "Just covering all the bases. And, for the record, I don't think you're a murderer, no. Heck, if you were gonna kill somebody, everybody in Crow Creek knows you wouldn't try and hide it."

Sara sits, folding her arms. "Thank you, Sheriff."

"Good." Brad tilts his hat so his blue eyes glisten under the brim. "Let's all stay civil now. This is just routine. I gotta ask my questions so I can clear y'all and get on with the real investigation. We good?"

Sara sighs. "Yeah, we're good."

"Miss Rossi?'

Gabriela jumps when Brad says her name.

(he's bent and shriveled but not old)

"Miss Rossi?"

"*Eh? Sì,* of course."

"Good." Brad flips through his notes again. "So, he visits you backstage. Visits with Gabriela. Five, maybe ten minutes. He's here looking for Meribel so he can get some comps for the Friday show. You're at your desk. Gabriela is. Sara, you're out back in, what did you call it, the scene shop?"

"Uh-huh." Sara picks her teeth. "Fixing to do some repairs on a buffet. Waiting for the head carpenter."

"This head carpenter." Brad scans a page. "This head carpenter, Doug Cousins. Doug wasn't with you at the time?"

"Nuh-uh. Not yet. He's here now, though. At the loading dock last I saw. About to make the repairs himself, unless you shut that down."

Brad nods. "Curly ran everybody outside while we taped off the crime scene."

"He's probably gone home then."

"Was there anybody else backstage at the time?"

Gabriela squeals, covering her mouth.

Brad lifts his eyes. "Miss Rossi?"

"Eh?"

"You okay?"

"Eh?"

"Somebody else back there with you I don't know about?"

"Back there?"

"Uh-huh," Brad says.

Gabriela's fingers find her *cornicello*. The dead man couldn't be real. Ghosts aren't real. It was probably her mind playing tricks on her. *Mamma* has an old saying about that, too. She's said so dozens of times. Said something about how you can't always believe what you see. Or what you hear. Not even ghosts backstage. All theatres have their own ghost stories, but they're never real. There's no such thing as ghosts or spirits or zombies or dead men walking and talking. Best to forget him. Forget his rotting eyes.

Gabriela shakes her head. "No."

"What do you mean, no?" Sara elbows her.

"Che chosa?"

"Terese was back in wardrobe. Terese and Anika."

"They still here?" Brad says.

"You tell me, Sheriff," Sara says. "Ain't your deputy sending everybody home?"

Brad scratches his chin. "Probably so."

"It's where I'd be right now if I hadn't come running into the house like I did as soon as I heard Meribel screaming her lungs out. Or hitching a ride on the next ambulance to the hospital like she did. Or *that*."

"You didn't find Mr. Patterson," Gabriela says.

"No, but I seen him," Sara says.

Brad silences a squawk on his radio. "You need medical attention, Miss Cooper?"

Sara grunts. "Either way, I'd be out of here."

"I'll follow up," Brad says. "Go on."

"Terese and Anika were back in wardrobe, like I said. I was by myself in the scene shop, but Connor was here. So was Deidre."

"Connor?" Brad scribbles on his pad. "Deidre?"

"Uh-huh."

"Who are they exactly?"

Sara bites her lip. "Well, go on, Gabriela. You're the stage manager now, ain't you? Don't you think you're the one who should be telling the sheriff who was here before calls and who wasn't? Ain't that your job? Or maybe this is all too much for you."

Gabriela clears her throat. "Yeah. I mean, no."

"Miss Rossi?" Brad says.

"Yes, it's my job. I know who was here." Gabriela glances at Sara. "But no, it's not too much for me. I'm just a little bit upset, you know. Like Meribel. Because of Mr. Patterson — he was bleeding."

"I understand," Brad says.

Sara groans. "Whatever."

"Connor. Connor Simmons," Gabriela says. "He's stage crew. But he's a lifer. He lives in this space. Almost as much as Tommy does. Tommy's an ASM, but I haven't seen him yet today."

"ASM?" Brad says.

"Assistant stage manager."

"Oh, right."

"Deidre works in administration with Mr. Patterson. She's our business manager. Sometimes she stocks concessions so we don't have to bother the volunteers. That's where I believe she was. Taking inventory for opening weekend. Nobody was backstage but me, though. And Meribel was in front of the house. The auditorium was empty. I'm sure of it."

"Except for Mr. Patterson," Brad says.

"Yes, he cut through the stage to go to the lobby."

Sara snorts. "Guess he never made it."

"No," Brad says. "Guess not."

"But nobody else was here," Gabriela says.

"Perhaps," Brad says. "Or not that you seen, anyhow."

Gabriela sinks on the bench. *"Sì."*

"Tell me, though." Brad stares at Sara. "Did anyone have any problems with Mr. Patterson that y'all know of? Present company excluded, of course."

Sara folds her arms. "Of course."

"How about this Tommy? The ASM you mentioned. He have any issues?"

Gabriela shakes her head. "No."

Sara flaps her lips. Sour breath warms Gabriela's cheek and burns her nostrils.

"Well, then." Brad stands and removes his hat. "Think I'm about done here for now. I'll need a list of everyone involved in the show regardless of whether or not you seen them here this afternoon. I'll need to verify their whereabouts."

"I can do that," Gabriela says.

"It can wait till tomorrow, though. I'll drop by before lunch. Make sure y'all are good to rehearse. How's eleven sound?"

(thank you eleven)

"Good, yes," Gabriela says.

"See you then."

Brad wanders through the double doors of the auditorium as two paramedics wheel Mr. Patterson's covered body across the lobby and outside.

Sara stands over Gabriela, wagging her finger. "What was that?"

"What?"

"When the sheriff asked about Tommy. What the hell was that?"

"What do you mean?"

"Why didn't you say anything about Tommy not getting the promotion?"

"Because I'm not about to place the blame on him or accuse anyone else." Gabriela stands, eyes slightly below Sara's. "And you better watch where you're shaking that finger. *Capisci?*"

Sara steps back and crosses her arms. "That so?"

"That's so."

"Or what? You gonna go all Italian on me with that phony accent of yours?"

"Phony?"

"You really know how to pour it on, don't you?"

"What are you talking about?"

"I seen the looks you gave the sheriff." Sara's eyes flutter. "Look at me, Sheriff. I'm so beautiful with my long dark hair and silky skin. You ain't fucked nobody like me before."

"Faccia da culo." Gabriela clenches her fists. "Quit it!"

"Gonna call your godfather to fix this?"

Curly enters the lobby from the auditorium, popping gum between thin lips.

"Funny," Gabriela says.

The lanky deputy crosses toward them. Unlike Brad, Curly wears gray cargo pants and a black tactical shirt, gunbelt cinched around his hip. Wavy hair spills out from under the matching cap.

"All clear backstage," he says. "If there's anything either of y'all need, I'm happy to walk with you. Still can't go back there on your own, though. Shouldn't be much longer."

"I'm parked out back." Sara twirls a set of keys on her ring finger. "I'll take the long way around, if y'all don't mind."

"Understood."

"Goodnight," Gabriela says, forcing a smile.

Sara returns the half-grin and leaves through the front doors.

"Miss Rossi?" Curly gestures with a sweep of his palm. "After you."

"Thank you."

Gabriela enters the auditorium. The last few rows of seats are taped off. The rough outline of James Patterson is spiked on the carpeted floor like stage furniture. The blood and vomit still haven't been cleaned.

But at least he's gone. At least *he* is.

"You okay, Miss Rossi?" Curly says as they approach the stage. "Look a bit pale. Like you seen a ghost."

(beware beware beware)

"I'm okay."

"Nothing to be ashamed of. Many folks lose more than their color when they seen what you did."

"Really, I'm fine." Gabriela wipes sweat off her forehead with the back of her hand. "Need to grab a few things."

"Of course."

Gabriela collects the promptbook off the stage manager's desk so she can study it tonight, closing the binder quickly to avoid the demon's stare as the pages flutter. She really needs to remove that sketch and run it through the shredder in the business office. Send the grinning demon right back where it came from. She heads to the break-room where the sheriff sits at the table beside Connor Simmons and takes notes. Connor runs his mouth about counterweights in a heavy drawl that makes Gabriela snicker.

When Brad winks, she dips her eyes. She grabs her purse from her locker and thanks Curly for the escort. He tips his hat and holds the back door for her as she heads out to the parking lot. A fast food wrapper rustles by the garbage bin and carries whispers of a dead man's voice that Gabriela ignores as she hops into her car.

Beware the wolf's mouth. He rises in the wolf's mouth.

Dark clouds of a late summer storm grow in her rearview mirror, echoing the sentiment as she drives home. She hustles up the steps and enters her apartment, kicking off her shoes by the front door. She tosses her keys on the kitchen table and grabs milk from the refrigerator before checking the pantry for a quick snack. She comes out empty-handed. Rehearsals haven't given her much time to do any shopping this past week. She taps her mobile so she can call *Mamma* but changes her mind. *Mamma* will pick up the cues that she's upset. What's the point in worrying her when she's thousands of miles away and can't help?

Gabriela snatches her laptop off the breakfast counter and hops on the sofa in the living room. She props her feet on the coffee table and opens Chrome. Lightning crackles outside. Rain patters on the windows. Maybe the storm will skirt to the west and miss Crow Creek. Lash Queensboro instead. She googles Orpheum Theatre. Upcoming events in Memphis, Los Angeles, and Boston dominate the results. She scrolls through three more pages and gets listings for every other major city but not Crow Creek. She narrows her search and finds the local website. The pages are easy to navigate. She only cares about their archives. The articles and photos go back until 2007. Not even fifteen years. Not long enough to find what she's looking for. *Who* she's looking for. Not even close. The ghost would be from an earlier era. If he's real.

Gabriela searches for Orpheum Theatre deaths. She gets eight hundred thousand results, the first few connected to Memphis, Los Angeles, and Boston. The next pages reveal deaths in other major American cities but nothing in Crow Creek.

Exhausted, she googles Orpheus and reads about the Ancient Greek singer whose wife Eurydice was fatally bitten by a viper while escaping the satyr that tried to rape her. Orpheus negotiated with Hades for his wife's conditional release from the underworld but stranded her when he wasn't able to uphold his end of the bargain. He looked back for her as he exited the land of the dead and lost her forever. Orpheus eventually died at the hands of Dionysus when the demigod ordered his carnal maidens, the Maenads, to slaughter Orpheus for being an infidel.

When Gabriela can no longer fight sleep on the sofa, she undresses and stumbles to bed, happy she forgot the promptbook in her car where the demon sketch can't taunt her. The storm wanes in the distance as she drifts into her dreamscape.

scene 3.

At ten o'clock the next morning, Gabriela parks downtown in front of DeVito's Bakery. As soon as she enters, Deborah pokes her head up from behind a glass display case and smiles.

"Gaby? *Buongiorno.* How are you, *mio dolce?*"

"Buongiorno, cugina."

"So nice to see you." Deborah engulfs her in a tight hug.

Gabriela gasps for air. "Nice to see you."

"You're early today." Deborah pulls back, squeezing Gabriela's shoulders. "What's wrong?"

Gabriela shakes her head. "Nothing."

"Gaby."

"Niente."

"Are you eating?" Deborah pinches her cheek. "You look thin."

A few customers drink coffee and eat pastries, holding polite conversations over checkered tablecloths. The walls, decorated with colorful Italy maps and grainy photos of old women wearing aprons, shroud the dining room like scenery in a box set. Through wide front windows, morning sunshine casts long shadows across the tiled floor.

"Can we talk somewhere?" Gabriela says.

Deborah claps both hands together, spraying a fine mist of flour into her graying black hair. "Talk?"

"Sì."

Whispering, Deborah narrows her eyes. "What's wrong?"

"I'm so glad I found you," Gabriela answers in Italian so nobody else understands. She sits by the *espresso* machine, eyes swelling.

"Oh, Gaby."

"I don't fit in here."

"Don't say that, *mio caro*."

"It's true." Gabriela sniffs. "Nobody likes me at the theatre."

"What makes you say that?"

"They're upset about my promotion."

Deborah waves her hand. "They'll get over it."

"I don't think they will."

"But I thought you liked it here?"

"Not as much as I hoped I would."

"Oh, honey." Deborah wraps a bundle of *pizzelles* in plastic. "Give it time."

Gabriela sighs. "I miss *Mamma*."

"I know. I miss my Tony. Our son Anthony, too. That's why God brought you and I together."

A customer peeps above a *cannoli*. Deborah removes a wet towel from the back of a chair and slides beside Gabriela, taking her hands. Gabriela stifles a sob.

"If only I could save enough money to send for her," she says.

"You know I'll help."

"No." Gabriela sniffs. "I can't ask you to do that."

"Gaby, please."

Gabriela chuckles. "*Mamma* would kill me."

"She'd never know." Deborah wipes a stray hair out of Gabriela's eyes.

"*Mamma* always knows," Gabriela says.

Speaking English again, Deborah pulls away. "Here, let me get you something to eat. Some cookies at least."

Gabriela catches her hand.

"Aspetta," she says. "There's more."

"More?"

"Sì."

Deborah sighs. "Tell me."

"Our producer died yesterday."

"Producer?"

"Yes, Mr. Patterson."

"James Patterson?"

Gabriela nods.

"*Gesù,* what happened?" Deborah asks.

"We found him in the theatre."

"Gaby, I'm so sorry."

Gabriela whispers. "I've never seen anything like it. Not even *Papà*."

Deborah makes the sign of the cross. "Did you call the police?"

"Of course."

"Sheriff Gleason?" Deborah wipes the table with the cloth.

Gabriela nods.

"What did he say?"

"Nothing yet. He asked a bunch of questions. I'm meeting him at the theatre at eleven so he can tell me whether or not we're allowed to rehearse today."

"At eleven?" Deborah checks a tiny wristwatch caked with batter. She wets her finger so she can clean the face. "You want me to go with you?"

"Eh?"

"I'll close the shop for the afternoon."

"You don't have to."

"I don't mind."

"I'll be okay." Gabriela dries tears with her palms. "Thanks."

"Of course."

A customer walks up to the counter shaking his credit card while grinning. Deborah jumps to the register and rings the order so Gabriela pours herself a cup of Americano. The first sip burns her tongue. Before returning to their table, Deborah checks the other customers, smiling and grabbing a *zeppole* for a child probably too young for school. His mom adjusts the paper napkin tucked in his collar and untwists a sippy cup for a quick milk refill.

"Are you sure I can't get you anything to eat, *cugina*?"

Gabriela sips again. "No, thanks."

"Nothing?"

"How did you do it?" Gabriela says.

Deborah raises an eyebrow. "Huh?"

"After you lost Anthony."

"Oh, Gaby." Deborah sighs. "Sometimes I can't remember. In many ways, losing Tony was tougher on me."

"Tougher than losing your son?"

"Kinda, yeah." Deborah shrugs. "Anthony had already left home."

How would *Mamma* feel if she were to die suddenly? Has the distance already made her forget? The time made her childhood seem like a dream?

"Oh."

"No, no." Deborah straightens a napkin holder. "Don't misunderstand. There's nothing worse. Nothing more horrible than the death of your own child. A part of me died that day. The day the towers came down. I carry his death with me every day. That's all I have now. That's all *we* have."

Images of the World Trade Center disaster flashed across small television screens in Italy that horrible September morning like they did everywhere else in the world. When she was a young child growing up in *Valle D'Aosta*, America seemed like a distant planet. Like a world Gabriela would never discover. Certainly not on her own.

"I can't imagine."

"When I lost Tony. . ." Deborah clasps her fingers and twirls her thumbs. ". . . I lost my soulmate."

Losing *Papà* hurt *Mamma* so much. She stopped eating for days and wouldn't leave the house for weeks. She wore black for a year and told Gabriela that even after her husband dies, an Italian woman never removes her ring or sleeps in another's bed.

"Tony woke up early that morning," Deborah says, lost now, where the dead pull the puppet strings of our memory. "He'd gotten up to use the bathroom. I waited for him to come back to bed. He never came. I found him lying down by the tub. His face was blue. Sorta purplish. His pajamas were around his ankles. They think maybe he crawled toward the door while it was happening. The medical examiner said so. Tony was probably trying to find me, he said. Hoping I'd help, but I never heard a thing. Maybe because he had the fan running in the bathroom. Who knows? Or maybe because he wasn't in bed snoring like he always did. How awful's that? My husband's dying and needs me, but all I did was sleep because I finally had some peace and quiet."

"It's not your fault, Deborah."

"No?"

"Of course not."

Deborah sighs. "Well, at least he went fast."

"Yeah," Gabriela says.

Not like *Papà*. The cancer ate him for years. He'd fight, then get better. Then get sick again. And come back. Fall sick again. Time and again, like a rollercoaster. Like the Edgar Allan Poe stories she read at the university in Italy when first learning English. *Papà* lost so much weight. He looked like a sack of bones when she found him under the sheet that cold gray morning in April.

(in the wolf's mouth)

"Look," Deborah says in English. "I'm fixing you something to eat, and I'm not taking no for an answer."

Gabriela chuckles. *"Bene."*

Deborah slips behind the display case and grabs some *biscotti* cookies. She places them on a small plate and sets them in front of Gabriela.

"Mangia," she says.

"Grazie."

Gabriela nibbles the cookies while Deborah returns to the kitchen and fixes a pepper-and-egg sandwich on Italian bread. She finishes her breakfast and hugs Deborah before leaving the bakery, grateful for her American cousin and the friendship the two have developed in the short eight months they've known each other.

scene 4.

Sheriff Brad waits patiently in front of the Orpheum when Gabriela pulls up at ten minutes before the hour. He tips his wide hat. She grabs her promptbook off the backseat where she tossed it last night after rehearsal was canceled and trots across the street. The large brick building looms beyond the sidewalk between a laundromat and yoga studio. Two crows glare from the unlit marquee, cawing at Gabriela from their perch in the middle of cursive letters. A pale green awning ripples in the summer breeze above the box office window. Posters for *Bury Me in Autumn* fill the oval glass and occupy the surrounding columns.

"Morning, Miss Rossi."

"Morning."

"We got you straightened out last night."

"Did you?"

"Yes, ma'am." Brad winks. "I told them to make it quick since your show opens later this week. Everything should be cleaned up by now."

"Grazie."

"Besides, it's not like we got much else to do."

"No?"

Brad shakes his head. "Nuh-uh, not usually. Crow Creek's a quiet place, if you can't tell. Been that way since Daddy was in charge."

Quiet. Would the sheriff feel that way if he'd been here yesterday afternoon when Mr. Patterson was stabbed? If he'd been backstage when the lights flickered and the hunched shadow crossed the stage.

"Oh."

"Better stay that way."

"Of course."

"I promised him, you know. Before he passed." Brad grins. "You mind?"

"Eh?"

"The door?" Brad rolls his eyes. "You do have the key, don't you?"

"Oh, *sì*. Yes, of course."

Gabriela digs into the front pocket of her jeans and opens the door. The stale odor of theatre paint lingers in the humid air. That smell lives deeper than any sanitizer.

Brad removes his hat. "Appreciate it."

"Certainly."

Gabriela steps in ahead of the sheriff, cradling the promptbook in the crook of her elbow and shifting into the large shadow he casts across the lobby. She punches the keycode to disable the alarm. Black collage frames featuring photos of recent shows line the sterile walls. Greek columns separate the lounge area from a concession counter trimmed with furrowed molding. Artificial cherry blossoms in ceramic vases decorate an enormous paneled window that opens to King Street. Pink flowery branches sprawl across the recessed ceiling.

"You know the one thing I can't figure out?" Brad says.

"What's that?"

"Well, we find a dead body in your theatre three nights before the show opens, and you theatre folks seem more concerned about the play going up as scheduled than the murder. At least everyone I talked with so far does."

Gabriela swallows. "I don't think that's true."

"No?"

"Nuh-uh. We all cared deeply for Mr. Patterson."

"Of course."

"Theatre is our life."

"Is it now?"

"We're a family."

(i thought you liked it here)

"Mmm."

"It's all some of us have, really."

(not as much as i hoped i would)

"I see."

"What else would we do?" Gabriela asks.

"Guess I don't know."

"Where else would we go?"

"I'm not sure."

"It's like this." Gabriela steps out of Brad's shadow so she can study his square jaw and honest eyes. "Since I've been in America, I've learned the truth about how much you worship celebrities, especially your athletes."

"*Worship,* Miss Rossi?"

"Well, maybe that's not the best word."

"I wouldn't use it."

Gabriela scratches her head. *"Idolatrare."*

"What does that mean?"

"They are your idols."

"Oh."

"In Italy, our farmers . . . our teachers and laborers are who we admire most. They're who we look up to. People like you, Sheriff."

"I see," Brad says. "But that doesn't answer my question."

"Please, sir." Gabriela grins and pats Brad on the arm. "Patience. I'm getting there. Italians love to talk, in case you couldn't tell."

Brad hitches his thumbs on his belt. "I'd be lying if I didn't say I enjoy listening."

Gabriela's face burns. *"Grazie."*

"Mmm."

"It's the way we deal with loss," she says. "Only our level of fame makes us different."

Brad nods and wipes the corners of his mouth. How warm his moist lips would be to kiss. Gabriela shakes her head.

"We've got a running back that plays football for the Panthers," he says. "He's an amazing athlete. Might be the best in the league this season. His son drowned in a swimming pool last week."

"How awful."

"He didn't miss Sunday's game."

"No?"

"First home game of the season, too."

"You see then?"

"I believe I do, yes."

"Plus, we've already paid so much money for the royalties." Gabriela smiles. "I don't think Deidre would let the publishing company off that easy."

"Deidre?" Brad says. "Your business manager."

"Now you're getting it, sir."

"Didn't even need to check my notes."

"Bravo."

Brad stifles his laughter. "Gabriela?"

"Yes?"

"Uh, you don't mind me calling you Gabriela, do you?"

"Of course not, no."

His face tightens. "Is that all *you* have?"

"Sheriff?"

"The theatre? You said for some, that's all they have."

"Oh."

"What about you?"

Long lines of tears streaked *Mamma's* pale cheeks the day Gabriela boarded the train to Milan where she caught her flight to New York and headed to the Pittsburgh Public Theatre to start her first gig in America.

"Sometimes I worry that it is," Gabriela says. "But I meet good people like you and know that *Mamma* would be happy for me even though we don't see each other every day."

"Thank you kindly," Brad says.

"Thank you, Sheriff."

"Please, call me Brad."

Gabriela nods. "Brad."

Brad claps his hat in his hands. "What do you say we walk through this place and make sure everything's okay? I'll still be needing that list of everyone who works here, of course."

"Of course," Gabriela says. "Let me get the lights."

Gabriela crosses the lobby to the far wall beside concessions. She flicks a set of switches, but nothing turns on. "Odd."

Brad shrugs. "Maybe they killed the breakers last night before they left."

"Is it normal for your deputies to do that?"

Gabriela tries the switches again, but the lobby remains dark.

"Nothing about this is normal," Brad says. "We should probably check the breakers."

"Probably, but I have another idea."

"Oh?"

"It will give us some light anyhow."

Gabriela enters the auditorium with Brad a few steps behind. She passes the last few rows where Meribel found James Patterson. The floor and seats have been scrubbed. The yellow caution tape is gone. Even the spiked outline of his body is no longer visible.

"Told you they're thorough," Brad says.

Gabriela must've stared longer than she thought. "Yeah."

She hops up two steps to the midhouse console and presses the top button on the Unison panel, which typically lights up the house. It doesn't this time.

"The fuck?"

"Ma'am?"

Brad's invisible in the darkness. His faint musk comforts Gabriela. The last time she was in the auditorium, she had an unexpected visitor. And James Patterson was murdered. At least she's not alone now.

"I'm not sure why I can't get the house lights on."

She presses a few more buttons programmed with simple rehearsal defaults. Nothing lights up. The stage stays dark. Only a faint outline of the living room is visible thanks to the ghost light shining behind the scenery. *Ghost light.* That fucking thing never goes out.

"Where's that light coming from?"

The solitary incandescent lamp rests on a wheeled tripod base that undoubtedly supported a followspot long before Gabriela came to the Orpheum. Apparently, Brad sees it, too.

"The ghost light."

"What's that?"

"The safety light."

"Safety light?"

"Yeah, it's so we can find our way in the dark backstage. It always stays lit."

"Well, there must be power coming from somewhere then."

"Sì."

"Plus, the AC's running. The breeze feels kinda nice. It'd be awful sticky in here if it weren't."

"I agree."

Gabriela presses the buttons on the Unison panel again. The lights stay dead. After she fires up the console, the computer hums to life.

"Trying something else?" Brad says.

Gabriela nods and slides the submasters. "The board."

More darkness. Like an old man snoring. He doesn't know how not to.

(beware)

"The screen says we're at full, but I've got nothing. I don't know what's going on."

Of course I do. The dead man who's not old just dead is waiting backstage for me again. Waiting for both of us this time. He's waiting with his rotten eyes and spoiled flesh. Waiting to grab me and hold me and never let me go. Then he'll come for Brad. He'll come for all of us. Only he won't be the dead man. He'll be Papà. *Because he rises in the wolf's mouth. That's where all the dead come from.*

"Could've had a power surge during the storm last night," Brad says.

Gabriela jumps. Something creaks on stage. Maybe the floorboards. Maybe worse.

"You hear that?" Gabriela says, mopping sweat off her brow with unsteady fingers.

"Uh-huh."

Brad unclips a flashlight and shines the narrow beam toward the proscenium. The living room remains untouched since yesterday afternoon.

Another creak. More like a moan. *Louder.* Not only in her ears. In her head now. Pounding and thumping.

"Think somebody else beat us here?" Gabriela says.

Brad lowers his flashlight and unclips his shoulder mic. "Possibly."

He calls for Curly. The hitch-pitched deputy squeaks on the other end. "Sheriff?"

"I'm down at the Orpheum right now with Miss Rossi."

"Check."

"Do me a favor, would you?"

"Sir?"

"Give Buzz Stanton a holler over at Duke Power. Talk to him directly and find out if we had any power outages in the area last night. Maybe lightning struck a transmission line or something."

"Yessir."

"Thank you."

"Ten-four." Brad clips his mic. "What do you say we take a look for ourselves?"

Gabriela swallows a thick lump. "Sure."

"If you don't mind," Brad says. "I think I'll take lead on this."

"Of course."

He chuckles. "Normally, I'm much more of a gentleman."

"I'm sure."

Brad pauses as they move along the house right aisle. "Maybe you'd let me take you out for dinner some night so I can prove myself?"

"Sheriff?" Gabriela coughs. "*Scusi.* Brad?"

"Prove that I'm a gentleman."

(she's about half your age)

Fuck you, Sara.

"Nothing funny," Brad adds. "Just thought maybe you could use a friend. Since you're new in town and all."

Gabriela grins in the darkness. "I'd like that."

Brad sweeps the flashlight across the aisle and keeps moving. Gabriela stays close beside his hip, reaching out with fingertips that brush his khaki shirt. When they reach the front of the stage, Gabriela gestures to the stairs to their right. Brad climbs, keeping the flashlight aimed at the stage. Gabriela follows, placing the promptbook on the stage manager's desk.

"You know where the breakers are?"

"I do, yes."

"Let's take a look then."

Gabriela moves to the stage and leads Brad behind the first set of legs. She signals with her fingers. "There's a mechanical closet off the back hallway."

"Right behind you."

Brad aims the light over her shoulders as she moves to the door. The ghost light radiates in the darkness behind the scenery. They exit to the hallway. After finding the correct key, Gabriela unlocks the closet. She hits the switch but nothing works.

"Here." Brad raises his beam to the metal panel as Gabriela slides the bar and pulls open the cabinet.

"Nothing's been tripped," she says. "But let me flip the lights anyhow."

"Fine."

Gabriela traces her finger along the breakers, careful to switch only the ones marked lights.

"Maybe that'll get us some power in the lobby, anyhow," she says. "And in here. The stage lights patch into dimmers. There's a separate closet for those backstage."

Brad nods and flicks the switch by the closet door. *Nothing*. He strokes the blonde hair of his toothbrush mustache. "Must be something else."

The backstage door slams shut.

Gabriela leaps in her workboots. "Brad?"

He unclips his holster and draws his firearm, holding the flashlight against the barrel so he can see where he's aiming.

"Stay right behind me."

Her heart pounds in the dark hallway. "I will."

Brad takes slow steps while she follows. His footsteps make no sound as he approaches the door.

"I'll move to the far side," he whispers. "On three, you open."

Gabriela nods as Brad moves into position. She reaches out and grabs the doorknob, steadying her hand around the warm metal. Brad counts. On three, she twists the knob and pulls back the door. He aims his weapon and steps through the opening. Brilliant light blinds her as she swings the door wide and follows. All the stage lamps burn. Brad lowers his flashlight and moves into the wings. He steps backstage of what would be a bedroom door if the scenery were real.

"Who's there?" he says, glancing above the walls.

The heat of the stage lights makes Gabriela dizzy. She clings to the metal rungs of escape steps that lead to the catwalks and finds her balance. Lights flicker across the stage as Brad reaches for the bedroom door.

"Brad?"

He pauses when the stage goes dark again.

"Brad."

He points his flashlight toward the pipes above the scenery. Tommy Nolan hangs from a batten, rocking in the breeze of the air conditioner. Both eyes have popped from his skull. His severed tongue drips blood as it dangles between clenched teeth. Gabriela heaves, leaning across the metal steps so she can vomit into a garbage bin. Brad holsters his weapon and runs to Gabriela.

"You okay?" he says.

Before she can answer, his radio squawks. They both jump.

"Sheriff?"

Brad unclips the mic. "What you got, Curly?"

"Talked with Buzz. No power issues last night."

"Ten-four."

Brad replaces his mic and offers Gabriela his hand.

scene 5.

By two-thirty, Gabriela has assembled the entire cast and crew of *Bury Me in Autumn* in the auditorium at Brad's request. Twenty-three people in all. They find their own groups. The administrative staff hovers house right but hasn't taken any seats. Meribel isn't with them. The cast and contracted crew, including Sara Cooper, sit orchestra center. They drink coffee but remain quiet. They don't seem to notice Tommy's missing. Or care. The full-time technicians linger house left, buzzing about the possibility of another missed rehearsal. Only one volunteer, Anna Hernandez, has shown up and stands with her twin daughters by the midhouse console, almost in the exact spot where James Patterson was found dead. She probably doesn't know. Gabriela winces. Anna works concessions but doubles as an usher when needed. Gabriela guesses that her girls aren't quite three.

"Thank y'all for coming," Brad announces. "If you could please take your seats."

Those standing scatter while Gabriela finishes checking the master list on her clipboard. "Only a couple missing."

"Not bad," Brad says. "Thanks for your help."

"Of course."

Brad signals for Curly to send the remaining deputies to the lobby. Curly nods and disperses the officers. They exit through double gold-plated doors. The stage is quiet. The pipe where Brad and Gabriela found Tommy hanging is about two meters lower than the rest. Gabriela wishes she could take the flyrail out where it belongs.

"Sheriff, can you please tell us what's going on?" Ellie Miles says, adjusting a flowery headband. She's the artistic director but hasn't been involved in the production since the design team finished their plans in early July. She has an exotic collection of gourds in her front office.

"Yeah," Deidre Worth, the business manager, says. Gabriela doesn't know if Deidre finished stocking concessions for this weekend. "Do you have any idea what happened to Mr. Patterson?"

Brad shakes his head. "Still waiting on Bob's report."

"Bob?" Ellie says, tapping her iPhone. Gabriela rolls her eyes when she sees the *Downton Abbey* case with its phony royal wedding. "You mean Dr. Cody?"

Brad nods. "Mmm."

"How long do you expect that to take?" Lynn Mayfield, the production manager, says as she washes two pills down her throat with Evian.

"Not sure. Another day. Maybe two."

"But we know for sure he was murdered, right?" Ellie says, still scrolling. Her eyes don't leave her screen. "We do know that."

"Uh-huh." Brad sucks his teeth. "Seems like it, yes."

"Well, how?" Lynn says. She gargles and swishes. "Surely, you know that much."

Tariq Lucas coughs. He's the lead. His caramel skin glows under the house lights. Sweat moistens his pencil-thin mustache. He's the first person outside the administrative staff to make a sound. Gabriela's been waiting for the director, Matt Leath, to interject, but he's been remarkably quiet. Except for teasing wiry hair with a metal net too much like a tennis racket to be a comb, he's motionless.

"Yeah, Sheriff," Tariq says. "How'd it happen? Can you tell us that much?"

Bad clears his throat. "He was stabbed."

The crowd gasps. Brad lets them settle. A few bury tears in tissues or palms. Even Ellie lowers her phone.

"Then why are you waiting on Dr. Cody?" Deidre says, pulling her heavy frame up the back of a chair so she can waddle to her feet.

Brad wipes the corners of his lips. "We're not quite sure what weapon was used."

"Not sure about the weapon?" Lynn says, capping her bottle. She rethinks and takes another swig. "So, you mean, it wasn't a knife?"

"Um, no. Not a knife."

"If not a knife, then what?" Lucas says, performing some acting ritual or Method exercise because he's full blown into his salesman character, lilting his vowels and tossing his hands almost the way Gabriela does naturally. "What else can you stab somebody with?"

"I don't know." Brad strolls up the house right aisle. "But I combed this entire theatre last night and couldn't find anything that looks like it could've been used as the murder weapon. Ain't that right, Deanna?"

Deanna Flowers, the props mistress, twitches across the auditorium when the sheriff calls her name. The nervous tic is more the result of her disability than Brad's shout. She's got clinical Tourette's. Her meds keep her even most days. She's the one they promoted instead of Sara. Maybe because of her disability, but Gabriela doesn't think so. Deanna does an outstanding job. Plus, she's actually pleasant.

"Yes, Sheriff, that's correct," Deanna says, addressing the house. Her shoulder pops in a small way. "I gave him access to every nook and cranny before they sent me home."

"And you didn't find anything?" Lynn says. "Did you check weaponry? We have a closet downstairs that we keep locked."

"We did." Brad smirks. "Quite impressive, for sure. But not what we were looking for."

"Besides, I checked our inventory." Deanna thins her lips. "Nothing's missing."

"But they could've gotten what they needed, cleaned up, and put it back before you checked," Lynn says.

Deanna shakes her head and glances at Sara, who sinks in her chair behind Tariq, lowering deep-set eyes. "Nobody goes in there but me."

Gabriela folds her arms. "None of those weapons could've done what was done to Mr. Patterson."

"What are you saying?" Doug Cousins, the head carpenter, says and tucks a pencil behind his ear. He adjusts the straps on his denim overalls.

"I've never seen anything like it," Gabriela says.

"Neither have I," Brad says. "That's why I'm waiting to hear back from the medical examiner before I jump to any conclusions."

"Where's Tommy?" Connor Simmons asks and stands. He's on the run crew but doubles as an ASM since Gabriela's promotion. The *lifer*. He pops gum. "Tommy might know something. Why ain't he here like the rest of us?"

"Yeah," King Boggs, the master electrician, says. Gabriela doesn't know how he got his nickname since that was before her time with the Holt Players. Probably because he thinks his shit doesn't stink. She wonders if *Mamma* knows an equivalent Italian expression.

King scans the house. His chubby face and white beard resemble *Babbo Natale*. The America version. Not the skinny Greek that looks like a Turk. Not *Befana,* either. The old witch who delivers gifts in Italy.

"If this here's an inquisition, don't you think all of us should be here?" he asks.

"Meribel, too," Deidre says. Struggling to stand under her own weight, she finds her seat.

"Now, hold up," Brad says. "This isn't an inquisition. As far as I can tell, I don't have any reason to suspect any of you. Not yet."

"What's that supposed to mean?" Joe Cox, the technical director, says. His hair's brighter blonde than

Brad's. His smile, merrier. His baby face is almost comical for an adult who spends his days implementing designs. "You actually think one of us killed our own producer?"

"No, that's the exact opposite of what he just said," Gabriela says. "Right, Sheriff?"

Brad grins. "Yes, ma'am."

"And Meribel hasn't even been released from the hospital yet," Gabriela says. "She was kept overnight for observation."

"Was she hurt?" Anika Vanhook, the wardrobe assistant, says. Across her lap, she repairs the torn pocket of a pair of Tariq's pants.

"No," Gabriela says. "She has minor heart trouble. The whole scene was a bit much for her. For both of us."

"That still doesn't tell us why Tommy ain't here," Connor says, popping gum louder now. He cracks his knuckles and doesn't sit back down.

Brad removes his hat and twirls it. "Well, that's another reason I had Miss Rossi gather y'all this afternoon."

Gabriela rubs her *cornicello*.

"What's wrong with Tommy?" King says, raising his chin so the point of his snowy beard forms a projectile awaiting launch.

Brad clears his throat and struts to the front of the house. "We found him this morning."

"*Found* him?" Anika says, stifling a scream.

Maybe she poked herself with her needle? Maybe she's the evil witch *Befana*. Maybe she dances with the dead and kidnaps children and stabs our producer and hangs our stage crew. *Beware the wolf's mouth.* Because it's one of them, right? The *wolf*. Doesn't it have to be? Doesn't the murderer have to be somebody sitting in the theatre right now? Wasn't that the purpose of the warning?

He rises in the wolf's mouth.

"You mean we've had two murders?" Ellie says.

"No, no." Brad bumps Gabriela with his elbow as he raises his hands. She bites her tongue to keep from shrieking. "We ain't sure Tommy's been murdered."

"Then what happened, Sheriff?" Ellie says.

Her *gourds*. Ellie, the artistic director. Her fucking gourds. The ones on the shelf next to her desk in her office backstage. You can sharpen one down and use it to impale somebody. She can. That's what she did, isn't it? She's *Befana*. She's the evil witch with her mobile phone that talks to the dead.

"We don't know yet," Brad says.

How well does Gabriela know any of them? She's only been here eight months. They could all be murderers waiting to make their next move. Waiting to make her their next victim.

"Looks like Bob's got his work cut out for him," Doug says and unbuttons the collar of his white Oxford shirt.

Da colpa nasce colpa. Deep calls to deep.

"Looks that way," Brad says.

The house grumbles. Curly steps inside the auditorium and pulls Brad aside. They whisper and point to the lobby before Curly leaves.

"Gabriela," Brad says.

She can't swallow. Or breathe. "Yes?"

"I need to go outside and hold off the press."

"Surprised they took so long," she says but isn't sure if her mouth formed words or if she's screaming somewhere in her mind so Brad can read her thoughts.

Brad nods. "Becky Stokes is giving Curly the runaround."

(she's always around the theatre when there's breaking news)

"Of course she is."

Talk about witch. The witch from the Crow Creek *Sentinel* with flaming red hair and heart of stone. *Mamma* always said, *"Quando il diavolo ti accarezza, vuole la tua anima."* Roughly: When the devil caresses you, he wants your soul. Or in this case, she does. *Becky.* Maybe she and Ellie have formed a coven. Or maybe Anika gave her needles to poke out Gabriela's eyes.

"Think you can manage without me for a few minutes?"

Gabriela's head swims. She grabs the lip of the stage. *"Eh?"*

"You okay?"

Gabriela shakes her head. "Yes, of course. What should I do?"

Brad narrows his eyes and scans the crowd. "Just a second."

"Sure."

Brad puts on his hat and raises his hands. "Listen, y'all. I need to step out into the lobby for a minute and take care of Becky Stokes."

Deep groans and lip smacking fill the space. A few curse words.

"I'm gonna leave y'all with Miss Rossi. While I'm gone, y'all need to come to some kinda consensus about what you're gonna do with this show."

"What we're gonna do?" Tariq says.

"That's right," Brad says.

"What's that supposed to mean?" Connor says. "You don't think we're still gonna do this play, do you?"

"Hell we ain't," Doug says. "You know how much time I got invested in this thing?"

"And money," Lynn says.

"Mr. Patterson is dead," Anika says.

"Yeah, so's Tommy," Joe says.

The room erupts. Words fly in a painful roar.

Brad looks at Gabriela. "I'll leave you to this."

"Thanks."

"I'm sorry," Brad says. "Give me a minute."

"Okay." Gabriela lets them argue for about thirty seconds. Enough time for her to regain focus and push away any suspicious thoughts of witches and dead men. "Quiet, please."

"Thank you," the crowd says and stops talking.

"Grazie," Gabriela says, genuinely grateful that the established attention signal works with adults. For safety purposes, every theatre should have one. At the university in Italy, they always declared *"Il silenzio, soprattutto!"* backstage, which roughly translates to "Silence, above all."

"I realize how stressful this is for everyone," she says. "But we need to be respectful and discuss this in a reasonable manner."

"Agreed," Ellie says. Gabriela's uneasy with her support. She'd be cautious if any of them took her side at this point. "There are plenty of reasons for and against going on with the show."

Matt raises a stiff hand above his wiry hair. "I've sat out of this discussion so far but would like to contribute."

"Thanks, Matt," Tariq says.

"Of course," Gabriela says.

The entire room nods, murmuring their agreement.

"As the director, I realize my work's almost finished," Matt says.

Gabriela knows the American rule. Once a director brings a show to opening night, they get paid and are no longer required to attend. That's not always the case in Italy, even in regional theatre. At least not where she's from. There are advantages to both.

"I'm excited about the work we've done," he continues. "About how much we've grown as a cast and as individuals. These last few weeks we've been on an incredible journey. Who would've thought that just three short months ago the Holt Players would've been granted the rights to an off-Broadway Lortel winner?"

"Straight," Tariq says.

Matt bows his head. "I've made some of the closest friends I've ever had along the way. For real, y'all."

The cast pats his shoulders and thanks him. The crew whispers solidarity. The staff smiles in favor of their hire. They are a coven. A gathering that abandons Gabriela.

Courtney Williams, who plays Tariq's onstage wife (she glows without makeup even when not under stage lights) says, "I love you, Matt."

"Love you, too." Matt's eyes swell as he surveys the house. "All of you. We can't do a show like this without the support of one another. Without tapping the human spirit and testing our limits as friends."

The oldest cast member, Ed Brown, clears his throat and widens his eyes. "As a family."

"As a family," Tariq agrees.

Matt bumps their fists. "What happened yesterday. What happened today. We can't go back and undo all that."

"Would if we could," Bianca Whitt, Ed's onstage wife, shouts. Her braided hair, knotted in a high bun, slants away from her sloped brown forehead.

Would if we could. Would Gabriela bring *Papà* back if she could? What if *Papà* wasn't the same when he came back? What if the cancer that took his life changed him in the after-life? Made him different. *Wrong.*

"Sure would." Matt nods. "Mr. Patterson and Tommy Nolan. They were part of who we are. Just like I am. Part of our family. For them and for us, we need to do this show, y'all. We need to finish what we started. The work we do now honors those we've loved and lost."

Silence sweeps across the auditorium. Those opposed before Matt spoke capitulate, and not so reluctantly. Gabriela doesn't reply. She's separate. Not a part. She wouldn't if she could because she wouldn't have the chance. They don't need her.

"So, where do we go from here?" Courtney says.

"Good question," Tariq says.

Gabriela clears her throat. "Our calls start at six tonight, if we're allowed to be here."

"Thank you six," Matt says,

"Maybe we can ask the sheriff to keep somebody on watch while we're here?" Lynn says.

"While we aren't here might be when that's needed most," Joe says.

"True," Doug says.

"I'll talk to him," Gabriela says.

"I've got ten past three."

"That gives us almost three hours."

"Maybe we can push the curtain till eight-thirty?"

"And what?"

"Calls at seven? Like we would've done last night?"

"We're adding full makeup tonight, so that sounds reasonable."

The chatter continues, faceless and nameless, until Deanna says, "Don't forget to check your props before going to makeup."

Deanna Flowers, the props mistress. Not Sara Cooper. Sara Cooper hasn't spoken a single word. She's been too quiet to trust.

Before Gabriela can recall any of *Mamma*'s sayings about how you can't ignore silence, Brad reenters the auditorium. Gabriela catches a glimpse of Becky Stokes when the auditorium doors swing wide. Her scarlet hair flaps in the breeze, exposing a slithering tattoo on the back of her neck like the serpent Sara has on her forearm. As the door closes, she flashes briefly, like an x-ray revealing muscles and bones. A fly saws the air near her ear. Gabriela rubs her eyes until Brad meets her at the bottom of the house. The cast and crew continue to buzz with their preparations in spite of Sara's reticence.

"You good?" he says.

Gabriela shrugs. "You?"

"Enough."

"Sorry."

"Don't be. What'd y'all decide?"

"They want to do the show."

"Figures." Brad checks his mobile. "Tonight?"

"If possible, yes."

"We can make that work." He sighs. "What time?"

"They want to start rehearsal by seven."

"Seven o'clock call, huh?"

Gabriela half-grins. "Thank you seven."

"I'll put Curly on. Maybe a couple of others. Keep an eye on things."

"I'm glad I didn't have to ask."

"Probably won't hurt to keep somebody on around the clock."

"Free publicity." Gabriela shrugs. "This'll be some show."

"You don't know the half of it."

"Eh?"

"Becky Stokes."

"What about her?"

"Local pastor's up to something no good."

"Pastor?" Gabriela says. "What are you talking about?"

"Just a second." Brad faces the rustling group. "Thanks for your patience. We'll do our best to help you get this show up and running by the weekend."

"Thank you, Sheriff," Matt says.

"But we're gonna be in your space. Ain't no other way around it. I can't compromise on that."

"Understood," Matt says.

"You heard the man," Tariq says. "Let's roll out."

Brad shakes hands and accepts gratitude as the house empties. A few say goodbye to Gabriela. Not many.

"I need to run," Brad says.

"Of course."

"Will you be here?"

"For the most part."

"I'll make sure we have two deputies on duty throughout the day."

"I won't be alone," Gabriela says. "The office staff is full-time. I'm sure Terese and Anika have plenty of costume work they'll be doing as well. And there's always last minute touch-ups on the set. Joe and Doug."

"Good." Brad pauses. "Gabriela?"

"Sheriff?"

"Think you might have time this afternoon to grab a bite before your call?"

"Eh?" Gabriela's blood thumps in her temples. "Today?"

Brad chuckles. "Yes, ma'am. If you ain't too busy."

"Not for you," Gabriela says. "I mean, I'm not too busy to eat. With you. *Sì.* Yes, I'd love to go. Where?"

"There's a great new Mexican place on Third. *Mi Despensa.* You know it?"

"Across from the bakery?"

Brad nods. "That's the one. How's five-thirty sound?"

Gabriela checks the time on her mobile. "I can do five-thirty."

"See you then."

Brad tips his hat, strides up the house and out the lobby doors. He never told her about Becky Stokes or the local pastor. Maybe that's why he wants to meet her for dinner. Maybe there's nothing more to it than that. Any butterflies or sweaty palms are pure fantasy. She's half his age, after all.

Gabriela stands alone in the cool auditorium. The crew who decide to linger or get work done have gone into the lobby or to the shops and dressing rooms backstage. Administration has filed away to their front offices. The cast is gone. A light flickers onstage. That same fucking light. The fucking source four.

We all have our own demons.

She should've asked King Boggs to check on it. That's what a master electrician does. He might think he's better than everyone else, but he's not too good to do his job. Gabriela will make sure of that. A glitchy instrument is nothing out of the ordinary this close to opening night.

King should check it. He's the fucking master electrician, not *Babbo Natale*.

The light flashes once more but stays on. The beam hits the spot where they found Tommy hanging. The pipe sways two meters lower than it where it belongs. Gabriela knows she should leave it as is and get out of the space. *Mamma* tells her to. *Quando vai in cerca di problemi ti trova.* Trouble finds you when you go looking for it. *Se guardi nell'abisso, l'abisso ti fissa di nuovo.* If you stare into the abyss, the abyss stares back at you. Gabriela doesn't need to hear *Mamma* to know that.

She climbs the stage left steps as she surveys the empty living room set. The light continues to radiate until the lamp pops. Burnt filament stings her nostrils. She turns the corner of the proscenium toward the flyrail and a frigid hand grabs her wrist. She screams. Putrid flesh drips off the bones as the lifeless fingers squeeze hard enough to bruise. Worms bubble under the pale skin.

"You didn't listen," the dead man says.

"What?"

"You didn't listen to what I told you," he says, gargling earth with each syllable.

"Let me go!"

"He rises."

Gabriela jerks her wrist loose, tearing the dead man's arm from its socket. It dangles in tatters as silky tendons stretch under his ripped suit. She screams and staggers toward her desk, catching her ankle. She pinwheels her arms for balance but topples, spilling her clipboard down the stairs to the orchestra pit below.

Keys rattle backstage right. A door opens. Connor Simmons enters.

"Connor?"

"Ma'am?"

Gabriela glances toward the proscenium arch. The dead man is gone.

"Connor."

"That you, Gabriela?"

"Mmm."

Connor rushes across the dark stage and helps her stand. She dusts off her hip.

"Thank you."

Connor nods but doesn't ask questions. He punches a button on the Unison panel so he can inspect an armchair that's off balance under the lights. Gabriela rubs her wrist before she crosses to the flyrail and adjusts the low pipe. *Tommy's* pipe. She decides not to collect her clipboard. Brad doesn't need to see the list anymore.

scene 6.

About twenty minutes later, Gabriela enters the public library on Cardinal Avenue. Wanda Butler sits at the circulation desk, nose deep in a shiny paperback. Wire-rimmed spectacles dangle from her ears off a thin gold chain. Gabriela smiles as she passes the librarian and heads to the reference section on the second floor. She scans both aisles but can't find anything local. The almanacs and directories are too modern for what she needs. She curses in Italian under her breath, and a mother about her age (holding the hands of two blonde children) rolls her eyes as they cross to a nearby reading lounge.

Gabriela navigates her way to the history books three aisles closer to the elevator but still finds nothing about Crow Creek. She pulls a Civil War text off a bottom shelf and flips through the pages, looking more at the pictures than reading the text. She scans a photo of African slaves in rural Arkansas mulling behind a crumbled shack and one of a battlefield in Missouri where a pile of soldiers lay bleeding and dead in black and white. Her history teachers didn't spend much time addressing the American war where she went to school in Italy, but how the slaves maintained their spirit despite generations of persecution in a land where they were dragged against their will always fascinated her. The Italian Civil War (*la guerra civile*) focused more on the socialist politics of World War II. Her great-grandfather fought as part of the *la Resistenza* prior to the national liberation and eventual start of the modern Republic.

She takes a deep breath and goes downstairs to the circulation desk.

"Good morning, dear," Wanda says.

"Morning."

Wanda closes her book. It's a recent text about the genetics of immune disorders. Not the pulp romance Gabriela was expecting.

"How may I help you?" she says.

"I'm not quite certain," Gabriela says. "I need to do some research."

Wanda's eyes brighten. "Why, I love research, sweetie. What're you thinking?"

"So, this might sound a little odd."

"Odd?" Wanda scoots closer to the desk. A small lump wriggles under her cheek. *Maybe she's poking around in there with her tongue?*

"Yes," Gabriela sighs. "I work at the Orpheum Theatre."

"The Orpheum Theatre?" Wanda says, removing her glasses. She straightens a decorative picture frame reflecting the photo of a large man missing an eye. "Awful what happened to James Patterson, ain't it?"

"*Sì*. It's very sad."

Be grateful you didn't see the hole in his chest. Or pull Meribel Sanchez out of his blood.

"I sat behind him at First Baptist every Sunday going on forty years now," Wanda says.

Or find Tommy Nolan hanging above the stage this morning. The rope severed his neck so deep it cut into his ears.

Gabriela clears her throat. "I'd like to study a little about its history."

"I see." Wanda straightens two pencils near a library card application pad. "Where are you from, darling? You ain't from around here, are you?"

"No," Gabriela says. "I haven't lived here long."

"Your accent's a bit exotic." Wanda flashes her teeth. "You sound like you might be from one of them countries in the Middle East. Like a Muslim country or whatnot with your hair so dark and wavy. Not that I'm judging. God gives all his children plenty of time to find Jesus, if they so choose."

"I'm from Italy," Gabriela says.

Wanda chuckles. "Well, that's close enough."

Gabriela bites her lip. "I already did a Google search."

"Google." Wanda cackles, bouncing in her chair. "I never did trust that Internet. The World Wide Web they call it. Web of lies, I say. Didn't find much, did you?"

"No."

"Not a surprise. I keep telling my son Helms it's a waste of time. Things that happen in Crow Creek tend to stay here, you know what I mean?"

Gabriela crosses her hands behind her back. Her library visit has gone longer than she wants. "So, the Orpheum Theatre?"

"Right." Wanda stands and wiggles her finger. "We cleared all our electronic databases before the Y2K scare, but you're probably too young to remember. Ever hear of it?"

The potential computer threat when she was four didn't really impact their village in the Alps. Her parents unplugged the weak dial-up connection on the early nineties model Hewlett-Packard they kept in the spare bedroom until Gabriela started *scuola secondaria* and required an upgrade. *Mamma* worked an extra shift at the shoe factory the entire summer to save for it.

"Some."

"I'll tell you what you can do." Wanda saunters around the circulation desk. "We donated all our old print newspapers to the *Sentinel*."

Gabriela checks the time on her mobile. Less than two hours before she needs to meet Brad for dinner. "The *Sentinel*?"

"For their archives." Wanda points a crooked finger toward the massive front window. "Mmm-hmm. Right around the corner across from the antique store on Ninth Street."

"I see."

"Becky Stokes will take care of you." Wanda walks Gabriela to the glass doors. "She keeps close to the willows, bless her heart."

"Close to the willows?"

"Tell her I sent you." Another lump squirms under Wanda's cheek. Not her tongue poking. Smaller and distinct like a maggot. "She'll know she can trust you."

Gabriela suspects Becky will be thrilled to talk with her since Brad and the local deputies shielded her from the Orpheum earlier today. She checks the time again. Not this afternoon, however. It's after four and she has dinner plans. She thanks Wanda Butler and trots out to her car so she can go home and freshen up. Wanda stares from inside the large glass windows until Gabriela drives away.

scene 7.

While waiting for Brad outside *Mi Despensa*, Gabriela can't help but feel like she's being watched. A pair of yellow eyes peak out behind a dumpster. Probably an alley cat. The shriek of her name slaps the brick buildings. More than likely the squeal of tires as a car brakes on King Street. Not demons laughing or the undead rising. Nothing like that.

Lightning flashes. Thunder claps. A summer storm kicks through the downtown streets, tossing her raven hair. She stands under the awning and watches rain fall in solitary drops, then as sheets. Her sneakers flood, soaking her socks. The cuffs of her jeans catch water. She scoots closer to the store window out of the microburst. Faces inside glow. Luminescent cartoons grin over her weary shoulders. Skeletal apparitions.

You didn't listen. What didn't she hear? *You didn't listen to what I told you.* What did he tell her? *Beware the wolf's mouth.* The wolf? *He rises.* Gabriela can't connect the dots. She no longer cares about whether or not he's real. James Patterson and Tommy Nolan are. *Who's the dead man? What does he want? Who rises?*

(beware)

By ten of six, the storm passes. Brad arrives. He parks his cruiser in front of the restaurant. He's not wearing khakis. He doesn't have his hat. Gabriela hides her *cornicello* under her collar.

"Sorry I'm late."

"You're fine."

"I wanted to wash up." He tucks a mauve crew neck into a pair of Wranglers. He's not wearing his gunbelt. "Probably didn't need to say that out loud."

Gabriela smiles. "You clean up nicely."

"Thank you." Brad grabs the door. "After you."

Gabriela enters and asks for a table. A round woman who could be Anna Hernandez, the Orpheum volunteer — but dressed in black slacks and a white button shirt, leads them to a booth. The restaurant is quiet. The tables line two aisles under an indoor veranda and false blue sky with white clouds. Large wooden trellises crown the ceilings where artificial vines spread out like leafy fingers. The few faces inside aren't glowing. They're not cartoons. They don't stare or watch her. Outside haunts her. She's safe here with Brad. The waitress brings their drink order. Brad talks in Spanish. Gabriela understands most of what they say. The menus wait closed in front of them.

"How'd the rest of your day go?" Brad asks.

She wants to tell him about what she saw. About her backstage visitor. But doesn't.

"Quiet, mostly."

"Good."

"You?"

"Pastor Aken wants to hold a vigil downtown on Friday night."

Gabriela chokes on her sweet tea. One of the few Southern delights she's usurped in the last eight months.

"Who wants to do what when?"

The waitress drops off a basket of chips and two sides of salsa, mild and hot. Brad lets her choose. She draws the mild.

"Pastor Aken." Brad dips into the hot bowl and snaps the chip between his two front teeth. "He's the pastor at First Baptist."

"I know who he is," Gabriela says. "A vigil? For James Patterson and Tommy? But why? And why does he want to hold it on Friday night? We open on Friday night."

Brad tilts his chin and bites another chip. "He does that."

Gabriela shakes her head. She knows the pastor is a local celebrity. His youth choir performed at the Orpheum for Memorial Day services and packed the house.

"Not this week, I hope."

"Becky Stokes seems to think so."

"What did you tell her?"

Brad sips his water. "Nothing, really."

"Nothing?"

(she keeps close to the willows)

The waitress takes their order. Brad selects the enchilada special with black beans, guacamole, and *pico de gallo*. Gabriela apologizes and pauses to check the menu. She settles for the chimichanga and Spanish rice with a small salad.

"My daughter died eight years ago," Brad says after the waitress leaves.

Gabriela freezes, tortilla chip scraping her pursed lips.

"Oh my god, I'm so sorry."

"She wrecked her car by the tracks on Ninth Street. Some believe she took her own life. Pastor Aken, for one. I don't. Never did."

"Brad, that's awful."

Deborah's son. Brad's daughter.

What would Mamma *do if she lost me? How does she feel right now while I'm halfway around the world? Does she pretend I'm dead to accept the distance?*

"The worst." Brad eats a chip. "But you live with it. Come to terms. That's the relationship you have. You're a parent to a dead child."

Isn't that what Deborah said?

(i carry his death with me)

"Same with me and Shana."

"Shana?"

"My wife. I'm the husband of a dead woman."

(an italian woman never removes her ring)

Gabriela reaches across the table and takes his hand. Her damp fingers tremble. "You're more than that."

(or sleeps in another's bed)

The waitress refills their glasses. Gabriela withdraws her hand, but not before Brad notices the bruise on her wrist.

"What's that?"

"Eh?"

"How'd you get that bruise?"

"Not sure."

Gabriela eats a chip. She doesn't like lying to Brad but doesn't want to tell him about what she saw. Not now. Not with all this talk of death and loss. He'd think she's insensitive. Or crazy, at the very least.

"We're always getting banged up backstage. I probably walked into a light boom. King Boggs keeps those in the wings when the instruments aren't lighting a dance recital."

Brad smirks. "Oh."

"You don't have any idea what I'm talking about, do you?" Gabriela says.

"No, but that's okay. Plenty for me to learn. I like that."

A server delivers their meals with plates lined up his padded arm.

"Gracias," Brad says.

Gabriela unwraps her silverware. "So, Pastor Aken?"

"Oh, right." Brad smothers his enchiladas with guacamole. "He held a vigil for my daughter after she died."

"What's so awful about that?"

"His vigils are more like rock concerts."

"Rock concerts?" Gabriela takes a bite of her chimichanga. "I don't follow."

"Let's just say, *Bury Me in Autumn* . . . that's the name of your play, right?"

"Mmm-hmm."

"Let's just say, *Bury Me in Autumn* won't be the only performance that night. And the good pastor'll draw a bigger crowd than that Orpheum theatre, even if you fill every seat."

"But you're not gonna let him, right? You're not gonna let him hold a vigil, are you?"

Brad puts down his fork. "I'm not sure I can stop him."

"But you're the sheriff."

"That doesn't mean I have the power."

A skinny young man with a greasy face, wearing a grocery store apron, surprises Brad with a tap on the shoulder. "Sheriff?"

"Huh?"

"Thought that was you."

"Yes."

"You look mighty different without that sheriff's uniform on. I love that shirt. What is it, pink? Luna won't let me wear pink, though. Says the color makes me look like I'm sick. Like I got cancer. You don't think I look like I got cancer, do you, Sheriff? Cause if you do, I'll need to get to the doctor right away. Like tomorrow. Because Mama'll kill me if she finds out I got cancer but ain't done nothing about it yet. Luna, too. She's my wife. Oh, but you probably knew that."

"Uh, excuse me, Clark." Brad tilts his head. "This here's Gabriela Rossi."

"Huh? Yes, yes. Of course. Sorry, ma'am. Nice to meet you." He extends his hand. "Clark Gufney."

Gabriela gives a quick shake.

"Clark Gufney." Brad says. "Miss Gabriela Rossi."

"Mighty nice to meet you, Miss Rossi, but I've seen you come into the Food Castle a time or two. You always buy gelato late at night. Dark chocolate or wild strawberry. Oh, Sheriff, did I tell you they put me on the swing shift? Mama thought it might be best. Luna, too. Keeps me out of the house during the evenings when the kids are home from school and need to get their homework done. Guess I horse around too much. That's what they say, anyhow. Mama and Luna. Not the kids. Not that I could ever ride a horse. Ever tell you about that one time I went horseback riding in Boone?"

"Uh, no, Clark. You didn't."

"Let me tell you, nastiest kick I ever got. Took one blow right behind the ear." Clark points. "Doctor said if that kick would've been three inches higher and two to the left, would've gave me brain damage sure enough. Or knocked my eyeball out. One or t'other. Now, wouldn't I look silly walking around with only one eyeball in my skull? Mama'd probably make me wear an eye patch or something. Luna, too. She's my wife. I mention that?"

Gabriela nods. "Yes."

"She's half-Japanese. Most beautiful woman I've ever seen. Still is. We weren't allowed to give our children Japanese names."

"Oh."

Brad clears his throat. "Clark?"

"Yessir?"

"Anything I can help you with?" Brad says.

"Wait a minute." Clark's eyes widen. "You're Gabriela Rossi?"

"I am, yes."

"The Gabriela that works at the Orpheum Theatre?"

"Mmm-hmm."

"Two blocks west of Gallagher's Pub off Route 119?"

"That's so."

"The girl from Italy?"

"Clark?" Brad dabs his lips with a napkin. "There a point to all this?"

"Well, that's just what I come over here to tell you about, Sheriff. What a small world! The world is so very small, for sure. If you could hold it in your hands, you could probably fold it up like a baby's diaper. But all my kids are out of diapers now, so I don't have to fold those no more. Mama always used to make me clean out the dispenser. What a mess! Rather clean chickenshit out of a coop." Clark slaps a hand across his mouth. "Oops, sorry. Let that slip. Sorry. Mama would blacken my hide if she heard me talk that way in front of a lady."

"It's no problem, really." Gabriela says.

Clark lowers his eyes. "I truly am tore up about Tommy Nolan. Him and me are kin. Were kin. Is it are or were? Maybe *is* kin. That's probably it. We's kin. Don't know the other fellow, but Tommy and me. My daddy and his daddy were second cousins. Something like that. I only know we was kin, and he always invited me to the family pig pickin on Memorial Day. Went there this past May. Played cornhole out back by the doghouses. He keeps his dogs out back along the creek. I played mostly with the young'uns so's they stayed out of trouble and didn't go near the roaster. Not my young'uns. Mama and Luna didn't go to the cook-out. They don't like my family much. Especially not my cousin Eli. The one who let me stay with him when Luna and me was fighting that one time she cheated on me with Mr. Sears. He's ex-military. Works on computers out of his house down the road."

"Clark?" Brad says, stirring the hot salsa with his spoon.

"Should I say kept? Can you talk about a person in the present tense when they ain't no longer in the present?"

"Think so, yes," Brad says.

"Which?"

"The past."

Clark's shoulders slump. "Oh."

(he's cousins with a dead man)

"Well, great seeing you, Clark," Brad says.

"Yeah," Gabriela says. "Nice meeting you."

Clark shakes his head. "But I didn't even get to tell you what I came over here to say in the first place."

"What's that?" Brad says.

"The vigil on Friday night."

Brad narrows his eyes. "You already know?"

"Whole town knows." Clark laughs and nods at Gabriela. "News spreads fast through Crow Creek."

"I see," Gabriela says.

"Anyhow," Clark says. "Few church members came by the store late last night hanging flyers. I was closing up by myself. Roy told me he'd stay — Roy's the manager — I told him I'm fine. Don't need no babysitting. I know how to lock a door. You remember what I did that one time them counterfeiters was passing off those phony bills?"

"I remember."

He unties his apron, untucks his shirt, and reveals a white scar above his hip. "Took a bullet."

"Gesù," she says.

"Crow Creek's my town." Clark lowers his shirt and puffs his chest. "Food Castle's my…well, my castle."

"Oh," Gabriela says.

"I'd say my home's my castle." Clark cups his mouth and squints over his fingertips. "But home's really just my home. Mama's castle, to be sure. Even more Luna's than mine. Even more the kids than mine."

"That's too bad," Gabriela says.

"No, it ain't. Not really." Clark digs deep into his front pocket and pulls out a crumpled piece of paper and hands it to Brad. "Here. I saved one so I don't forget, but I'll snag another off the window. Might even close the store early. If Roy lets me. He should. He goes to First Baptist. Knows Pastor Aken as well as anyone. Once that show starts, ain't nobody gonna be nowhere else. Not the grocery store or nowhere."

"Yeah," Brad says and unfolds the flyer.

"But don't you worry, Sheriff." Clark says, smile cutting to his ears. "I'm part of the volunteer firehouse off Fry Avenue."

"That so?" Brad says.

"Uh-huh. Over by Houndstooth. Chief Riddle put me on a crew."

"Right."

Clark props his hands on his hips. "Well, guess I better get back to the store. I really enjoy having this hour to myself for dinner now that I'm working the swing. Makes a big difference. Eat here nearly every day. Except for when I can't take a full hour cause we're too busy and I run over to the Subway. It's in the same strip mall as the Food Castle."

"Go there plenty," Brad says.

"Get their footlong tuna when I go. Well, I did. Mama says the tuna makes my breath smell something awful when I come home from work on the nights I go to Subway. She's right, of course. Luna won't kiss me till I brush my teeth. I eat the footlong steak and cheese now. Hold the onions." He winks at Gabriela.

"Hold the onions," she says.

"And the peppers." He winks again. "For Luna."

"Probably a good idea," Brad says.

"Catch you later," Clark says and bustles toward the front door. He stops to give the hostess a hug on his way out.

"He's sweet," Gabriela says.

Brad nods. "Lots of energy."

"So many names and places."

"And yet he manages to keep track of them all."

"Reminds me of home."

"Does it?"

"Of course," Gabriela says. "Small towns are the same. We all know everything and everybody. What's the flyer say?"

Brad shows her the crumpled paper. The poster announces the upcoming vigil. Pastor Aken is prominent above the center line and in full color. He's bigger than both black and white photos of James Patterson and Tommy Nolan. Over sculpted hair, he wears a blood red John Bull tophat with several crow feathers protruding from a copper band. A sable cloak drapes his charcoal gray suit. A matching red ascot dangles loosely around his neck. Varnished Giorgio Brutini boots add several centimeters to his immense stature. He spreads his arms above his head, posing with slender hands in the air above a crowd not visible in the live shot.

He's gorgeous. Gabriela can't stop looking at him. His caramel complexion's flawless. His aquiline nose slopes graciously. His beard's trimmed to a fine point. His masculine jawline and delicate features make him androgynous. Gabriela wants to touch him. Or better yet, be touched by him. For the first time since she moved to Crow Creek, she's seen a man better looking than Brad. A hole forms in the pit of her stomach. She hangs her head in shame.

"Gabriela?" Brad says. "What's wrong?"

"Eh?" She nibbles a bite of rice. "Nothing."

"You look like you seen a ghost."

"I'm . . . I'm fine."

Brad folds the paper and shoves it into his shirt pocket.

"You sure?"

Gabriela swallows. Something's not right about the pastor. She knows it. *Feels* it. Believes Brad does to. *When the devil caresses you, he wants your soul.* The *cornicello* burns her chest under her shirt. She can't wait any longer.

"What if I told you I saw somebody backstage?"

"Did you?"

She puts down her fork and drinks her tea. "Yes."

"And you think this person might be responsible?"

"What?" she says.

"For Mr. Patterson and Tommy?"

"No, no sir. You misunderstand." Gabriela leans across the table. "What if I told you I believe I did see a ghost?"

"A ghost?"

"I know this sounds crazy, but I'm . . . *aspetta*." Gabriela rolls up her sleeve. "You asked about this bruise."

"Yes?"

"That's where he grabbed me."

Brad inspects her wrist. His gentle touch warms her arm. He stands. "Come with me."

"Brad?"

"Please." Brad offers his hand. "This'll only take a second."

Gabriela follows. Brad pauses to tell the hostess they'll be right back. He takes her outside where the sun has shifted west toward fresh storm clouds that build on the horizon. A constant breeze slaps her face as they hurry down King Street. He walks her out to the center of the quiet intersection at Cardinal Avenue.

"Here." Brad drops her hand. "You feel it?"

She does. A slight buzz. Not the vibration of traffic. Something different. Something deep in the earth but not of this world. Gabriela nods.

“And look.” Brad traces the perimeter of a bright circle that forms a scar on the pavement around the crossroads.

She follows with her eyes as an old pickup truck honks when it passes. Brad waves.

“I see,” she says.

“You asked me if I believe in ghosts.”

“Yes.”

“I’m not sure what I believe anymore.” Brad touches her shoulder. “But sometimes when I drive over this spot, my daughter calls for me.”

“Brad?”

His eyes swell. “And I know I ain’t imagining it.”

“You’re not,” Gabriela says.

“This place, this spot. I don’t know. There’s an energy.”

(the wolf’s mouth)

“I feel it,” Gabriela says.

“It’s where he . . .” Brad draws her closer. “Where the pastor held the vigil. Where he always holds them. Not just my daughter’s. All of them. Something’s not right here.”

“I’m glad you showed me,” Gabriela says.

Together, they walk back to the restaurant in silence where they finish their meals. Gabriela offers to split the check, but Brad tells her not to worry as he digs a few bills out of his wallet. She can cover next time. Gabriela thanks him.

She arrives at the Orpheum ten minutes before her call. *When you’re on time, you’re late.*

Maybe *Mamma* said that.

scene 8.

Rehearsal ends shortly after midnight. Gabriela’s the last to leave. Two deputies escort her to the parking lot and watch as she drives away. An evening storm approaches from the west, whipping up leaves and turning over lawn chairs. She gets to her apartment and hurries to the stairs as the rain starts. A small package with a note taped on top sits by her front door. She unlocks and goes in, dropping off her keys on the buffet in the front hall. A solitary light left burning above the stove guides her to the kitchen where she kicks off her shoes. She removes socks still damp from the earlier storm and sits barefoot at the table with her package. Thunder cracks in the distance. She pulls off the note. It's a thoughtful message from Deborah telling her she's always there for her.

Gabriela smiles as she unwraps the pastry box and digs in, shoving a mini rum *baba* down her mouth in three quick bites. Few places have been as sweet and delicious as home. Colangelo's in Pittsburgh where she enjoyed the sidewalk seating after her long hours in the theatre each day. When she stopped at Rocco's Pasticceria in Greenwich Village on her three-day excursion to New York City last Christmas before moving to Crow Creek. And Deborah's.

She reaches for a cream puff and takes a bite before going to the refrigerator for cold milk. She pours a glass and turns on the TV for background noise. An improvisational show where four best friends from high school play practical jokes on one another emerges out of the dark screen. While trying not to laugh, they read ridiculous names to unsuspecting guests who wait for an imaginary focus group. Gabriela loves that the art form derives from the Italian *commedia dell'arte* of the late Renaissance that she studied at the university back home. She curls up on the sofa, tucking cool toes under her legs as she sips milk and watches the program. Lightning dances outside her front window, sizzling before a loud crack of thunder makes her jump. The image on the TV blinks. The kitchen light flickers. Lights have been flickering too often lately.

To echo her thoughts, a flash of lightning causes another surge and flutter.

Dress rehearsal went well tonight. As well as can be expected under the circumstances. The performers didn't have as much energy as they should've, but that's excusable. With only two rehearsals left, they'll need to step up their game for the opening on Friday. She's confident Matt Leath will guide them. He's a solid director. As far as she knows, this is his first gig with the Holt Players. He'll be invited back. They've made him feel more welcome at the Orpheum than she does. Connor Simmons took all the cues as the stand-in for Tommy Nolan without any trouble. There aren't any major scene changes, so the backstage crew spends most of its time in a vamp. Even the board ops have it easy beside her at the console.

The technical demands didn't make the run-through difficult for Gabriela. Her inability to quit thinking about Brad did. What's going on between the two of them? She's half his age. That's not Sara Cooper talking. That's the truth. The cold facts. How could Brad possibly be interested in her? *Why* would he be? Is she even serious about him? He's the town sheriff. He's a widower. His late daughter might've been older than she is. Gabriela's from another country and has lived in America fewer than two years. What could they possibly have in common? Maybe she's reading signals that aren't there. His touch is gentle and affectionate, but maybe he's just a nice guy. There are still gentlemen left in the world, aren't there? Despite what social media and the politics of her generation spout about toxic masculinity. Isn't there something of value in a man who treats a woman like she's a woman? Who'll hold a door for her and pick up a dinner tab? Maybe her views are Old World because she was raised Old World by *Mamma* in the shadows of the Alps where farming is a way of life, there are no suburbs, and news of The Beatles breaking up still hasn't arrived.

Well, that's not totally fair. But close.

Wind howls outside as rain pounds the apartment. She raises the volume on the TV. The pranksters toss fruit over their shoulders at a grocery store. She goes to the kitchen table for the rest of her cream puff. Lightning flashes. She sits on the sofa and draws a pillow over her lap.

What about Pastor Aken? She'd be lying if she didn't admit that not only did she find herself more hungry for sex than she's been in a long time when she first saw his picture, but that she wants to attend the vigil if only to see him in person. That's the best way to describe the difference between Brad and the pastor, isn't it? She wants Brad to romance her. She wants the pastor to *fuck* her. And she knows she's a horrible person for wanting both of those things. But how long has it been since she's had sex?

Since Pittsburgh and Josh West. He worked on the run crew at the Pittsburgh Public Theatre. Nothing more than a grip that shifted scenery, but he was cute. The light eyes and fair skin more typical of the Northern Italians where Gabriela grew up. Not the best in bed but cute and respectful. Definitely not mature enough for her, however. They only slept together three or four times. Mostly, she taught him what to do. He probably wasn't a virgin but might as well have been. He was very intimidated by Gabriela and her foreignness. She always felt distant when they were together. Like she wasn't really there.

So over eight months. More like ten months since she's had sex.

What if the pastor were here right now?

Gabriela finishes the cream puff and licks her fingers before stretching out on the sofa. She reaches for the remote control, presses the mute button, and closes her eyes. She finds Pastor Aken in the darkness. His sensual snarl apparent even in the still photograph. She pulls down her jeans and slips them over her feet. They drop off the edge of the cushions and to the carpet. Her quivering hands move along her inner thighs and tug her underwear. She finds her clit and rubs, moaning and spreading both legs with her feet in the air. Lightning crashes but distant now. Not because the storm is passing but because the outside is lost. Gone somewhere like faded dreams and distant memories. She only has Pastor Aken now. He's on top of her, pressing his full weight. Sleek as a snake, drawing hips low and close until he penetrates. She gasps while he pumps, rubbing harder and faster. Pinning her hands above her head with one strong fist, he strokes her cheek with a slender finger along her jaw and down her neck.

Her neck. Her *cornicello*.

Gabriela's eyes snap open.

Her *cornicello*?

She pats her chest and neck, searching for the charm. It's gone. She pulls up her underwear and twists over the cushions, throwing them aside as she searches for the tiny red horn and gold chain.

Lighting spits, driving the power away for good. The silent image on the TV folds, swallowing the four clowns. The kitchen light pops. Gabriela bumps her knee on the coffee table and falls to the living room carpet in the darkness.

"Fanculo."

On her knees, she digs through the sofa but finds nothing. She crawls to the kitchen and pulls herself up to the table, tossing the pastry box and flipping the grapevine placemats, but can't find her charm. The charm *Mamma* gave her for Christmas before she shipped out from Milan. The one that protects against evil.

(beware the wolf's mouth)

Gabriela scrambles across the floor to where she dropped her jeans so she can dig through her pockets. In theatre, they call this kinesthesia. From the Greek for sensing movement. The ability the muscles have to find their way without the need of the other senses. Muscle memory. Find your way. In the dark.

She grabs the jeans.

Maybe she stuck her *cornicello* in one of the pockets when she was with Brad? When they were out at the intersection walking the perimeter of the scar in the pavement. The circle that buzzed with its own electric current. Yes, that's when she put it there.

No, it was during rehearsal. That's it. That's when she did it. It's clear now. She was at console and didn't want to lose it, so she put it in her pocket. No, it was backstage at the desk. Probably then. No, it was when she was by the flyrail. By the steps to the pit where she dropped her clipboard. Backstage near the dressing rooms. That's when. It'll be there.

She checks her pockets.

It's not.

Of course, it's not in there because Gabriela never takes off her *cornicello*. The only reason she tucked it under her shirt when she saw Brad walk up to the Mexican restaurant was because he wasn't wearing his hat, and she thought it was silly to have her *cornicello* out because she's a grown woman and doesn't need a fucking good luck charm, and *oh my god I lost it. I lost* Mamma*'s gift.*

Gabriela jumps into her jeans and shoes, skipping the damp socks. Her toes squish. She grabs her keys off the buffet, careful not to knock over the twisted ficus tree in the dark, and runs out the front door. Rain pelts her face, blurring her vision as she hurries down the steps and into the parking lot. Lightning cracks above. By the time she gets to her car, she's soaking wet.

She heads out. The drive takes fifteen minutes in the pouring rain. The roads are empty. She parks in front of the theatre. The police cruiser across the street flashes its lights without the siren. Gabriela groans. She forgot about the extra security. Maybe if she had parked out back, she would've been able to enter without being seen. But they probably have guards posted out back as well. Why wouldn't they? Or maybe they rotate. Who knows?

Focus, Gabriela. *Mamma* would say, *Non perdere di vista ciò che ti sta di fronte.* Don't lose sight of what's in front of you. Or something like that.

Gabriela takes two deep breaths and goes out into the rain. Water coats her shirt, flooding the small of her back and crack of her ass. She protects her face with her forearm. *Giove* rocks the heavens with another bolt of lightning. Gabriela flinches. It's obvious the deputies have no intention of meeting her halfway. They sit in their cars with their red and blue lights swirling. The driver lowers her window a crack. Gabriela doesn't recognize her dark features. She rubs her buzz cut.

"Help you, ma'am?"

"Eh?" Gabriela says. "Oh, no. I work for the theatre."

The partner cranes his neck to look out the window at her. He's as young as she is. Light blonde hair, not as thick as Brad's. His black tactical cap rests in his lap.

"Awful late for you to be out here, ma'am."

Wind swirls down the street. Gabriela staggers. Rain sprays under her arm. She chokes on a mouthful.

"Ma'am?" The driver shines her flashlight. "Don't you think you oughtta go back home?"

Home. If only she knew where home was. If only Gabriela could go home right now.

"No." She moves closer to the window. "I mean, I'm sorry. This'll only take a minute. I'll just run in real quick. I left my . . ."

Can she tell them what she's really looking for? Can she tell them about her *cornicello*? Won't they think she's crazier than they already do?

"Ma'am?"

"My notes," Gabriela says. "Yes . . . my notes. I left my notes backstage. I need to post them online before I go to bed tonight."

"Notes?"

"Yeah, I'm the stage manager." She bites her lip against the next lie. "I didn't give my notes to the crew tonight so we could all go home early."

"Is that right?" the driver says.

"Under the circumstances," Gabriela says.

The partner chuckles. "Stage manager?"

"Mmm-hmm."

"What exactly does a stage manager do?"

Gabriela peeks up at the clouds. "Look, I'll only be a minute. I promise."

"Where are you from?" the driver says, aiming the light at Gabriela's eyes. "You don't sound like you're from around here."

Gabriela squints, cupping both hands around her face. "One of you can come with me if you want. Both of you can."

The driver laughs and points her flashlight toward the sky. "In this storm? You must be joking."

"No, ma'am."

The driver and her partner exchange glances. She flicks her light at the theatre. "Go on."

"Thank you, officers."

"We'll be here," the partner says. "Don't forget."

Gabriela turns away and sprints across the street. She fumbles for her keys and drops them on the sidewalk. She curses, grabs them, and opens the door. The alarm chirps. She punches the code and disables the system. Shapes form in the darkness of the lobby as her eyes adjust. The ticket counter, the waiting area where she sat with Sara Cooper when Brad first talked to them, the concession stand, the display case filled with trophies from local competitions, portraits on the walls that archive previous shows. Water drips off her clothes and soaks the carpet. She staggers, hands out in front of her, and opens the custodial closet beside the box office. She switches the lights, but nothing turns on.

"Fanculo." Italian now. No time for English. *"Che cazzo?"*

She flicks the switch again but can't power the lights. She feels for the towel rack and grabs what she hopes is a clean one off the top. She dries her face and hair (thinks twice before closing the door), removes her bra, and sets it on the ticket counter. She grabs a second towel, stares out the front window to make sure the police officers aren't shining their lights her way, and blots under her shirt, soaking as much she can. She drops the towel and dresses. As she walks toward the auditorium doors, the air conditioner rumbles to life. The cool breeze gives her the chills under her wet clothes. She pulls her mobile out of her back pocket, hoping the shield's kept it dry. It has. No stagehand's dumb enough not to have a phone protector. She pushes the flashlight icon as she goes into the house. The doors swing closed behind her. She aims her single beam of light along the back of the house as she climbs into the console.

Find the cornicello *and go home. This doesn't have to take long. Find it and go.*

She searches the lightboard and monitor, feeling with her hand, as her eyes follow the light she points toward the soundboard. She pushes cables and headsets aside. Lifts scripts and cue sheets, but can't find her charm. She hits the Unison panel, hoping for stage lights, but gets none. Not even the ghost light. The alarm system chirps in the lobby for a ten count, rearming now that it's after hours. Gabriela leaps off the console in the dark and moves down the right aisle, following the glow of her mobile phone until she reaches the stage.

Floorboards creak behind the living room scenery. A door slams.

Please. Not again. Not now.

Gabriela races to the stage manager's desk and shakes her promptbook, wishing the demon won't cackle as the pages blur, but it does. Hoping the tiny red horn falls out, but it doesn't. *Or did it? Was that a sparkle?* More footsteps drag backstage. Heavier now. Closer. A shadow ripples. Sagging flesh swims in a tattered black suit.

"Beware the wolf's mouth." The oozing skin. The rope burns around the neck. *"You didn't listen."*

Gabriela drops, crawling on the floor by the flyrail until she gets to the top of the stairs near the orchestra pit. She shines her light. The clipboard she dropped after the production meeting is still at the bottom of the steps. A light flickers. Not the source four on stage. Below. In the pit.

"The fuck?" she says.

Something moans. She can't tell if it's above or below. From her knees, she traces the backstage wall with her light until the beam is lost beyond the proscenium. The floor vibrates and ripples, pulsing through her body. Not unlike the feeling she had with Brad when they walked the perimeter of the downtown crossroads outside *Mi Despensa*. Goosebumps sprout along her spine. She scoots to her feet and goes down into the pit, tracking the path below with her mobile until she reaches her clipboard. When she bends to pick it up, she spots light bleeding through cracks in the brick wall under the stage. The light forms a box about two feet wide by three feet high. She runs her fingers along the light. It's a trapdoor she's never noticed before. On the far side of the pit, she sees a similar glowing box within the brick wall. A pair of trap doors leading directly under the stage.

Have they been there all this time? What would they have been used for?

Maybe the theatre had a crawl space back when it was first built. Surely, it has a concrete foundation under the hardwood by now.

A slight hum builds within the shimmering light. Gabriela wants to run. Wants to turn, go upstairs, and drive back to her apartment. Or go for the police.

We'll be here, they said. *Don't forget.*

She can't run. Even if she doesn't find her *cornicello*, she needs to know what's behind the door. She runs her fingers along the crack, searching for a catch or lock. Her fingers trip a spring. The door lifts and opens. On her knees, Gabriela snags the edge so she can peek inside the narrow gap. Several metal girders mounted below the stage obstruct her view. A few steps lead down to a dirt subflooring. Above, a pulsing dome of electrical cables sends power along radiating glass cylinders to a mainframe stacked on a handtruck in the upstage corner.

Connor Simmons stands at the center of the space above a well. But not really a well. It's more like a conduit or what she imagines an oil rigger might use to tap the bottom of the ocean. King Boggs hovers beside him, stroking his snowy beard. His head is only centimeters from the joists above that support a composite steel deck. A woman Gabriela doesn't recognize slouches on the floor against a beam. Her eyes shift from Connor to King, but she's motionless in a heap propped in the dirt. Connor points a large curled horn at King.

"We must've made a mistake," Connor says.

"I know," King says.

"We need more blood."

"Maybe."

"We can't be responsible for what he did."

"And the other?"

"I'll deal with her if I have to." Connor looks down at the crippled woman. "She doesn't have much longer."

"What if they find out?" King says.

"They won't."

The trapdoor creaks on its hinges as the edge slips away from Gabriela's grip. Connor lifts his face toward her. So does King.

"The fuck?" he says.

"Who's there?" Connor says.

Gabriela bounces off the door and kicks it closed. She runs, slamming the pit door behind her as well. She stumbles on the steps but keeps her footing as she reaches the top. A flash under the railing catches her eye. Her *cornicello*. She has no idea how it got there. Maybe it slipped off before the show. Or after the show. She doesn't know. The charm has never come off before. Not since *Mamma* first placed it around her neck that Christmas morning so long ago. Before dead producers and hanging run crew and backstage ghosts. Maybe she shouldn't have bothered to hide it when she met Brad at the restaurant.

She shouldn't be ashamed of who she is or where she's from. Mamma always told her, *Te stesso.*

Be who you are.

Gabriela pancakes and stretches, brushing the tiny horn with her fingertips. It slips to the edge of the staircase and threatens to topple.

"No!"

She stretches her arm as far as she can. A black boot steps out from behind the proscenium and blocks her hand. Gabriela screams.

"You shouldn't be here," Sara Cooper says.

Gabriela looks up. "Sara?"

"Come on."

Sara tugs her, but Gabriela shakes loose to collect her *cornicello*. The pit door opens and closes. Footsteps barrel up the stairs. She bumps the horn and it slides off the edge. Gabriela gasps, flattening her palm on the backstage floor to catch the gold chain before it falls. She winds it around her wrist and pushes away as tilted heads emerge from the darkness below.

"Sara?" Connor says in the dark.

Maybe they didn't see me. Maybe they won't know I was here.

Sara hoists Gabriela to her feet and pushes her down the backstage hallway to the rear exit. They crash through into the pouring rain. The alarm howls, blasting its siren. Gabriela doesn't look back.

Act II

Thunder Underground

scene 1.

"The fuck?" Sara Cooper says as she drives.

"The fuck what?"

"What the fuck were you doing there?"

"My car," Gabriela says, adjusting her necklace. "I need to go back to my car."

Sara turns left on a rural road away from downtown. "Are you crazy?"

"Where are we going?"

"Nowhere."

"The police," Gabriela says.

"What about them?"

"They saw me go into the theatre. They know where I left my car."

"That's not good," Sara says.

"No, I need to go back."

"You can't." Sara screeches to a halt. "No fucking way."

Wipers slosh across the windshield.

"Please."

"There's no fucking way I'm going back there. You can walk back if you want, but I ain't. They don't know I was there."

"*They* don't know?" Gabriela says. "Connor? King?"

"Yes, Connor and King. Who the fuck do you think I'm talking about?"

"What were they doing there?"

"What were *you* doing there?" Sara says.

"I couldn't find my *cornicello*."

"Your what?" Sara shoves her car in gear and drives. "English, princess."

"My lucky horn."

"*Horn*?"

Gabriela clasps her charm and shows Sara. "This."

"You gotta be fucking kidding me."

"Why?"

Sara drives west on Route 119 toward Queensboro. The rain tapers as they head into the rural darkness of early morning.

"Did you see?"

"What?" Gabriela asks.

"Did you see them? Did you see what the fuck they were doing down there?"

"What they were doing down where?" Gabriela shakes her head. "Under the stage?"

"Yes, under the fucking stage. What's wrong with you? Did you forget to take your slow pills this morning?"

"Slow pills?"

Sara throws her hands up. "Where the fuck are you from?"

The car fishtails.

Gabriela lowers her chin. *"Italia."*

"You don't know how to split beans, do you?" Sara says.

"Eh?"

"Jesus."

"Please," Gabriela says. "Tell me what's going on."

"You don't wanna fucking know."

"Then at least tell me why you're helping me."

Sara slows, pulling into a narrow driveway. She winds through the dense woods to a single wide trailer parked on an open patch of grass and parks in gravel.

"Let's go inside." Sara kills the ignition. "We'll have a drink. I'll catch you up."

"Drink?"

"They do that where you're from, don't they?"

Gabriela nods. "Wine."

"That'll do." Sara opens her door.

"Sara?" Gabriela says.

"Huh?"

"Thank you."

Sara smirks. "I wouldn't say that just yet, darling. We're not out of the woods. Neither of us. And I realize we're in the fucking woods."

Sara gets out of the car, and Gabriela follows. They climb two steps and enter the unlocked trailer. The space inside is tight and dark. Sara turns on a lamp that reveals shag carpet and yellow wallpaper peeling in strips. Sara offers Gabriela a seat in a wide armchair. She curls up with a musty cushion.

"Let me get that wine," Sara says and goes to the kitchen. She pops open a bottle and sets two glasses on the counter as she pours.

"You live here?" Gabriela says.

"Nuh-uh." Sara puts Gabriela's glass down on an end table and plops into a denim sofa, kicking up dust in brown clouds. "I'm not that dumb."

"Dumb?"

"In case they come looking for me."

"You think they followed us?"

"Doubtful." Sara props both boots on a rickety coffee table and drains her wine. "Once that alarm went off, they would've run."

"You think so?"

"I do."

Sara jumps to her feet and pours another class. Gabriela sips hers. American wine has no flavor.

"Whose place is this?"

"Meemaw's."

"Meemaw?"

"Oh, excuse me." Sara chuckles as she sits back down. "That's how we say Grandma around these parts."

"I see."

"How do they say that where you come from?"

"Grandma?"

"Mmm-hmm."

"Nonna."

"Nonna?"

Gabriela nods.

"I like that," Sara says, removing her boots before she places her feet back on the coffee table. Gabriela's pummeled by the cheesy scent of Sara's dirty socks. She gags.

"What's the matter?" Sara says and adjusts her nose stud. "Don't like the wine?"

"Eh?" Gabriela takes a quick swallow. "No, it's fine. Not bad at all."

Sara raises an eyebrow. "You ain't a good liar, Miss Rossi."

"Sorry."

Sara stretches her arms behind her head. Her armpits are also ripe. Gabriela squirms.

"No," Sara says. "This here's Meemaw's. Well, it was. She passed away about six years ago. Left the whole place to me and my brother, but he's worthless. Spends more time in jail than out. Anyway, the house's paid off. Property taxes are cheap as dirt. I can come and go when I please."

"That's nice."

"Yeah, but I keep my apartment in Braxton Lake. Rent's a bit high over there, but it's a damn sight nicer than this dump." Sara glances to the ceiling where stucco crumbles. "Sorry, Meemaw. Anyhow, if they're gonna come looking for me — for us — they won't come here."

Gabriela sets down her wine glass. "Thank you."

"Yeah, you probably think I'm a bitch."

"No, I didn't. I don't."

Sara slides to the front of the cushions and tilts her glass. "Believe me, you don't have to lie. I know I can rub people the wrong way and come off as downright pissy, but I ain't. At least not on purpose. I only speak what's on my mind. Most country folks do."

Some people talk because they have tongues in their mouths.

"No, I get it," Gabriela says.

"Do you, though?"

Gabriela nods.

"Hey, relax." Sara stretches out. "I'm only fucking with you."

"Oh."

"So, you wanna know what those guys were doing down there?"

Gabriela clears her throat. "I'm not sure."

"That's okay, cause I'm not so sure I can explain it. Not really."

"Who's the girl?"

"Oh, you saw her, too?"

"Yes."

Sara sighs. "The fucker."

"What's wrong with her?" Gabriela says.

"Not *her*. I mean, I don't know what's wrong with her. She's sick. Well, obviously. I meant Connor. That fucker. I can't believe he keeps putting her through that shit."

"She's sick?"

"Yeah."

"But you don't know what's wrong with her?"

"Not exactly. Birth defect, I think."

"Can she move?"

Sara shakes her head. "Nuh-uh."

"Who is she?"

"Connor's sister."

"Minga," Gabriela says. "His sister?"

"Uh-huh. Older sister. Been sick as long as I've known Connor."

"How long is that?"

"Not sure. He and I went to middle school together. So, twenty years?"

"Middle school?"

"Yeah, they don't you have that where you come from?"

The schools at home are divided almost the same way as they are in America, but they're only compulsory until the age of sixteen, which makes sense in an economy that relies on agriculture and manufacturing.

"Scuola media."

"Yeah, that shit sounds about right."

Gabriela rubs her *cornicello*. "What's he doing to her?"

"Connor?"

"Mmm-hmm."

"What's he doing to his sister?"

"Sì."

"That's the million dollar question, ain't it?"

Gabriela slips off her shoes and dries her bare feet on the carpet, hoping they don't smell as bad as Sara's. Not that either would notice.

"Is he trying to help her?"

"Help her?" Sara coughs. "Guess you could say that, yes."

"Was Tommy part of it?"

Sara stands and walks to the front door. She splits the miniblinds with two thick fingers as she peeks through. She doesn't look at Gabriela when she answers.

"Yes."

Gabriela crosses the small room and stands behind Sara. Outside, the world is quiet and still. The storm long gone. Crickets chirp. A toad bellows. Gabriela checks the time on her mobile. It's half of three.

"How?"

"I hated lying to the sheriff," Sara says.

"You lied?"

"Well, I didn't tell him the truth. Not all of it. To be fair, I didn't know that Tommy had killed Mr. Patterson by then. Only figured as much."

"Tommy killed Mr. Patterson?"

Sara turns and faces Gabriela. She comes as close to tears as Gabriela's ever seen. As close as Gabriela's thought possible in the eight months they've known each other.

"You know how upset I was when you got that promotion?"

"I don't understand what you mean."

"When Heather took that job up in Boston? Fucking Heather. If she hadn't left, none of this would've happened. At least not all of it. Connor still would've been fucking around with that collider King hooked up for him, but they wouldn't have gone for blood. Tommy was just so fucking angry about it."

"I don't understand," Gabriela says and takes Sara's hand.

"You know the fuck of it?" Sara clears her throat. "It was my idea."

"Your idea?"

"Yeah. Well, kinda."

"To kill Mr. Patterson?"

Sara nods. Now the tears spill. "But I was joking. I fucking swear. I didn't mean it."

"Of course you didn't."

"And that dumb shit, Tommy. He didn't have to listen to me, did he? For fuck's sake, I joked about you, too."

"Me?"

Sara nods.

"You told Tommy to kill me?"

"Huh?" Sara steps back toward the kitchen. "No, not kill. The blood. Connor thought blood would help. Thinks it will."

Gabriela follows. "Yes, I heard them talking about that. About needing more blood."

"So, I told them, wouldn't it be funny if we made some type of sacrifice? Like in the old days. I didn't think they'd actually fucking do it."

"The old days?"

"Yeah, I mean Dionysus and shit. The Ancient Greeks. Didn't you study all about that when you went to school?"

"Of course."

Dionysus, the foreign god. The Outsider. Half-god, half-human. Zeus sewed Dionysus into his thigh to shield him from the gods who killed his mother. He was known as Bacchus in Ancient Rome. The massive festivals honoring Dionysus produced works by some of the greatest playwrights in human history. Sophocles, Euripides, Aeschylus, and even Aristophanes (despite how the Greeks undervalued comedy, unlike the Romans). Their rituals included sacrifice. The bleeding of a bull. The goat given to Thespis, the first actor to step away from the chorus. Before him, all theatre was music. Song, dancing, and instruments. Many believe the word *tragedy* comes from this offering.

"Did you know that he could cross over?" Sara asks.

"Eh?"

"That Dionysus could go back and forth between life and death?"

(he rises in the wolf's mouth)

"His mother was human." Gabriela nods her head. "Semele, the princess of Thebes. The other gods often mistreated him because of his lineage."

"That, too."

Gabriela walks back to the armchair and sits. "Did Tommy kill himself?"

"That's what I thought." Sara shrugs. "At first."

"But you don't anymore?"

Sara shakes her head. "Nuh-uh."

"Why not?"

"The batten."

"What about it?" Gabriela says.

"He would've needed somebody else to fly him out."

And the pipe was two meters lower than it should've been.

"Oh, right." Gabriela finishes her wine. "There would've been somebody else on the rail. Somebody who doesn't normally operate it."

"And whoever the fuck it was, they had to be strong. They didn't add any bricks. The pipe was out of balance with Tommy's dead weight."

"King?" Gabriela says.

"Doubtful. I don't think he or Connor would've gotten their hands dirty."

"There's somebody else involved then?"

Sara shakes her head. "Not with Connor, no. That circle's closed. Even I'm out."

"But somebody else who knows?"

"Mmm-hmm."

(the dead man)

Dead men can't hoist linesets. Gabriela rubs the bruise on her wrist. *Maybe they can.* She reaches for her shoes. "I really need to go get my car. Think it's safe?"

"Sleep here tonight." Sara sits on the arm of the chair. "You can go get your car in the morning. In the daylight."

"Are you serious?"

"Gabriela," Sara says and slides into the wide armchair so their hips touch. "You haven't been in Crow Creek for very long. I've lived here my whole life. There's something wrong about this place. Something's off, deep where the underground currents flow. I've always felt it."

"What are you talking about?"

"Trust me, okay? We'll share Meemaw's bed. It's not big, but it's better than this filthy sofa." Sara punches a cushion.

"Sleep together?"

"Trust me, dear, you'll be fine." Sara winks and unwraps a pack of cigarettes before lighting up. "You're not my type. Cute and all with that sexy foreign accent, but I prefer redheads."

Gabriela drops her shoes beside the end table. "Funny."

"You can call your boyfriend in the morning," Sara says as she inhales.

"Boyfriend?"

"Brad."

"Oh."

"He can take you to get your car. A police escort. How perfect would that be?"

Gabriela groans and smacks Sara with a sofa cushion. She wishes she could shower. Or that Sara will. A cloud of blue smoke from Sara's cigarette shrouds the compact living room of Meemaw's trailer.

scene 2.

Gabriela doesn't have to call Brad in the morning. He calls her at eight o'clock. She jumps and pulls her mobile out of her back pocket. The charge is almost gone.

"Ciao?"

"Miss Rossi?"

Not Gabriela. Not even a hello.

"Yes?"

"This is Sheriff Gleason." Not Brad or Sheriff Brad. His rank. And last name. "Need a few words. Where's a good place?"

Gabriela glances at Sara, who hasn't moved. She cuddles a pillow while she snores.

"The theatre?"

"That works. How's twenty minutes? You need a ride?"

"*Eh*? No . . . I mean, yes, I can be there."

But she wants to take care of something else while she's downtown so early. Find answers the living haven't been able to provide.

"Give me an hour, please," she says.

"See you then."

He hangs up. Gabriela rolls to her side and shoves Sara.

"The fuck?"

"Sheriff Brad."

"What about him?" Sara groans. "I'm still sleeping."

"I need to meet him at the Orpheum at nine o'clock."

"Fuck," Sara says and kicks the sheets off.

She wears only panties under the covers. Tattered purple ones. Gabriela doesn't remember when Sara took off her clothes. A bright rose tattoo stretches between her breasts, which are both full and quite pleasant, especially compared to Gabriela's small ones. Wrapped around the rose's stem is the name *Becky* inked in black.

(she keeps close to the willows bless her heart)

After they swig sour orange juice and shove dry corn flakes down their mouths, Sara takes Gabriela to Luke's Hardware about five blocks from the theatre.

"Mind walking the rest of the way?" Sara asks.

"No, it's fine."

"Might not be such a great idea for the sheriff to see me drop you off."

"Probably not."

"Calls at six tonight?"

Gabriela steps out of the car. "For previews."

Before the run last night, Deidre Worth mentioned something about how they're expecting roughly eighty for the final dress, mostly invites from the senior center in Houndstooth.

"Thank you six," Sara says before she leaves Gabriela standing in the middle of the parking lot.

A toothless elderly man (probably escaped from the senior center) smiles and waves as he drags himself along the pavement on a wooden cane. The sky above is bright. The sun already warms the downtown streets. To her left, she spots DeVito's Bakery. Deborah opens early. Maybe she should grab some coffee? It would be nice to see Deborah and thank her for last night's pastries, if nothing else. But Brad's waiting, and she has another stop to make first.

Not *Brad.* Sheriff Gleason.

Why was he so cold and distant when he called? Maybe he was at his desk in the sheriff's office? It can't be easy for him to be open about his feelings in front of his staff. How long did he say his wife's been dead? Two years? And what feelings? That's crazy. *Pazzo.* Brad has no feelings for her. He's a police officer with a job to do in a small town that normally gives him nothing to do. And he didn't sound thrilled on the phone.

She turns right on Cardinal Avenue away from the bakery and walks to the newspaper office. She has forty minutes before she meets Brad. A tall woman with flaming red hair and freckles stands by an open file cabinet, shuffling folders with slender hands. She wears a loose fitting sheer blouse tied off above hip hugging jeans. Her light eyes swirl as she greets Gabriela.

"Morning."

"Good morning."

"How may I help you?"

"I'm Gabriela Rossi." She extends her hand. "I work at the Orpheum."

"Of course you are." Becky Stokes closes the file cabinet and shakes with a soft cool grip. "Pleasure to meet you."

"Grazie."

"Have a seat." Becky offers a chair opposite a metal desk.

Gabriela sits. A rooster clock above stacks of newspapers reads half of nine.

"I must say — " Becky scoots in a squeaky rolling chair facing Gabriela. "I didn't expect you so soon. Sheriff Gleason has been rather strict about protecting the theatre folks."

"I'm sure he has."

Becky leans back and nibbles the end of a sharp polished fingernail. "Unless you have another reason for dropping by."

"I do."

"How exciting." Becky grins. "Maybe we can help each other?"

"That's what I'm hoping for."

Becky unfolds a newspaper on her desk. "Glad we're on the same page."

Gabriela snickers.

"Sorry. I couldn't resist the joke," Becky says. "Newspaper humor and all."

"It's fine."

"What if I start?"

Gabriela nods.

"So, you're the stage manager at the Orpheum?"

"I am."

"Oh, just a moment." Becky taps her phone. "I almost forgot. May I record this?"

"Sure."

"Great. Thanks." She presses an app. "So, you're the stage manager?"

"Yes."

"And how long have you been at the Orpheum? Not quite a year?"

"That's correct. Eight months."

"Eight months? Wonderful." Becky narrows her eyes. "I'm detecting an accent."

Gabriela sighs. "Look, I don't mean to be rude, but I can make this go a lot faster. Save us both some time."

"Oh?"

"I found James Patterson *and* Tommy Nolan."

Becky croaks and covers her mouth with a closed fist. "Both? I didn't realize."

"Yes, ma'am." A fly buzzes Gabriela's ear. "Well, I wasn't alone, but yes. I was there."

"And you sure you're supposed to be talking to me?"

"They're both dead," Gabriela says. "What does it matter?"

"Good point." Becky props her elbows on the desk. "Can you share the details?"

"Mr. Patterson had a hole carved out of his chest. Tommy was hanging from a batten. Can we move on?"

"I like your style, Miss Rossi," Becky says.

Gabriela can't help but notice how pretty she is. Her high cheekbones and narrow nose look porcelain. Her full moist lips, succulent. She's almost a ginger version of Pastor Aken. If this is Sara's Becky, Gabriela wouldn't be surprised. Sara prefers redheads. Becky always seems to find her way around the theatre. The math adds up. Why wouldn't Sara tell her? Maybe Gabriela didn't need to know.

"Thank you."

"Hole in his chest?"

Gabriela scratches her chin. "Yes."

"That's about what the sheriff gave us." Becky pushes away from the desk and grabs a pot of coffee off a small formica table behind her. "Care for a cup?"

Not a bad idea. Gabriela's rolling on less sleep than she normally does during show week. She should already be on her third cup this long after she's out of bed.

"Please."

"Per favore?" Becky says. "Am I right?"

"Sì."

Becky smiles bright and wide. "I have an ear for accents."

"Maybe you should work at the theatre," Gabriela says.

"I'm not as far away as you think."

"Only a few blocks, right?"

Becky laughs and pours Gabriela a cup of coffee before pushing cream and sugar across the desk. Gabriela sips hers black. Tastes like burnt office brew. So few Americans know how to make coffee, except Deborah. She prefers *Mamma*'s homemade *espresso*. The caffeine gives her a quick jolt, however.

"Tommy?" Becky asks.

"What else do you want to know?"

"Does it look like he did it to himself?"

Gabriela pauses. Sara doesn't think so, but the pipe isn't the most convincing evidence.

"As far as I can tell," Gabriela says. "But I can't say for sure."

Becky sighs. "Well, that's more than the *No comment* Brad gave me."

Brad. Not the sheriff this time. Not Sheriff Gleason. *Brad.* Maybe Becky's been making her rounds? Curly was rather pushy when pulling Brad out of the auditorium to meet with her yesterday.

"Last question," Becky says. "Then I'll give you what you need."

How does she know I need *anything?*

"Sure," Gabriela says.

"How do the rest of the cast and crew feel about you being the stage manager?"

"Eh?"

"Well, it's been less than two weeks since Heather Danby left." Becky taps the folded paper she set aside. "We ran a feature on her two Sundays ago. The Huntington Theatre in Boston sounds like a golden opportunity. We had no idea who Heather's replacement would be when we went to print. Having you step in at the last minute might rub some of the locals the wrong way."

Gabriela swallows. "Time will tell."

"Fair enough." Becky flutters her eyelashes and leans closer, flashing ample cleavage. It's not difficult to see why Sara would find her attractive. She oozes sex. "So, what can I do for you?"

"You mind?"

"How's that?" Becky says.

"Your mobile?"

"Oh, of course." Becky taps her phone and stops recording. *"Scusi."*

Gabriela snorts. Becky knows more Italian than she should, even if her words are basic. Gabriela doesn't know of any Italians in Crow Creek besides Deborah. That's probably why her bakery stays busier than Starbucks. Her pastries are a privilege. Starbucks seems more like an entitlement to Americans.

"I need some information about the Orpheum."

"What kind of information are you talking?"

"I need to know if there have ever been any deaths in the theatre prior to this week."

Becky slides a laptop across her desk. "You already do a Google search?"

"And checked the library." Gabriela sips stale coffee.

"Wanda Butler do you any good?" Becky says.

How would *Mamma* answer?

"Only good enough to cook my goose."

Becky grins. "Not sure that's how we'd put it around here, but I get it. She's a hot mess."

"I didn't mean to insult her."

"Don't worry." Becky waves her off. "If you think she's odd, wait till you meet her son."

More than likely, the one-eyed giant in Wanda's picture frame is her son. Gabriela can't imagine any circumstances where that would come true. Maybe he's the reason Wanda was reading a book about genetic disorders. Seems a little late for that, however.

"Is that so?"

"Mmm-hmm."

Becky refills Gabriela's cup. The clock inches toward eight-forty.

"Any other ideas?"

"Think so." Becky pushes back from the desk. "Come with me."

Gabriela ignores her full cup of coffee and follows Becky as she swivels her hips through a glass door at the back of the office. They take a narrow hallway and go down a flight of stairs into a cold storage room lined with dozens of file cabinets.

"We keep all our archived prints down here," Becky says, scraping a fingernail along the metal cabinets. "They go back decades."

Gabriela releases a noisy breath of air that reverberates in the frigid space. "Oh."

"But I'll return the favor and save *you* some time."

"You already looked?"

"I'm a journalist, Miss Rossi." Becky rests her slim fingers on a handle two rows down. "What do you think?"

"Grazie."

Becky pops open the drawer and pauses, grinning. "Dionysus was twice-born."

Gabriela shudders, raising the hair on the back of her neck. *"Che cosa?"*

"That's why they never liked him."

"*Who* never liked him?" Gabriela staggers closer to the file cabinets. "The gods? So? What are you talking about?"

As Becky walks to the stairs, she flashes like the irritating source four in the Orpheum catwalks, bones and muscles visible beneath her clothes and skin.

"Aspetta." Gabriela shakes her head, rubbing the bridge of her nose. "What do you mean?"

"Careful what you wish for."

Becky disappears up the steps.

Sounds like something *Mamma* would say. *Fai attenzione a ciò che desideri.*

Gabriela drops to her knees and opens the drawer all the way. She flips through the hanging newspapers one at a time from the back forward until she finds the headline she's searching for from an issue dated November 8, 1957. **Local Theatre Manager Hangs Himself Opening Night.** She recognizes the man in the photograph as the apparition she's met twice backstage at the Orpheum. His features are unmistakable and quite handsome (without the decaying flesh), especially his high cheekbones and oiled hair. The caption identifies him as Ralph Delacourt, age 36. She reads the article but learns little about Delacourt beyond his four-year tenure as house manager and premature demise. He didn't have any immediate family and was survived by his parents and unmarried younger sister,

Peggy. His funeral was held at First Baptist, where he was laid to rest on the morning of the thirteenth.

Gabriela scratches her chin and sits with her legs folded as she studies the old photograph. Delacourt poses with guests at the Orpheum on opening night. The caption names the show as *Orpheus Descending* by Tennessee Williams. It's not a title Gabriela recognizes, but she's familiar with the playwright, whose work she studied at the university in Italy.

As she starts to slide the newspaper back into the file cabinet, another face standing beside Delacourt in the photograph catches her eye. She blinks in doubt and traces the profile with a shaking finger.

Pastor Aken.

She'd recognize him anywhere now that she's seen him on the flyer the grocery store clerk gave Brad at the Mexican restaurant last night. She can't forget his chiseled jaw or rippling gaze. His high-bridged nose and lofty forehead. His complexion smooth and glossy like snakeskin. Like Becky's. Gabriela makes the sign of the cross.

What's Pastor Aken doing in a photograph dated November 8, 1957? He can't be more than forty years old. There's no way he was born by 1957, much less an adult. That would make him a hundred years old at the very least if alive today.

Gabriela rubs her eyes. Pastor Aken remains in the newspaper photo, leering over Ralph Delacourt's left shoulder like a guardian angel. Or a pouncing demon.

(we all have our own)

Gabriela closes the file cabinet and trots up the stairs. By the time she leaves the newspaper office, it's five of nine and Becky Stokes is nowhere to be found.

scene 3.

Outside the theatre, Brad's cruiser is parked behind her car. He leans against his rear fender and scrolls through his mobile. He stands when he sees her and tips his hat.

"Morning."

"Sheriff."

"Have a rough night?"

"Kind of."

"You look a little worse for wear."

"Sorry."

"Don't apologize," Brad says. "Unless you got something you're sorry for."

"I don't."

"My deputies saw you go into the theatre last night."

"I know."

"They didn't see you come out, though. Not even when the alarm tripped. Something you wanna tell me?"

Two crows caw as they watch from above, bobbing and weaving on the edge of the marquee. Gabriela nods.

Brad walks to the theatre. "Guess we better go inside and chat then."

"Yessir." Gabriela unlocks the door and punches the code to silence the beeping keypad. She picks up the towel she dropped by the ticket booth last night and returns it to the custodian closet without bothering to check the lights.

Brad waits by the doors. "Through here?"

"Bene."

They enter the dark auditorium. Shadows flicker across the scenery from the ghost light shining backstage. Gabriela hops to the console and presses the Unison panel. All the lights come up.

"At least they're working," Brad says.

"For now."

She adjusts the settings so the stage stays dark and plugs her phone into a charger above the soundboard since she's at sixteen percent.

"Mind if I sit?"

"Help yourself, sir."

Brad takes a seat in the back row and gestures for Gabriela to sit opposite him across the right aisle. She does. The bright house lights bounce off the paneled walls and ceilings where old slats of hardwood flooring were repurposed as part of the decade-old renovation that Gabriela's glad she missed. The chair in front of her is named for Everett Jackson, a generous deacon at First Baptist. Gabriela gathers the bottom of her shirt and rubs a speck of blood off his gold plaque, installed as part of the fundraising campaign that assigned donors seats in the auditorium during the remodel.

"Look," Brad says. "I don't believe you killed Mr. Patterson or had anything to do with Tommy Nolan."

"You don't?"

"Of course not." Brad removes his hat and runs his fingers through his thick blonde hair. His eyes sparkle. "But I need you to tell me what's going on. We got both reports back from the medical examiner last night. Patterson was impaled by an animal, and Tommy was dead before he got hung on that pipe."

"By an animal?"

"You heard right." Brad stretches his neck as he scans the auditorium. "And correct me if I'm wrong, but I ain't seen no wild animals running through your theatre lately."

"Connor was holding a horn."

"Ma'am?"

"When I came here last night, I found Connor under the stage holding a goat's horn."

A *goat*. The word *tragedy* comes from the goat given Thespis at the *City Dionysia*.

"Connor was here last night?"

"He was. So was King Boggs. They were together under the stage."

Brad pulls his notepad out of his khakis and flips through the small yellow pages, licking his fingers as he does so.

"Connor Simmons. He's the assistant stage manager, right?"

"ASM. Yes. He is now. Now that Heather's gone, and I'm the stage manager."

"And this King Boggs? He's what you call the master electrician?"

"Yes, he hangs and focuses the lights."

Brad raises his eyes toward the catwalks where the source fours mounted above the house stare lifelessly from their perch like sentinels.

"Lights?"

"Mmm-hmm. He takes care of our lighting equipment."

"Interesting." Brad says.

"But he didn't kill Mr. Patterson," Gabriela says.

"He didn't?"

"Neither did Connor."

"No?"

"Tommy did."

"Tommy?" Brad squares his shoulders. "He killed Mr. Patterson?"

"Sì."

"What happened to Tommy then?"

"I don't know who killed him or how he died."

"No?"

Gabriela swallows. "I'm sorry."

"How do you know he killed Mr. Patterson then?"

"Connor told King last night."

Not exactly a lie. *We can't be responsible for what* he *did. He*'s Tommy. *What he did* was kill Mr. Patterson. That's what Sara told her as well. But what if Sara's wrong? Then the killer's still out there. What if she's right? Then who killed Tommy and why? And can she tell Brad about Sara? I'll deal with *her* if I have to. *Her* is Sara. That's who Connor was talking about, right? Can she betray Sara after she saved her life last night?

Brad dabs a pencil on his tongue before he takes notes. "When they were both under the stage?"

"Sì."

"You realize how crazy this all sounds, right?" Brad shifts, facing the aisle, and rubs his boots on the carpet. "Even to me?"

"There's more," Gabriela says.

Brad scratches his head. "More?"

"Remember the ghost I told you about?"

"Uh-huh."

"I know who he is." Gabriela ignores another speck of blood on the back of Everett Jackson's chair. "Ralph Delacourt."

"Delacourt?" Brad scratches his chin. "Name doesn't ring a bell."

"He was a house manager here in the 1950s. He hanged himself on opening night."

"That doesn't ring any bells either."

"That's not all," Gabriela says.

"Had a feeling you might say that."

"I found an article about him in the newspaper."

"Wait a minute." Brad clears his throat. "You went to the *Sentinel*?"

"Sì."

"Becky Stokes?"

"Uh-huh." Gabriela wipes away the speck of blood. "I didn't tell her anything she didn't already know."

"That so?"

Gabriela nods. "Pastor Aken was in the picture with Mr. Delacourt."

"Pastor Aken?"

"*Sì.* Yessir."

"*Our* Pastor Aken?" Brad shuffles in his seat. "You're certain?"

Gabriela rolls her eyes. "Well, I've only seen the poster your friend gave you at the restaurant last night, but it was him. I'm sure of it. *Certamente.*"

"That doesn't make any sense. You realize how old that'd make him?"

"But you believe me?"

Brad tugs his shirtsleeves. "I don't know."

"Maybe I should show you?"

"What you seen last night?" Brad stands, setting his hat back on his head, and pockets his notepad and pencil. "Probably so."

scene 4.

Gabriela leads Brad to the stage. They pass the desk where she sits when she's not at console. It's where Tommy would've sat during the run. Connor sits there now. It's where she must've misplaced her *cornicello*. Could Connor have gotten his hands on it? If so, why would he have left it on the floor? No, she must've dropped it. Or maybe the clasp came undone when she tucked it under her shirt at dinner, and it took a while to slip off on its own. At least she didn't lose it at the restaurant or out on the street where it never would have been found. Out on the street where Brad walked the circle around the intersection. Where the currents under the pavement hummed.

The promptbook stirs as they go by. The flipping pages reveal the demon she sketched the day Tommy murdered James Patterson. The flames in the eyes burn red. Gabriela shivers and goes down into the pit. Brad follows.

"Always this dark down here?" he says.

"I'll get the switch."

Gabriela turns on the lights. The fluorescents cast an eerie glow, lighting up the conductor's platform (for when they stage musicals) and supplemental platform pieces that can be arranged to make a false apron in front of the master curtain for extra dance space. The Holt Players have only produced one musical since Gabriela first arrived last winter, *The Drowsy Chaperone*. The absurd parody of the Jazz Age delighted audiences but didn't sell as many tickets as a Disney musical or a popular title like *Hairspray* would. It's always a risk when planning a season. Gabriela played no part in selecting the current lineup, but you need those big splashy shows to fund smaller artistic ones like *Bury Me in Autumn*. Without them, any theatre — community or regional — won't survive for long. That's why the theatre in Italy where Gabriela worked closed before she left for Pittsburgh. They didn't build profitable titles into their season for too many years to count and eventually dissolved. Maybe that's why James Patterson was giving comps to Raleigh Regional. Maybe he was worried about the Orpheum going under and wanted to entice potential investors.

Brad walks to the center of the orchestra pit. "Here?"

Gabriela shakes the cobwebs out of her head. "No sir."

Without the glow of light from beyond, the secret doors are difficult to spot. Gabriela traces her fingers along the brick wall until she finds the catch on the closest trap. The door lifts and creaks open.

"Here."

Brad slides his flashlight off his belt and enters first, descending the two steps with caution. Behind him, the antechamber looks even more cramped than last night in the single beam he casts. Gabriela can't figure out how King Boggs could fit under the rafters. The steel joists bend down from above with little clearance, knocking Brad's hat loose. He snatches it out of the dirt and whacks it against his hip.

"You're saying Connor and King were down here last night?"

Gabriela nods. "Yes, and Connor's sister."

"His sister?"

"Sì."

Brad pauses and scratches his head. "I've heard about her."

The dirty air tastes sour on Gabriela's tongue when she opens her mouth. "You have?"

"Amanda Simmons." Brad nods. "She's crippled."

"That's what I thought."

Brad faces Gabriela and shines the light between their eyes like he's telling ghost stories around a campfire. "About thirty years ago, Entech ran clinical trials on a cancer drug. No, maybe closer to forty years ago now. They're a local drug company. Anyhow, it's well documented around these parts. Well, at least, it was. The children of those lab rats had all sorts of problems. Birth defects, autoimmune diseases, you name it."

"Birth defects?" Gabriela pictures Wanda's eyeless son. "That's awful."

"The worse side effects were the ones you couldn't see."

"Che cosa?"

Brad taps the side of his head with his flashlight. "Some of them were plumb crazy. Only one oar in the water, you know? But at least they could get treated or institutionalized. The others? Well, it's the ones you can't tell are sick that are the most dangerous."

"You *can't* tell?"

"That's right." Brad sweeps the room with his flashlight. "Those are the worst of all."

Gabriela's stomach pings. *He's talking about Connor, isn't he?* Connor's sister has a visible defect. Maybe Connor's illness runs deep like the vibrations under the earth on King Street.

She leans against a column. *"Vedo."*

"How do they describe folks like that where you come from?" Brad asks.

How would *Mamma*? She had an expression for everything. *Has* an expression. A lump forms in Gabriela's throat. Mamma *didn't leave me. I left her.*

"Quando il diavolo ti accarezza, vuole la tua anima."

(when the devil caresses you he wants your soul)

Brad sighs. "I sure hope you don't mind me saying this, but I could listen to you speak all day long. English or otherwise. You just have the sweetest voice I've ever heard. Tickles me, really."

"Glad I amuse you," Gabriela says.

"No, ma'am." Brad half-grins. "Not that kinda tickle."

"Sheriff?"

"Pardon me." Brad's face turns bright red in the dim light. "That was rude. I didn't mean anything by it. Please forgive me, Miss Rossi."

"Of course."

Brad digs his bootheel in the dirt. "Really, I'm sorry."

"I'll live."

"Appreciate it." Brad paints the brick walls and steel girders with his flashlight. "So, you're saying they squeezed three down here?"

"Not just that." Gabriela circles around a post and points to the center of the space. "Right here. Right here they had some type of equipment."

"Equipment?"

"Yessir."

"What equipment?"

"I don't know, like an oil rig or a drill or something they were driving into the ground. And up here." Gabriela reaches above and taps between the rafters. "Here they had an electrical conduit with lines running to a terminal in the far corner. Like a nuclear collider or reactor."

Brad aims his flashlight. "Over there?"

"Yes, but it's all gone now."

Brad shakes his head. "I want to believe you, Gabriela, but this all sounds so crazy. What do you think they were doing down here?"

"I don't know, but you remember what you showed me out on King Street?"

Brad nods. "Of course."

"Last night while I was down here watching . . . while I was watching the three of them, I had the same feeling I had when we were standing at the intersection. The same kind of buzz. Or hum."

"Like a current?" Brad says.

"Sì."

Brad bends down in the center of the crawlspace and runs his hand through the dirt, revealing the small hole where Connor and King had plugged the tap into the earth. His flashlight flickers and goes out.

"Brad?"

The trap door swings shut behind them on squeaky hinges. The antechamber is pitch black. Gabriela can't see her hand in front of her face.

"Brad!"

A brilliant flame erupts from the earth, knocking Brad off his feet. He drops his hat. Gabriela thrusts her forearms in front of her face to block the heat. Above, the composite steel rattles. Gabriela drops to her knees and crawls to Brad. He writhes on the floor, rubbing both hands over his eyes. He convulses two, maybe three, times and freezes. The fire from the earth puffs out as quickly as it appeared. The flashlight sputters and turns back on. The beam points toward the far corner opposite where Connor and King had stacked their mainframe. Gabriela sees the dead man walking. *Ralph Delacourt.* His stooped shoulders and tattered suit. The peeling, rotten flesh. He disappears. The red eyes of the demon follow him in the darkness and fade.

(into the wolf's mouth)

Brad moans on the dirt subfloor. "Gabriela?"

"I'm here," she says. "I'm here, Brad. Are you okay?"

Brad struggles to sit up. The peripheral glow of the flashlight washes his bright red cheeks where he's lightly burned. "Think so, yes."

"What can I do?" Gabriela says.

Brad blinks. "Give me a minute."

"Okay."

Gabriela pants in the dim crawlspace, struggling to catch her breath. Sweat drips off her hair and runs down her cheeks. She can't unsee the sunbolt. Its fading scar streaks her vision. She pinches the bridge of her nose.

"Gabriela?"

"Yes, Brad, it's me."

Brad reaches out and takes her hand. "Are you okay?"

"Yes, yes, I'm fine." She rubs her blackened forearms. "I'm okay."

"What happened?" Brad says.

"I don't know," Gabriela says. "The hole. That's where Connor and King buried their pipeline or whatever it was."

"Did you hear?"

"Did I hear what?"

Brad coughs as he searches for her face in the dimness. "My daughter called for me."

"You heard your daughter?"

"Yes." Brad adjusts his duty belt and shoulder strap. "When the light hit me. Did you hear her?"

Gabriela picks up Brad's hat, twirling it in her hands. "No, I didn't."

"She was here. In the light."

"I believe you."

"That's not all."

"No?"

"No."

"What else did you see?"

Brad blinks. "I saw *me*."

"You?"

"Yes."

"I saw myself in the light." Brad reaches for his hat. "How's that possible?"

Gabriela rubs out a smudge with her palm and gives it to him. "I don't know. Was it like a memory?"

"No, it wasn't in my head. *She* wasn't. *I* wasn't."

"Where then?"

"Here." Brad crawls to the hole and digs away the dirt. "In the earth."

"You heard your daughter calling your name from a hole in the ground?"

Brad nods. "And saw myself in the flame."

"It's funny," Gabriela says, clenching her *cornicello*.

"Funny?" Brad stands. "What is?"

She takes his hand and climbs to her feet. "Minutes ago, you were doubting what I've seen and heard. *Capisci?*"

"I'm sorry."

"Don't be, sir." Gabriela swallows. "Not unless you've got a reason."

"Right."

Gabriela moves closer to the hole. "Where do you think this leads?"

"I don't know, but I wouldn't get any closer."

The hum of the earth builds under the ground and in her bones. Gabriela stops about a meter away.

scene 5.

Brad crosses the antechamber and collects his flashlight, tilting the beam over Gabriela's shoulder. "What's that?"

Gabriela moves to the far corner of the crawlspace where she saw Ralph Delacourt fade after Brad got knocked down. Ralph Delacourt and the red eyes. "What?"

"Looks like another trapdoor." Brad walks past her. "Was it here before?"

"I'm not sure."

"Do you think it's another secret entrance to the orchestra pit?"

"No, it can't be. The pit's still behind us." Gabriela spins on her heels and points. "Over there."

Brad shines his light so they can see the vague outline in the bricks.

"So, where does this one lead?" he says, tracing his finger around the threshold.

"I don't know."

The door is larger than the other two. Tall enough for Brad to walk through without his hat. Like the trapdoors, the wooden panels are held together by a metal framing set flush within the brick foundation. Brad pops the spring on the lock so it creaks open. He flattens his hand and pushes until it swings wide. The hallway beyond, lit only by his flashlight, declines into an earthen abyss not unlike the Parisian catacombs Gabriela visited during the Easter holiday of her senior year at the university. She can't tell what they mined in Crow Creek to create this underground artery or if the path will be paved with bones the deeper they go.

"Gems," Brad says.

"Eh?"

"That's why they would've cut into the earth under Crow Creek."

"Oh."

"I could see you were thinking about it." Brad rubs his eyes. "Rubies, emeralds, even turquoise. Though you find more of that out west, like New Mexico and Arizona."

"I see."

"More recently, natural gas."

She's read enough about hydraulic fracturing and shale gas since she moved to America, especially when she lived in Pittsburgh, to understand the dangers and political concerns.

"Fracking?"

"Uh-huh. They do that in *Valle D'Aosta*?"

He remembers where I'm from.

"No."

Brad chuckles. "Am I pronouncing that correct? *Valle D'Aosta.*"

Not quite.

"Close enough. *Valle D'Aosta.*"

"I like the way you say it much better," he says.

Gabriela blushes. *"Grazie."*

"Thing is . . ." Brad unsnaps his firearm and rests his palm on the grip. ". . . where they mined for gems in Holt County ain't nowhere near downtown. Fracking's a bit closer, over by Scott Lumber on Highway 77, but not here. This tunnel ain't been used for either of those. Bet my life on it. This leads somewhere else."

Gabriela nibbles a fingernail. "Where?"

"About to find out." Brad presses the mic on his shoulder radio. "Curly?"

"Boss?"

"I'm over at the theatre with Miss Rossi. I need you to send a couple deputies out this way. Who you got on duty this morning?"

"Camille and me are sitting at the station right now. Got Katie and Austin over in Houndstooth."

"Katie and Austin?"

"That's right."

"What's going on over that way?"

"Domestic issue. Nothing big. Probably about finished by now."

Brad checks his watch. "They'll do."

"They're supposed to make their rounds anyhow," Curly says. "Last crew cut out about six."

"Fine," Brad says. "Tell them to hurry over, but keep the chatter to a minimum. I don't want Becky Stokes catching wind. She's the last one I need snooping around."

"Ten-four."

The radio squawks. Brad presses his mic again. "Oh, Curly?"

"Yessir?"

"Tell them to stay outside in their patrol cars like they've been doing."

"Sheriff?"

"We don't need to worry the locals neither. I have my radio. I'll holler if I need them. You good?"

"As a pig in sunshine."

"Ten-four." Brad releases his radio and glances at Gabriela. "You can go back if you want. Probably not a bad idea, actually."

Gabriela shakes her head. "I've come this far."

Brad draws his pistol. "Stay behind me then."

"Yessir."

"Oh, one more thing."

"Sì?"

Brad hands her his hat. "You mind?"

"Of course not."

She rolls up her hair and sticks the hat on her head so it tilts up high enough for her to see under the brim. The weight comforts.

"Not a bad fit," Brad says.

Gabriela smiles. "Not bad at all."

Brad aligns his flashlight with the barrel of his gun as he descends. She follows. The tunnel is less like the Parisian catacombs than she first thought. They've been carved into packed red clay rather than stone so they're dank and slippery. Small rivulets run along the path like bloodstreams.

"Mind your footing," Brad says.

He's getting better at reading her thoughts when he can't see her face.

Italian slips out: *"Anche tu."*

"I will," Brad says.

He's also getting better at understanding her language.

After several hundred meters, the path levels so they're no longer declining. The water pools at what appears to be a circular clearing or intersection. Several paths branch off from the center and into darkness.

Brad stops. "I was afraid of that."

"Of which?"

"Both."

"How deep do you think it is?" she says.

"Can't say for sure. Probably not more than a foot or two. You ain't worried about ruining those boots or getting your jeans wet, are you?"

They're still damp from the night before. It didn't take her long to learn that nothing dries in North Carolina.

"No." Gabriela shakes her head. "How many tunnels do you think there are under here?"

"Not sure. Daddy never told me about none of them, if he knew at all." Brad shines the light ahead. "Guess we better pick a direction."

Gabriela squats and studies the mouths of the new paths.

"See something?" Brad asks.

"Uh-huh." She nods and points at the mud. Footprints and tire tracks. "Third tunnel on the right."

Brad squints. "Looks like we found our heading."

"I agree."

Brad takes his first step.

"Stai attento," she says.

"Yes, ma'am."

Gabriela grins. "You're getting good at that."

"Ain't as dumb as I look."

"You've said." She smiles and follows. "But I don't think you look dumb, either."

"Really?"

"Of course not!"

"Didn't think a rough and tumble hillbilly would be your type." Water ripples at his ankles. "Regardless of age."

"No?"

"Don't those European boys wear tight suits with the legs rolled up high?"

"I'm from the mountains, not the city."

"Oh." Brad rolls his eyes. "Come to think of it, maybe I should've tucked up my pant legs. My boots are getting squishy."

Gabriela's halfway to the middle of the intersection and up to her knees when something wriggles in the water beside her, brushing up against her leg. She jumps and splashes.

"Gabriela?"

After emerging from the tepid water, a pudgy rat waddles into the darkness ahead.

"I'm fine."

"I ain't gonna lie." Brad chases the rat with his beam. "Spooked me, too."

"Good to know."

"At least he ain't going where we're going."

Brad stops at the deepest part of the crossroads and faces the third tunnel on the right. The muddy water splashes above his calves. Gabriela's thigh deep. Her heavy jeans cling to her.

"Feel that?" Brad says.

Vibrations rise from the center of the circular pool, thumping through Gabriela's boots and up her legs. Her hands tingle and teeth chatter.

"Uh-huh."

Brad shines his flashlight at the clay dome where water drips from leaky pipes. "Get the feeling we been here before."

"Here?" Gabriela says.

Brad raises his chin. "Up *there*."

"The intersection at King Street?"

"Think so." Brad shines the flashlight back toward the murky pool. "But I'm more concerned about what's below us."

The humming builds into a pounding that resonates in Gabriela's temples. Her ears ring. A few more squeaking rats skirmish out of the water and disappear down different tunnels.

"They agree with you," she says.

Brad narrows his eyes. The flashlight radiates dying embers in each pupil.

"Can't be easy," he says.

"What can't be easy?"

"Leaving home like you did. Don't think I could ever do it. Go someplace I've never been where I don't know nobody."

Gabriela struggles for breath in the stale air. Her heart outraces the pulse of the earth. *Why does he care about why I left home? Why now?* Red eyes stare back at her from the stagnant water. Demon eyes. Her demon. *Does Brad see? Does his daughter call for him in the water?*

"Gabriela?" he says.

What about Mamma*? How do I tell him about how* Mamma*'s long face broke my heart when I headed through security at the airport in Milan?* She'd lost *Papà* twenty months earlier. Then Gabriela left her. *What daughter leaves her mother alone?*

"I needed to find a job," she says, wishing she could pull Brad's hat down over her face.

"I get that." Brad relaxes his shoulders and lowers his gun. "Maybe it's easier to walk away than to have everything taken from you."

A wave of nausea punches Gabriela's gut. She tightens her stomach and clenches her jaw. This is much worse. She lost *Papà*. How does that compare to losing what Brad lost?

"I'm sorry," she says.

"Thank you."

He doesn't tell her not to apologize.

"You said your daughter died in a car accident?"

"That's right." Brad takes his first step up the path and out of the crossroads. "Eight years ago. Uh-huh."

"How old was she?"

Brad swallows. "Not quite nineteen."

Two years older than Gabriela.

"Your wife?" she says.

"Shana?" Brad ascends from the pool and reaches the muddy path, careful not to tread on the existing footsteps. "Most beautiful woman I've ever seen. Well, except for my daughter. My heart died when I lost her. The both of them. Didn't think a person's heart could die twice. And of course there's Mama and Daddy. They're both gone. But that's different. You expect to lose your parents at some point, right?"

Papà*'s dead.* Papà*'s dead and I left* Mamma *all alone.*

Gabriela stands beside him in the mud. Water runs down her pants and trickles toward the pool. "We don't have to talk about this anymore."

"You know what? I've kept quiet about it for so long. Kinda feels nice to tell somebody. But I get what you're saying." Brad takes a deep breath. "Try to avoid those tracks if you can. At least until the ground's not so wet. We might need to come back and take another look."

Gabriela grabs his arm as he starts to walk up the tunnel. "How?"

"Mmm?"

"How did your wife die?"

Brad clicks his tongue. "That's the funny thing."

"What happened?"

"She got bit by a spider."

Chills run up Gabriela's spine, standing the hair on her arms. A gust of air moans from behind, carrying the stench of sour eggs or a burnt matchstick and tilting the sheriff's hat. She staggers and bumps Brad as he raises his flashlight and pistol. Seeping water down the red tunnel walls reflects his beam.

Gabriela adjusts the hat. "Spider?"

"Yeah, we don't think she knew."

"She didn't know she got bit?"

"Nuh-uh."

"I didn't know that was possible."

"Me neither," Brad says. "She went to bed complaining about a pain in her hip. She took some ibuprofen and went to sleep. Never woke up."

"No redness?" Gabriela says. "No swelling?"

"Nothing that she noticed. Couple of pinpricks. Bite marks. Bob Cody showed me. He's the medical examiner."

"I remember."

"Said she must've had an allergy."

"That's awful."

"Had I known, maybe I could've done something. Maybe we could've had an EpiPen at the house like for when you're allergic to bee stings or peanuts. But who knows if that would've worked? How can you tell if you're allergic to something like that until you get bit? Probably the only way to find out."

"I don't know."

Brad sighs. "Anyhow, I think we're here."

"Eh?"

"Look."

Brad shines his light on a closed door at the end of the tunnel resembling the one they entered under the theatre. Gabriela reaches for her mobile but remembers she left it charging at the midhouse console, so she can't check the time or gauge the distance.

"How far do you think we walked?"

"Not very," Brad says. "Probably been down here about thirty minutes. Maybe forty since we stopped to chat. How long then? Maybe a mile and a half. Two at the most. But that's overstating it more'n likely."

Two miles. *Three kilometers.*

Gabriela nods. "That means we're still downtown."

"And there are plenty of places within a two mile radius of the theater." Brad lowers his ear to the door. "What do you say we go in?"

"We've come this far."

Brad grins. "I like your spirit, Miss Rossi."

More words hang on his lips. Gabriela can't be sure what he wants to say. She can't read his mind or guess his thoughts, English or otherwise. Is he thinking about her? His wife? His daughter? Maybe that's giving this more weight than she should. Maybe he's just worried about what they're going to find on the other side of the door. Maybe she should start paying more attention and stop worrying about whether or not the sheriff has feelings for her.

(she's half his age)

(don't think i could ever do it)

(didn't think a person's heart could die twice)

"Gabriela?"

"Yes."

"Might be best if you pop the door and get behind me."

"Of course."

Gabriela reaches up for the spring and trips the lock. The door shifts and opens toward them. The tunnel's too narrow for her to find shelter behind Brad.

He grunts low. "Forgot about that."

"I'll be okay."

Brad keeps his eyes on the door. "I ain't gonna let nothing to happen to you, Gabriela."

Tears spring from her eyes. Not so much his words. She believes him.

They enter. Daylight from the top of an unfinished staircase on their left spills below and casts an unsettling glow. Brad pockets his flashlight and levels his gun. The space is less of an antechamber (like the subfloor under the theatre) than it is a cellar. Gabriela gags at a stench even more putrid than what was in the tunnels. Under wooden joists, thick glossy webs cover the gaps between girders. Flies jump, avoiding capture, along the swirling cone of light. Above the center, the dome of electrical cables Connor and King assembled below the stage connects glass cylinders to the mainframe stacked on a handtruck below. The collider remains quiet and dark, attached to a similar shaft in the wooden floor.

"Connor?" Brad says, soft and low.

Gabriela nods. "And King."

As they move closer to the stairs, plump spiders wiggle for position in their wake. Brad doesn't react. If he's thinking about his wife, Gabriela can't be certain. Cardboard boxes damp with mildew line metal racks under the staircase. A green cooler rests padlocked on the center shelf beside loose Christmas tree branches. A hunched shadow, suit in tatters, flickers between the racks but disappears.

(the dead man)

"Where are we?" Gabriela says.

"I'm not quite sure." Brad reaches the stairs. "But I feel like I've been here before."

"Should we go up?"

Brad nods. As he places a boot on the bottom step, a door closes above. Not at the top of the stairs, but close. Chairs drag. Talking and laughter follow. Brad places an index finger against his lips as he ascends. The boards creak three steps up. He freezes and waits. Above, the conversation continues without interruption. The stair moans when he takes his next step. He curses under his breath and waits for a reaction from above. None comes.

"Let me go," Gabriela says.

Brad wrinkles his brow. "Okay, but first noisy step and you're out."

"Deal."

Gabriela slides past on his right, supporting herself against the wooden railing as she climbs. The stairs, so far, don't reject her weight. She looks over her shoulder where Brad keeps his gun poised (but not aimed) and avoids the line of fire. He nods. Four steps from the top, polished Italian boots on her right rest beside the legs of a chair. She recognizes the Giorgio Brutinis from the photograph. *Pastor Aken.* Laughter, loud and threatening, shakes the staircase. Gabriela squeals, dipping her head out of sight, and clutches the railing. She peeps back at Brad. He props his finger against his mouth again. She nods, lifting her eyes. The angle to her left gives her a better view under the brim of the sheriff's hat. Ornate bookcases frame the small office. Each shelf holds an exotic animal horn resembling the one Connor held under the stage the night before. Across a mahogany desk, an open window gives light. A crow on the ledge dips its head several times and caws. Pastor Aken pushes back from his desk and swats at the bird until it flies away. She can't see his face while he stands. Only up to his hips. He pulls the window down with slender fingers and circles back to his seat until he's only a pair of boots. The suited shoulders opposite his desk slide closer. A stout hand digs into a bowl of hard candy beside a copper lamp. Pastor Aken offers a Lysol wipe. Gabriela presses her chest against the stairs and cranes her neck but needs more height to see the other person's face. She digs in her heels and pushes, clinging to the steps as she moves up. They moan. She freezes and buries her face in the wooden slats, hoping the sheriff's hat muffles her gentle yelp. Brad's gun clicks behind her. Her heavy breaths fill the cellar. She squeezes her eyes and listens.

"I'm so glad you came through," Pastor Aken says.

"Where else would I go?"

Gabriela knows the second person.

"Friday then," Pastor Aken says.

"Wouldn't miss it."

Who? Who the fuck is that?

"Don't let Becky see you," Pastor Aken says.

Becky. Becky Stokes. The news reporter.

"Of course not." Deep laughter. "That would be awful."

I know who that is. I need to see his face.

Gabriela lifts her eyes above the tread, straining as she pulls herself up. She glances back once more at Brad. He raises a palm.

"Easy," he mouths.

She nods and pulls. A wide neck appears above the shoulders. He pushes away from the desk, but only for a second, before slipping back into view. Her spine burns as she arches. Her back muscles scream, straining in resistance.

A bald head dips into the light.

James Patterson.

"The fuck?" she says.

Mr. Patterson freezes, hard candy near his open mouth. He rotates his face to the stairs, making eye contact with her. With red demon eyes.

Gabriela doesn't move. Heart racing, she stares back at what must be another apparition. Another ghost. Another dead man walking. *How can James Patterson be alive?* She saw his dead body. Heard Maribel scream. Saw the blood. The gaping hole in his chest. The paramedics wheel him away.

Mr. Patterson glances across the desk at the hidden pastor and mumbles. Pastor Aken pushes back in his chair. His boots disappear behind the door. Gabriela braces, hugging the shadows of the railing. Under the brim of her hat, she sees Brad slip off the stairs and stand behind a girder, pointing his gun. She grits her teeth as the pastor pulls open the door. He doesn't speak. She can't tell if he notices her. She only sees how striking he is, even in the backlight from the window. How enchanting his smooth complexion and elegant features are. His aquiline nose and lobeless ears. Her pelvis throbs and mouth goes dry. Before closing the door, Pastor Aken shimmers like a dying candle, his bones and muscles visible beneath his clothes and skin.

(becky becky becky)

Gabriela jumps and slides down the steps, passing Brad. She runs for the exit but doesn't look back until she's in the tunnel. The shambling dead man haunts the distance beyond the brackish water, tattered clothes swaying in the breeze. Brad's behind her, pistol at his hip wrapped tightly in both hands. He swings the door closed. They pause, catching their breath.

"They see you?" Brad says.

Gabriela nods. "I think so. I don't know. Maybe. *Non lo so!*"

"Just breathe." Brad cocks his firearm. "If they come, I'm ready."

Gabriela closes her eyes, struggling for air in the warm dank tunnel. She finds *Mamma*'s face in the darkness.

Sono qui. Anche mentre sei via, sarò sempre con te.

("I'm here," *Mamma* says, wiping tears off Gabriela's cheeks. "Even while you're away, I'll be with you." The airport bustles around them.)

Mi mancherai, Mamma.

(I'll miss you, *Mamma*.)

Non sarò mai lontano.

("You'll never be far away," she says, drawing her kerchief up to her eyes. White hair frames her delicate face. Gabriela releases her hand and kisses *Mamma*'s cheek.)

Ti amo.

("I love you.")

Ti voglio bene, mia dolce bambina.

("I love you, my sweet child.")

Gabriela weeps in the darkness and pulls herself into Brad's arms.

"Who did you see?" he says, holding her.

She stifles a sob. "Pastor Aken."

"First Baptist, of course." Brad nods. "I've been in that cellar plenty of times. Helped decorate for Christmas. The homecoming potluck. Dairy Days every April. In and out of there plenty. I've never seen that set up, though. All them wires and tubes."

Gabriela's chest heaves. "He wasn't alone."

"Who?" Brad rubs her shoulders. "Who else was with him?"

She pulls back and searches for Brad's face as her eyes adjust. She runs her fingers along his cheek and touches his lips. "I saw James Patterson up there."

Brad flinches. "James Patterson?"
"Uh-huh."
"But you couldn't have."
"I did."
"He's dead."
"I know."

After a minute, Brad unclips his flashlight and points the beam down the tunnel. Together, they walk back to the theatre, wading through the stagnant pool. The earth pulses in the clearing, making her chest and temples pound, but they don't stop. The stage is quiet when they return. She hands Brad his sheriff's hat and thanks him. He tells her he'll see her tonight after the preview. Says he knows where they need to go next. She doesn't question him, only nods and squeezes his hand as they go to the console for her mobile. She punches the code in the lobby to the set alarm. Brad walks her to her car and joins the two deputies parked across the street.

Gabriela says goodbye and drives home. The cool shower soothes her aching back and feet. She sleeps without dreams for several hours and heats up a small bowl of *pasta e fagioli* when she wakes. She tightens the clasp on her *cornicello* and goes back to the theatre for her six o'clock call.

scene 6.

Gabriela parks out back and checks the callboard for early arrivals. Terese and Anika are already in wardrobe. Deanna does a prop check. Doug Cousins is the only other crew on deck. He places bricks on the lineset carrying the upstage cyc.

"Added two instruments," he says. "Makes a stronger blue for the nighttime scenes. Might need a different moon gobo, though. I'll have King check when he shows up."

Gabriela nods and goes to her desk. She flips to the back page of the promptbook so she can remove and shred her demon sketch. She never should've drawn it in the first place. She's tired of seeing the red eyes. We only have our own demons if we believe we do.

It's missing.

She searches the backstage floor surrounding the desk where she dropped her *cornicello* but finds nothing. A quick glance to the bottom of the pit also reveals no sketch. Only darkness. Darkness Gabriela has no desire to revisit. Not down there or beyond. She's finished with ghosts and dead men and secret tunnels and hidden rooms.

The entire cast arrives slightly before six and signs in. They pass by her desk on the way to the green room for warmups. They offer greetings. Director Matt Leath follows, hair teased high above his glowing face.

"Should've met us for dinner," he says.

Gabriela forces a smile. "Where'd you go?"

"Gallagher's."

Gabriela's been to the pub once before. It's a cop bar, but she didn't see Brad while there. Maybe he used to go with his wife before she died. Gabriela watched Dante Rose headline their Fourth of July party. He fronted the hard rock band Thorn about twenty years ago. As a teenager, she bought their debut album on vinyl. They had a decent following in Italy until their lead guitarist broke off to form his own group. Either way, Gabriela went alone and didn't really feel like she belonged. Perhaps, Sara Cooper would've gone with her. If she'd only known to ask back then.

"Sorry I missed it."

"Hey," Matt taps her desk. "Got a moment?"

"Eh?"

"Let's take a walk."

Gabriela follows Matt to the green room where he tells his assistant director Paula Bradley to start warmups. She shouts a few commands, giving the performers five minutes to do individual stretches before they circle up.

"I haven't gotten a chance to thank you," Matt says.

"Thank me?"

"Uh-huh."

"For?" Gabriela checks the time on her mobile.

A toothy grin splits his full lips. "For stepping up."

"Oh."

"It's difficult to fill in the way you did."

"It hasn't been easy."

Matt shakes his head. "No."

Gabriela sighs. "Poor Tommy."

"And Mr. Patterson."

What if you knew the truth about Mr. Patterson?

"They'll be missed," she says.

I'm still not sure I believe what I saw.

"They'll always be with us."

Gabriela chuckles. "More than you know."

"Anyhow, I wanted to tell you that I really appreciate all you've done for the show."

Gabriela smiles. *"Grazie."*

"She wasn't sure how you came through."

Gabriela shakes her head. "What?"

"I told her not to worry."

"Her?"

Paula huddles the cast in a large circle and leads deep breathing exercises until she's ready for vocal warmups. They start with a series of tongue twisters before alternating between voiced and voiceless consonant repetitions.

Matt claps his hands. "How long we got?"

"Who did you tell not to worry?" Gabriela asks.

"Oh, forget I said anything." Matt teases his hair with a steel pick. "I'm so excited for tonight. You ready?"

Gabriela bites her bottom lip. *"Sì."*

"Great. How long?"

"Twenty minutes till wardrobe."

Matt bows his head. "Thank you twenty."

Gabriela half-smiles and leaves when the cast starts an energy jump that builds while they count to ten. Her bootheels click as she walks the quiet backstage hallway.

How you *came through.* Like a magic trick. As if she was a wild bunny rabbit that some trained magician pulled out of his hat. She returns to her desk by the orchestra pit. Connor Simmons stands in the wings beside the props table, picking his teeth with his fingers.

"Great run last night, huh?" he says.

"Eh?"

"Rehearsal went well."

"Oh." Gabriela swallows. "Yes, great run."

He steps closer. His breath is warm and sour. "Can't believe we're already at previews."

"I know," she says

"Doesn't feel like it's been that long since the read-through."

"No, it doesn't."

"Going to the party at Ed Brown's after the show tonight?"

"I don't know."

"You should." Stained crooked teeth emerge between his taut lips. "His wife serves a mean barbecue."

"Does she?"

He digs into his back pocket. "Might give you something else to do."

"Che cosa?"

"So you can get to know everyone better, I mean." He unfolds a sheet of paper. "Now that you're the stage manager and all."

"Oh, right."

King Boggs enters the wings from the electrical closet carrying a wrench and a source four PAR. He stops beside Connor. "About to replace a light on the stage right boom. Give me a hand?"

"Just a sec," Connor says.

Gabriela clears her throat. "Did Doug tell you about the two instruments he added?"

"Nope." King belly laughs. "Can't say he has."

"I'm sure he'll find you."

"Sure he will." King waddles off behind the scenery toward the rolling ladder.

"Ever tell you about my sister?" Connor says, tugging greasy locks off his forehead.

"No." Gabriela reaches for her *cornicello*. "You haven't."

"She's sick."

Gabriela raises an eyebrow. "Hope she feels better soon."

Connor snorts and smacks the paper against his thigh. "Not that kinda sick."

"Oh?"

"Born that way."

"Oh."

"Ain't like she got the flu or nothing."

"Right."

"Mama fucked up."

"Did she?"

"That's right." Connor checks the tension on a lineset. "Amanda didn't deserve what happened to her."

"I'm sorry," Gabriela says.

Connor stares at her, brooding eyes swirl. "Don't need to be."

"Connor?"

He steps closer, flashing the sheet of paper. "You know why the gods didn't like Dionysus?"

Gabriela licks her lips. "Dionysus?"

"You heard of him where you're from, right?"

Gabriela nods. *"Certamente."*

"He didn't belong," Connor says.

"What?"

"Some things are better left alone, you know?"

He hands her the sheet of paper. She doesn't look at it.

"I don't know what you mean," she says.

"Go to the party tonight," he says. "At Ed's house."

"The party?"

"Don't mess this up for her."

Sania Cortez, the lightboard operator, swings around the corner of the proscenium, carrying a clipboard and pencil. She hums under her breath and adjusts the collar on her black button-down shirt. "Gabriela?"

"Sì?"

"You ready?"

Gabriela glances at Connor. He cracks his knuckles.

"Am I?" she asks.

Connor smirks. "I'm gonna see about King and that light he needs help with."

Gabriela checks the paper in her trembling hands and flinches when she sees the red eyes. *Don't mess this up for her. I told her not to worry.* She wads up the sketch of her demon and tosses it into the trashcan before she grabs her promptbook.

scene 7.

Gabriela follows Sania to the midhouse console where they meet the soundboard operator, Cherlynne Lawrence, to test run their cues. Cherlynne is elbow deep in a bag of Doritos, dusting the soundboard with crumbs and nacho cheese. When she sees Gabriela, she rolls the bag and tucks it under the counter before sweeping off the controls with the front of her black t-shirt.

"Sorry," she says. "Didn't get a chance to grab dinner."

"Va bene." Gabriela places her headset around her neck. "Are you ready for a dry run?"

"Of course."

Cherlynne swivels in her chair and grabs her headset. Sania sits beside her and powers up her lightboard before taking down the lights with the Unison panel. As soon as the monitor flashes, Gabriela opens to the first page of the promptbook and calls for preshow warmers and the house to half. Sania punches keys, establishing the look.

"We'll go slow." Gabriela holds her place in the script with her finger, waiting to shift to the next sticky note.

"Works for me," Sania says.

"Same here," Cherlynne says and pulls a bottle of Dr. Pepper out from a small refrigerator between their knees.

Gabriela rolls her eyes.

"I'll put it right back," Cherlynne says.

"You're fine," Gabriela says.

King Boggs clamors downstage right as he drags the source four PAR across the boom. Connor steadies the ladder and avoids looking at the console. When Gabriela calls the next cue, the stage goes dark.

"Fuck," King says.

Gabriela moves the mouthpiece off her chin so she can shout off headset. "Keep your harness secure until we can get some light on you. I don't want you falling off that ladder."

"Understood." King chuckles. *"Boss."*

Connor laughs in the darkness.

"Stronzino." Gabriela clenches her fists and turns to Sania. "Unison?"

Sania punches the keypad. "I'm not getting anything."

The source four in the catwalks blinks, casting its beam right of center in the living room. Gabriela searches for Ralph Delacourt in the darkness but doesn't find him. *Maybe he's done what he needed? Maybe there's nothing left to tell me.*

"Looks like you got another instrument to replace when you're finished on the boom," Connor says.

"Looks like it," King says.

Sania howls with laughter. "Oh, fuck."

"What's so funny?" Gabriela says.

"I must've wrote a blackout into the cues."

"A blackout?"

Sania punches the keypad on the lightboard and takes the stage to the proper cue.

Gabriela nods. "We're moving on."

King gives the thumbs up before Connor and he clear the stage and disappear behind the scenery. As Gabriela transitions through the cues, she hears them clanging up in the catwalks. She continues calling the sequence, asking Cherlynne to adjust the volume on a crash effect used near the end of act two that's overly loud.

"That should be coming out of the upstage monitor, not the house," Gabriela says. "So it's practical."

"I agree." Cherlynne spins a knob. "Input probably came loose."

"Possibly."

Cherlynne stands, swatting away bright orange crumbs. "I'll run down and check."

Gabriela strains to look into the catwalks, rubbing her sore neck. "King's still busy up there."

Cherlynne trots away.

"Only take a minute," she says over her shoulder.

Gabriela repeats the warning to Sania, who reclines and scrolls through her mobile as King steps to the railing above the house.

"Gabriela?"

She pushes the mic away from her mouth and looks up. "Yes?"

"I can't find the source four," King says and leans with both elbows across the pipe. He wipes his glasses with a small white rag.

"What do you mean?"

"We have plenty of source fours up here on the bridge but nothing at that angle."

"Are you sure?"

"Not at that angle." King shakes his head. "Not the one we just seen light up."

"Is Connor up there with you?" Gabriela asks.

"Connor?"

She doesn't know why she asked about him. Maybe Connor knew she was down in the pit after the rehearsal last night, but King doesn't seem to know. Or care. *And what the fuck is going on? First the blackout. Then the audio failure. Now, there's no source four?* Gabriela searches the stage for Delacourt. *Where the fuck are you, old man?* She flattens her hair under the headset where the folding hinge pulls. *Don't mess this up for her. I told her not to worry.*

"Yes, Connor."

"Nope." King puts his glasses back on and smiles. "Not sure where he ran off to. Why? Don't you trust me?"

"Eh?"

"Don't you think I know our default plot?"

"I didn't say that."

King leans down over the bar. "Hey, Sania, bring up our plot, will you?"

"Everything?" Sania places her mobile beside the board. "Now?"

"Yeah."

Sania looks at Gabriela. "Okay with you?"

Gabriela checks the time. The house opens in less than thirty minutes.

"Okay, but make it quick."

"About to get very bright in here," Sania says, tapping keys on the board.

She takes the stage out of the current cue and goes dark before she brings up the dimmers. Once the gridiron's burning, she powers the bridge until every instrument in the catwalks is lit. King steps away from the railing. Gabriela waits. He returns to his position above the console and swipes a hand across his throat to cut the lights. Sania takes down the plot and brings up the general worklights so the stage isn't completely dark.

"Found it," King says.

"What?" Gabriela says.

"Don't know how I missed it." King laughs. "Guess I'm getting old."

Sania snorts. "You can say that again."

"Give me a minute so I can replace it," King says.

"You got a minute," Gabriela says, staring at the living room again.

Where are you, Delacourt? Any minute now you're gonna sneak out from behind the scenery and issue your warning. Or I'm gonna turn a corner and you're gonna grab my arm. Gabriela rubs her wrist and thinks of *Mamma*. What would she say about all this? Where are her comforting words when Gabriela needs them? Even *Mamma* has gone dark.

Cherlynne trots down the stage steps and back up the aisle to the console. "Should be all set."

"Bene," Gabriela says but doesn't ask what was wrong. She doesn't need to know because she doesn't want to mess this up for her. He told her not to worry. Whoever the fuck *she* is.

"Probably a loose input jack," Cherlynne explains anyhow. "But I couldn't find anything. Mind walking me back to that cue?"

"Of course not." Gabriela adjusts her mic. "Sania, you on cue seventeen?"

Sania hits a few keys. "There now."

"Warn lights eighteen," Gabriela says.

"Thank you eighteen."

"Eighteen go," Gabriela sits down. "Sound four go."

Sania and Cherlynne execute their cues. Lights and sound move forward without a hitch. Gabriela finishes the cue-to-cue and gives her board operators fifteen minutes until the house opens. They thank her and scatter from the console while Gabriela resets her promptbook for the opening. Anna Hernandez pokes her round face into the auditorium through the lobby doors.

"Good to open in ten?"

Gabriela nods. "You're on house tonight?"

"Si." Anna walks to the console. "Meribel's not coming in."

"Can't say I blame her for that," Gabriela says.

"I'll probably work the run."

"Thank you." Gabriela steps down from the console. "Maybe Deidre can build a stipend into the budget for you?"

"Maybe," Anna says. "I'm not worried about it."

"You should be." Gabriela thumbs through a drawer on the side of the console for spare batteries in case the headsets drain out during the preview. "I'll talk to her. You've got mouths to feed at home. It's a lot of time to volunteer for free."

"Gracias."

"Prego," Gabriela says.

Anna returns to the lobby.

scene 8.

When the doors open, the buzz of the invites bleeds into the house. Gabriela manages a grin. Previews should be exciting. They finally get to show off what they've been working on for six weeks. Isn't that the purpose of theatre? The reason for art? Her university professors always told her the world is a better place because we don't keep our talents to ourselves.

Gabriela hustles backstage to check the callboard before the house opens. Sara Cooper is the only one who hasn't signed in. She scrolls through her unopened text messages but hasn't gotten anything from Sara. Everyone else who contacted Gabriela while she was at the console is already at the theatre.

Where's Sara?

Gabriela shoots off a quick text to see if she's okay but doesn't wait for a reply. She heads to the props closet where she finds Deanna Flowers tinkering with a breakaway lamp. Gabriela startles her. She twitches and almost drops the lamp.

"Sorry," Gabriela says.

"Don't be." Deanna sets the lamp down beside a prop starter pistol used in act two. "I'm a little more jumpy than normal since we have an audience tonight."

"I shouldn't have snuck up on you."

Deanna waves her off. "I'm fine. What's up?"

"Have you heard from Sara?"

"Don't think so." Deanna scratches her chin and taps her mobile. She gurgles deep in her throat and shifts her right elbow. "No, I haven't."

"Oh."

"I'm sure she's fine." Deanna lifts a wallet off the prop table. "This really should go over to wardrobe. Ed needs it in his back pocket for when he throws cash at Tariq."

Gabriela nods. "Five minutes to house."

"Thank you five," Deanna says.

Gabriela sweeps backstage and the dressing rooms, making calls to let everyone know the house is about to open so she'll be at console until bows if anyone needs her. She finds Connor in the break room talking to the technical director, Joe Cox, and asks him to get on headset at the desk backstage right to listen for cues. He nods and rubs out a cigarette on the metal table. She doesn't bother to remind him that he's not supposed to be smoking indoors. The cast and crew have a designated area outside by the dumpster. She wants to avoid another confrontation this soon before curtain.

Once the crew finds their assigned spots, Gabriela trots up the aisle to the lobby doors and gives Anna the signal to open. She meets Cherlynne and Sania at console as the crowd wanders in. Mostly seniors from Houndstooth, but Brad's with them, out of uniform in a light blue Oxford dress shirt and dark slacks. He's nearly a foot taller than the rest. His wavy blonde hair rustles in the air conditioner. His fuzzy mustache shines. Maybe he polishes it?

He salutes when he passes the console but continues to his seat on the house left side about five rows back from the stage. A few other prominent locals arrive. Some she knows by name. Fire Chief Riddle. Everett Jackson (the elder at First Baptist). Stan Krulikowski, the sordid bank manager at the Savings and Loan off King Street. Many others she doesn't recognize. There are close to seventy in total by the time she calls the cues to take out the stage warmers and start the pre-show address.

Pastor Aken isn't in the crowd. She's not sure whether or not she wishes he was. Her heart and mind tell her she's glad he's not. Her passion tells her to go fuck her rational thoughts. She makes the calls to start the show. Her phone buzzes in her pocket. She can't take her eyes off the opening scene to check. Not yet. Maybe it's Sara. Everybody else is here. She scans the first few pages of the script looking for the next break. Her phone buzzes again. As soon as she gives the warning for the upcoming light cue, she sneaks a peek. Her touchscreen is blank. She zigzags the combination to unlock but doesn't have any notifications for texts or direct messages on her apps.

"Should I go?" Sania says.

"Eh?"

"The first scene just ended."

Gabriela blinks and shoves her phone in her pocket. "*Fanculo.* Lights go, yes."

The stage goes dark. The delay might've been three seconds. The audience didn't notice. Three seconds is a fucking eternity for the actors, but the audience has no clue. This is her first night in front of an audience with this show. She's fine. She's got this.

Her phone buzzes again. Steady now. Not a text or a message. A call. She can't dig it back out. Not now. Not in blackout. But what if it's *Mamma*? What if *Mamma* needs her? She lets it ring out and tells Sania to start scene two. No delay this time. Courtney Williams is right on cue. So's Cedric Young. He plays Tariq's onstage younger brother, Clay. Her phone vibrates once. Probably a voicemail. She flips through the script. Scene two is short but doesn't have any cues. She can see who called, even if she can't listen to her voicemail or respond. Maybe it's not *Mamma*. Maybe it's Sara telling her she's running late. She pulls her mobile out again. The lock screen is blank. She opens. No notifications. No voicemail. No fucking call.

"Gesù."

Cherlynne slides her mic away from her mouth and covers it with her palm. "You okay?"

"Fine, yes." Gabriela nods. "Cue eight go."

Sania moves to the next cue.

"Gabriela?" Connor says over the headset after they transition into scene three.

"Connor, go."

"Sara Cooper's here."

"She is?"

"Yes," Connor says. "Showed up about five minutes before curtain."

"Oh."

"Couldn't get her car started. Had to Uber. Sorry I didn't tell you sooner."

"Where is she?" Gabriela says.

Connor snickers. "By the props table, giving me the middle finger right now."

Sounds like Sara.

"Let's keep the channel clear." Gabriela clears her throat. "Warn sound cue four."

Cherlynne nudges her MacBook with her knuckles, poised for the call as soon as Gabriela passes it along. The energy builds through the rest of the first act without interruption. The audience, illuminated by the peripheral shine of the stage lights, absorbs the action until Gabriela calls for blackout and walks the show into the intermission. When the house lights are up, Brad glances her way. She half-smiles and nods.

"Let's take fifteen," she says over headset.

"Thank you fifteen," Connor says backstage. "I'm going for a smoke."

Cherlynne and Sania remove their headsets but don't walk away from the console. Sania digs wax out of her ear. Cherlynne dives back into the Doritos, crunching half-buried under the console. She licks her fingers and smacks her lips.

"I'm going to the bathroom," Gabriela says. "I'll be right back."

Sania opens her phone. "That works."

Cherlynne mumbles, spewing crumbs.

scene 9.

In the lobby, the line to the ladies room is ten deep. Gabriela needs a break from the crew more than she needs to use the toilet, so she doesn't wait. She grabs a bottle of water from Deidre, who supervises the volunteers at the concession counter.

"Going well," Deidre says.

Gabriela unscrews the cap. "Thank you."

The elderly guests also offer their appreciation but probably have no idea who she is. Wanda Butler, the peculiar librarian with the wire-rimmed glasses, wobbles out from the middle of the group and greets Gabriela with a bright smile. Beside her, a hunched giant ambles on a cane. The left side of his face sags. His eye socket is empty.

"Well, looky who it is," Wanda says. "Thought I might find you here. Show's great so far."

"Thank you."

"That Cedric Young's a hoot, I tell you." Wanda waves the program. "You didn't tell me you were so important."

"Didn't I?"

"Stage manager." Wanda howls. "Sounds mighty official to me."

"I call the cues."

"Of course you do, dear." Wanda grabs the deformed man by his elbow. "Oh, I almost forgot. This is my son Helms. Say hello, Helms."

(if you think she's odd)

"Evening, ma'am." Helms extends a quivering hand. Gabriela shakes his dry palm. He has no fingernails.

"Nice to meet you."

(wait till you meet her son)

"Named after our great senator," Wanda says. "God bless his soul."

Gabriela doesn't know any senators named Helms but nods politely. She can't help but remember what Brad told her at dinner about the drug experiments in Holt County decades ago and how the children had side effects. Is that what happened to Helms? Was the librarian a test subject whose son paid the price? Like Amanda Simmons. Like Connor?

(the ones you can't tell are sick are the most dangerous)

Wanda glances sideways and draws Gabriela closer with her bent fingers.

"You find Becky Stokes like I told you yesterday morning?"

Gabriela nods, choking on Wanda's flowery perfume. Her nose tingles as she's bumped and elbowed by older spectators jostling for the snack line. Helms buckles a knee and catches himself on his cane. His voided eye socket wrinkles.

"She give you what you went looking for?" Wanda asks.

Ralph Delacourt.

"Sì."

"Knew she would."

The skin under Wanda's right ear bubbles. Gabriela gags. *Did the experiments do that to her? Is that* her *side effect?* Brad didn't mention anything about what happened to the parent test subjects. Maybe they have skin disorders like lesions or psoriasis.

Lesions don't squirm. Psoriasis doesn't wriggle.

"Thanks for coming," Gabriela says, lifting her face.

Wanda grabs her hand. "Delacourt died for a reason."

"Eh?"

"Delacourt." *How does she know about Ralph Delacourt?* "Don't go searching for things you ain't meant to find."

"What?"

"You don't belong here."

Gabriela breaks loose of her grip and staggers backward into a water fountain.

"Well, I better get back to my seat before the second half," Wanda says. "Can't wait to see how this finishes. Come along, Helms."

The old librarian disappears into the throng of guests meandering back to the auditorium with her misshapen son beside her.

scene 10.

Sania flashes the lights in the lobby for the two-minute call Gabriela misses. When she returns to the console, Deanna Flowers stands by her chair, blinking and clearing her throat repeatedly.

"Deanna?"

"We still ain't heard from Sara."

"What do you mean?"

Deanna yelps after a twitch in her shoulder. "Sara still hasn't shown up."

Deanna's as old as Wanda Butler. Maybe the nervous tic isn't Tourette's. Maybe she was also a test subject. Gabriela scans her face for slithering lumps and worms but finds nothing.

"Sure she has," Gabriela says.

"Where?" Deanna says.

"Connor told us she was backstage when the show started." Gabriela looks at Cherlynne, then Sania. "He told us over headset, remember?"

Cherlynne shakes her head. "Not that I heard."

Gabriela looks at Sania.

"I didn't hear anything."

"Are you kidding?" Gabriela asks.

"Gabriela?" Deanna says.

"We all heard him right after the show started. We all heard him tell us that Sara was backstage giving him the middle finger."

Cherlynne chuckles. "That sounds like Sara, but I didn't hear Connor say anything on headset the whole first half."

"Me neither," Sania says.

"Figlio di cagna!" Gabriela slams her headset on the console. "Don't touch anything or start without me."

Sania's eyes widen. "Okay."

"Cherlynne?" Gabriela says.

"Standing by." Cherlynne swishes her Dr. Pepper and dives into the Doritos.

Gabriela points at Deanna. "Follow me."

She doesn't wait for Deanna's reply. She hustles down the aisle, ignoring the blank faces, including Brad's, as she hops up the stage left steps and rounds the proscenium. In all the years she's done theatre, she can't remember ever having broken the fourth wall during a live show or even a dress rehearsal.

(i never break the legs)

But she doesn't care. She's had enough. If Connor wants a fight, he's got one. She rolls up her sleeves.

Connor sits at the desk backstage on headset, holding his place in his script with a pencil. She wants to tear that fucking smirk off his face. Shove the crumpled demon sketch down his throat. Hold his *coglioni* over the shaft in the earth beneath the stage until the sunburst that singed Brad's face scorches them.

"Where the fuck is she?" Gabriela shouts.

"What are you talking about?" Connor says.

Joe Cox staggers out of bluelight and away from his position on the rail.

Gabriela raises a finger. "Stay where you are, Joe. You don't need to get involved."

"Gabriela?' Joe says.

"You heard me."

Joe retreats, adjusting his gloves. "Sorry."

"Where's Sara?" Gabriela says, breathing on Connor now. Spittle spews off her lips and splashes his forehead.

"How should I know?" Connor says. "Aren't you the stage manager?"

King Boggs and Doug Cousins enter through the backstage door. Deanna follows. She took the long way around. The hallway Gabriela ignored. The performers gather in the wings, murmuring. They all want to know what's going on. Why Gabriela's so upset. Maybe she should tell them about James Patterson. Let them know he's leading the good life, throwing back hard candies with Pastor Aken.

"This is your last chance." Gabriela squeezes her fists. "Tell me where she is."

Connor sets down his pencil. "I don't know. And I don't appreciate your threats."

"Fuck you."

Gabriela pounces. She claws at his face, slicing with her fingernails.

"The fuck," he says and rolls off the chair. The back of his head smacks the railing above the pit.

King rushes past the desk to help Connor. The others close in. Joe grabs her from behind.

"Settle down, Gabriela," he says. "We'll work this out."

"Bastardo!" She struggles but can't escape his grip. "Let me go!"

"Calm down!"

Gabriela smashes Joe's foot with her boot. He squeals and loosens his grip. She squirms out from under his arms and raises her palms, sweeping the entire backstage.

"I don't know what the fuck's going on here," she says. "But Sara better be okay."

"The fuck?" one of the actors says. Possibly Cedric, the youngest cast member.

"Since when are you and Sara so tight?" another says. Probably Tariq.

Have they all fucking turned against her? Where's Matt? Where's the director? Didn't he tell her before tonight's preview how grateful he was for the job she's done stepping in for Heather at the last minute? That he told her not to worry. What the fuck is going on?

Connor stands. "Relax, everybody. I'm fine. Gabriela's a little on edge. I'm sure she doesn't mean anything. We're all stressed. It's understandable with all that's happened. We'll find out what's going on with Sara, and everything will be good to go. Did anybody text her?"

Deanna pulls out her mobile. "Yes. About six times."

"And?" Connor says.

"And I still haven't heard back."

Squawks rattle the headset on the desk. Connor puts them on and checks his watch.

"I know, Sania." He glances at Gabriela. "Crowd's getting restless."

Gabriela catches her breath. "Fine. Let's get back to work. I'm sorry I lost my temper."

Connor nods and speaks into his mic. "Tell Cherlynne Gabriela's on her way back."

"If anybody hears from Sara, please let me know immediately," Gabriela says.

Except for the performers waiting to make their first entrances of act two, the crowd disperses backstage.

Gabriela rushes out the side door and circles the auditorium through the escape hallway so she doesn't have to break the fourth wall again. Best guess, the audience has been in a hold for five or six minutes. Not unbearable but definitely suspect.

When she climbs to the console, she sees Brad lift his chin and shrug his shoulders. She's happy he's concerned. At least there's one person in this fucking theatre who gives a shit about her right now. Even if he is twice her age. Even if he doesn't have feelings for her. If it weren't for Brad, Deborah would be the only person in Crow Creek who offers Gabriela any comfort. And she spends her life at the fucking bakery because *she's* all alone.

Gabriela wants to call *Mamma*. Instead, she calls the cues to finish the second act.

scene 11.

Sara Cooper doesn't show. Gabriela texts her as soon as the play ends before she goes into the lobby to greet the audience and celebrate with the cast and crew. *Celebrate* isn't exactly the word she would use. *Tolerate* sounds more accurate. Sara doesn't respond. A few seniors, including Wanda Butler, drink champagne and eat fresh fruit. Wanda's defected son Helms sits on a lounge chair near the front windows, propping himself on his cane so he can close his one cyclops eye and rest while he waits. Brad doesn't take long to pull her aside.

"You okay?"

Gabriela shakes her head. "No."

"How soon can you get out of here?"

"Very soon," she says. "I'll tell Joe I'm not feeling well."

Not exactly a lie.

She asks Brad to meet at her apartment. He agrees. When they get to the parking lot, she doesn't invite him up. Probably for the best. She's not in any condition to host or share tiny space with Brad or anyone else right now. Mixed signals or not. Feelings or no. He waits in his utility vehicle while she changes into fresh clothes. As soon as he drives away, she asks if he can take her to check on Sara.

"Sara Cooper?"

Gabriela nods. "I know you have somewhere else you want us to go right now."

"That can wait." Brad adjusts a knob on his police radio. "What's going on?"

"She didn't show up for the run tonight."

"And you didn't hear from her?"

Gabriela shakes her head.

"You know where she lives?" He digs in a breast pocket and pulls out his yellow notepad. "I have it in here somewhere."

"She's not at her house."

"No?"

"No."

"Where then?"

"Queensboro."

"Got it."

Brad flips a switch on an instrument panel across his armrest. The lights flash and the siren howls. He races west down Route 119, following the directions as best as Gabriela can remember them. They miss what she believes is the turnoff. He backtracks after u-turning in a driveway near a cow pasture and kills his siren when she's sure they're on the right path in the woods. The trailer appears in moonlight after a kilometer on the winding road. A single interior light shines through broken miniblinds in what Gabriela believes is the living room. The door hangs loose on its hinges.

"That can't be good," Brad says.

Gabriela hops out of the car and jogs to the trailer. She hears Brad follow but doesn't wait to go inside. The door swings unevenly when she pulls. An eye hook dangles from a broken latch. Sara must've known trouble was coming. Why else would she have locked the door? She didn't when they spent last night together.

The lamp on the end table reveals the damage. Sara fought hard. The arm chair's toppled, the coffee table overturned, one leg on the sofa collapsed. A small hole in the faded paneling might be from a stray fist or an ashtray.

"She wasn't expecting company," Brad says, pointing to the whiskey bottle and solitary tumbler on the kitchen counter. The wine glasses Sara and Gabriela drained await rinsing in the sink.

"No," Gabriela says, bending down to examine drops of blood on the shag carpet.

Brad squats beside her. "How'd you know about this place?"

"She took me here last night."

"Here?"

"It's her grandmother's." Gabriela slaps both thighs and stands. "She didn't think anyone else knew about it."

"Where do you think she is?" Brad says.

"I have a couple of ideas."

"A couple?"

"Either Connor got to her," Gabriela says.

"That's what I'm thinking."

"Or Pastor Aken did."

Brad nods. "I need to radio this in. We'll stay here until we've got one of my deputies on sight. Then we'll see about making a visit of our own."

"Shouldn't we go after her first?"

"You think she's already at the theatre?"

Good point. Gabriela doesn't need to check her watch to know the Orpheum hasn't cleared out yet. Not even Connor would be stupid enough to keep her locked under the stage during tonight's performance. Even if he could've muffled and restrained her, there's a chance somebody might've wandered into the pit and seen or heard something. And any chance is too big.

"Not yet," she says.

"First Baptist then?"

"Maybe."

But she knows there wouldn't be any reason or cause to go there yet. Pastor Aken clearly told James Patterson that their plan, whatever it is, won't happen until Friday. The downtown vigil is Friday. That must be what he meant. If Pastor Aken has Sara somewhere else, they still have time to find her.

"I'll take you wherever you want to go," Brad says.

"No," Gabriela says. "I trust you."

She's not so sure she feels the same way about the rest of Crow Creek.

Brad smiles. "We'll go back to the theatre as soon as we can."

She rubs her *cornicello*. After Brad steps outside, *Mamma* finds her in the empty trailer. *Non pensavi di poterti fidare di Sara.* She didn't think she could trust Sara. *Mamma's* right. It's too soon to cast judgment on an entire town for the erratic behavior of a few. How would that be any different than what she feels they've been doing to her? Instead of being judged as the outsider, she's condemning the locals. She still doesn't know how James Patterson fits into all this. Maybe where Brad plans to take her will shed some light.

scene 12.

Gabriela leaves the trailer and rejoins Brad while he waits beside his cruiser. A rusty bicycle leans against a broken chain link fence at the bottom of the hill. Did Sara take bike rides in the country when she was a child the way Gabriela did when she grew up in the mountains of Northern Italy? How similar are the two different worlds despite their obvious distance?

Curly shows up in his patrol car about ten minutes later. Brad tells him to notify Queensboro PD and the Holt County Sheriff's Office. Together, they can decide whether or not to arrange for state detectives to investigate.

"Out of our jurisdiction," Brad says.

"Sure is," Curly says.

"For now."

Curly unclips his shoulder mic. "More you ain't telling me?"

"Could be," Brad says and signals Gabriela that it's time to leave.

They jump into his cruiser and drive away from the trailer. Brad goes left on Route 119 back toward Crow Creek but veers north on Frye Avenue into Houndstooth. They cross the Bragg Bridge and move along a narrow country road bordered on both sides by wild underbrush until they reach a wooded neighborhood with homes set deep behind the trees. Brad parks along the curb in front of a single story home with a rickety porch and faded siding. He trots up the steps and knocks on the door while Gabriela waits on the gravel drive. A large mastiff trots out from beside the house and slips through a broken chain link fence before sniffing her shoes and sitting proudly at her hip. Brad cups his hands against a front window so he can peek into the darkness inside. The mastiff offers a few friendly barks until Brad hops down from the porch and follows the dog through the fence, taking Gabriela's hand so that she isn't left behind. They move through uncut grass and weeds toward a crumbling shotgun shack under a wide cottonwood tree. Gabriela sees the dog's watchful eyes flash within its black facial mask as it barks twice in the shadows of the moonlight. Low chanting from within the shack ceases, and the slatted door creaks open. A massive shape with a face as black as the mastiff's appears in the threshold. Crickets chirp in the nighttime silence.

"Brad?" the shape says. "That you?"

"Darrell?"

Brad releases her hand as Darrell steps into the yard and envelopes the sheriff in a warm hug. The mastiff disappears inside the battered shack, bumping the door with her hind quarters so a small amount of light spills to the yard. Darrell wears a peacap and a checkered flannel too heavy for a summer evening. His bearded features relax as he withdraws from Brad.

"When you texted you needed to see me, I didn't realize you meant this soon."

"Sorry," Brad says, placing his hand on the small of Gabriela's back. "This is Gabriela."

Darrell grins. "The one you told me about?"

Brad nods. *He's been talking about her.*

"Nice to meet you," Gabriela says.

"Pleasure's mine," Darrell says.

"Darrell and me been friends since high school," Brad says.

"Played football together." Darrell's deep laughter is a growl. "Next to each other on the offensive line."

Gabriela doesn't know the positions or how American football differs from the *calcio* played back home except that they touch the ball with their hands and kick the ball between goalposts instead of into nets. Either way, she feels more comfortable on the slopes than she ever did on any field.

"All the way through college," Brad says.

"And the Gulf War," Darrell adds.

"The first one."

Gabriela can't be sure whether or not they mean the one that killed Saddam Hussein when she was ten years old but guesses they're probably talking about an older war fought before she was born. They don't seem to care if she knows. The exchange is more for the two of them as they fast forward through a shared history now merely a blip in their subconscious.

"We're old, ain't we?"

"Those were the days."

Darrell lowers his mouth. "How long's it been?"

"Since high school?"

"Either."

"Wolfpack, class of eighty-nine. Thirty-one years last spring."

Gabriela cares less about their graduation year (she *is* half his age) than the team mascot. The *Wolf*pack.

He rises in the wolf's mouth.

"You're getting old," Darrell says.

"We both are," Brad says.

Darrell whistles. "Not me."

The mastiff trots out of the shack where Darrell bends over and rubs her belly.

"Thea keeps me young and sharp."

"So she does," Brad says. "Glad you have her."

"Goes on every run with me," Darrell says.

Brad looks at Gabriela. "Darrell drives a big rig for Scott Lumber."

"Oh," she says.

"Ain't seen you since the funeral." Darrell flattens his brow and purses his lips. "But you don't seem like you're alone no more. Shana would approve."

Brad turns red and shrugs his shoulders. Gabriela hasn't seen him embarrass so easily.

"Excuse me if I'm overstepping," Darrell says. "Tell me why you dropped by."

"Gabriela works for the Orpheum."

"The theatre downtown where they found them two bodies earlier this week?"

"Word travels fast," Brad says.

"Even when I'm out on the road, I don't miss what happens in Crow Creek. Been here long enough to know this town has a lifeline."

This town has a lifeline.

(this place this spot there's an energy)

(something wrong about this place deep where the underground currents flow)

(if you stare into the abyss)

"She was there," Brad says.

"Both times?" Darrell says.

Gabriela nods.

"Jesus ain't playing with you, girl," Darrell says. "Maybe you should come on in."

Brad takes Gabriela's hand as they enter after Darrell. Unsteady candlelight reveals stone coffins piled and stacked on shelves in the front room of the shotgun shack, surrounding a hand-woven Moroccan rug in the center. A rectangular arch nearly the width of the hut opens to an abandoned kitchen. A doorless refrigerator serves as a shrine to a crucified saint Gabriela doesn't recognize. A statue stands atop the bubble condenser laced at the wrists to a miniature tree made of black marble. The exposed steel cabinet contains unlit votives, prayer beads, dried blood, and a few daguerreotypes of African slaves not unlike those Gabriela studied in the Civil War library book yesterday. Skulls arranged in pantries, on broken tables and chairs, and in a large, cast iron stove populate the rest of the galley.

"You should sit here," Darrell says, offering her the center of the oracle rug.

Gabriela folds her legs under her hips and faces the edge of the rug where a deep scar in the hardwood disappears beneath the frayed edge. Brad stands in the corner beside a homemade bow with a quiver of branches honed into jagged arrows.

"Brad?" she says.

"You'll be fine," Brad says. "Let Darrell do what he needs to do. You can trust him."

Gabriela takes deep breaths as Darrell slips into the kitchen and unwrinkles a sheet of parchment paper kept under what looks like a petrified tongue. He cracks several raw eggs into a tall glass and opens a jar filled with thick purple jam. He scoops out a large glob, separating the thick mass into two. Jamming his thumb into either a lemon or a lime (Gabriela can't quite tell in the candlelight), Darrell squeezes juice over the entire mess. He stirs the glass with his fingers and recites a soft prayer before returning to the rug.

"I need to know what you know," Darrell says. "From the beginning."

Gabriela slows her heart rate as she gathers her thoughts. The persistent hum that rises beneath the rug lulls her into a trance.

"It's only been a few days," she says. "I started working as the stage manager on Monday."

"Before that?" Darrell says, taking a knee with his mastiff at his side. He sets the glass on the hardwood floor.

"I was the assistant stage manager. I've only been at the Orpheum for eight months."

"Why did you come here?"

"For the job. That's why I left home."

"You left loved ones behind?"

"Mamma."

"You miss her?"

"Molto." Gabriela clears her throat. "Pardon me. I miss her very much."

"What else?"

"I could only get crew work in Pittsburgh where the theatres are bigger. They have more deckhands moving up the ladder. I wanted to go someplace small like where I came from."

"You found Crow Creek?"

"Not exactly."

"Crow Creek found you?"

Gabriela nods. "I have a cousin who lives here. Deborah DeVito. She owns the bakery downtown. She told *Mamma* she'd let me know if she could help."

"She told you about the job?"

"Yes."

Darrell snaps his fingers at the mastiff. The large tan dog curls in the corner next to Brad, whose face disappears in shadow.

"Let's jump to this week," Darrell says.

"Okay."

"I need you to focus. Tell me what you know."

Gabriela squeezes her eyes. Words flow from her mouth in her native tongue because English doesn't suffice. Her inner tempo matches the rhythm of the earth's pulse.

"Meribel . . . Meribel, she's the house manager — she found Mr. Patterson dead in the auditorium right after he talked to me about a possible merger with Raleigh Regional. But not before I met Ralph Delacourt. I didn't know who he was, not until I found an article about him in the newspaper this morning. He hanged himself in the theatre over sixty years ago. Just like Tommy Nolan did two days ago. Or what we thought Tommy did. Sara doesn't think he killed himself. Sara's a props assistant. She's my friend, only I never knew. She's missing now. She thinks somebody else murdered him but doesn't know who or why. I found a secret room under the stage where Connor Simmons tapped a hole in the ground with some kind of gravity drive. Connor Simmons, he took over for Tommy at the theatre. I'm not sure what he's trying to do, but I think it has something to do with his crippled sister. There's another tunnel under the stage that leads to First Baptist, and when Brad and I went through, we found Mr. Patterson on the other side talking to Pastor Aken. But he's not a true pastor, not holy. He has red eyes like a demon, like the demon I sketched, and I don't know what the fuck is going on. I'm losing my mind, aren't I? I'm going crazy because nobody wants me here, and I never should've left home or left *Mamma* alone after *Papà* died."

Gabriela falls on her side, gasping for air. Her forehead swells with sweat. She can't slow her heart rate because the earth thumps too fast beneath her. Darrell rubs a gentle hand through her hair, begging her to keep calm and find a peaceful light so they can proceed.

"Please, Gabriela," Brad says in the darkness of the shack. "Let Darrell help."

Gabriela sits up.

"That's better," Darrell says.

Gabriela opens her eyes and speaks English again. "Okay. I'm okay. I'm sorry."

"You're doing fine," Brad says.

"We need to continue," Darrell says. "We don't have much time."

"Okay." Gabriela stifles a sob. "I'm ready."

Darrell leans closer, steaming her face with his warm breath. "What do you believe?"

"Scusi?"

"What do you believe?"

"Non lo so."

Darrell slaps both palms on the rug. "Tell me."

"Non so in cosa credo."

Brad steps into candle light. "Tell him, Gabriela. Tell him now!"

She catches her breath.

"Papà." A single word. "I can't forgive myself."

Gabriela explodes in tears. The shack quakes. Gabriela yelps as she topples to her side. The floor undulates beneath her, lifting the rug and separating along the scar in the hardwood. Darrell forces the glass into her hands.

"Drink!" he shouts.

Gabriela raises the potion to her lips and tilts. She gags as the raw eggs lodge behind her tongue. The weight of the berries carries them down, burning her throat as she swallows. The warm mixture drops into her stomach before a burst of sunlight erupts from the fissure, blinding Gabriela. Darrell wails and rolls off the rug. The stone boxes topple, spilling their ashes and splintered bones. Skulls animate on the kitchen shelves, popping their jaws and chanting in harmony with Darrell as he laments, eyes rolled up in his head.

Brad wraps Gabriela in his arms. "I'm here."

An apparition floats within the brilliant light. *Ralph Delacourt.* Gabriela reaches for his youthful face, ghostly and beautiful, no longer sagging with rotten flesh or marked by death wounds. His oiled hair glistens in the solar glow.

"You are the key, my child," the spirit says. "You must do what I couldn't."

"What?" Gabriela says. "Tell me what I need to do."

"Close the door before it's too late."

"Close the door?" The earth's thump rattles her bones. "What door?"

"We live in the shadows," the ghost says. "He can't come through."

"*Who* can't?"

Delacourt glides to her along the writhing hardwood. "Close the door forever."

"How?"

"It might already be too late."

Gabriela wrestles free from Brad and steps to Delacourt, clenching her fists.

"No more riddles," she says. *"Dì la verità."*

"He rises in the wolf's mouth."

"Dì la verità!"

But Gabriela knows the truth. She's known all along.

Delacourt takes her bruised wrist. Gabriela winces as her skin sizzles.

"It might already be too late," he says again.

The ghost ascends into the cramped space above the rug in a shimmering vortex. The earth belches and burns before puffing out. Delacourt disappears, sucked back into the vent in the hardwood. Darrell collapses, silent except for heavy panting. The skulls wobble until they're motionless on the dusty kitchen shelves. The floor stops beating. Brad drapes his arm around her shoulders.

"We need to go," Gabriela says, rubbing her wrist. "We need to find Sara."

Brad nods and crosses the threadbare rug to Darrell, careful to step over the split floorboards. The large truck driver pulls himself to his feet and wipes sweat off his brow. They shake hands.

"Thank you, Darrell," Brad says.

With their hands locked, Darrell draws Brad near.

"They come back wrong," he says.

Brad shakes his head. "Huh?"

"Let her rest," Darrell says.

"Who?"

"You'll know."

Brad escorts Gabriela back to his cruiser. The mastiff barks as she chases bats under the cottonwood tree. They don't look back at the shotgun shack or speak until they cross the Bragg Bridge out of Houndstooth.

scene 13.

After midnight, Gabriela studies an image forming on her bruised wrist as Brad drives with his lights flashing. She recognizes the Greek letters and the layering from her days in Sunday school at *Santissima d'Annunziata* as a Chi-Rho, the crucifix Constantine witnessed over the burning skies of Gaul before the legendary Battle of the Milvian Bridge. The mythic prophecy declared that the ruler would become the world's greatest conqueror, as long as he kept faith in the one true God. As long as he believed.

"You didn't tell me Darrell was a conjurer."

"Didn't I?" Brad says.

"No."

Brad chuckles. "Some folks say he has the face of Jesus in the stained glass windows at First Baptist, but I don't see it."

"Neither do I." Gabriela adjusts her seatbelt harness. "How much do you know about theatre folklore?"

"In a word?"

"Mmm."

"Not much."

"I'll give you the abridged version," Gabriela says.

"That'll do." Brad turns left on Highway 77 toward downtown Crow Creek. "I ain't never been much of a scholar."

"No?" Gabriela's not sure why that surprises her. Brad has keen intuition. Maybe that's something you can't learn from a textbook.

"Except for law enforcement, but Daddy taught me everything I know. If it weren't for the football scholarship, I probably never would've gone to college. Then the war came, and I didn't finish."

"Fair enough." Gabriela watches evergreens pass her window in a blur. "Theatre has its roots in storytelling, like all performance art. That's universal. It doesn't matter what part of the world you study."

"People sit around and tell stories," Brad says. "They change their voices and act out different characters. I get it."

"Exactly." Gabriela traces her finger on the glass, tracking dew drops. "Early theatre included songs with dancing and musicians. For the Greeks, this meant festivals and competitions."

"Kinda like rock concerts?"

"Kind of. But imagine if they went on for weeks at a time."

"Kinda like Woodstock."

Gabriela's not familiar enough with the hippie festival to recall any of the performers (she'd probably recognize some names if told) but knows of its cultural importance to radicals in late 1960s America. "Maybe. But they were scripted. They involved rituals and sacrifice."

"Oh."

"That means religion. *Capisci?*"

Brad nods. "So these stories they told were about their beliefs? About their gods?"

Gabriela smiles. "Now you're catching on, sir."

"Like Sunday services. The pastor tells stories about Jesus. We play music and sing songs to praise him."

"Correct," Gabriela says. "Communion is our modern sacrifice."

"How so?"

"We eat the body and drink the blood."

"Of course." Brad slows at a red light but drives without stopping. "We reenact the Last Supper."

"Yes," Gabriela says. "But in a primitive culture, the sacrifices were different."

"They were?"

Gabriela rubs her forehead as she searches for the right word in English. "They were…*viscerale*."

"Visceral?" Brad says.

"*Sì,* visceral. For theatre, they slaughtered bulls as an offering. So imagine if we couldn't start our Sunday worship without killing an animal first."

"Visceral in the literal sense."

"Mmm-hmm." Gabriela clasps her *cornicello.* "Dionysus was the god of theatre. The Romans called him Bacchus."

"I've heard of Bacchus." Brad presses the gas pedal. "Shana and I went to New Orleans plenty before she passed. He's the god of drinking and partying."

"Right, but part of the tradition was lost when the Romans adopted Hellenic culture as they conquered Europe."

"Lost?"

Gabriela nods. "The dark part of the story."

"Dark part?"

"Dionysus had the power to cross back and forth between the world of the living and the world of the dead."

"Oh?"

"To spite his rival Apollo, he would allow demons to cross over with him."

"Demons?"

Brad turns on Ninth Street. Gabriela wonders how close they are to where his daughter died on the railroad tracks.

"The Maenads," she says.

"I'm not gonna try and pronounce that one."

"Ravishers, in English. That's the closest translation anyhow. They disguised themselves by wearing fox pelts or wolf skins."

"Beware the wolf's mouth?" Brad says.

Gabriela shudders. *In bocca al lupo.* "The wolf's mouth, yes. It's where our modern concept of the werewolf comes from."

"As in the wolfman?"

"Not quite," Gabriela says. "The Maenads were all female."

Brad sighs. "Female demons?"

"They tortured their victims, often dismembering them, including Orpheus."

"The same Orpheus your theatre is named after?"

"Sì."

"But what does all that have to do with us?" Brad parks in front of the Orpheum. "With Crow Creek?"

"When I talked with Delacourt, I understood." Gabriela takes Brad's hands after he shuts the ignition. "Pastor Aken plans to summon Dionysus at the vigil tomorrow night."

"He plans to summon Dionysus?"

"Yes."

"But I thought those were all myths and legends."

"So did I," Gabriela says.

"What about James Patterson?"

"I'm not quite sure. Maybe because he invited investors from Raleigh?"

"You think Pastor Aken doesn't want any outsiders?"

"I don't know, but I believe the vents under the church and the theatre are somehow connected."

"The intersection where the Pastor holds the vigils," Brad says. "The underground currents must join there."

"They must," Gabriela says. "And if he can summon James Patterson . . ."

Gabriela steps out of the cruiser without finishing the thought. Brad follows.

scene 14.

The street in front of the theatre is dark. Crows lining the marquee caw, protesting their early morning arrival. Brad runs to the patrol car parked across the street for a quick exchange (tells the deputies to stay alert and proceed with caution if they hear or see anything suspicious) before returning.

"There's still one thing I can't understand," he says.

Gabriela unlocks the doors. "What's that?"

"I can't figure out how Connor Simmons and his sister are involved."

"They aren't." She punches the code to disarm the system. "Pastor Aken has no idea what they've been up to."

Brad shines his flashlight in the lobby. They walk through the auditorium doors. For the first time this week, Gabriela doesn't want stage lights so she avoids the console and leads Brad down the dark aisle, pursuing his beam. They round the proscenium, passing between the ghost light and the stage manager's desk. The ghost light brightens as if happy to see her. The promptbook flaps its pages, revealing her demon sketch. The sketch she crumbled and tossed in the trash.

The last fucking thing she wants to see right now are those wicked red eyes. How the fuck did that get there? Will Delacourt show up next? Hasn't he told her what he needs to tell her? Can't he move on? That's how the land of the dead works, right? If the source four starts blinking again, it better be the fucking dimmers for real.

Gabriela shakes her head. Outsider or not, she has Brad by her side. And Deborah's not far away. Although she's not quite sure what her American cousin could do to help, unless Italian pastries are the ancient god's weakness.

Find Sara. That's first. *Prima di tutto.*

They reach the bottom of the steps to the orchestra pit and open the door. The space reeks of mold, musician sweat, and foul breath. Not a delightful combination. She scrunches her nose but can't see if Brad does. He traces the closest trapdoor with his fingers until the lock pops. Pulsing light bleeds through the cracks. Brad draws his firearm. He's not in his uniform, but Gabriela's learned that his weapon's always within reach. Like the officers at home in *Châtillon*, he keeps his concealed while off duty. He holds a finger over his lips as they move in.

Connor and King stand at the center of the antechamber. Connor holds the goat horn like the last time. His sister Amanda lays crumpled beside him. Once again, the collider is poised; cables and tubes thread into a processor on wheels against a steel girder in the far corner opposite the secret door to the underground tunnels. The same processor she and Brad found under First Baptist. The one Connor's been stealing behind the pastor's back.

The earth buzzes.

"Simmons." Brad aims his gun. "Hands where I can see them."

"Sheriff?" he says.

"Same, Boggs." Brad levels his firearm as he slips between girders. "Don't move."

Nodding, the bearded master electrician raises his plump hands.

"Where's Sara?" Gabriela says.

"How the fuck should I know?" Connor says, gritting his teeth.

Gabriela shuffles through the dirt. "Tell me!"

"I don't have any idea. This isn't about her."

"You said you would deal with her," Gabriela says.

"What?"

"I heard you and King talking down here last night."

"That was *you*?"

"What did you do to her?"

"I wasn't talking about Sara."

"You're lying!" Gabriela slaps him. Her hand stings. He drops the horn and grabs his face, more responsive to this strike than the earlier scratch she gave him backstage.

"Go back where you came from, you bitch," Connor says. "You don't belong here."

"Vaffanculo."

"Take it easy," Brad says. Gabriela can't tell if he means her or Connor or both. "Nobody's going anywhere. Not until we get some answers."

"That's what you think," Amanda says, shrill and harsh.

"Amanda?" Connor says.

Her gnarled fingers wrap around the bent horn Connor dropped as she pulls herself off the dirt floor using a metal post for support. Taut skin on her cheeks stretches, exposing bones and teeth.

"You don't know what you started, brother."

Amanda plunges the bent horn into her gut and shrieks. Blood paints the room. Sparks cascade through the cylinders. The earth drops, shifts, pauses, and skips as sunlight bursts through the portal in the dirt, toppling the computer equipment and knocking Gabriela to her knees. The rest of the group tumbles.

"Brad?"

He finds her in the brightness as two human figures emerge from the hole and spill into the light. Gabriela can't tell who they are. The room vibrates, pounding with the heartbeat of the earth's core. Gabriela thrusts her hands over her ears. The dirt floor expands, holds, and contracts, sucking all the light back into the tap.

Silence fills the room.

Amanda stands below the electrical dome, both hands outstretched. Lightning dances across her slender fingertips.

Amanda but not Amanda. A different Amanda. Amanda, not crippled or shriveled or depleted at all. A powerful Amanda, chest heaving and eyes swirling.

(they come back wrong)

The crippled Amanda lies crumpled and dead in a growing pool of her own blood. Beside her, an older man Gabriela's never seen before (not unlike King Boggs but fitter) lays unconscious in the dirt. More like Darrell maybe, with ragged jeans and a thick flannel. But neither. Somebody *new*. His chest rises and falls. A faded Chi-Rho tattoo glistens on his sweaty forearm. Gabriela rubs her bruised wrist where the matching symbol burns.

"Amanda?" Connor whispers.

"I found God," she says.

Without warning, Amanda grabs the bent horn and drives it into Connor's eye socket. The point bursts through the back of his skull, spraying King with blood and chunks of brain. Connor collapses lifeless beside the unconscious stranger. Brad raises his gun, but before he can say anything, Amanda flicks her palm in his direction.

Lightning explodes off her fingertips and knocks Brad against the brick wall of the orchestra pit. He drops his firearm and slumps as he moans and grabs the back of his head.

"Brad," Gabriela says and crawls to his side, cradling his shoulders.

The trapdoor to the orchestra pit swings wide as the two deputies parked in the patrol car in front of the theatre arrive, firearms leveled. The female officer with the buzz cut leaps behind a steel girder when she sees Amanda spin on her heels toward her.

"Austin!" she yells, but the tall blonde officer is too slow to react. Amanda rotates her wrists and cocks her hands. A bolt surges off her fingertips and drives the young deputy against the far wall, cracking his back. He collapses in a heap.

Brad scrambles for his gun, but his eyes roll up into his head when he moves. Gabriela heaves his shoulders across her lap to keep him out of sight as Amanda strides the length of the antechamber toward them.

The female officer arches her back and pushes off the girder, wheeling as low as she can and aiming her gun. Amanda launches another electric strike that passes overhead and scorches the surrounding bricks. The deputy fires twice. Each round catches Amanda in the chest. She recoils, clenching her fists and screaming as her entire head erupts into flames. The deputy fires a third time, but the bullet goes stray because Amanda's on her, tearing away at her throat with sharp teeth. Blood squirts. Gabriela screams as Amanda drains the limp deputy and deposits her wasted carcass on the subfloor.

Brad's eyes flutter. He moves his mouth, but Gabriela places her hands over his lips so he's quiet. She trembles and shivers, gritting her teeth to stop the chattering. *Please keep us safe. Please God. I want* Mamma. *Please. I'm so afraid because I'm all alone and I don't belong here and* DIO MIO DIO MIO *DID YOU SEE WHAT SHE DID? SHE BIT HER AND DRANK HER BLOOD!*

(deep calls to deep)

Amanda says nothing and appears unharmed by her bullet wounds, especially now that she's fed. She relaxes her fists, splaying the fingers of her exposed palms, and elevates herself a few centimeters off the dirt floor. The antechamber trembles, shaking the composite steel deck above. Dust and dirt shower Gabriela, salting her eyes. The center girders buckle as Amanda continues her magical rise, cracking open the cement foundation beneath the stage floor. She disappears. The sofa and coffee table slide into view, threatening to spill over the edge. A lamp rolls in and crashes on the sparking mainframe. The lamp that Bianca Whitt breaks in act two. The resulting shatter sounds nothing like Cherlynne's canned effect.

scene 15.

"Gabriela?" Brad blinks. "You okay?"

"Yes," she says. "I'm fine. You?"

Brad shivers. "Been better."

She massages the goose egg on the back of his head. "You need ice."

"Probably so."

"We have some upstairs."

"Give me a minute." Brad grabs his gun and drags himself across the dirt until he finds the blonde deputy. He checks for a pulse but shakes his head. He moves into the center of the room where King lies under the electrical dome.

"Sheriff?" King mutters.

Brad grabs King by the collar of his blood-soaked crew shirt. "You better tell me what you know."

King pushes away. "Let me go."

"I ain't messing around, King."

"I don't know nothing."

Brad presses the barrel of his gun against King's forehead. "Last chance."

"Okay, okay." King sits up. "Take it easy."

"Start talking." Brad lets him go and lowers his gun.

King catches his breath. "Connor came to me about four months ago. Told me about what he seen in the cellar at First Baptist while setting up for Easter brunch. Said he thought it could help his sister. Maybe ease her pain."

"Tommy Nolan with you?" Brad says.

"We all were at the church." King nods. "Except none of us went down there but him."

"Tommy?" Gabriela says.

King sighs. "No, Connor."

"Wait a minute," Brad says. "If Connor was the only one who went into the cellar, why kill Tommy?"

King shrugs. "You'd have to ask Pastor Aken."

"Did the pastor kill Mr. Patterson?" Brad says.

"Nuh-uh." King swallows. "Tommy did."

"Tommy?" Brad says. "That can't be possible."

"I ain't lying," King says.

Gabriela breathes. "It's true."

"Gabriela?" Brad says.

"Sara told me."

"Why didn't you say anything?"

"I didn't want her to get in trouble."

"In trouble?" Brad says, her betrayal reflecting in his doleful stare.

"She knew what Connor seen," King says. "He asked for her help, but she didn't want no part of it. All I did were the hookups. Connor did the rest. We didn't break no laws, though. Not really. Not like killing or nothing. We only borrowed the gravity drive so I could connect it for him and help Amanda."

"Help Amanda?" Brad flexes his arm and lifts his gun. "*Help* her? This is your idea of helping? We've got two officers down. They're both dead."

"We didn't know anything like this would happen, I swear," King says. "We put the collider back each time. We would've put it back tonight if y'all hadn't showed up."

"And you didn't think the pastor would notice this missing?" Brad waves his gun. "This time machine or whatever it is?"

"Ain't a time machine," King says.

Gabriela scoots closer. "What is it?"

"Best I can tell now, a portal."

"A doorway?" Brad says.

(close the door)

"Suppose so, yes." King peels a bloody chunk of Connor's skull off his snowy beard. "Connor thought the energy from the earth's core might heal his sister. I never thought it would work, to be honest."

"Amanda calls it the Bridge," the stranger says, coughing as he rolls over and pulls up the sleeves of his checkered flannel.

Gabriela's bruise flares again. The Chi-Rho darkens. Brad shifts his aim to the older man rustling in the far corner. Gabriela doesn't recognize him. He's scruffy but muscular. His white hair pulls back from a receding hairline in thin strands. The cleft in his knobby chin's about as deep as a button. His eyebrows form two bony arches over sunken gray eyes.

"Good to see you, Brad," he says.

Brad relaxes his grip. "Do I know you?"

"Probably don't," the old man says, studying the collapsed stage floor. "Not unless y'all got a B-52 parked out back. I'm thinking, no. Where is this anyhow?"

"B-52?" Brad recoils. "The bomber?"

"That's right."

"Daddy flew one out of Guam during Vietnam," Brad says. "Operation Arc Light. But why would we have one parked out back?"

"Nevermind." The old man stands, extending his hand. "Frank Edwards. No relation to the senator from Bethlehem that got caught cheating on his dying wife."

Brad shakes. "Who?"

"So he doesn't exist in this world? Or Bethlehem don't," Frank says. "Probably for the best, either way. Am I still in Winter?"

"Winter?" Gabriela says. "As in the season?"

"No, the place. About thirty miles south of Crow Creek. Where they dropped the nuclear bomb in the 1960s. Tried to kill Jack Kennedy with it. Failed, as it were, till the *Mafia* got him." Frank offers his hand to Gabriela. His tattoo ripples. "You must be the sheriff's daughter. Heard plenty about you. All secondhand, though. Most of my time's spent on the road driving my truck. You're prettier than they said, though. Love your dark curls. Like my Jeanette. My late wife. We never had no kids."

"Uh, no." Gabriela's face warms. "I'm not Brad's daughter."

"Sorry, Sheriff," Frank says. "Hoped she would still be alive in this world. Ain't she?"

Brad tilts his brow. "No."

"Lose her life on the tracks?"

"Mmm-hmm."

"Huh." Frank scratches his knotted chin. "Some events must overlap."

Gabriela tugs Brad's shirt. "Mr. Patterson."

"What about him?" Brad rubs the bump on his head.

"He wasn't a ghost."

"How's that?"

"If Connor could bring Amanda through the portal, then the pastor could bring Mr. Patterson through."

Footsteps shuffle above near the cracked stage floor. A soft flutter. Gabriela's not sure if anyone else hears.

"Connor didn't bring Amanda through," King says. "I told you. He only wanted to make her better. Everything he tried failed."

Frank clears his throat. "I can't say much about what's happening on your end, but Amanda didn't need no help coming through. She did what she needed on her own and crossed over. I only gave her a little push. Never thought we'd end up here, though."

"You're saying she found this place?" Brad says.

"Either by choice or by chance, yes." Frank narrows his eyes. "And what's this business about a pastor?"

"Pastor Aken," Brad says. "Ever heard of him?"

Frank nods. "Met him once. Once was enough. Held a rally at the Elks Club in Winter. Led an effort to rebuild the city decades after the bomb fell. More like a rock concert. Where I first met my wife, truth be told. My Jeanette. He makes you feel numb inside. Like you ain't got any control over your desires, if that makes sense."

"I've felt that," Gabriela says.

"You have?" Brad says. "But you don't even go to First Baptist. Have you ever met him?"

"No." Gabriela swallows. "From the photos. He drugs you somehow. It's unlike anything I've ever felt."

Frank half-grins. "Looks like we got the Devil in both worlds."

More footsteps above. Maybe someone shouting. In the distance. A flash of light.

That can't be Delacourt.

"Or two devils in one," King says.

"We need to get out of here." Brad tries to stand but loses his balance and plops in the dirt. "Guess I took a harder hit than I thought."

Gabriela takes his hand. "What about Sara?"

"I don't know. We've ruled out Connor, so that still leaves the pastor." Brad rubs his bruise while looking at King. "Think he's got her somewhere?"

King climbs to his feet. "Can't say for sure."

"What about Amanda?" Brad says.

"Amanda?" Gabriela says. "Connor's sister? What would she want with her?"

"You seen what she could do," Frank says.

"We all did," Brad says, hoisting himself up against a girder.

"Back in our world, she did worse."

"Worse than kill her own brother?" Brad says.

"Destroyed her mother. Amanda brought her entire company to ruins."

"Her *mother*?" King says.

"That's right." Frank dusts off his jeans. "She worked for a drug company. Amanda's mother. Had a bright red birthmark across her face. Easy to recognize."

"Like a demon's wing," King says.

"Same in this world then."

"Uh-huh." King unplugs an electrical cable from the center dome, avoiding the split in the composite steel. "Peggy Simmons."

"Peggy?" Gabriela says. *Where do I know that name?* Footsteps closer. Right above their heads. *Why can't anyone else hear that?*

Frank shakes his head. "Not Simmons. Not where I'm from. And she didn't have a son. Not that I'm aware of. Course Jeannette worked with her for over twenty years so I believe she would've known."

"Not Simmons?" Brad says.

"Ganis," Frank says. "Margaret Ganis. Why?"

King shakes his head. "Come to think of it, Connor's mom doesn't go by Simmons. She uses her maiden name."

"Maiden name?" Brad says.

"Mmm-hmm. Ever since she got the promotion at Entech."

"Entech?" Brad says. "The drug company in Queensboro that got in trouble for their experimental cancer drug?"

Experimental cancer drug. *Wanda Butler.* Her misshapen son Helms.

Furniture slides across the stage. The buffet. Maybe an armchair. Or both.

"Uh-huh." King dismantles a large cylinder. "Can't believe you're old enough to remember that. Don't look it."

"Well, at least they work for the same company in both worlds." Frank says.

"Connor's mother took the drug," Brad says.

"That's why Amanda was sick," King says.

"What's her maiden name?" Gabriela says.

King scratches his beard and discards another chunk of skull. "Can't quite recall."

Peggy. Where do I know that name? Above, shouting. Calling. A burst of light.

"Probably not important," Frank says.

"Wait a minute," King says. "I got it. Delacourt. That's her name. Peggy Delacourt."

Of course. *Delacourt.* The newspaper article. Ralph Delacourt's obituary. He was survived by an unmarried younger sister, Peggy. Delacourt had more to tell Gabriela after all.

Something glistens above the cracked stage floor. Her head swims. Brad hooks her elbow and keeps his balance against the girder so she doesn't fall.

"That's where she's going," Gabriela says.

"Stands to reason," Frank says. "If she destroyed her mother in one world."

"Think she'll do the same in both?" Brad asks.

"I'm not certain, honestly." Frank scratches his protruding forehead. "She'll wanna go to her mother, if nothing else. We're pack animals after all."

Brad narrows his eyes. "Why should we trust you?"

A loud bang above. Like a door slamming or scenery toppling.

"Don't see as you have a choice," Frank says, looking up.

Brad signals for everyone to take cover. A gleam descends through the fractured composite steel.

"Sheriff? That you?"

Not Ralph Delacourt. Not a ghost. Not the different and powerful Amanda Simmons.

"Curly?" Brad says.

Gabriela recognizes the deputy holding the gun.

"Uh-huh," Curly says. "You all right down there?"

"Hope so," Brad says.

"Katie called in a 10–18. She good?"

Brad lowers his eyes and shakes his head.

"Austin?"

"No."

Curly groans. "Both of them?"

"Sorry," Brad says. "Weren't much we could do."

"Coming down," Curly says.

"Use the stairs backstage," Brad says.

Curly peeks over his shoulder. "Got it."

The deputy disappears above the stage floor. Brad takes a few steps and stumbles. Frank and King grab his arms so he's stable.

"I won't be of much help if I don't get some rest." Brad props himself against a post and drops his forehead in the crook of his elbow. "I'm sorry."

Gabriela kneads his back with her palm. "What do we do?"

"I don't know," Brad says.

King stacks the remaining tubes and cables on the handtruck. "For what it's worth, I'll help however I can."

"Grazie," Gabriela says.

Curly enters through the trapdoor and holsters his firearm. Brown hair spills in waves under his black tactical cap. He rushes to Gabriela so they can lower Brad to the subfloor.

"Thank you," Brad says.

"What's going on, Sheriff?" Curly says, shining a flashlight. "This place looks like a war zone. Who else's down here? Miss Rossi, that you?"

Gabriela nods.

Curly widens his eyes as he surveys the room. "What in Jesus . . . ?"

"Amanda Simmons," Brad says.

"Amanda Simmons?" Curly tugs his ear. "Why do I know that name?"

"Connor's older sister."

"Connor who works here at the theatre?"

Brad takes a few deep breaths and stretches his back. "Uh-huh."

"Few years ahead of me in school. Weren't his older sister ill or something like that? Crippled in some way. Maybe she had that Lou Gehrig's disease? I can't remember."

Brad points. "That's her."

"On the floor over yonder by the machinery?" Curly says.

"Uh-huh."

"That her brother next to her with the spike in his head?"

"Mmm."

"She's responsible for this?" Curly steps to Katie and lifts her wasted arm. "For Katie and Austin?"

"It's not what you're thinking," Brad says.

"I don't know what I'm thinking right now," Curly says.

Frank steps out of the shadows. "You'll need an army to stop her."

"Sir?" Curly says.

"You heard me."

"An army?" Brad says.

Frank nods. "Know where you might find one?"

"I think so, yes," Brad says.

"Brad?" Gabriela says.

He turns and faces her. "Might could use some ice, Gabriela. That offer still good?"

"We have some upstairs in the freezer."

"Take me upstairs, please."

Curly waves his hands. "Oh, no. Ain't nobody moving you nowhere, Sheriff. I gotta call this in and get you an ambulance right away. Get this mess cleaned up. Y'all hang tight."

"Okay," Brad says and eases back against a girder. He closes his eyes. "Gabriela?"

"I'm here," she says.

"Glad you are."

Frank helps King assemble the rest of the equipment. Once it's stacked, King says he's taking it back to First Baptist. For now, they can only hope Pastor Aken doesn't know what they've been up to. Gabriela agrees. Frank stays with Brad and Gabriela until the paramedics arrive. They strap Brad on a stretcher and remove him from the subfloor and out the orchestra pit. Gabriela follows. Police cars and emergency vehicles line King Street in front of the theatre. The rolling red-and-blue lights wash the downtown buildings in the darkness of early morning. Beyond a police barrier, Becky Stokes stands outside her newsvan with a camera operator. Red hair cascades off her pale shoulders and gothic sundress. Gabriela squeezes Brad's hand as they lift him into an ambulance. He whispers words she can't hear or understand. Maybe he asks for his wife. Or his daughter. Gabriela's eyes swell. Frank waits for her under the marquee as officers and medical personnel move past in a blur.

"I don't know where I'm supposed to go," the older man says. His eyes twinkle.

"Sorry," Gabriela says.

"There's no Winter in this world. That means there's no Jeanette. If there's no Jeanette, there's no me."

Gabriela takes a deep breath. "You're an outsider."

"How's that?"

"You don't belong."

Frank rubs his forearm. "May I see your wrist? If I ain't being too forward."

Gabriela reveals the bruise and her matching Christogram.

"Maybe I do," Frank says.

"Eh?" Gabriela says.

"Maybe I belong here with you."

Gabriela half-grins. She doesn't have the energy or strength to smile bigger. She still doesn't know where Sara is or have any idea where to go looking for her. Not unless Amanda has her at Entech, but why? How would Amanda even know who Sara is? The new wicked Amanda wouldn't, even if the dead one did. And there's no guarantee she's going to Entech. Just because she destroyed her mom in one world doesn't mean she plans to do the same thing here. *Non ne ho idea.* But she has an idea about Frank. And for now, it'll have to do.

scene 16.

After a deputy that Gabriela doesn't recognize gives them a ride back to her apartment, she goes to her bedroom and crashes for several hours. She lets Frank sleep on her sofa. He's no threat. If he is, she has no will to stop him. But he's not. There's something about the marks on their arms that bonds them. She doesn't quite know how or why.

Deborah opens her bakery at seven o'clock. Gabriela enters with Frank.

"Cugina?" Deborah says.

"Deborah."

They embrace. The gentle caress of Deborah's arms and her warm scent comfort Gabriela and remind her of *Mamma*.

"You're early today."

"I know."

Deborah greets Frank with an upturned chin.

"Who's this?"

How do I explain? Where do I begin? Maybe Deborah doesn't need to know the whole truth or even part. Not yet.

"A friend."

Deborah pulls out a chair. "Sit."

Frank thanks her.

"I'll fix you breakfast," Deborah says.

"Grazie," Gabriela says.

"Non farò domande."

I won't ask questions. Mamma would say, *Pensa ai tuoi affari e alle tue maniere.* Mind your business and your manners. Maybe Deborah knows the same proverb. She retreats to the kitchen. When Gabriela helps herself to *espresso*, her mobile vibrates.

"Ciao?"

"Gabriela."

"Brad?"

"Yes. It's me." He's quiet and foggy.

"How are you?"

"I'm fine."

"You don't sound fine."

"I am."

"Where are you?"

"Waiting to be released from County Regional. They kept me here for observation."

"Are you okay?"

"I have a mild concussion." Brad clears his throat. "About what I figured. When can you meet?"

Gabriela burns her tongue as she sips. "Brad?"

"I can't sit this out," he says. "We need a plan."

Deborah returns to the dining area with a plateful of pastries. She sets them in front of Frank with a napkin and serves him a cup of black coffee before returning to the kitchen.

"What can we do?" Gabriela asks.

"We need to find Sara, right?"

"Yes, of course."

"We'll go to Entech and see what we can learn."

"And if she's not there?"

"We'll go someplace else."

Brad excuses himself and mumbles. More than likely, he cups a hand over his phone.

"That's a start anyhow," Gabriela says.

"I agree."

Gabriela peeks out the front window of the bakery. Life wakes up on King Street. A shop owner opens her miniblinds along Antique Row. Another feeds a cat a bowl of milk while smoking a cigarette on a metal folding chair out front. Two teenagers wait for a city bus. Either they're skipping class or they've dropped out. Sunshine sprawls across Cardinal Avenue. Gabriela can't see as far as the Orpheum.

"Where?"

"How about the *Sentinel* at eight o'clock?"

"The newspaper office?" Gabriela says.

"Yes."

Brad smothers the call again. Gabriela bites a jagged fingernail.

"Brad?"

"About to get discharged," he says. "Eight o'clock?"

"Eight o'clock, fine. But why the *Sentinel*?"

"You need to let Becky know there's not gonna be a performance tonight."

Gabriela raises an eyebrow. "I don't follow."

"You're the stage manager, right?"

"*Sì,* but somebody from the front office will handle all that."

"Nuh-uh. You're going to. Right away. With me."

"Why?"

"She won't be able to run anything in print on short notice, but she can post online. That'll be enough."

"And?"

"Pastor Aken's holding his vigil tonight, right?"

"Right."

"He wants to be a rock star? Let's make sure he believes he's the only show in town."

The only show in town?

"Brad?"

"Frank said we need an army to stop Amanda?"

Gabriela's not sure an army will be enough even if they have the old Vietnam War bomber Frank asked about.

"Sì."

"Let's get one then."

"Scusi?"

"Don't worry," he says. "I'll explain. Eight o'clock at the *Sentinel*. Don't be late."

"I won't be."

"We'll find Sara," Brad says. "I promise."

"Eight o'clock."

Gabriela hangs up. Deborah returns with fresh fruit and *prosciutto*.

"Mangia," she says.

Gabriela sits opposite Frank and snags a *sfogliatelle* drenched in powdered sugar.

"Good choice," Frank says, dabbing the corner of his mouth on a cloth napkin.

Deborah busies herself with a surge of customers, juggling tables with the cash register as she takes orders and serves the early morning rush. A few faces wrinkle when they see Gabriela but don't interact. News travels fast in small towns, so the tragedy at the theatre last night has probably escaped plenty of hasty lips, even if in half-truths. No doubt the death of the two officers is already breakfast gossip. She doubts word of Connor and Amanda has traveled, however. Not unless Curly ran his mouth, to use a Southern expression Gabriela isn't entirely fond of. Possibly the news that Amanda and Connor are dead, but nothing about the different Amanda that came through from Frank's world. Curly wasn't there when that happened and King won't talk. Not even to Pastor Aken. He'd have to admit his own culpability. Gabriela doesn't know much about Crow Creek, but she knows the power Pastor Aken wields over its citizens. She's felt it, if only through photographs.

She watches Frank slurp his coffee.

"Cat got your tongue?" he says.

"Eh?"

"Oh, beg pardon. It's an expression we use here in the States."

"Is it?"

"Means you're awful quiet." Frank cracks a biscotti and dunks. "Can't say I blame you."

Deborah pauses by their table since the rest of the customers appear content wolfing pastries and guzzling coffee without anyone begging at the counter.

In Italian, she asks, "Can you tell me what's going on?"

"Non lo so."

Deborah tilts her forehead. "What about him?"

"Qui." Gabriela swipes a palm across the table.

Deborah smiles and sits beside Frank. "Mind if I join you?"

"Not at all," he says, tucking the last of his biscotti behind thin lips.

"Deborah," she says. "Deborah DeVito."

"Nice place," he says.

"Thank you." Deborah wipes crumbs into her hand. "From out of town?"

Frank chokes and almost spits out his coffee. "You could say that."

"Your wife visiting with you?" Deborah says.

"Huh?"

"Your wife?" Deborah drops the crumbs into an apron pocket. "Your wedding ring."

"Huh?" Frank sets down his mug and taps his finger. "Oh, this? Yes, my ring. Uh-huh, I'm married. Well, I was. Thirty-two years. She passed away last week."

Deborah blushes. "I'm sorry."

"Don't be."

(not unless you've got a reason)

"Last week?" Gabriela says. "I had no idea."

Frank waves. "How could you?"

Deborah excuses herself so she can take a *cappuccino* order from an older woman wearing a white cardigan. Possibly a schoolteacher needing her early morning jolt.

"What happened?" Gabriela says.

Frank lifts coffee to his face and peers over the cup. "I killed her."

Gabriela gives her head two brisk shakes. *"Scusi?"*

Frank slides one seat to his right so he's closer to Gabriela. She shivers but doesn't move. The bruise on her wrist spasms.

"In my world, I did things I'll never forgive myself for. Putting my Jeanette out of her misery ain't one of them."

"Out of her misery?"

"You heard me." Frank drapes a hand over his mouth so the other customers can't read his lips. "What Amanda did doesn't sound so crazy now, does it?"

"That depends," Gabriela says.

"On?"

"The rest of your story."

Frank traces the Chi-Rho on his forearm with a crooked finger. "She was ill, but not like you're thinking. Working for Entech made her sick."

"Entech?" Gabriela says. "The drug company?"

"That's right. They create monsters."

"Like Amanda?"

Frank swallows. "By the time Jeanette died . . . by the time I took her life, she wasn't human no more. You seen what Amanda did to that officer?"

(she bit her and drank her blood)

Gabriela nods.

"Then you understand why I did what I did."

Deborah returns. Frank slides back to his seat.

"Mrs. Hart," Deborah says. "What a dear. Teaches second grade at Crow Creek Elementary. Stops by every morning on her way to school. Bless her heart."

Bless her heart. Another Southern expression Gabriela's not fond of. Clearly, Deborah's lived in Crow Creek too long. Or maybe Gabriela hasn't lived here long enough to appreciate it.

"Bless her heart," Frank echoes.

"So, last week?" Deborah says.

"Eh?" Gabriela says.

"No, Frank. You were saying your wife passed away last week?"

"Yes, ma'am. Quite awful. Rare blood disease. Doctors did everything they could."

"Hope she didn't suffer long."

Frank stares at Gabriela. "She didn't."

"How do the two of you know each other, anyhow?" Deborah asks.

"The two of us?" Gabriela says.

"Mmm."

Frank rolls down his sleeve, covering his tattoo. "We met at the theatre last night."

"Last night?" Deborah says. "Oh my God, Gabriela. Last night. I almost forgot. Been so busy this morning. Were you at the theatre last night when all those police officers and firefighters showed up downtown?"

"Was I there?" Gabriela looks at Frank and shakes her head. "No, I was long gone."

"Grazie Dio." Deborah rolls her eyes. "I can't believe what's happening to our town."

Gabriela reaches across the table and takes Deborah's hands. She speaks in Italian. "I need a favor."

"Of course," Deborah answers.

"Frank needs to stay here with you today."

"Here?"

"Until the vigil tonight."

"But I close at three."

"Please."

Deborah studies Frank. "You're sure I can trust him?"

(don't see as you have a choice)

"Yes."

"Okay."

Gabriela leans across the table and kisses her cheek. *"Ti amo."*

"Ti voglio bene, cugina."

Deborah scurries off to clean a table so a new group of customers can sit. They wear flowery scrubs and flash bright teeth. Dental hygienists from Holt Family Dental. Gabriela rises.

"What time?" Frank says.

"What time what?" Gabriela says.

"You're leaving me here, right?"

Gabriela nods.

"What time can I expect you back?"

"Pastor Aken's holding a vigil at seven tonight for the people who died this week."

Frank clears his throat. "There were others besides the ones last night?"

"Yes, two. Well, one."

"One or two?" Frank says. "Which is it?"

Gabriela squats beside Frank and whispers. "I'm not sure I can answer honestly anymore, but the crowd will think two."

"Fair enough."

Gabriela wants to hug the old man but doesn't. He reminds her of *Papà.* Not the sick *Papà.* But not a healthy *Papà*, either. Different.

(they come back wrong)

Gabriela shudders. Is Frank wrong? Is her intuition off? If he's come back wrong, where did he come from? And in what type of world is it ever right to kill your wife, even in a mercy killing? But still, they are connected. Her bruise proves it. She knows it. Feels it deep in her bones where words don't speak. Instincts do. *Kinesthesia.* He grabs her arm as she turns.

"Cavalli," Frank says.

"Eh?"

"Do you know what that means?"

"Of course," Gabriela says. "Horses. *Cavalli* means horses in Italian."

Franks shakes his head. "There's a deeper meaning. We share a bond."

The image on her wrist flares. An outline flames around each of the layered Greek letters.

"We're an ancient order," he says. "Ghosts, you might say."

"Ghosts?"

Frank strokes his dimpled chin. "Does Brad have the marking?"

"No, I don't think so." Gabriela tries to remember. "I'm not sure. I've never seen one."

Franks sips his coffee. "He does in my world."

Gabriela's entire body warms. A sharp light fills her. The earth's core builds up from her soul and spreads along each of her limbs and through her appendages in high definition. *Brad has the Chi-Rho.* She closes her eyes and listens. For a moment, for a brief second, for maybe as long as the space between seconds, she hears a single word calling from a disembodied voice. *"Daddy."*

(my daughter called for me in the light)

A single word. A disembodied voice. *Daddy.*

"Do you think you know?" Gabriela says, soft and low.

"Know what?" Frank says.

"Do you think you know when you die in one world if you can feel it in the other?"

Frank reaches for a chunk of cantaloupe. "All worlds are joined along straight and crooked lines. Only some of us embrace the one we're in."

"Cavalli."

Frank bites. "You're never really an outsider."

Gabriela pats Frank on the shoulder and waves to Deborah as she leaves the bakery.

scene 17.

Brad waits outside the newspaper office by ten of eight. He leans with his foot propped against the brick façade, wearing black pants and a Carolina blue athletic shirt.

Gabriela smiles. "You look nice out of uniform."

Brad shrugs. "Supposed to limit my activity for three days."

"That won't be easy."

He rubs his head. "Never is."

Gabriela hugs him. They hold each other tight until she needs to breathe and withdraws.

"Thank you," Gabriela says.

"For?"

"For being my friend."

Because that's what they are, right? Because any other way to define who they are would be absurd. Not because of their age or any feelings. Worlds join in straight and crooked lines. We embrace the one we're in.

Brad blushes. "I feel like I should tip my hat."

"Maybe you are." Gabriela rubs her *cornicello*. "Somewhere."

"Maybe so."

"Brad?"

"Yes?"

"I heard her."

"Huh?"

"When we were under the stage the other night, I heard your daughter calling for you."

His eyes swell with tears. "Gabriela?"

"I don't mean to upset you."

"You're not."

"I want you to know before anything else happens to us. I heard your daughter calling your name. She was there."

Brad wipes his face with his hand. "Why didn't you say anything then?"

Gabriela licks her lips. "Because I didn't know I was listening."

Becky appears behind the glass in a flurry of pale skin and rolling ginger locks, making Gabriela jump.

"Brad?" she says.

"You ready?"

Gabriela nods.

Brad holds the door open as they enter the newspaper office. Becky greets them with straight white teeth and sparkling eyes. She wears the same gothic sundress she wore earlier this morning when the police and firefighters swarmed downtown. A strap slips off her freckled shoulder. Maybe she lives in the newspaper office? How many times has Gabriela spent the night in the bowels of a theatre working on a show? How many times has she stayed in the same crew clothes from one day to the next? Some people are married to their jobs. Maybe Becky Stokes is. Maybe the *Becky* tattoo across Sara's breasts is some other Becky. Some Becky not connected to the *Sentinel* or the theatre or Crow Creek. Some *other* Becky. A different one.

"You're early this morning," Becky says.

"The job calls," Brad says.

Becky keeps her grin bright. "Wasn't talking to you."

"Oh?"

"Didn't Miss Rossi tell you?"

Brad gives Gabriela a sideways glance. "Tell me what?"

"We're old friends." Becky slips her arm, snake-like, across Gabriela's hips. "How're things, Miss Rossi?"

Gabriela inhales Becky's stinging perfume and rolls her eyes. "Could be better."

"Find what you were looking for the other day?" Becky says and struts to her desk.

"I did."

"You know, I've always believed that if you look long enough or search deep enough, you'll find what you're looking for. Ain't that true, Sheriff?"

"Not always."

Becky sits and offers the chairs opposite. "Please."

"No, thanks," Brad says. "Can't stay long."

"Such a pity. I rarely get company this early."

"Shocking," Brad says.

"Don't be obtuse, Sheriff. We each have a job to do. Yours isn't the only one that calls."

"I'm sorry." Brad smirks. "Haven't I been transparent about what's been going on at the theatre this week?"

"You have, sure. If you can call the scraps you gave me *transparent*." Becky rises and circles her desk so she's orbiting Gabriela again. "Specifics, Sheriff. The art is in the details. If this lovely angel hadn't made herself available on her own, you would've had me talk to nobody at the theatre. Nobody at all. I'd have been forced to find my own leads."

Brad arches an eyebrow. "Made yourself available?"

"I told you." Gabriela waves. "Ralph Delacourt."

"Oh, right." Brad clears his throat. *"Delacourt."*

Becky bites her lower lip and peeps over Gabriela's shoulder. "Lovers keeping secrets, are they?"

"Huh?" Brad wrinkles his nose. "What? We have no secrets."

"Interesting." Becky crosses her arms and taps her foot. "Not the denial I was expecting."

Gabriela snorts. "We're canceling the show tonight."

"No show?" Becky says.

"No."

Becky returns to her desk. "Now that's news."

"Come on," Brad says. "Did you really think I'd let them?"

"So, you're shutting them down?" Becky says. "That's even bigger news."

"We have six dead bodies."

"Six?"

"Do I need to spell it out for you?" Brad says.

Becky winks. "Maybe I should record this conversation so I don't forget?"

"Tommy Nolan, Connor and Amanda Simmons, James Patterson. My deputies. *Six.* Are you happy?"

"Six." Becky rolls on her chair and grabs the coffee pot. "Oh, right. I forgot about poor old Mr. Patterson. Shame when money takes it on the chin, huh?"

"Let me see." Brad strokes his thick mustache. "What word did you use? *Pity.* That's it. Such a pity."

"You're aware that would've been Sunday's headline, right? Local show producer sells out to Raleigh theatre." Becky slips a hand beside her mouth so she can direct the next line to Gabriela. What's called an aside in melodrama. "I know you're not from around here, but our print editions are only available on Wednesdays and Sundays."

Gabriela swats a fly. *"Capito."*

"Twice a week. That's a big enough workload when you're the entire staff. Well, almost. I do keep that incessant photographer around to do my bidding."

"At least you're not alone," Gabriela says.

"Is that empathy I'm detecting in your voice, dear?" Becky sips her coffee. "Because, believe me, I'd drop that *scemo* in a minute if you're ever available to take my photos."

"Is that so?"

"Mmm. I find working with women to be a lot more dangerous. Wild, even." Becky wiggles and jumps to her feet. "After all, isn't that why Brad keeps you around?"

"Desideri," Gabriela says.

Becky licks her lips. "I do wish, Miss Rossi."

Brad raises his hands. "Look, can we just get this over with? I don't keep anyone around, okay? Gabriela's a grown woman who handles herself as well as any man I've ever met."

"Can I quote you on that?"

"Of course."

"How gallant of you, Sheriff."

Gallant. Gabriela pinches the bridge of her nose. What was the word Frank used? *Cavalli.* We're an ancient order. Ghosts, you might say. Not horses. Knights. *Cavalli* are knights.

The symbol on her wrist glows. Two Greek letters overlapping. *Chi-Rho.* The icon Constantine saw burning in the sky before he converted to Christianity. The first Roman Emperor to embrace the faith. His imperial army founded Constantinople and defended all Christians in the kingdom. The birth of the Teutonic Order. The Order of the Cross. Does Brad have the marking?

(he does in my world)

Gabriela searches. She studies his face and neck and arms and hands. She can't see anything that resembles the Christogram. Maybe he doesn't have his yet? She wasn't born with hers. Delacourt gave it to her when he grabbed her wrist. Frank's is a tattoo, also not natural. Maybe you earn it. Like knighthood.

"So, what else is there to tell?" Becky says, taking her seat.

Gabriela blinks. *"Eh?"*

"You're not having your performance tonight?"

"Um. That's correct, yes."

"On whose authority?" Becky purses her lips. "For the record."

"Mine," Gabriela says.

"Yours?" Becky picks at a cuticle. "Doesn't that need to come down from above your head? Present company excluded, of course."

Brad grunts and rolls his eyes.

"No," Gabriela says. "It doesn't matter whether or not Brad . . . the sheriff . . . wants us to cancel. We're not going up. We can't."

"You can't? But you haven't lost any of your performers."

"That doesn't matter."

"Aren't the backstage crew replaceable?" Becky smiles. "Again, present company excluded."

Gabriela grits her teeth. "We're canceling the show because I want everyone involved in our production . . . no, everyone who works for our theatre . . . to attend Pastor Aken's vigil tonight."

Becky's mouth drops open. "Is that so?"

Brad clears his throat. "Yes. The entire town should be here."

"I must say, I'm surprised to hear that coming from you, Sheriff," Becky says.

"Yeah?"

"Well, considering how disgraced you were after the one he held for your daughter . . ."

Brad massages the back of his head. "I wouldn't say I was disgraced."

"Oh, no? What would you call it?"

"I'd call it my daughter was killed, and I was fucking heartbroken."

Has Brad ever cursed in front of me?

"Excuse me," Brad says and looks at her.

He hasn't.

"So, that's the hook?" Becky says. "After a series of murders at the theatre this week, you're canceling tonight's show?"

"We don't know for sure that all six deaths were murders," Brad says.

"No?"

"And we don't know how long until we'll be able to perform," Gabriela says. "We might have to cancel the entire run."

"I know you're going out on a limb, Miss Rossi," Becky says. "So I'll only mention tonight. That'll give me some time to talk to Lynn and Deidre in the front office. Sound good?"

"Va bene."

"Tonight's all that matters anyhow. Pastor Aken's gonna bring down the house. I think that's the right expression."

Brad grins. "Hope so."

"Guess you'll have to see for yourselves what all he's got planned."

"Can't wait," Brad says.

"Me neither," Gabriela says.

Becky smirks. "He gave me the inside scoop, of course."

"Of course," Brad says.

"Let's just say you won't wanna miss it."

"Don't plan on it."

Becky winks. "Never know who's gonna show up."

"Suppose not," Brad says and starts to leave. "Gabriela?"

"Coming."

Becky slithers out of her chair and cuts off Gabriela as she exits. The door closes behind Brad, trapping him outside. Becky gives the deadbolt a swift turn.

"What are you doing?" Gabriela says.

"Tell me, Miss Rossi," Becky says. "Where does the tradition of giving roses to the performers really come from?"

Gabriela flinches. *"Eh?"*

"After the show. Was it Italy?" Becky trumpets. "The great Roman theatre?"

"I don't know."

"Or maybe it was the Greeks?"

"Not every culture gives roses," Gabriela says. "Before or after the show."

Becky grabs Gabriela's arm and sniffs her neck. "I see the cute little bruise you have. Brad might think you can handle yourself, but I wouldn't do anything foolish if I were you."

Gabriela yanks loose. *"Lasciami andare."*

"You don't know what you think you know about who runs the show in this world."

Brad grabs the armbar and pulls. The door rattles on its frame. His shouts are muffled outside.

"Don't I?"

"I keep bringing him back because he listens."

"Who does?"

"Your friend should do the same." Becky flashes, exposing teeth and bones beneath her skin. "That would make things so much easier for the both of us."

"*Vai a farti fottere.* Go fuck yourself!" Gabriela jostles past Becky and slams into the door before scrambling to unlock it and run outside.

"What's wrong?" Brad says.

"See y'all tonight," Becky says as she stands in the doorway. "Look for me in the crowd."

Brad doesn't reply. Gabriela can feel him on her heels as she turns the corner and collapses against the side of the building in tears.

"Becky has Sara," she says.

"Becky does?" Brad says.

"Yes."

"How do you know?"

"She just told me."

"Becky told you she has Sara?"

"Not in those words exactly."

"Gabriela." Brad squats beside her. "In what words exactly?"

Gabriela catches her breath, stifling her sobs by cupping her hands over her face. "I don't know how I missed it. The signs were there."

Brad rubs her shoulders. "With all that's going on?"

Gabriela curls a fist and punches her thigh. "We don't even know where she is."

"We'll find her."

"It doesn't matter." She climbs into Brad's arms. "I should've known."

Brad strokes her cheek. "Daddy used to say I couldn't see the forest for the trees."

Gabriela sniffs. "Your father used expressions like that?"

"All the time." He chuckles. "He was a regular Ben Franklin."

"Ben Franklin, *eh?*"

"Oh, a famous American." He brushes wet hair out of her eyes. "A long time ago."

Gabriela chuckles. "I know who Benjamin Franklin was."

"They teach that in *Châtillon*? Am I pronouncing that right?"

Gabriela nods. "Mamma says funny things all the time. She says I can't see the nose in front of my face. I miss her."

"Daddy said that one, too. Funny." Brad drops a knee. "How do you say it in Italian?"

"Non riesci a vedere il naso davanti alla tua faccia."

"Your words match your beauty."

"Thank you."

Gabriela stares at herself in Brad's tranquil eyes. She doesn't look or feel beautiful. Her face sags, her eyes sink in swollen pockets, and her lips are peeling and dry. Brad leans closer. If he wants to kiss her, she won't stop him. He pauses after tilting his head.

"Maybe in another world," he says.

Gabriela sighs. "Maybe."

Brad helps Gabriela to her feet and holds her hand as they walk to his cruiser.

scene 18.

Brad shuts off the police radio and closes the laptop on the console between them.

"Becky has Sara," he says.

Gabriela latches her seatbelt. *"Sì."*

"We know why she has her so that buys us some time."

"Because of tonight's vigil?" Gabriela says.

Brad nods. "Whatever they have planned for Sara probably won't happen until then."

"I agree, but where do you think she's keeping her?"

"I don't know." Brad taps the digital clock on the dashboard. "That should give us eight hours."

"Lo fa, sì."

"And you think you know what Pastor Aken plans to do?"

(you don't know what you think you know)

"Summon Dionysus," Gabriela says. *He rises in the wolf's mouth.* "Frank Delacourt showed me last night when your friend Darrell conjured him in his ossuary."

"Sara and Mr. Patterson will be part of that," Brad says. "Even if they're unwilling participants."

"Mr. Patterson didn't seem so unwilling, but yes."

"When they summon your Greek god, his demons will come through?"

"The Maenads?" Gabriela says. "Possibly, yes."

Brad flips open his palm Italian style. "There's our army."

"Our army, sir?"

"Frank said we need an army," Brad says. "So now, the only trick is to get Amanda where we need her."

Gabriela squints. "Brad?"

"Ever been to Entech?"

"I can't say that I have."

Brad pushes the ignition. The cruiser roars to life, lifting the bonnet.

"Well then," he says as he puts his utility vehicle in gear. "Let's go for a ride."

Brad drives away from the *Sentinel* and cuts through downtown until he merges with the interstate west toward Queensboro. He doesn't spin any lights or sound his siren. Gabriela's not sure whether or not he's on-duty. She also doesn't know whether or not a police officer's ever off-duty, especially in a small Southern town. Bright sunshine fills the sky as they creep along with rush hour.

"Probably headed to Winston-Salem," Brad says. "Maybe all the way down to Charlotte."

"Eh?"

"The traffic. Can't believe how busy it's got over the past ten, fifteen years. Plenty of folks moving out this way."

Gabriela watches a murder of crows circle a carcass on the shoulder. Beyond, rolling fields of poppies and uncut summer grass end at a line of dense evergreens. Kudzu perennials blanket most of the underbrush in thick viney clusters. On the surface, beautiful.

(something wrong about this place deep where the underground currents flow)

"Like me," she says.

(deep calls to deep)

Brad exits the highway and joins the service road for two kilometers until he pulls into an industrial park. Entech looms on the horizon like Dracula's castle. Two gray towers on either end bite into the sunshine with enormous fangs. The massive windowed structures divide a complex bridged by elevated rows of glass teeth. Brad follows the turnaround in the front parking lot and stops in the visitor's center.

"Do you have a plan?" Gabriela asks.

"Nothing rational." Brad shakes his head. "But then again, if you'd told me last week I'd be sitting with you in this parking lot right now under these circumstances, I would've looked at you like you're from another planet."

"Maybe I am," Gabriela says.

Brad shuts the ignition. "For now, we'll see if we can find her mother."

"Peggy Delacourt?"

"Mmm-hmm. She might have some answers. I don't know."

"She might give us more questions."

"Probably so."

When Brad steps into the parking lot, he pops on a pair of sunglasses from his breast pocket.

"Feel naked without my hat," he says. "These'll have to do till we get inside."

They enter the sliding glass doors. The circular lobby has two spiral staircases on opposite sides and an elevator bank at the far end. Wild Madonna lilies frame the reception desk at the center. Gold molding braided into ribbons trims the rounded walls. Potted plants with fresh flowers sit in ceramic vases, like Grecian urns, below the plate glass windows. The receptionist wrinkles her sallow brow when they approach the desk. She drapes long brown hair across her left shoulder. Her right arm ends at a stump visible in her sleeveless turtleneck.

"Good morning," she says. "Welcome to Entech. How may I help you?"

Brad pockets his sunglasses and flashes his badge. "Peggy Delacourt, please."

"Of course, Sheriff," the receptionist says. "Hope there's no trouble."

"None on my end."

The receptionist offers a phony grin. "I'll see if she's available."

"You do that," Brad says and taps Gabriela so she'll follow.

They walk over to the front windows and wait. The urns are larger now that Gabriela's closer. Probably three feet tall. Soldiers wage war through raging flames on the nearest one.

Brad ties a loose bootlace. "If she sees us, Amanda's here."

Gabriela nods. On cue, a large woman with writhing white hair descends the spiraling stairs, grinning. She wears a Duke blue brocade business suit with a pointed collar and clutches a knotted cane in her spotted hands. The hue of her flat, pearly-white choker matches her dry flaky skin. Pale pancake makeup conceals the winged birthmark on her cheek behind a transparent Halloween mask. Under the painted visage, Gabriela sees Ralph Delacourt's square features and Connor's shifty eyes. A thick lump wriggles on her jaw, squirming beneath the high neckline. *Psoriasis doesn't wriggle.*

"Good morning, Sheriff Gleason," Peggy says as she descends, spreading her flabby arms in a royal sweep. "So good to finally meet you."

Brad rolls his eyes. "Likewise."

"And who's this lovely creature by your side?" Peggy asks when she reaches the bottom step, standing slightly higher than Brad.

"Gabriela Rossi," Brad says.

"Yes, Miss Rossi. Of course," Peggy says. "I believe I saw you this summer at the theatre where my son works."

Gabriela doesn't recall seeing Peggy Delacourt at the Orpheum. A wretched face like hers would be impossible to forget.

Connor's dead. Should I correct her verb tense?

"Which show?" Gabriela says.

Peggy shrugs a shoulder and plants the cane at her feet under lumpy knuckles. "Why squabble over details, dear? A funny one, a sad one. A show with song and dance. They all blur when you're as timeless as I am and have witnessed so many."

"Don't cheat yourself," Brad says. "The next show is always the best one."

"How prophetic, Sheriff."

"Call me Brad."

"Brad." Peggy raps her cane twice on the tile. "What brings y'all to Entech?"

"Your daughter."

"Amanda?" Peggy says. "I see."

"Don't act so surprised," Brad says.

"Curses!" Peggy shakes a fist. "All that money I spent on acting lessons down the drain. Maybe Miss Rossi could give me a few pointers?"

"I don't act," Gabriela says.

"You don't break the legs, huh?" Peggy says.

(you know where that expression comes from)

"No, ma'am. I always get paid."

"What about the wolf's mouth?" Peggy smiles a rotten uneven mess. "Ever go in there?"

(beware)

"More often than you know."

Peggy drops a heavy hand on Brad's shoulder and cackles. The receptionist peels her eyes away from the mobile she navigates with her useful hand as laughter reverberates across the vestibule.

"Oh, Brad, I like this one," Peggy says. "She's got spunk. Reminds me of me when I was her age."

"You don't seem to have lost none of yours," Brad says.

"If only you knew, dear boy. Now I make way for a younger generation."

"I see," Brad says.

"Come then." Peggy whips around and gallops up the steps as she spouts the next line over her shoulder. "We have much to discuss and plenty to see."

Gabriela trails Brad as he follows Peggy up the winding staircase and along a tiled hallway. They reach her executive suite and are swiftly ushered into a conference room where an onyx marble table fills the space between gothic windows and a garish ceramic bookcase lined with exotic horns that aren't dissimilar to those in Pastor Aken's office. While propped on her cane, Peggy offers Brad and Gabriela seats in a white leather sofa.

"Let's cut to the chase, shall we?" Peggy says. "I know you're here for my daughter."

Brad lifts an eyebrow. "I'm sorry?"

"Don't think I'm a fool, Brad. That would only make things worse for the two of you."

"And to think I intended to break the news that your daughter's dead," Brad says, biting his grin.

"That wretched waste?" Peggy cracks her cane against the tiles. No longer a celebratory tap. The demon flaps its wing across her cheek. "I should've offed her when she was born. My new arrival is a delight. I should exist in her world."

(back in her world she did worse)

"Not so sure you'd be welcome there," Brad says.

"I'm always welcome everywhere I go."

Gabriela clears her throat. "And your son?"

Peggy hisses. "What good did he ever do?"

"He tried to cure his sister, for one," Gabriela says. "That's more than you can say."

Peggy shakes her cane in Gabriela's face. "Don't presume to know my intentions, dear. You don't know half of what we're developing in our labs."

"No, I don't," Gabriela says.

"You shall see soon enough."

"That so?" Brad stands. "Sounds like a threat."

"I'd stay seated if I were you, Brad," Peggy says. "Oh, there's the threat you needed."

Gabriela pulls Brad back down beside her.

"Good girl." Peggy slurps her lips. "I wasn't lying when I told you I like this one."

"Where is she?" Brad says.

"I'm happy to take you to Amanda," Peggy says. "That's all part of the plan."

"Good," Brad says.

"But first I need to know *your* angle." Peggy shakes a fist. "Awww, did I do that wrong? Am I not supposed to put stress on a pronoun?"

Gabriela shakes her head. "No, ma'am."

"Rats, I'll try again." Peggy clears her throat and closes her eyes, finding her moment in the silence. "Here goes. First, I need to know your *angle*. Better?"

Gabriela sighs.

Brad rolls his eyes. "What makes you think I'm willing to share?"

Peggy chuckles. "Well, I don't think you would've come all the way out here to Queensboro with your little girlfriend in tow if you didn't have some sorta plan."

"Maybe I don't," Brad says.

"Highly unlikely." Peggy nudges Brad out of the way so she can sit between the two. Her breath is warm and sour on Gabriela's face as she talks. Gabriela gags. "Indulge me for a moment, sweetie."

"About?" Gabriela says.

"Acting theory. Let me know if I've got this straight." Peggy winks at Brad. "I do love good theatre, you know?"

"Naturally," Brad says.

"So, these actors . . . they must first identify their objectives. What do they want? What's their goal? Like that. Those come in layers, of course. Each scene forces the actors to pursue specific objectives. For example, you coming to visit me. That's a beat, right? But there's also an overarching objective. The super-objective, am I right?"

Gabriela nods. "I suppose."

"Oh, goodie," Peggy claps her hands now that she can prop the cane between her legs. "Embedded within those objectives are motivations. Why do we want the things we want? That's the logical component. The rationale. And, of course, there are always obstacles. Ooh, now those are the most exciting part, aren't they, because they drive the conflict."

"Yes," Gabriela says.

"What would a world be like without conflict, I often wonder. But nevermind that. Let's continue our lesson."

"Is this making a point anytime soon?" Brad asks.

"Oh, Brad, don't be such a spoil sport. What good are any of us without a thirst for knowledge? I never made it to the stage, but what's the harm in an old lady trying to discover whether or not she has the chops?"

"Please," Brad huffs. "Continue."

Peggy narrows her eyes, elongating the crow's feet. "In each scene, actors take risks to determine what they're willing to lose to reach their objectives. In other words, is what they want worth fighting for? Well, in a fictional narrative, it always is; otherwise, what would be the point in writing the story? But in real life, conflicts don't always have such universal stakes. But forget that for now. Once the conflict unfolds, the outcome's revealed."

"Usually, yes," Gabriela says.

"In a comedy, the actors succeed. At least the one the audience cheers for does." Peggy winks at Brad again, giggling. "I always picture myself onstage with a twirling mustache, so I guess I'd be the villain. Shame, that is. I would definitely lose in a comedy."

"Uh-huh," Brad says.

"But in tragedy things are a little different, aren't they? The protagonist fails because of some fatal flaw. Isn't that so? The infamous *goat song*."

"È vero," Gabriela says.

"Alas, the villain wins!" Peggy abruptly grabs Gabriela's bruised wrist. "So you have to ask yourself, dear, are you starring in a comedy or a tragedy?"

Gabriela winces. *"Vaffanapoli."*

"Time will tell." Peggy releases Gabriela. She pulls herself up on her cane and swirls on her heels to face Brad. "What do you want with my daughter, Brad? Tell me the truth, and I'll take you to her."

Brad swallows. "I need her to come to Crow Creek tonight."

"Tonight?" Peggy says.

"You heard correct."

"I'm intrigued." She straightens a rhino horn on a nearby shelf. "Do explain why."

"Pastor Aken's holding a vigil for those who died at the theatre this week."

"Ahhh, Pastor Aken. I've heard the lovely pastor's at it again. How did that go for you when your daughter died?" Peggy says.

"Not well," Brad says.

"Care to tell me why things would be any better this time around? Not only for me, but for my daughter?"

"And your son."

"My *son*?"

"You heard me."

"That's a twist I wasn't expecting," Peggy says.

"Sorry to be the one to break the news."

"No matter." Peggy choreographs a brief grapevine behind her desk. "Who was it that said 'Good riddance to bad rubbish' when Elvis died?"

"I don't have any idea," Brad says. "I wasn't even ten. I don't remember him. Only that Mama enjoyed his movies and his records."

"His records, yes. Especially the early ones when he sang like a dog in heat. The movies? Never. Poor boy would've benefited from some serious acting lessons. Even then, he would've been no Marlon Brando." Peggy growls. "Now there was a catch!"

Gabriela coughs. “Mr. Patterson.”

“How’s that?” Peggy says, crossing her hands over the knob of her cane.

“Mr. Patterson . . . James Patterson, the producer.”

“What about him?”

“Pastor Aken brought him through.”

“I don’t follow, dear.”

“The pastor brought Mr. Patterson through the same way Connor brought your Amanda through.”

“Interesting.” Peggy scratches a wriggling worm under her chin. It’s less of a scratch and more of a tuck. She shakes open a bottle of pills on her desk. “So my Amanda’s not the only one who’s crossed the Bridge?”

“No,” Brad says. “We’re concerned the pastor might try again.”

“Tonight?” Peggy says, popping a purple capsule in her mouth and swallowing without water.

“For something bigger.”

“Bigger, huh?” Peggy hobbles to a window and stares. “Of course he will.”

“All of Crow Creek will be there,” Brad says.

“The whole town?” Peggy says. “Now that might be worth seeing.”

“We even canceled our show,” Gabriela says.

“How awful for you,” Peggy says.

Brad stands. “Can we see her now?”

“Of course, Brad. I’m happy to oblige as promised.” Peggy raps on the private door beside the bookcase. “But, if you don’t mind, we’ll need an escort.”

The door swings open. A hefty police officer wearing tan pants and matching shirt fills the threshold, clasping a white handkerchief against his lips and wheezing. He staggers into the conference room and unsnaps a revolver dangling off his wide hips. He pockets the rag and drops plump fingers on the handle.

“Sheriff Osbourne,” Peggy says. “How nice of you to join us. He’ll show y’all how we run things here in Queensboro.”

"Firearm, Sheriff Gleason." Osbourne extends a meaty palm. "Nice and slow, please."

"Oh, he prefers Brad," Peggy says and winks.

Osbourne taps his foot but says nothing else. Brad digs into his pocket and delivers his firearm to the large sheriff. Gabriela's mobile vibrates in her pocket. Peggy sniffs the air when Gabriela reaches to see who's texting her so she relaxes her palm without checking.

"Shall we go for a walk then?" Peggy says and exits through the private door.

Brad keeps Gabriela in front of him as they follow with Osbourne panting and gasping at the rear.

scene 19.

They move down a dark corridor and descend a private set of stairs until they reach a glass door where Peggy slides her ID, punches a code, and presses her palm onto a flat monitor to register her fingerprints. Osbourne stumbles when they enter. Scientists wearing blue Tyvek suits nod as they brush past their lab tables without detaching themselves from their work.

Gabriela's mobile buzzes in her pocket again, but she ignores it.

A laboratory assistant with a misshapen cleft palate and clubfoot waits for them when they reach a metal door labeled **SECTOR ONE** above a royal blue flame. She hobbles aside as Peggy leans over the biometer and completes her retinal scan. Once the computer identifies her as Margaret Delacourt, Executive Director of Operations, the lock releases and the self-activating door opens with a slight hush, sucking air inside the hallway. They make their way down an adjoining corridor and into an elevator that Peggy opens by inserting a special snub-nosed copper key.

The transport descends about thirty meters and leads them into a sterile alcove. Peggy directs both Brad and Gabriela to step into Level B HAZMAT suits with Velcro neck enclosures and hanging plastic facial masks strapped over their heads. The gear also includes miniature high-pressure air tanks and plated mouthpieces fitted with voice-actuated radios.

"Y'all hear me?" Peggy says.

Brad and Gabriela nod.

"The three of you?" Brad asks. "You don't need the suits?"

Peggy throws her head back and cackles. "Nothing here can harm us anymore, I assure you. All the damage has been done."

"The damage?" Brad says.

"Don't play dumb with me, Brad." Peggy swipes at his feet with her cane. "You're old enough to remember the drug tests and how savagely they failed. Only a few of us remain. Us and our mistakes."

Osbourne tightens his grip on his revolver.

"Your mistakes?" Gabriela says.

"They came out wrong, dear." Peggy frowns. What can only be sorrow wounds her pallid face. "At least Connor gave me hope. Little that it was."

"Connor?" Brad says.

"Wanda Butler, the others. He's the only one of our children who didn't have any birth defects. None that we could see anyhow."

"The worse side effects are the ones you can't see," Brad mumbles.

"I'm afraid so," Peggy says. "Such a weakling. I suppose I should be more grieved that he's dead. Perhaps, we can pull another Connor across the Bridge? A more virile and diligent Connor like the Amanda he brought through. But then I'd be cheating another me out of a valuable son, wouldn't I?"

"I suppose you could look at it that way," Brad says.

Peggy starts to turn.

"Ms. Delacourt?" Gabriela says.

Peggy freezes, ruffling her lofty white hair. "Yes, dear?"

"Deanna Flowers?"

"Deanna Flowers?" Peggy wrinkles her brow. "Where do I know that name?"

"She works at the Orpheum with Connor and me." Gabriela scratches her lip. "With *me* now."

"Oh, of course," Peggy says. "Rather pleasant woman. Obsessive, but pleasant nonetheless. What about her?"

"Was she one of the test subjects?"

"For us?" Peggy smiles. "No, dear, she wasn't. Some mistakes belong to nature."

Gabriela's mobile buzzes a third time but with an extended ring, not a text. Under the Tyvek, Gabriela has no chance of answering even without Peggy's watchful eyes. She lets it ring out until it burps with a voicemail.

Peggy guides them through a portal divided by large plastic strapping and into **SECTOR ONE**. Inside her HAZMAT suit, Gabriela shivers from the chill. The deformed laboratory assistant punches a few keys on a nearby mainframe until lights beep and flash on the screen. She pushes away from the computer and crosses to a panel with a series of sliders and buttons not unlike the Unison controls at the Orpheum.

"On your word, Ms. Delacourt," she mutters to Peggy while holding a nailless finger above the console.

"Thank you, Miriam," Peggy says. "We can begin now."

Miriam presses a quick combination until the room hums to life. Sirens ring in a whirl of red lights as large metal doors part on electronic gears. Beyond the hatch, Amanda rests naked at the top of a metal scaffold about five meters high. Suspended from a glowing dome, an intricate nest of tubes and cables intertwine through a collider until they connect to ports dotting Amanda's exposed body from her forehead to her bare feet. Dark fluid flows intravenously through the fittings and conduits while Amanda remains catatonic. Below, a shaft connecting her table to the concrete floor taps the earth. Energy surges through the portal in pulsing waves.

Gabriela covers her ears as the earth's vibration intensifies, Tyvek tickling her soft lobes.

"Someday I dream of harvesting the sun," Peggy says. "For now, we drain the earth's core. Look familiar?"

"The underground currents?" Gabriela says. "Like those under the theatre and First Baptist?"

"Precisely what my Connor found but didn't know how to cultivate."

"What are you doing to her?" Gabriela says.

"Preserving her, of course. She's the prototype. I've been waiting for her."

"Why?"

"*Just because I can* would be too trite an answer, wouldn't it?"

Gabriela nods.

"My dear, you've been nothing less than honest with me and deserve to know the whole truth about my motivation." Peggy drops a corpulent arm across Gabriela's shoulders. "Some power destroys. We feed for eternal life. This is our communion. Think of what the Greeks and the Romans did. The Christians. How are we any different?"

Brad strides toward Amanda until he's stopped by the click of Osbourne's revolver.

"Far enough," the obese sheriff wheezes. "Unless you want to be next for clinical trials."

Brad scans the steel catwalks that crisscross the laboratory above the dome. "What are you feeding her?"

Peggy whinnies. "Blood, of course. What did you expect?"

(she bit her and drank her blood she bit her and drank her blood)

Brad widens his eyes. "Whose blood are you giving her?"

(her blood her blood her blood)

"We're a laboratory. We have unlimited donors."

"You're using the blood that people *donate*?"

"For now. Until we can develop a more efficient way to drain." Peggy grins. "Great job with inflection, by the way. Are you sure you're not an actor?"

"But that's intended for hospitals." Brad clenches his fists. "For transfusions. The injured and the sick need that blood."

"And what are we, Brad?" Peggy tucks another wiggling maggot into the turkey flap dangling from her chin. "Look around you. We're all defects. We don't belong. Don't you understand what those drug tests did to us? If *we're* not sick, who is?"

Osbourne wheezes, clutching his revolver with pudgy fingers.

"But how?" Gabriela says. "How does it work?"

"Smoke and mirrors, my dear child," Peggy says. "This isn't science fiction. I can't reveal all my secrets. It's like those plays you stage manage, an illusion of the first time."

Gabriela spots the segmented bladder throbbing on the gridiron above the dome. The elongated headless body resembles a giant pill bug seething with yellow mucus in its rotating cradle. Ductwork wide enough to fit an enormous HVAC system connects the bladder to the dome like a diseased umbilical cord.

"What is that?" Gabriela says.

Peggy grins. "We call her the *Skull.*"

"Why?"

"She holds the blood," Peggy says. "The blood, and the power of the stars."

Gabriela shivers and looks at Brad. "We need to leave right now."

"I know," he says.

"The earth's lines connect." Peggy spins, launching into an elaborate tapdance and clicking her heels. "Straight or crooked, they connect."

(our worlds join along straight and crooked lines)

Brad faces Osbourne. "Get us out of here."

"We don't control that," Peggy howls. "We take what the universe offers."

"Now."

"Why don't you stay?" Osbourne slides the barrel of the revolver between his teeth and pulls the trigger repeatedly. The hammer clicks without firing any rounds. "Don't you trust us?"

"Brad?" Gabriela says.

"I'm no demon, Miss Rossi." Peggy waves her cane high above her cascading blanched hair and performs a cha-cha. Her birthmark flaps and sizzles. "Neither's Amanda."

(we all have our own demons)

Gabriela tugs Brad's shirtsleeve. "Brad!"

"We're all stars," Peggy cries and erupts into an elaborate freestyle shuffle. "Each and every one of us. Even you, Brad. And Sheriff Osbourne. Miriam, too, that defective whore. Even you and me, Miss Rossi. We're all stars. Stars, do you hear me? STARS! STARS! STARS! WE'RE ALL FUCKING STARS ACROSS THE UNIVERSE! WE'RE ALL FUCKING STARS ACROSS THE UNIVERSE! DON'T YOU LIKE MY SONG? WE'LL SING AND DANCE FOREVER AND EVER!"

Brad grabs Gabriela's gloved hand and pulls her through the plastic stripping into the decontamination chamber where they're hit with intense steaming chemicals. As soon as the cleanse finishes, they step out of their HAZMAT suits and masks. Brad hits the plunger to open the security door. Peggy's shouts fade as they hustle down the corridor, climb a flight of stairs, and push through an emergency exit. An alarm blares. They emerge in the sunshine on the opposite end of the visitor's parking lot in the shadows of Entech's twin towers. Devil horns stab the clear blue sky. They run to Brad's cruiser.

Gasping, Gabriela leans against the rear bumper to catch her breath. "Do you think she'll come tonight?"

"Amanda?" Brad hangs his head and props his palms on his inner thighs. "She wouldn't miss it. Not in a million years."

Gabriela digs into her pocket to check her messages. Both texts are from Deborah. The first bubble says *Something's wrong with Frank.* The second reads *Can you please call me?* in Italian.

Gabriela taps her phone and listens to the voicemail.

Deborah speaks rapidly. "Please come quick. I don't know what's happening. Frank needs help. What should I do? *Dio mio.* Where are you, Gabriela? Please hurry."

Gabriela texts Deborah that she's coming now but doesn't wait for a reply. She tells Brad they need to get to the bakery as fast as possible. They jump into the cruiser and drive away. Brad hits the lights and blares the siren.

scene 20.

When they park in front of the bakery, Brad opens the glove box and grabs a black pistol to replace the one he left behind with Sheriff Osbourne. Gabriela leaps out of the utility vehicle and rushes inside. The tables are empty. Several customers stand around the far corner of the dining room near the coffee counter. Deborah emerges from the crowd, wiping her hands on a wet towel.

"Cugina," she says. "I don't know what's happening."

"Where is he?" Gabriela says.

Deborah tilts her head. "Back there."

The group parts for Brad, muttering their relief that he's finally on the scene. Gabriela follows him. Frank gasps, half-propped against the wall under the counter, his face a sickening blue. He claws at his neck with shivering hands, desperate to remove whatever infects him. A thin smile crosses his swollen lips.

"Came through wrong," he says.

Brad kneels beside him and takes his pulse, shaking his head.

Gabriela places the back of her hand against his forehead. The old man burns with fever. "How can we help you?"

"You can't." Frank coughs up thick yellow phlegm. "You shouldn't."

"Don't say that," Gabriela says. "We can call for an ambulance. Brad can take you to the hospital."

His chest hitches. "Let me pass."

Deborah gives Gabriela's shoulder a gentle squeeze. "He wouldn't let me help either."

"He's not gonna last much longer," Brad says.

"Don't want to," Frank says, gouging an open sore on his forearm above his tattoo.

Gabriela reaches up to the counter and grabs a coffee mug. She bumps her way through the customers and pours fresh water from a carafe near the register.

"Here."

She places the mug against Frank's distended lips until he laps a swallow.

Frank coughs. "Back where I'm from." His eyes roll under his eyelids.

"Yes?" Gabriela sits on the tiles beside him. "What about it?"

"Back where I'm from, they all were sick."

The crowd retreats, shooting sour glances at one another. Many depart without finishing meals or paying bills. Deborah doesn't stop them.

"Who?" Brad says. "Who was sick?"

"My wife Jeanette," Frank says. "Maybe I picked it up. Maybe we all will die."

The remaining customers gasp until the final two scramble out the front door.

"No," Gabriela says. "The jump across the Bridge caused this."

"Gabriela?" Brad says.

"Darrell told us. He told you they come back wrong. That's why he doesn't want you searching for your daughter on the other side. You know that's true. Look at Amanda."

"Amanda was wrong from the start," Frank says.

(some mistakes belong to nature)

"He's right," Brad says. "His world's leaking into ours."

Frank convulses and cracks his head against the wall until blood runs from his ears.

"Frank?" Gabriela cradles the sick man's shoulders, dipping her hand into steamy mucus flowing from his mouth and nose. Vomit builds up in her throat, but she forces it back down with a violent swallow. "Frank!"

"I dreamed of this. Of *you*." Frank hisses with closed eyes. "I dreamed of a world where our souls connect the way lightning strikes the earth from the clouds."

Gabriela squeezes his bony hand. "Don't leave, Frank. Our world can still be what you dreamed."

"No," Frank whispers. "It's too late. We've bled through. *I* did. I shouldn't be here, but I can't go back and don't want to take you with me."

"Nobody can tell you where you belong," Gabriela says.

"I'm scared."

"So am I."

Frank pauses between each word, stretching every syllable into a painful whisper. "I'm. So. Scared. Scared. I. Won't. Be. With. Jeanette. When. I'm. Done. Here."

"You will be."

"I'm. Scared. She. Won't. Want. Me. No. More. No. More. Cause. Of. What. I. Done. What. I. Done. To. Her."

"She will."

Frank's eyes flutter until Gabriela sees cold blue crystals. "The sickness doesn't come from the radiation. It comes from us."

"No," Gabriela says.

Frank gulps as his head juts to the side, dislocating. His neck tethers the rest of his fractured body. He heaves and arches his back until he slices his frayed lips, smashing his mouth closed.

He babbles incoherently. *". . . soop . . . soop . . . krah . . . krah . . . soop . . . soop . . . krah . . . krah . . ."*

"What's he saying?" Brad asks.

Gabriela leans closer. "I can't tell."

Frank's bloody lips split unevenly. *". . . sooper, karah, sooper, karah, sooper, karah, sooper, karah . . ."*

"What's that mean?" Deborah says, crouching over Gabriela.

Gabriela clutches Frank's rigid body. "I don't know."

He purrs in her ear. "Find your friend."

"My friend?"

Frank gasps one final time and expires in Gabriela's arms.

"He's gone," she says.

"I'm sorry," Deborah says.

"I know what he meant."

"Gabriela?" Brad says.

Becky Stokes bursts through the front door of the bakery, followed by her bearded camera operator. She bumps a table and sends salt and pepper shakers askew. She yanks at Brad's shoulders. Her flaming locks rollick in the breeze.

"What's going on, Sheriff?" she asks. "You can't shut me out on this."

Gabriela charges. "You have her."

"What?" Becky jumps back and knocks her camera operator to his knees. He continues recording.

"Puttana," Gabriela spits as she lowers her shoulder. "Where is she?"

Before Becky can reply, Gabriela dips into her ribcage, tackling. They hit a table and crash to the floor. The table tilts on its base and topples. Deborah screams. Gabriela doesn't stop. She flails her arms and curls her fists, striking the news reporter on the chest and chin. Becky wails but can't shake loose. Gabriela's hands find her throat and start to squeeze.

"Tell me where she is."

But Brad grabs her and heaves until she flies loose. Gabriela kicks her feet in midair while Brad swings her away from Becky. She knocks over the *espresso* machine. Brad pins her against the pastry display window.

"Stop!" he shouts. "Gabriela, pull it together."

"No," she says, tossing her head and shoulders. "She has Sara. I want her back now before it's too late. Let me go. I'm not waiting any longer. *La ucciderò.*"

"Gaby, no," Deborah says.

"I mean it," Gabriela says. "*Porco cane.* I'll kill her."

"Gabriela, quit!" Brad yells.

Becky picks herself up off the floor, cupping her swollen chin with slender fingers. "No, Sheriff. She's right."

"Becky?" the camera operator says, lowering his shutter.

"Wait for me outside," she tells him. "And don't share that footage with anyone."

He nods, slips out the front door, and waits under the red-and-green awning.

Becky wraps long satin hair over an exposed shoulder. "Y'all want Sara? I'll take you to her. It's about time, but I'm warning you. You won't like what you see."

"You don't get to decide," Gabriela says.

Becky snorts. "I've been calling the shots so far."

"That ends now," Gabriela says.

"We shall see." Becky glances at Frank. "Who's he? He looks awful messed up."

"A friend," Brad says.

"One of yours?" Becky asks.

"You could say that, yes."

Becky circles the overturned table. "Or does he belong to you?"

"Me?" Gabriela says.

"Mmm."

"He doesn't belong to anyone."

"Cute, dear," Becky says. "Did he work for the theatre?"

"What does that matter?" Gabriela says.

"We'll see, won't we?"

"No," Brad says. "He doesn't work at the theatre. He didn't. Like I said, he's a friend of mine. Drives linehaul. Well, he did. Darrell Mebane introduced us."

"Darrell Mebane?" Becky says.

"That's right."

"That two-bit shaman from over in Houndstooth?"

"He conjures," Gabriela says.

"Oh, you know him, too?" Becky says.

"Un po."

"Well, this keeps getting more interesting by the minute," Becky says. "First, we have a dead stranger that looks like Deborah's run him through a cheese grater."

"Leave me out of this, Stokes." Deborah tosses the spilled salt shaker over her left shoulder and straightens the table. "If you know what's good for you."

"My apologies." Becky runs a finger along the coffee counter as she approaches Gabriela. "And now you're both making friends with Darrell Mebane? Looks like we got a genuine mystery to solve."

"Ain't no mystery," Brad says, assisting Deborah while she stands the table. "Darrell helped me through a tough time after my daughter died. And after I lost Shana."

"*That* worked out well for you." Becky stops in front of Gabriela. "And what about you?"

"She lost her Daddy," Brad says. "Darrell just gave her some comfort's all."

"Wanna hear it from her, darling." Becky grins. "If you don't mind."

Brad nods. *Don't tell her the truth.* That much is obvious. *She can't know why we visited Darrell.* A fly whizzes past Gabriela but she avoids it.

"*Papà. Papà* died. I've been struggling since we lost him year before last."

"I see." Becky scoots away. "Y'all better be telling the truth. Hate for there to be any secrets between us now. Not now that we've come this far. You wouldn't want to meet the same fate as Travis Boggs."

"*King* Boggs?" Brad says.

"Some people don't get second chances." Becky shrugs. "They stay gone and can't come back."

Gabriela starts for the front door. "What about Sara?"

"Can you still get us into the theatre?" Becky says.

Gabriela raises an eyebrow. "Brad?"

"Fine with me. If there's any police tape, I'll give Curly a holler and check the status."

"Then, yes," Gabriela says. "I can get us in."

"Shall we?"

Becky steps outside without waiting for a response. She meets her camera operator and starts lecturing. Brad tells Deborah to call 911 to remove Frank.

(you remove dead bodies)

"I will," Deborah says.

"I imagine he has an ID, but that probably won't help much," Brad says. "They'll end up treating him as a John Doe, which is just fine. I don't think he would've minded."

"You don't think?" Deborah says.

Gabriela shakes her head. "I'm certain he wouldn't."

"Okay."

"Cugina?" Gabriela says.

"Gaby?"

Gabriela hugs Deborah. *"Grazie."*

"You be safe," Deborah says, but she looks at Brad. "You take care of her."

"Yes, ma'am."

scene 21.

Gabriela and Brad step out into the sunshine as Becky finishes explaining to her camera operator that he needs to return to the office and lock up the equipment until he hears from her later this afternoon. She expects him to be downtown for the evening vigil by six o'clock sharp.

"That'll give us an entire hour to set up before the festivities," Becky says.

The camera operator agrees and turns the corner at Cardinal Avenue. Brad keeps Gabriela by his side as they walk up King Street to the Orpheum. He scrolls through his mobile and sends a text. Gabriela doesn't know who he's contacting. She doesn't ask. He has a life outside of hers. Even with all they're going through. He must.

The front of the theatre is calm. The crows aren't perched on the marquee. Maybe they're hiding. Gabriela takes out her keys and unlocks. The alarm hasn't been set. Not a huge surprise, if the police were the last ones here this morning. But still, they would've needed a key to lock the door. Worse, however, the lobby lights are on. They cross into the auditorium. So are the house lights. And the stage is lit.

"We have company," Brad says.

Gabriela climbs to the stage and peers into the severed composite steel deck where Amanda emerged into their world. The antechamber is empty. "Not down there."

"Oh, we'll need to go a bit farther," Becky says and circles the proscenium so she can descend the stairs into the pit. "Come."

Brad and Gabriela follow. As King promised, the electrical equipment and machinery have been removed. So have Connor and the crippled Amanda. The two dead deputies. Becky walks the length of the subfloor, examining the impressions in the dirt.

"I've spent several hours down here since last night," she says. "But still can't figure out exactly what happened."

"How did you get down here?" Gabriela says.

Becky ignores her and points along the earth where Amanda crossed before levitating. "Shots fired. Two officers down. Connor and Amanda both impaled. Connor through the skull. Amanda, the abdomen. That last wound self-inflicted. Did she off herself after executing her brother? Seems logical. But why the police and the gunshots? The crack in the stage floor? Care to enlighten me, Sheriff?"

She doesn't know. She doesn't know what Connor did. That Amanda came through.

"You tell me," Brad says.

"So, you wanna play that game?" Becky bites her lip.

Gabriela chuckles. "You don't know what you think you know."

"Clever girl."

Becky springs the lock on the secret door to the tunnels and slips into the darkness. Brad draws his weapon and flashlight as he follows. Gabriela keeps a few paces behind while they descend toward the underground pool. The muddy stream splashes her ankles once they're level.

Gabriela spots the theatre group standing in a circle in the middle of the water holding hands and chanting, soft and low. The entire cast and crew are assembled. The front office staff. Even James Patterson. Sara hangs from above, strapped to pipes crossing below the intersection. She's thigh deep and naked. Gabriela can't see if her feet touch the surface. The shackles bite into her wrists, leaking blood and tinting the pool a sickly red. Brad's flashlight shines on her breasts, illuminating the thorny rose named for Becky.

"Sara?" Gabriela forces her way through the circle. Sania and Cherlynne, the board operators, rejoin hands without noticing. "What have they done to you?"

Sara, too weak to talk, smacks her lips and flutters her eyes.

"Cut her loose." Brad waves his gun. "I ain't playing."

"Not so fast," Becky says and passes between Anika and Terese. The wardrobe technicians don't open their eyes. Like the rest, they're awake, but unconscious. Becky melds through. "I still need her."

Sara coughs and lifts herself, struggling for breath until Gabriela wraps her arms around her and holds her as tight and as high as she can.

Becky shakes her head. "How long do you think you can keep that up, Miss Rossi?"

"Let her down," Brad says and aims his gun, still standing outside the chanting chorus.

"I told you I can't."

"Why are you doing this?" Gabriela says, straining her back and neck.

Becky presses against her chin with a narrow finger. "What if you could replace the people in your life with better versions of themselves?"

"I warned you." Brad crashes through the circle, knocking Doug Cousins under water. The head carpenter splashes but doesn't stop his cadence or open his eyes. He wades through the ruddy muck until he finds his rightful place between Joe Cox and Deanna Flowers and takes their hands. The wordless recitation continues. "This ends now."

"Is that so?" Becky says.

In the near darkness, Brad rests the gun barrel against Becky's temple. "Last chance."

"But then you'll never know why," Becky says. "And these poor people will never know who *she* is."

"*Who* she is?" Brad says.

"You heard me."

Gabriela's grip loosens. "Who *I* am?"

Sara sinks, kicking below the surface so she can jump up for another breath. Gabriela squeezes her hips and bends her knees for leverage to keep Sara from submerging.

"Why won't they know who I am?" Gabriela asks.

"Because you don't exist in their worlds."

"What?"

"Or in any other world."

Gabriela gasps. "Brad?"

Is that even possible? If there are other worlds, and from this vantage point and the events that unfolded last night, the only rational conclusion is that there are multiple, how could she only exist in one world?

(i saw me)

"Sheriff?" Becky peeks out of the corner of her eyes at Brad's gun. "May I?"

Brad lowers his firearm. "You have thirty seconds."

Becky runs her hands through the dirty pool. "The people you know, those you care about, your loved ones. What if you could find better versions? Would you take that chance?"

"Better versions?" Gabriela says.

"What do you mean?" Brad says.

"Different ones." Becky soars her hand in the dense putrid air. "Across the multiverse. Ones that you prefer."

"Why?" Gabriela says.

Becky scoffs. "So they'd be better suited to your needs, of course. So they'll do exactly what you tell them to do. Isn't that the purpose of every relationship? To subject others to your will? Why else would you puny humans interact with one another? Isn't dominance and submission the ultimate goal?"

"You're sick."

"Maybe," Becky says. "But would you trade for them?"

"*Trade* for them?" Brad says. "I don't follow."

"I've crossed worlds, Sheriff. Looking for the very people you see all around you to help me complete a very specific task."

"To do your *bidding*?" Gabriela snaps.

Becky nods. "That's right. I've brought them here. Most have been exchanged. Their counterparts now roam distant worlds innocent and free, living their lives as the gods intended. Some, like Tommy, do not."

"Tommy?" Gabriela says.

"Yes," Becky says.

"You killed Tommy?"

"Surprised?"

Brad rotates as Becky orbits Sara and Gabriela inside the circle of chanters. "Why?"

"Because he wouldn't play along and did something he shouldn't have done. He was like a child who wouldn't listen." Becky leans over Gabriela as the weight of Sara drives her deeper into the water. "But you wouldn't know anything about that, would you?"

"You took him from every world?" Brad says.

The earth's natural vibration bumps in intensity under Gabriela's feet. The humming of the cast and crew increases in volume as they bounce in place to the rhythm.

"That's what he deserved," Becky says. "He had no right to interfere."

"Because he killed James Patterson?" Gabriela says.

"Because he fucking questioned my authority." Becky gathers herself. Takes a deep breath. Straightens her ebony jumper. "But, yes. That. Tommy kept complaining about not getting his promotion and worrying about the investors from Raleigh. Like it matters what job he has backstage or where the money comes from to run this place. Like this place matters. Not any more than any other place of worship. You think the Greeks and Romans took issue when they slaughtered their sacrificial lambs? Maybe Tommy never understood my endgame, but I didn't need him to understand. I don't need any of them to understand.

Or you, whoever the fuck you are. All I need is their song. The ritual. And that's still going according to plan. Made even easier now that you've canceled tonight's show. Now that we don't have to do everything under the cover of darkness."

"Your thirty seconds is up." Brad raises his weapon.

"Your daughter, Sheriff," Becky says.

Brad gasps. "What about her?"

"What if you could bring her back from some other place? Take her away from some other you? Would you? Could you? Would you let that *other* you suffer just so you could find some peace? So you could love again?"

"You fucking bitch," Brad says.

But Gabriela hears the soft voice now. The soft voice rising up from the undulating blood water. The underground pool stained by Sara Cooper as she hangs.

"Daddy."

Brad lowers his gun and screams. "No, Maddie! No!"

"Daddy. It's me. Your little angel."

"Go back, sweetheart."

The earth drops, shifts, pauses, and skips as a beam of light erupts from the center of the pool, enveloping Sara. Gabriela falls away and swims to the chanting perimeter. Sara writhes and coughs while she hangs, spitting up blood until her face quivers and melts. A teenage face emerges after the metamorphosis. A striking young blonde with Brad's innocent eyes and loving smile.

"Daddy?"

"You don't belong here."

"Don't you love me anymore?"

Brad drops to his knees. His chest hitches as he starts to sob. "Please, no."

"Why am I here?" his daughter asks and pulls at the restraints. *"Help me, Daddy. Get me down."*

"Maddie, I can't."

"Why not, Daddy? It hurts."

Brad wails. "Please make her stop."

"I'm your little girl, Daddy. Don't you remember me?"

Brad reaches for his daughter.

"Take her," Becky says. Like an instant camera, her skin flashes, revealing bones and muscles underneath. "Hold your child one last time and all the pain will go away. You'll be with her forever and ever."

The earth shakes, blasting energy from its core and tossing Brad closer to his daughter. The bright light casts undulating shadows on the tunnel walls as the chanting chorus sways to the rhythm.

"No!" Gabriela screams, shielding her eyes.

(they come back wrong they come back wrong they come back wrong)

"I see the man with the flies, Daddy."

Brad shakes his head. "Don't look at him, Maddie."

"I hear the train coming."

"Get away from the tracks, sweetheart."

"Don't let me die again."

"Please, Jesus, no. Take me. Don't take my child."

Brad runs for his daughter, but Gabriela leaps, blocking his path. He grabs her shoulders.

"Don't you understand?" he says. "I can't lose her again. Not again."

"That's not her, Brad," Gabriela says. "That's not your daughter."

Brad staggers away, pinching his nose as tears flood his eyes. "I miss her. And my wife, Shana. Every day without them is another day I would trade. Becky's right."

"No," Gabriela says. "She's not. Don't you see? That's what she wants you to believe."

"I don't care."

"Go to her, Brad," Becky whispers.

"*Lascialo solo!* Leave him alone."

Gabriela rushes Becky, her legs drudging through the cesspool, but fierce hands grab her and pull her tight. She screams, kicking and spinning. Connor Simmons flashes a sickly grin in her stunned face and squeezes.

"Connor?" Gabriela says.

He opens his eyes. They glow red in the darkness.

(my demon my demon my demon)

"I told you," Becky taunts. "He doesn't know who you are. How could he? He's only been with us for a few hours now. He hasn't met you yet."

(you don't exist in their worlds)

"Connor!" His unchanging, dull stare mocks her with contempt. "What did she do to you?"

"I found him," Becky says, laughing. "I keep finding them. All of them, until they're exactly what I want them to be."

Brad stumbles toward Gabriela and drops a lead hand on Connor's shoulder. Connor doesn't blink. The red eyes continue their unyielding burn.

"Let her go," Brad says.

Becky cackles. "I don't think so, dear."

Maddie jerks in her restraints, twisting and writhing until her face contorts. She screams one last time for Brad as Sara returns to her body. Maddie disappears.

"Maddie, no!" Brad shouts. "Don't go."

"You should've listened when I told you," Becky says "Now your time's up."

Brad drops to his knees and buries his face in his hands. Gabriela shoves Connor in the darkness and bumps Sara, who rocks like a swinging pendulum. The light from the earth's core subsides until the thunder underground is a blip in Gabriela's subconscious. A pulse kneading her celestial soul. The chant of the circle dulls, the bounce of the cast and crew diminishing as their shadows stretch and peter out.

"Beware the wolf's mouth, Gabriela," Becky says.

"Eh?"

"You're standing in it."

The earth rumbles again, draining the stagnant water from the tunnels into the shaft beneath Sara. Becky howls, signaling the cast and crew to converge. Brad raises his head and jumps for the pipes above Sara. He yanks down hard. Metal cracks and hisses, blasting the swarming circle with steam. They recoil. Gabriela wrenches herself free from Connor's grip and grabs Sara. Brad swings his gun but can't fire because flailing hands and arms return as quickly as they dissipated. They seize him, embracing while they moan and chant and rasp. He shouts for Gabriela as he's wrestled away. Gabriela drags Sara toward a tunnel, but Becky leaps on top of them.

She snorts, gnashing her pointy teeth. "Not so fast."

Gabriela loses her footing and collapses on top of Sara, who lands unconscious on her side, her mouth barely above the waterline.

"Listen to me," Becky hisses. "Listen to *me* now."

(did i do that wrong am i not supposed to stress a pronoun)

"The gods drove their mortal-born into exile where he waits for us," Becky says, her soft warm lips brushing Gabriela's face. "You think Pastor Aken's going to unleash hell on earth? You're mistaken. He'll do what I need him to do, like the others. I keep close to the willows. Did you forget? I *am* hell on earth."

Becky convulses, extending her neck and jaw as sharp teeth sprout. Thick crimson fur mushrooms along her spine, rippling through her black sundress and covering her back and shoulders. Her hands elongate until serrated claws glisten, replacing her fingernails. Gabriela shields her neck and throat. She bucks her hips, unable to shake Becky loose as Brad shouts from the center of the pool, tossing the catatonic cast and crew off his shoulders. He levels his gun and fires, catching Becky-wolf in the hind quarters. It screeches and rears its salivating mouth until the howl shakes the underground cavern. Brad fires again, but Becky-wolf pivots and pounces with lightning agility, tearing into Brad's face and shredding his neck. Gabriela screams.

"Run!" Brad shouts.

Becky-wolf drives him underwater as the cast and crew stagger zombie-like into the red clay walls, clearing space for their master.

"Brad, no!"

He bubbles under the surface, emerging with Becky-wolf clinging to his body and biting deep into his clavicle. He reaches up with both hands, pulling at thick fur and pummeling the tight muscular frame. When Brad opens his mouth, Becky-wolf forces him under again. Only bright eyes and wet hair are visible as he fights for his life until the flailing ceases. Becky-wolf throws its head back and roars.

Gabriela moves. She hooks Sara under the shoulders and drags her through the mud and up the nearest tunnel. But Becky-wolf springs.

"Vaffanculo!"

Brad's mud soaked hand emerges from the murky pool and catches Becky-wolf's rear leg. She snorts and growls before rotating to face him again.

"Please, Gabriela," Brad says.

Please, Gabriela. But it's more with his face. More in her mind. More than anything he could ever say or speak or she could ever hear. Only that she knows and he knows because in this moment they're together. *Please, Gabriela.*

"No, Brad," she whispers. "I can't go without you."

No more words, only please run and save yourself. Save yourself and Sara. Don't let this be the end. Not after all we've been through. Not after the journey we've taken together. Please, Gabriela. Please please please Gabriela please please please Gabriela run run run go go go because you don't settle you conquer AND IT HURTS SO MUCH TO KNOW YOU'RE OUT THERE WATCHING ME

DIE RIGHT NOW, AND I NEVER GOT TO TELL YOU THAT NO MATTER HOW MANY WORLDS YOU CROSS YOU WILL ALWAYS BELONG WITH ME.

That's it. No goodbye. Nothing more.

Please, Gabriela.

His last words. Two more words than he ever got to tell his daughter before she died at not quite nineteen years old on the railroad tracks across Ninth Street in this world and in every other world where they existed, do exist, or ever will exist.

scene 22.

Gabriela doesn't look back. She tugs Sara until she reaches the end of the tunnel. She pops the spring, but the door drops on its hinges without budging.

"Cazzo!"

She doesn't see any handle or latch to pull. Can't find anything to grab hold of in the dark. Sweat dripping off her forehead blurs her vision. The crack along the threshold is too thin to penetrate. She punches the door and screams. Voices echo down the abandoned tunnel. Probably her own. Maybe Becky-wolf. The theatre zombies. She doesn't know or care because she needs to get through.

Maybe the door opens toward the other side?

With her hands wrapped around Sara's hips, she heaves with her shoulder, but the slatted wooden door doesn't move. She heaves again. Only a slight give. Shoves a third time. The door rattles and slides the width of her fingers. Humid tunnel air gets sucked through in a whistle. Something on the inside shakes. Whatever's blocking the door. Whatever's blocking the fucking door on the other side shakes.

"Fanculo."

Gabriela sets Sara down, leaning her against the wall. Sara's head lolls. Gabriela needs to move fast. She drops to the red clay floor and sits with her legs crouched so her boots are flat against the door. With both hands planted behind her, she scoots her hips and drives with all her strength, gritting her teeth and whining. The door teeters. She recoils her feet and hits until she loses count, and the door swings. A loud, fierce crash shakes the dirt beneath her. But the gap's wide enough now. She rolls and stumbles to her feet, grabbing Sara and pulling them both through to safety.

Act III

Into the Wolf's Mouth

scene 1.

After she shuts the door, Gabriela's eyes adjust. She recognizes where she is more because of what she smells than what she sees. Sara lies beside her, unconscious but gently breathing. Gabriela unwraps Sara's laces and gathers her shirt so she can dab Sara's sliced wrists to ease the bleeding. Sara moans. Gabriela searches the cellar and grabs a large flat bag of flour that slid off a toppled heavy-duty storage rack. She props Sara's head. A harsh light pops on above. Footsteps descend the stairs. Deborah's concerned face drops into view below the overhead joists.

"Gaby?"

"Cugina." Deborah trots down the steps into the cellar beneath the bakery. "Sheriff Gleason?"

Gabriela shakes her head.

"Where is he?" Deborah says.

"I left him behind," Gabriela says.

"Behind where?"

Gabriela tosses her head toward the cellar door. "Back there."

"The mines?" Deborah says.

Gabriela nods.

"But nobody goes down there." Deborah listens by the door. "What were you two doing?"

Gabriela shakes her head. "I don't know."

Deborah glances at Sara. "Who's that?"

"Please help her."

Deborah leans over Sara's face, checking her breath and pulse. She lifts each closed eyelid and sighs.

"What happened to her?" Deborah says.

"Becky. Becky Stokes."

Deborah pulls a dark green tablecloth off a fresh folded stack and covers Sara. "The newspaper reporter who was here with you this morning? What about her?"

"She's trouble."

"Well, everybody knows that," Deborah says. "She always sticks her nose in where it doesn't belong. You learn to live with it. I did, and I've been here for over forty years now."

Mamma. Gabriela's almost too weak to remember her saying. *Pensa ai tuoi affari e alle tue maniere.* Mind your business and your manners.

Deborah grabs a white dishrag and rinses it under the shop sink beside a dormant furnace before returning to Sara and dabbing her lips and cheeks.

"Forty years?" Gabriela says.

"Yes, of course, *caro*. You know that."

"No," Gabriela says. "Forty years. Becky's been here that long? Since you moved here?"

Deborah scratches her chin. "Come to think of it, I'm not really sure. That can't be possible, no. Maybe?"

"But she's not that much older than I am," Gabriela says.

"Sure she is," Deborah says.

"No, she's not."

Sara moans, and Deborah scrambles for a styrofoam cup that she fills with water. She lifts the cup against Sara's pursed lips. Sara's eyes flutter as she sips. Deborah rinses the rag and cools her face again.

"Grazie, cugina," Gabriela says.

"What's going on?" Deborah asks.

Before Gabriela replies, the cellar door rattles. Gabriela jumps, scooting toward a storage shelf. She grabs a can of baking powder and cocks her arm as the spring on the lock pops. When the door swings wide, Darrell Mebane appears in the threshold, a quiver of homemade arrows slung across his back. In his broad arms, he cradles Brad, caked with mud.

"Brad!"

Gabriela drops the can and scrambles across the floor to where Darrell sets him down next to Sara.

Deborah rushes to her side. "Sheriff?"

The lacerations on Brad's face and throat gush blood. His left eye swells below a deep jagged scratch. Deborah grabs more hand towels and rinses before applying them to Brad's wounds. He gurgles.

"Brad?" Gabriela says, her eyes squirting tears. "I thought I lost you."

"Almost did," Darrell says.

Gabriela raises her chin. "But how did you know?"

Darrell shrugs. "Had a feeling."

"He texted you, right?" Gabriela says. "While we were walking to the theatre?"

Darrell lowers his brow. She catches a glimpse of his neck. The right side. Under his ear and behind his tight beard. The Chi-Rho. She must've missed it when they went to his ossuary.

"Your neck," Gabriela whispers.

"Gabriela." Deborah mops up more blood on Brad's chest. "We need the first aid kit. It's upstairs under the register. Hurry!"

"Yes, of course."

Gabriela runs upstairs. The steps lead to a door near the restrooms. She sprints down the back hallway, through the kitchen, and into the dining room. The bakery is empty. The tables still haven't been cleared. The closed sign hangs in the front window facing King Street. Deborah must've shut down the store while they were removing Frank. A chalk outline on the tiles designates where he expired. Gabriela makes the sign of the cross before she grabs the red medical box and hustles back downstairs. Deborah rinses more towels as Darrell cuts away the tattered remains of Brad's blood-soaked athletic shirt.

"Qui!" Gabriela says, fumbling with the latch before she pulls out antiseptic and bandages.

Deborah drops the towels in the sink and rushes to Gabriela. She digs through the first aid kit and peels open a small pouch with large folded dressing pads.

"Hand me the tape," she says.

Gabriela gives Deborah several strips so she can secure the loose bandages. She stretches the biggest across a gouge in Brad's chest.

"He needs to go to the hospital." Deborah digs through her apron for her mobile. "I'll call for an ambulance."

"No," Darrell says, resting his fingers on Deborah's hand as she starts to tap her phone.

"Darrell?" Gabriela says.

Darrell strides to the storage shelves and sifts through the ingredients. He collects a jar of honey, a can of almonds, a container of apricot preserves, and salt. After he spreads them out across the metal countertop, he pulls a small pouch out of the breast pocket of his flannel and sprinkles spices across Brad's nose. Brad groans and sneezes. Darrell ignores him.

"Eggs?" he asks Deborah.

"Also upstairs."

Gabriela hurries up the steps, feet sloshing in her muddy shoes, and pulls a carton two-thirds full out of the refrigerator in the kitchen. After she returns, Darrell takes two, pauses, then grabs a third. He cracks each into the emptied almond can before combining all the elements and stirring with two wide fingers. He wipes his hand on a damp towel and kneels beside Brad so he can smear the cluster across each of the major wounds and as many of the minor abrasions as he can locate. Brad winces each time Darrell lifts the bandages and touches his mutilated skin.

"How do you know this will work?" Gabriela says.

Darrell doesn't answer. He draws a homespun arrow out of his quiver and pokes the tip of his finger before smearing a single stroke of his blood across Brad's forehead.

"Y'all might want to stand back," Darrell says.

"Darrell?" Gabriela says.

Deborah tugs her elbow and drags her behind the furnace where Gabriela keeps her eyes at an angle below the gas valve so she can watch from a safe distance. Deborah gapes over her shoulder as Darrell grabs a tablecloth and covers Sara's face. Sara might as well be at a morgue with her naked body concealed the way it is. But she's not dead. She has a pulse and breath. She'll wake up. Brad needs attention now. He's shredded and losing blood.

While hovering over Brad, Darrell recites prayers under his breath that Gabriela can't hear. Or if she hears, she can't understand. He orbits Brad a few times, sprinkling more spice from the tiny pouch but pauses to examine the cellar space. He walks the length of the floorboards from the stairs to the escape door until he finds the center. He raises a hand and estimates the width by swiveling his thumb and pinky finger on his wrist, reminding Gabriela of the hang loose Hawaiian greeting that she's seen before in a romantic comedy on Netflix.

"What's he doing?" Deborah whispers in her ear.

"I'm not sure," Gabriela says.

Darrell takes a knee. He knocks several times on the floor until he loosens one of the boards. He sits and pries the plank loose. It can't be more than a half meter long and six centimeters wide. He slides his hand under and pulls several loose until he's able to stoop far enough to see below. Content with what he finds, he climbs back to his feet and collects Brad, sweeping him up into his arms in a cradle similar to when they first arrived. He carries Brad to the center of the cellar and lowers him to the floor, shifting his body until Brad cups the exposed subfloor in the fetal position. Darrell returns to his knee and drops one heavy hand on Brad's thigh and the other on his shoulder. The large truck driver tilts his head back and closes his eyes. Nothing happens at first, but Gabriela feels a single wave roll under her feet not unlike the prefatory tremors that shake the Alps when earthquakes rattle her village.

Deborah squeezes her shoulder.

"You feel that?" she asks in Italian.

"Sì."

The earth starts to hum, picking up speed and intensity. She knows what comes next. She's seen enough in the last two days to expect what the earth is about to do. Gabriela covers her ears but won't hide her eyes. She wants to see. Even if the light from the core burns her retinas, she needs to witness its healing power. She believes in the energy regardless of how Becky corrupts and distorts what the universe offers. She must believe.

"I believe," she whispers.

"Huh?" Deborah says.

The earth's buzz caterwauls, shaking the entire cellar and spilling the contents off the storage shelves. Boxes and containers crash. Glass breaks. Light explodes from the floorboards, swallowing Darrell and Brad in a singular shaft. It blinds Gabriela, but she fights to see. Shadows dance in the intense light, crouching as they writhe until they squeeze and caress Brad. He coughs and gags beneath Darrell's clenched hands, spewing blood between his teeth. His body jerks and hitches. He arches his back and tenses. Darrell prays or chants or counts or does whatever he needs while Brad endures one final spasm and relaxes, breathing deeply. The intense light sucks back into the hole in the floor. The earth stops pounding. Darrell, glistening with sweat, drops his head and collapses beside Brad, gasping for breath.

"Where am I?"

Not Brad. Not Darrell. *Sara.*

Sara Cooper sits up in the dank cellar, clenching the tablecloth against her breasts.

scene 2.

Gabriela rushes to her side.

"Gabriela?"

"It's me."

"Where am I? What's going on?"

"You're safe now," Gabriela says.

"How'd I get here?"

Gabriela sweeps matted hair off Sara's forehead. "Take it easy, please."

"I was home."

"I know."

Sara clears her throat. "Becky."

"She's gone now."

"Gone?" Sara coughs. "She never leaves."

Deborah stands beside Brad as he sits up and rubs his neck. "Gabriela?"

Darrell Mebane gathers the few arrows that spilled from his quiver and drifts into shadow. Gabriela gives Sara a quick squeeze on her shoulder and runs to Brad. He falls in her arms as he climbs to his feet.

"I thought I lost you," Gabriela says.

Brad half-smiles. "So did I."

"What happened back there?"

"Darrell," Brad says. "He found me."

Gabriela looks at the two bright eyes shining in the dim corner by an upright freezer. "How?"

Brad hugs her tight. "We stay connected."

"On straight and crooked lines?"

"Something like that, yes," Brad says.

Deborah taps Gabriela. "Like you and me, *neonata*."

"Cugina?"

"I'm always with you." Deborah cups her face with a soft palm. "This is where you belong."

Gabriela drifts out of Brad's arms and into Deborah's. *"Ti amo."*

"Now then." Deborah claps her hands. "Anyone care to tell me what's going on?"

"Same," Sara says, clinging to the tablecloth at the base of the storage shelves.

"Brad?" Gabriela says. "Did you stop her?"

As soon as Brad starts to speak, Gabriela sees the mark on his forehead where Darrell streaked a thin line of his blood. *Chi-Rho.* Brad's knighthood. The Order of the Cross.

"Gabriela?" Brad says.

Gabriela reaches up and strokes the Christogram with gentle fingers. Her wrist tingles.

"The sign," she whispers. "You have it now. Darrell gave it to you."

Darrell grumbles deep and low. "I didn't give you anything you didn't earn."

Brad clasps her fingers as they trace the outline together. "Well, it ain't gonna make for a pretty picture."

"Do you think you already have that mark in other worlds?" Gabriela says.

Brad swallows. "If I do, maybe I saved my daughter somewhere."

"Maybe," Gabriela says.

Sara groans. "At least I was right about something."

"What's that?" Gabriela says.

"You two." Sara tweaks her nose stud. "Still going at it like you're sharing coffee at Starbucks."

"Hey, watch it," Deborah says. "You don't know how hard I fought city council to keep the evil empire out of downtown."

Sara arches her unibrow, thicker and more tangled than before she disappeared. "Sorry."

"She's not gone," Darrell says and folds his arms.

"Darrell?" Brad says.

"Becky Stokes," Darrell says. "All these years I thought the pastor was our curse. I was wrong."

"I've never trusted her," Deborah says. "But I get it. She has a way of showing up where you don't want her."

"By hiding under the cover of the *Sentinel*," Brad says.

"He's no joy, either," Deborah says. "That Pastor Aken."

"No," Darrell says. "But she pulls his strings. That's clear now."

"Maybe Sara knows more than we do?" Brad says.

Gabriela crouches beside Sara. "Do you?"

"I don't know what to say." Sara pulls the tablecloth up to her chin. "We were together at Meemaw's before the dress rehearsal. The next thing I know I woke up here."

"That's not what I meant," Gabriela says. "How did you meet? What did she tell you?"

"I'm not sure." She wriggles her plump toes out from under the tablecloth. Dried mud flakes off. "Seems like we've always been together. I can't remember not knowing her."

"The tattoo with her name," Gabriela says. "When did you get that?"

Sara peeks under the tablecloth. "I don't know, really. I've always had it."

"She brought her through," Brad says.

"Huh?" Sara says.

"Do you remember what she told us, Gabriela?" Brad asks.

Gabriela nods. "She replaced her."

"Replaced me?" Sara tries to stand but can't quite keep her balance and plops on the floor. "What the fuck are you talking about?"

"Becky Stokes crosses over," Darrell says.

"Crosses over?" Sara says. "I don't follow."

"Yeah, neither do I," Deborah says. "Gabriela?"

"Most get pulled," Darrell says. "Becky goes through on her own."

"Goes through?" Deborah says. "Goes through where?"

"Other worlds." Brad says.

"Other worlds?" Sara says. "You're telling me my girlfriend is from another fucking world?"

"No," Brad says.

"What then?"

"You are," Darrell says.

"I am!" Sara shouts and dives into a coughing jag. "What the fuck are you talking about?"

Gabriela clears her throat. "Becky told us she was replacing everyone in the theatre."

"*Replacing* us?" Sara asks. "How? Why?"

"Trading you for others that will do what she wants," Brad says.

"All of us?" Sara says.

Brad shakes his head. "No, not all of you."

"Who?" Sara says. "Who didn't she replace?"

"Me," Gabriela says.

"You?" Sara wrinkles her brow. "That doesn't make any sense."

"None of this does," Deborah says.

"No, I mean, you're the only one I remember coming here," Sara says. "About eight months ago from that theatre in Pittsburgh."

"*Sì,* Pittsburgh Public," Gabriela says, her days on their run crew fading to a distant lifetime in her memory.

"That's exactly why it does make sense," Brad says.

Sara drops her shoulders. "Huh?"

"I don't exist anywhere else," Gabriela says.

"Gabriela?" Deborah says. "What are you saying?"

"This is me, *Cugina*. This is who I am. This is who I'll always be."

"Non capsico," Deborah says. "Isn't that true for all of us?"

"No." Gabriela shakes her head. "*Mamma* used to tell a story about an old woman in *Châtillon*. I never understood it until now."

"What story?" Deborah says.

"A myth." Gabriela lowers her eyes. "An urban legend, really."

"You're not talking about the old woman boiling pasta?" Deborah waves her hand. "That foolish story."

"I am."

"Wanna clue us in?" Brad says.

"The old woman kept a portrait of the *Madonna* on the wall," Deborah says.

"Madonna?" Brad scratches his head. "The pop singer from the eighties? I knew she was an Italian, but I didn't think she was good enough that I'd call her a legend."

"Not Madonna," Gabriela says. "The *Madonna.*"

"Mary," Darrell says. "The mother of Jesus."

"Oh." Brad's face warms. "*That* Madonna."

"Jeez, Sheriff." Sara chuckles. "Even I knew that one."

Brad snorts. "Guess I am as dumb as I look."

"She believed she saw the *Madonna* crying in the portrait," Gabriela says.

"How's that?" Brad says.

"Tears," Gabriela says. "She saw tears in the Virgin Mary's eyes."

"Oh," Brad says. "I've heard of that. Like weeping statues."

"Or images of Jesus that bleed the *stigmata*," Deborah says.

Brad nods. "The wounds where he was crucified."

"The old woman summons a monsignor to come out to her home to verify what she sees." Gabriela thins her lips. "A monsignor is the Catholic equivalent of a pastor in the Baptist church."

"But only out of respect," Deborah adds. "There's no real designation or appointment. They're priests like any other."

"Oh," Brad says.

"So, the monsignor requests the assistance of a bishop because he can't draw any rational conclusions on his own and believes he's witnessing a miracle," Gabriela says.

"The bishop oversees many churches in the Catholic faith," Deborah says. "He's more of an authority than a local priest."

"Does the Baptist church have bishops?" Gabriela asks.

"Depends on the church," Darrell says.

"Not traditionally," Brad says.

"Anyhow, they end up consulting with the Vatican," Gabriela says.

"The pope?" Brad says.

"Mmm," Gabriela says.

Deborah waves a hand. "They take it all the way to the top. Funny hat and all."

"The pope sends a special envoy up to *Châtillon* to investigate," Gabriela says. "When he arrives, he studies the kitchen where the portrait of the *Madonna* hangs and asks the old woman to boil pasta."

"Odd request," Brad says. "But I guess I'd want pasta if I ever go to Italy."

"When in Rome," Sara says.

Gabriela shrugs. "The old woman does as she's told. As soon as the water starts boiling, the *Madonna* begins to cry."

"This would be an awful time to crack a joke about not liking her cooking," Brad says.

"I'm glad to see death didn't kill your sense of humor, Sheriff," Deborah says.

"He wasn't dead," Darrell says, unblinking.

"Well, wherever I was, I'm sure glad you pulled me out," Brad says.

Gabriela rolls her eyes. "The point is that the boiling water created condensation on the portrait that made the *Madonna* look like she was crying. *Capisci?*"

Deborah sighs. "A bedtime fairytale."

"With a valuable lesson," Gabriela says. "You can't always believe what you see."

(you don't know what you think you know)

"Or trust your senses," Darrell says.

"Darrell?" Brad says.

"You need to know beyond what your senses tell you," Darrell adds.

(kinesthesia)

"Is that how you found Brad?" Gabriela asks.

Brad chuckles. "No, I texted him."

"I would've found you anyhow," Darrell says.

"Probably so," Brad says.

"If Becky isn't who I thought she was," Sara says. "Who is she?"

"And what does she plan to do?" Deborah says.

"Becky plans to use the cast and crew to perform an ancient ritual at the Orpheum tonight," Gabriela says.

"At *our* theatre?" Sara says.

Gabriela nods. "She's already begun."

"This all sounds crazy," Deborah says. *"Pazzo!"*

"I know," Gabriela says. "I'm not sure I would believe it if I hadn't seen it with my own two eyes."

"Seen it?" Deborah says.

"She's already started," Brad says.

"I only slowed her down some," Darrell says.

"I'm sure she's back on track by now," Brad agrees.

"But what kinda ritual?" Deborah says.

"Yeah," Sara says. "Why would she need everybody at the theatre?"

"Are you familiar with how the Ancient Greeks sacrificed animals before the start of the *City Dionysia*?" Gabriela asks.

"Of course," Sara says.

Gabriela spreads her palms. *"That."*

"What?" Deborah says.

"Wait a minute." Sara manages to pull herself up to her feet while keeping the tablecloth draped over her shoulders to cover her naked body. "*I* was the sacrifice? I'm her animal?"

"It would appear that way," Brad says.

"The goat," Darrell says.

"Her communion," Brad says.

Gabriela nods and crosses to Sara. "I'm sorry."

"Fuck that bitch," Sara says and brushes past Gabriela toward the hidden door in the cellar. "She's this way?"

Darrell steps in front of her and blocks her path. Sara spins toward Brad.

"You're not gonna let me do anything about it?" she asks.

"Well, you're naked, for starters," Brad says. "And we need a plan. The last time we went down there, I nearly died."

"But you saved my life!" Sara says.

Brad nods. "Well, Gabriela helped."

"Sheriff?" Sara says. "Did you?"

"Huh?"

"Save my life?"

Brad shrugs his wide shoulders. Sara pulls back abruptly from a hug, shooting a crooked but snarky glance at Gabriela.

"Not because of you." Sara shakes the tablecloth. "I just don't want anything to fall out and embarrass him. I'm packing."

Gabriela smirks. "You sure are."

"Aspetta." Deborah points her finger at each of them as she speaks. "Becky Stokes intends to complete some type of ancient ritual that requires a human sacrifice? Of this young girl, to be specific, because she works at the theatre?"

"Sounds about right," Brad says.

"But why?" Deborah says. "What does the ritual do?"

Darrell flexes his chest. "I don't intend to find out."

"But we have to let her finish," Gabriela says.

"Gabriela," Sara says. "Are you crazy? Do you know the history behind those rituals?"

"I do."

Deborah holds up both palms. "I'm no expert on the theatre, but I'm thinking that anything that involves a human sacrifice needs to be stopped."

"No, we can't stop her," Gabriela says. "Right, Brad? We need an army."

Brad strokes the quivering caterpillar on his top lip and glances at the cellar door. "After what I seen down there, I'd rather face Amanda alone."

"You won't be alone," Darrell says. "There are five of us."

"Thank you," Brad says. "But I don't think I can put any of you in harm's way. Not again."

"Try and stop me," Darrell says.

"Brad?" Gabriela says. "Are you serious?"

"I'll reach out to Curly," Brad says. "See who we got down at the station."

"But you saw what she did to those two deputies last night," Gabriela says.

"Amanda?" Sara says, scratching her forehead.

"We'll need more than police officers," Darrell says, plucking an arrow from his quiver. "I'll melt down some silver back at the house. Soak the tips."

"For Amanda?" Sara says. "Amanda *Simmons*? Connor's sister?"

"Silver?" Gabriela says.

"What's she gotta do with all this?" Sara says.

"She came through wrong," Brad says.

"But she's crippled, ain't she?" Sara says.

"Not anymore," Brad says.

"The fuck?" Sara says.

"Silver won't do anything against Amanda," Gabriela says. "Will it? She's not like Becky."

Darrell sheaths his arrow. "Silver has ancient properties for defense against all evil."

"Why would you need silver to stop Becky?" Sara asks.

"Dionysus," Gabriela says. "The ritual."

Sara rubs the wounds on her neck. "The Maenads?"

Gabriela thins her lips. "Mmm-hmm."

"She's a fucking werewolf?" Sara says. "How's that even possible?"

"How *is* that possible?" Deborah asks.

"Their world is leaking into ours," Gabriela says. "But Delacourt was wrong. Or at least what he showed me was."

"Delacourt?" Deborah says.

"Who the fuck is that?" Sara says.

"He tried to warn me about Becky, but he was wrong."

"Who the fuck is he?" Sara says.

"We met at the theatre," Gabriela says.

"When?" Sara says. "Does he work there? Why don't I know him?"

Gabriela slumps. "No, he doesn't work there. He *did.* A long time ago."

"A ghost?" Sara's eyes inflate. "You've been talking to a fucking ghost?"

"Gabriela?" Deborah says. *"Ti rendi conto di come suona?"*

"I know how this sounds, *cugina*. But it's true."

"It's true?" Sara says. "There are werewolves and ghosts in Crow Creek?"

"And don't forget about vampires." Brad snickers. "Or whatever Amanda is."

Deborah coughs. "Vampires?"

"Yes," Gabriela says. "And I'm afraid they're all here because of me."

(you don't exist in any other world)

"But he wasn't wrong," Brad says. "Delacourt wasn't wrong."

"No?" Gabriela says.

"He showed you the ritual?"

"Sì."

"Pastor Aken summoning the Greek god Dionysus?" Brad asks.

"Mmm."

"Maybe you saw it wrong."

Gabriela swallows. "How's that possible?"

"We stopped Becky from sacrificing Sara," Brad says.

"We did."

"Thank Jesus," Sara says.

Deborah makes the sign of the cross.

"Why do you think she chose to sacrifice Sara in the first place?" Brad asks.

"Please don't say because she loves me," Sara says. "I might puke. If I don't punch you in the face first."

"Not because she loves you," Brad says.

"She's not capable of loving," Darrell says.

"You can say that again," Sara says.

"As far as we know, she's taken years to find you," Brad says. "The *right* you. The one she could use for her own purposes."

"I suppose," Sara says. "But that's not very comforting."

"No?"

"Not particularly. How would you feel being traded around like a discarded piece of meat or unwanted trash."

"Fair point," Brad sighs. "But you two were close."

Sara tightens her grip on the tablecloth. "Wild, if you wanna know the truth."

"I don't think I do," Deborah says.

"And you have a passion for the stage, which I imagine is a key element of the ritual," Brad says.

Darrell nods. "Desire is always the key element to a practical conjuring."

"Brad's right, Sara." Gabriela licks her parched lips. "Look at how upset you were for not getting the promotion."

"Fuck you," Sara says.

"See?"

Sara relents. "Oh."

"And who else is Becky Stokes close to?" Brad asks.

It only takes Gabriela a blink. "Pastor Aken. Tonight's vigil."

(he rises in the wolf's mouth)

"He's always the star of his own show," Brad says. "Believe me, I know."

"She's gonna sacrifice the pastor?" Deborah says.

"She's gonna sacrifice the pastor," Brad echoes. "That's what you saw, Gabriela."

"He's not summoning Dionysus," Gabriela says. "The pastor is Becky's sacrifice."

"Exactly."

"I did see it wrong," Gabriela says.

Brad leans against the metal counter. "It appears that way."

"But what if he's not the sacrifice?" Darrell asks.

Brad thins his lips. "You know something I don't?"

Darrell shrugs. "Hard to tell."

"Guess we'll find out then," Brad says.

"So what do we do now?" Sara says.

"Talk to Pastor Aken," Brad says. "Force him to cancel tonight's vigil."

Gabriela checks her mobile. "We only have a few hours. Do you think that's enough time?"

"It'll have to be," Brad says. "At least long enough to try."

"Do you think it'll work?" Deborah asks.

"Honestly?" Brad says.

Deborah nods. So does Sara.

"No." Brad looks at Darrell. "Back here by six?"

(thank you six)

"Six," Darrell says and tips his peacap as he sneaks out the cellar door and into the abandoned mines.

"Why's he going that way?" Deborah says.

"Always best not to ask," Brad says.

"What about me?" Sara says. "I can't exactly go outside like this."

"Deborah?" Gabriela says.

"Sì?"

"Can you take Sara home so she can get dressed?"

Deborah carries a pile of bloody towels to the sink and drops them in. "What about you?"

"I'm going with Brad."

"Back by six?" Deborah says. "All of us?"

"Sì."

"I'll see you at six then."

Gabriela thanks Deborah and hugs Sara before she and Brad leave. The walk to First Baptist takes less than ten minutes.

scene 3.

Brad pulls open the enormous copper doors to the entrance on the Jefferson Street side of the building. The receptionist greets them at the front desk of the fellowship hall. She sits at a wide marble desk, has short peppery hair, and wears sunburst frames. An elegant arcadia rug (inset with a plain gold cross) sprawls across the lobby in front of her desk. From a visitor's angle, the cross is upside down. Portraits of church elders smiling in glossy black frames line the stark white walls.

"Afternoon, Sheriff."

"Afternoon," Brad says.

"You look worse for wear."

"Yes, ma'am."

"And out of uniform?"

"Mmm."

"Almost didn't recognize you without your hat." She leans across the desk. "And ain't she a sight?"

Gabriela half-grins.

"How can I help y'all today?"

"Looking for Pastor Aken," Brad says. "He in?"

"Sure is," she says. "Can I ask what this is all about? He's quite busy, as you can imagine. With the vigil tonight and all."

"Of course. Won't take but a minute."

She removes her glasses. "You sure I can't tell him what this is about? Maybe I can help y'all so we don't have to bother him. He could be deep in prayer."

"Appreciate the offer," Brad says. "But I really need to speak to the pastor directly."

"Oh." She coughs and mutters under her breath. "Must be official police business then."

"You could say that, yes."

"Well, give me a minute then. Let me see what I can do."

She disappears behind a large ebony door with rectangular tray panels. Shortly after, Pastor Aken comes through without her. Dressed in all black and as tall as Brad, the pastor radiates beauty. Gabriela squirms. Not so much because she can't control her impulses; the pastor seems to notice and relish the attraction. Lobeless ears frame a near feminine visage punctuated by a pale aquiline nose. He strokes the fine point of his beard.

"You two are a mess," he says, lilting his vowels hymn-like. "We need to get you cleaned up before our chat."

Brad glances down at the soiled mess Gabriela and he are. "Oh?"

She doesn't take her eyes off Pastor Aken.

"Gents down the hall," he says, pointing with two fingers. "Ladies, follow me."

He turns without interruption, heels clicking on the polished tiles as he avoids the welcome rug and leads Gabriela down a bare hallway with crisp grooved columns and copper trim. When he reaches the women's restroom, he whips a moist towelette out of his pocket and wipes the handle before pulling the door open for her. His teeth glisten in a soul-penetrating smile as she passes by, transfixed.

"Don't be long," he says.

"I won't."

She doesn't know if she actually spoke and can't tell where her thoughts stop and words begin. Every surface of the bathroom is as polished as the tile floor. Not a single fingerprint blemishes any of the copper fixtures. No water spots or soap drips stain the porcelain sink. Either she's the first person to use the bathroom this century or there's a custodian always on duty. The stark contrast to the backstage bathrooms at the Orpheum would sicken Pastor Aken. She'd be ashamed to let him see those. She'd have to take him home to her apartment instead where the floors are always scrubbed (pristine, really) and the bed linens always fresh and clean. In case he wants to spend the night and sleep with her. Keep her warm under the covers. Hot under the covers, really.

Gabriela shakes her head and runs the tap water until it's warm enough to rinse her face and hands. She can't let the pastor taunt her desires. Becky Stokes might run the show, but Pastor Aken's the star. Any weakness on her part, any submission whatsoever, will only reduce her ability to defend herself and put the entire town at greater risk. The ritual must be stopped. There's no other option.

She catches a glimpse of her reflection in the mirror. Her wavy black hair runs askew. Mud streaks the nooks of her ears where she scrubs again with warm water. Her black crew shirt is stretched and filthy. She tucks the hem into her jeans and dusts off as much of the dry mud as she can, littering the waxed floor. She dabs broken chunks with the tip of her finger and uses toilet paper to wipe the rest. She flushes the waste down the toilet because there isn't a single tissue or solitary piece of trash in either of the two shiny rubbish bins. Even the toilet seats sparkle. She wonders if Brad finds the men's restroom to be as immaculate. It can't possibly be. The men's dressing rooms backstage are always a disaster after a show. And the smell. *Gesù.* Nothing is worse than the stench of male body odor after two hours under stage lights. That's why she avoids the costume shop before laundry hour.

She pokes and prods her hair into place and cleans her *cornicello* with a licked finger. After a deep breath, she steps back into the hallway where Pastor Aken waits for her. He offers Gabriela a handwipe.

"For any germs you might've missed," he says.

"Oh."

She swabs both hands and pockets the towelette as she follows the pastor back to the lobby. Brad stands beside a large artificial maple tree in a rectangular copper basin. The receptionist has returned to her desk and smiles while watching her mobile. Gospel harmony emanates across the serene lobby from her phone speaker.

"Shall we?" Pastor Aken says, extending his hand toward the ebony door. Again, he avoids the arcadia rug. Maybe the gold cross is directly above the shaft in the cellar where the pastor keeps the gravity drive to the earth's core. The one Connor stole and used to gate Amanda through the portal.

She and Brad follow. The pastor offers seats in his office across from his desk in the exact same place where James Patterson sat two nights earlier when she and Brad climbed up the cellar stairs for a peek. The door remains closed. An empty spot looms on the row of animal horns on the bookshelf behind Brad. Maybe the pastor doesn't notice?

He slides the bowl. "Hard candy?"

"No, thank you," Brad says.

Gabriela keeps her eyes low and doesn't reply.

"You haven't introduced me to your delightful friend," Pastor Aken says.

"Oh, excuse me." Brad shifts to allow an introduction. "Gabriela Rossi."

"How lovely," Pastor Aken says, stroking her hand across the varnished desk. "Why haven't we met sooner?"

Gabriela shrugs.

"No doubt she has a tongue so she can speak for herself?"

(sometimes people speak because they have tongues in their mouths)

"Of course," Gabriela says.

"Brava ragazza." Pastor Aken sucks his lips. "You are Italian?"

"I am."

"So that explains the symbol."

"Hmm?"

"On your wrist," Pastor Aken says. "I couldn't help but notice the markings."

"Oh, yes. Sorry."

"The Order of the Cross." Pastor Aken struts to a lofty shelf near the door and plucks a tome. "I always found Constantine to be the most remarkable of all the Roman Emperors."

"Is that so?" Gabriela says.

"Sì." Pastor Aken switches to Italian as he thumbs through the text. "To move the seat of a vast empire and rename the conquered city for himself. Can you imagine the impudence?"

"I believe so," Gabriela says.

"You intrigue me, *mio dolce*."

"It's better to notice than to forget."

Or as *Mamma* would say, *Meglio notare che dimenticare.*

Pastor Aken returns the book and finds his chair. "Oh, my apologies, Sheriff Gleason. Would you have preferred I speak in Latin? Those rural colloquials can be tedious, I know."

"Latin?" Brad says.

"Well, surely you've learned the papal language by now."

"How's that?"

"The symbol on your forehead." Pastor Aken dabs his hand on a disinfectant wipe. "You've converted to

Catholicism to honor your precious young ward, have you not?"

Brad smirks. "Not yet."

"Well then, you might be vigilant the next time you join us for Sunday service. Keep your hat on, if you must. Most folks won't appreciate the scar. Those who recognize it for what it is, anyhow." Pastor Aken lowers his voice. "You might not know this, Sheriff, but some Baptists don't believe the Catholics are Christians."

"Is that so?" Brad says.

"I, for one, find the notion preposterous. The Vatican is a desecration, at the very least." Pastor Aken winks at Gabriela. "Please forgive me if I offend."

She answers in Italian. "I value the words as greatly as I do the speaker."

Another of *Mamma*'s aphorisms.

He ignores her slight. "But for better or worse, our church has roots there."

"Indeed," she says.

"Alas, we've grown up. And our branches spread so high and wide that we barely remember the dirt from which we sprung."

"Obviously," Gabriela says, finding his charm less potent the longer she's in his presence. Well, the more he opens his mouth, anyhow.

"Now then, Sheriff." Pastor Aken claps. "What brings you here this afternoon? As you know, I'm a busy man. We have another vigil tonight. The biggest one yet. Six lost souls."

"Gabriela works at the Orpheum," Brad says.

The pastor's eyes widen. "Well, why didn't you say so in the first place? But, of course, I should've known."

"No. How could you?" Gabriela asks.

"Every good shepherd leads his flock." Pastor Aken smirks. "Perhaps, your mother taught you something similar when you were young?"

"Perhaps," Gabriela says.

"So, what do you do at the theatre?"

"I'm the stage manager."

"Of course you are." Pastor Aken digs through the hard candy. "I would expect no less."

"We've canceled tonight's show."

"I've heard." Pastor Aken unwraps the perfect butterscotch. "Such a tragedy."

"Mmm."

"But we'll make up for it, won't we? Now you'll be free to join us and give the audience what they wish for. Like always."

Brad clears his throat. "That's why we're here."

Pastor Aken places the wrapped candy under a handwipe and chuckles. "Believe me, I appreciate the offer, but I'm confident the cast and crew will provide as much support as they possibly can."

"You don't understand," Brad says.

"Don't I?"

"No, we need you to cancel the vigil."

Pastor Aken cackles high and loud. His twisted countenance is quite repulsive as he does so. *How did I ever find him attractive?* Let alone, sexy. Lobeless ears. Hooked nose. He's hideous. A carnival freak.

"Pardon me, Miss Rossi, if I allow myself that minor indulgence."

Gabriela raises an eyebrow. "Laughter?"

"Well, yes. That might seem like an odd request to one as dainty as yourself, but mine is a serious business. I try to avoid excessive guffaws whenever possible. It's a bigger sign of weakness than tears, I'm afraid. It's why the ancients never entered comedies into their competitions, as I'm sure you're aware."

Gabriela rolls her eyes. "Of course."

"Comic relief, as the saying goes. Relief from quotidian turmoil. The mundane, as it were. The stuff of life's tragedy, *mio caro*."

"No doubt."

"A good pastor needn't search for such relief."

"So, that's a no?" Brad asks.

Pastor Aken taps the point of his beard with a solitary finger. "Allow me to show you something, Sheriff? Your beguiling friend as well."

"Sure," Brad says.

"This way then." Pastor Aken sweeps away from his desk and opens the cellar door. He flicks a light switch and trots down the stairs. Silky webs glisten in the fluorescent beams. "Forgive me for not yielding the right of way, but I thought it best for me to arrive down here ahead of you lest the machinery displease. Or, worse yet, unsettle and disturb."

Gabriela sighs. "I'm fine."

"Chivalry need not be dead, *bambina*. Even in these arduous times."

Brad clears his throat. "Gabriela can handle herself, Pastor."

"Indeed."

Gabriela grins. "But I appreciate the gesture."

"Splendid." Pastor Aken flips both palms. "You might wonder what it is you see before you."

If only he knew.

"Do tell," Brad says.

"What is it that man has desired since the beginning of his existence, my dear friends?"

Gabriela smirks. "To know how to talk to a woman without making a fool of himself?"

Brad chuckles. "Good one."

"Ahhh! You jest." Pastor Aken rubs both hands together. "Quite clever, but notice how I control my indulgences and resist tittering? That might make you reconsider the next time one of those sly quips runs across your lips."

"Sorry," Gabriela says.

"No reason to be," Pastor Aken says, circling the borehole. "The hunger to cheat death is what I meant, naturally. Immortality itself."

"Of course," Brad says.

"You don't seem so convinced, Sheriff."

"Believe me, I am."

"Then why such a nonchalant response?"

"Maybe I've cheated death enough for one go-round."

"Because of your darling wife and beloved daughter?"

"You could say that."

"Yes." Pastor Aken nods. "I do understand. You might think me brutish, Sheriff, but I certainly wish we could've had this technology prepared in time to return your departed."

"Don't do me no favors," Brad says.

(they come back wrong)

"But whom, if not you Sheriff, deserves the chance to be reunited with those you've lost?"

"If I ever see my wife and child again, Pastor, it'll be on God's terms, not yours. Or even mine. I've gone through hell once and have no intention of looking back a second time."

"How exquisite!" Pastor Aken grins. "An Orpheus reference to keep your theatrical Catholic in the loop. You truly are a considerate lawman. I don't believe the public at large would be as complacent, however. Nor should they."

"We'll see," Brad says.

"With this collider, we shall cross worlds," Pastor Aken says. "Surely, you can see the possibilities?"

"Clear as a bell," Brad says.

"You don't seem so convinced." Pastor Aken drops his shoulders. "You, Miss Rossi?"

"Oh, I think we know more than you might realize."

(you don't know what you think you know)

"How's that?"

"About time we come clean," Brad says.

Pastor Aken crosses in front of the blinking mainframe processor so he's backlit by its flashing lights. "Please do."

"We've already seen your contraption at work."

"But that's not possible." Pastor Aken wrinkles his brow. "Tonight's launch will be the first time we go public."

"Wrong," Brad says.

"Is this another of your catty jokes? The entire town will watch us bring James Patterson back from the dead. You of all people should be excited, Miss Rossi. He's your cohort."

"I don't think so," Gabriela says.

"But how can you be so obtuse?" A fly buzzes, dodging a thick spider, and lands on the shoulder of the pastor's Stygian suit. "The sheriff, I understand. But you, Miss Rossi? You're a Catholic. You might as well be a mystic. Don't you worship the saints as equal to our Lord and Savior Jesus Christ? This type of pedestrian resurrection should fit in keenly with your polluted concept of miracles."

Gabriela smacks her forehead. *"Mio Dio."*

"We believe your collider works, Pastor," Brad says. "I told you. We've seen how it operates. I just don't intend to let it happen again."

Pastor Aken shakes his head. "All our tests have been under private discerning eyes with only one singular success. James Patterson. And he will make his entrance on cue as proof of our validity. And once the town sees him, we'll bring back the others. Tommy Nolan. Connor Simmons. Your deputies, Sheriff. You wouldn't stop us from returning your colleagues?"

"You're wrong about that," Brad says.

"How about Amanda Simmons? She deserves another chance at life, doesn't she? Given the cards she was dealt. You don't blame God for her lot, do you? Those miserable lab tests made her the victim beyond the reach of our Lord. Don't you see? I can correct what God couldn't. I can be her Savior. Isn't that why I've been put here?"

"Shame on you, Pastor." Gabriela spits at his feet. "You don't get to play God."

"Wretched creature!" Pastor Aken recoils as if stung. "Foul heathen. How dare you step into my holy house and make such damning accusations!"

"You really have no idea what's going on here," Brad says. "Do you?"

"I'm starting to." Pastor Aken nods. "You've entered here as a blasphemer attempting to infect my authority with your sacrilegious Catholic witch."

"Nel culo, stronzo," Gabriela hisses.

Pastor Aken crosses both arms in front of him. "Repent, demon!"

"*Becky*, Pastor Aken." Brad sighs. "We're here because of Becky Stokes."

"Becky Stokes?" Pastor says, lowering his brow in what appears to be genuine sorrow. "Please don't tell me some evil fate has befallen our town's esteemed messenger? My heart mustn't be subjected to any further pain after this irreverent mock trial."

"How much do you really know about her?" Brad says.

"Becky?"

"Mmm."

"I know everything about her. Why?"

"Maybe I should ask it this way," Brad says. "How long have you known her?"

"For as long as she's been here, of course."

"Of course."

"What are you implying?" Pastor Aken asks.

"She's not who you think she is."

Pastor Aken chuckles. "She's exactly who I think she is, Sheriff."

"She's not."

The pastor smirks. "What makes you so confident?"

Brad tilts his head toward the shaft in the floor. "She brought you through."

"Huh?"

"Multiple times, would be my guess. Until she found the perfect you."

"This is absurd," Pastor Aken says. "Some malevolent trick on your behalf to fool me."

"I wish it were."

"But it can't be true."

"It is." Gabriela's hip bumps the locked green cooler, ruffling an unboxed artificial Christmas tree. "She plans to sacrifice you tonight."

Pastor Aken clenches his jaw. "Me?"

"Yes," Brad says. "And not to bring back Tommy Nolan or Connor Simmons or anyone else you might expect."

"No?"

"Her plans are far worse than you can imagine," Gabriela says.

"But that's not possible," Pastor Aken says. "She would never want to kill me."

"She does," Brad says.

Pastor Aken wags a slender finger. "But now it's you who doesn't understand, Sheriff."

"Me?"

"Nor you, Miss Rossi." Pastor Aken stares at the dome of tubes and cylinders. "Becky Stokes would never want to harm me."

"And why not?" Brad says.

Pastor Aken expels an unforgiving gasp of air. Gabriela catches a whiff of the sweet candy scent.

"Because I'm her father," he says.

"Her *father*?" Brad says.

"Afraid so."

"You're her father!" Gabriela gulps. "Then that gives us even more of a reason to stop you from holding tonight's vigil. Family blood will only increase the chances of her success."

"Gabriela's right," Brad says. "I can't let you go out there."

Pastor Aken scoffs. "What are you going to do, Sheriff, arrest me? Get a court order? The entire town demands my presence. You couldn't stop me if you tried. They'll hunt you down and tear you apart."

Brad brushes his mustache and glances at Gabriela. "He's right. You haven't seen one of his vigils before."

"Rock concerts?" Gabriela says.

"Quite the spectacle, yes," Pastor Aken says.

Brad folds his arms and bites his bottom lip.

"Brad?" Gabriela says.

"What's your next move?" Pastor Aken says.

"We'll add more security detail to the stage." Brad shakes his head. "The show must go on."

"Are you serious?" Gabriela says. "You're giving in that easily?"

"I don't see any other way."

Pastor Aken claps. "Well, now that we've had our little chat, I've got a revival to prepare for. Perhaps the two of you can find your way out?"

"Yeah," Brad says.

"See you after a moment," Pastor Aken says. He trots up the steps and pauses, turning once more before he leaves. "Oh, nice to have met you, Miss Rossi. Do come again, won't you?"

Once the pastor's out of earshot, Gabriela asks, "But what about Amanda?"

"We'll use our own army," Brad says without hesitating.

"What are you saying?"

Brad takes her hands. "You trust me?"

"Sì."

"Come on then."

Brad leads her up the stairs and out of Pastor Aken's office. They cross the lobby, passing directly over the arcadia rug, but don't stop to say goodbye to the bespectacled receptionist who doesn't lift her head out of her mobile, smiling as the gospel harmonies haunt the fellowship hall.

scene 4.

Darrell Mebane arrives at the bakery at a quarter of six. He stands by the espresso machine sorting arrows. Deborah and Sara sit at a table near the pastry display. Brad, wearing the tan uniform and hat he picked up at the station, watches out the front window with his arms folded. Gabriela paces the center of the dining room between rows of tables.

"Please don't make me go there, Brad," she says.

"There's no other way."

Gabriela nibbles her fingernails. "But there's gotta be."

"They'll be expecting you."

"Why? You heard Becky. They don't even know who I am."

"No." Brad shakes his head. "They didn't know you in their other worlds. They know who you are now and will expect you to join them at the vigil since the show's canceled. Same goes for Sara."

"Me?" Sara jumps out of her seat. "But you already said they tried to sacrifice me."

"Becky did," Brad says. "And if she wanted you back, she would've already come for you. Pastor Aken's her target now. He's the move."

"Maybe so," Gabriela says. "But you saw the cast and crew the same as I did. They were like zombies. What if that happens to us? What if she puts us into a trance once the ritual starts?"

"I don't think that'll happen," Brad says.

"How can you be so confident?" Gabriela says.

"Because it never happened to Sara," Brad says. "She was attacked. She wasn't under her spell. There's a difference. I don't know why or how, but it means something."

"And me?" Gabriela asks.

Darrell clears his throat. "She has no power over you."

"Darrell's right," Brad says. "That's why you weren't included from the beginning. She's working around you. She never anticipated your arrival here in Crow Creek. That plays to your advantage somehow."

"Somehow?" Sara says.

Gabriela grabs Brad's elbow. "But how?"

"I don't know, but we have no other choice."

"Fine." Gabriela stomps her foot. "We'll make our six o'clock call at the Orpheum. What about you three?"

Brad peeks out the front window again. "We'll spread out and stay in contact using our phones."

Darrell sheepishly pulls out his flip phone. "Uh, Brad?"

Brad rolls his eyes. "We'll see each other."

"But how will we know where you are or if you're okay?" Gabriela says.

"Deborah will stay close to the bakery so she can find safety if she needs it."

"Forget about it." Deborah puffs her chest. "I'm not hiding anywhere."

"You won't be hiding." Brad winks. "Just have an easy escape plan if it comes to that."

Darrell crosses to Brad and points out the window. "I'll take the high ground over Gallagher's Pub. The fire escape will get me to the roof."

"That works."

"Here." Darrell extends his leathery palm. A small object glistens in the center. "I only had time to fashion one. Use it wisely."

"Silver?"

"Mmm-hmm."

"Nine millimeter?" Brad takes the bullet and grins while narrowing his eyes. "Perfect."

"But what are *we* supposed to do?" Gabriela says.

"You'll know when the time comes," Brad says.

"But we don't have any weapons."

Darrell taps the side of her head. "This is your strongest defense."

"That's ridiculous," Gabriela says. "I want a gun or a bow and arrow like you two have."

"Have you ever shot a gun?" Brad asks.

Gabriela sighs. "No."

"Or a bow and arrow?"

Gabriela lifts her face and nods quickly. "Yes, at summer camp. At summer camp in *Valle D'Aosta*. We shot arrows and rode horses."

"I see." Brad raises an eyebrow. "And how old were you the last time you went to summer camp?"

Gabriela drops her shoulders. "Twelve."

"Cugina," Deborah says.

Darrell takes her hands and rubs her wrist. "You have strength greater than any weapon of man."

Gabriela rolls her eyes. "How boring, sir."

Brad caresses her cheek. "When the time comes, you'll know."

"So you said."

"We should get going," Sara says, circling the table. "Before you two start smacking lips."

"I guess we should then," Gabriela agrees.

"Don't worry," Sara says. "I got your back."

Gabriela smiles. "And I have yours."

"Gabriela?" Brad says as she pushes open the door.

"Yes?"

"Stay safe."

"You, too."

"I'll find you after."

"Okay."

scene 5.

Gabriela and Sara step out into the late afternoon sunshine and head down King Street toward the Orpheum. Police cruisers line the curbsides as deputies set up barricades to contain the approaching crowd. Fire trucks and emergency vehicles are parked on opposite ends of the intersection at Cardinal Avenue. Technicians dressed in black lay cables across a massive stage erected by the storefronts along Antique Row while they run sound checks and prepare for the vigil. The deck includes a sizeable drum kit and Marshall half-stacks for three guitars. Mic stands (probably SM58s) dot the apron. A portable truss system anchors enough source fours and par cans to light the intersection long after sunset. The scar circling the pavement, above where Gabriela and Brad found Sara hanging a few short hours ago, already glows in the heat. There's no sign of Becky Stokes or her camera operator.

Not yet.

A familiar face turns the corner one block shy of the theatre and greets Gabriela with a generous smile. She can't pinpoint his name.

"Miss Rossi?"

"Yes?"

"It's me, Clark Gufney."

"Clark?"

"From the other night at *Mi Despensa*, the new Mexican place on third. You were with Sheriff Gleason. I probably don't look the same on account of how I'm dressed."

Gabriela sighs. "Of course."

Sara nudges her with an elbow. "You two went to dinner and didn't tell me?"

"Oh, it weren't nothing," Clark says. "Sure hope you didn't get the wrong idea or whatnot. She and the sheriff's just passing time. He's twice her age and all. Mama always told me once a man gets to be a certain age, he can have younger lady friends because it ain't no threat no more. He's probably at that age by now. I'm still young, so we can't be friends yet. You and me, Miss Rossi. Not Mama and me. We were never friends."

"That so?" Sara says.

"Sure is."

"Good to know," Sara says.

"See, Miss Rossi?" Clark places both hands on his hips and exhales. "Told you I was gonna be a volunteer firefighter tonight. Chief Riddle gave me the green light. That's him over yonder."

Gabriela looks where Clark points and spots the burly fire chief under a yellow hat barking commands at a small group of volunteers. "I see."

Clark waves a hand to show off his baggy cargo pants and dark blue crew top. "Like my get up? Sure does beat the store apron, I think. I work at the Food Castle, in case you forgot or I never told you, but I think I did."

"Most certainly," Gabriela says.

"The suspenders are my favorite." Clark snaps his pair against his chest. "Mama always told me that only circus clowns wear suspenders, which we know ain't true because I'm wearing them right now and I ain't no clown. Of course, I can't speak for the rest of them volunteers, but they seem like they got their act together to me. For the most part."

"Seems like it."

Clark curves his hand around his mouth in a classic aside. "You like how I used that theatre metaphor, Miss Rossi? Figured you'd appreciate it."

"I did and I do."

"Gufney!" Chief Riddle shouts from across the street. "Get over here with the rest of us. You're late!"

Clark scratches his head and checks his mobile. "Hmm. I got five of six."

"If you're on time, you're late," Gabriela says, repeating the lesson *Mamma* taught her before she left home.

"Gufney!" Chief Riddle hollers again.

"Guess that's my cue." Clark chuckles. "I'm full of theatre jargon today, ain't I? Nice seeing you again, Miss Rossi. And nice meeting you, Miss Rossi's friend. Sorry I didn't catch your name. Maybe next time."

Clark trots across the street and falls in line as Gabriela and Sara continue toward the Orpheum.

"He's quite the chatterbox," Sara says.

Gabriela nods. "I think he's adorable."

"Me, too."

scene 6.

When Gabriela and Sara enter the theatre, the cast and crew of *Bury Me in Autumn*, along with the front office staff and volunteers, fill the lobby, buzzing with energy. They don't wear the catatonic faces Gabriela witnessed under the street. Would they have finished the ritual this morning if she and Brad hadn't shown up with Becky? Did Becky intend to leave Sara strung up all day until tonight's vigil, bleeding her? Was it a type of pre-ritual ceremony? Certainly the Ancient Greeks and Romans combined multiple sacraments in their efforts to satisfy their gods, especially Dionysus. Maybe they were doing a dry run? Like onstage. A rehearsal of sorts.

It doesn't matter. The script has changed now. The objective remains the same but with brand new tactics.

Joe Cox, the technical director, approaches first, wavy blonde hair squeezed under a black ballcap. He sucks a toothpick.

"Shame about Connor," he says.

"Awful," Gabriela says.

The blank stare on Sara's face tells Gabriela that she genuinely has no idea about what happened when Connor tried to use the collider to cure his sister. Only that they're both dead. How could she know? She was fighting her own battle against Becky. Fighting and losing.

"Yeah," Sara says.

"You know how?" Joe asks.

"Not really," Gabriela lies.

"I heard it was a murder-suicide."

"That so?"

"Uh-huh. Crew's been talking. Involved his sister somehow."

"Wasn't she sick?" Sara asks.

Gabriela can't tell if she's asking truthfully or playing along. Sometimes, technicians make better actors than performers. The difference is that they live in the shadows. They're the ninjas of theatre.

Joe nods and snags his toothpick. "Crippled. Multiple sclerosis, I believe. She couldn't walk near the end. Must've been painful for Connor to watch her suffer that way."

"Yeah," Sara says.

"And to kill his sister before taking his own life." Joe rears his lips. "Rough."

"Oh," Gabriela says. "That's what you think? That Connor killed his sister? Not the other way around?"

"Well, yeah," Joe says. "If it were a murder-suicide, like they say. Isn't that what you think? That Connor killed his sister. You know, to end her suffering."

"Yeah." Gabriela shakes her head. "Of course. Probably."

"After the police showed up, he probably had no choice but to kill himself so he didn't have to spend the rest of his life in prison for what he done." Joe replaces the toothpick in his mouth. "I don't blame him."

Doug Cousins, the head carpenter, sidles up to Gabriela. She doesn't believe she's ever seen him not wearing denim overalls, even in the tunnels this morning. Now, he cleans up in dark slacks and an Oxford, pencil still tucked behind an ear.

"Ciao."

"Talking about Connor?" he asks.

"Uh-huh," Joe says.

"I don't blame him neither. I wouldn't let my sister suffer that way. Poor girl. What was it? Cystic fibrosis, I believe. Diabetes?"

Joe nods. "Something like that, yeah. One of those."

"He done the right thing."

"Sure did."

"Must've taken those deputies out before he killed himself," Doug says.

"Eh?" Gabriela says.

"Oh, you didn't hear about the two officers that died?" Joe asks.

"No, I heard," Gabriela says. "I just didn't think Connor was responsible."

"Well, he must've been," Doug says.

"Yeah, you're right." Joe shoves his hands deep into the pockets of his overalls. "How else would they have died?"

Gabriela shrugs. "I don't know."

"There was a big brawl onstage," Doug says.

"I heard they knocked over the scenery," Joe says.

"Connor probably got a hold of one of their guns and shot them both."

"It's the only way he could've done what he did." Doug folds his arms. "Pretty bad-ass, if you ask me."

Deanna Flowers, the props mistress, joins the conversation, right arm twitching at the shoulder. *Some mistakes belong to nature.* "Y'all talking about Connor?"

Joe nods. "Mmm."

"He's a hero for what he done," Deanna says, yelping deep in her throat.

"Say that again," Doug says.

"Pastor Aken's doing right by him," Joe says. "That's for sure."

"For sure," Deanna says. "Vigil's gonna be the most beautiful one yet."

"Can't wait," Doug says.

Deanna squeezes Gabriela's shoulder, steadying herself. "You're in for a real treat."

"Mmm."

"Your first one and all." Deanna's squeeze becomes a full-blown hug. "I'm so happy you're here with us."

"So am I."

Sara scans the lobby. While wrapped in Deanna's embrace, Gabriela follows Sara's gaze to the yellow police tape that seals the auditorium doors. A deputy she doesn't recognize guards the doors, cradling an assault rifle across his chest.

"Hey, you guys seen King?" Sara asks.

Joe adjusts his cap. "Who?"

"King." Sara wriggles her nose stud. "You know, King *Boggs*?"

Doug glances sideways at Sara. "You feeling okay?"

"Huh?"

"I don't know nobody by that name," Joe says.

"Me neither," Doug says, shifting a pencil from one ear to another.

"What do you mean you don't know King?" Sara says.

Gabriela breaks Deanna's grip and makes a slashing motion across her throat. "Sara."

"King Boggs!" Sara says. "Our master electrician?"

"Nope," Joe says.

"Connor's been running all the electrical work for this show," Doug says. "Well, he was."

"Yeah," Joe says. "Ain't had a master electrician at the Orpheum since forever. Not that I can remember, anyhow."

Doug laughs. "Yeah, if we did, maybe they'd fix that channel up in the catwalks that keeps burning out all our source fours."

"Are you fucking crazy?" Sara spreads her fingers across her unibrow. "Deanna? You remember King, right?"

"Sara, please," Gabriela says.

"Deanna?" Sara says.

Deanna shakes her head. It's not a twitch.

"The fuck?" Sara shouts.

Gabriela tosses an arm over Sara's shoulder and walks her away from the group. The others shrug, drifting off into other conversations.

"The fuck was all that about?"

"They don't know who King is," Gabriela says.

"Obviously. Why not?"

"Becky took him away."

Sara pushes back until they stop walking. "What did you say?"

"Becky took him away."

"No, I heard what you said." Sara pokes her tongue into the side of her mouth. "How is that even possible?"

Gabriela sighs. "It's not easy to explain."

"Wait a minute." Sara wipes her lips with the back of her hand. "You know what? I don't even wanna know. I don't even wanna fucking know right now. This is all too crazy."

"I don't blame you," Gabriela says. "It's about to get worse."

"No doubt," Sara says. "I need a fucking cigarette."

The crowd in the theatre waits another ten minutes before Matt Leath, the director, offers a formal welcome. Standing on a concrete step by the box office, he's dressed in a charcoal suit and bowtie.

"Our company has really taken it on the chin this week," he says.

"That's one way of putting it," Cedric Young, the cast member who's not quite as funny offstage, says.

A few of the cast and crew mutter, cocking their heads like crows or chickens.

"Nobody here today, or elsewhere, could've imagined what we've been through," Matt says, eyes swelling. "I can't tell you how much it means to me to be a part of this family."

"Love you, Matt," Ed Brown, the oldest cast member, says.

Matt winks. "Love you."

"You're the best," Tariq shouts, picking his high hair.

"Thank you." Matt thumps his chest with a closed fist. "Means so much."

"We couldn't do this without you," Bianca Whitt shouts while standing beside Ed, her onstage husband.

"Thank you now," Matt says. "Everyone of y'all. And I promise we'll figure out how to get this production back on its feet one way or another. We've worked too hard and too long to let it disappear after one preview. We didn't come here to die."

Tariq pockets his comb. "Truth."

"So, let's stay strong for one another now. Let's keep it together for those we've lost. Y'all hear me?"

The crowd murmurs and nods, clapping hands and slapping thighs.

"For Tommy and Connor and Mr. Patterson," Matt says.

"And King," Sara mutters.

"They're our brothers," Matt says. "And we won't ever forget them or what they meant to this show."

"Never," Gabriela whispers.

"I'm no preacher, y'all," Matt says. "But can we please take a moment to hold hands and bow our heads?"

The group huddles in silence at the foot of the step, awaiting Matt's prayer. Gabriela keeps her eyes open. So does Sara.

"Dear Heavenly Father," Matt says. "We know you always keep watch over us, in good times and in bad. We ask that you pick up the pieces of this show, of our lives, and guide us on the path to salvation as only you can do. Thy will be done, Lord. Please give us the courage to live honest lives in these trying days. Inject us with your Holy Spirit so that we might be a light to others and keep us on the righteous path to your kingdom. We ask you this in Jesus's name. Your only son who died on the cross for our sins. Amen."

The crowd bursts into an echo of amens, wrapping one another in tight hugs. Gabriela and Sara skirt the perimeter, joining the invocation so they don't look suspicious.

"The fuck?" Gabriela says, once they're out of range.

Sara smirks. "You ain't seen nothing yet."

"The vigil?"

"Mmm-hmm. I've been to every single one. You'll think it's Easter morning."

"That bad?"

Sara nods. "In Golgotha."

(we call her the skull*)*

"Gesù."

"Pretty much."

scene 7.

Once the cast and crew disperses, Matt leads the processional out of the Orpheum and down King Street toward the intersection at Cardinal Avenue where the deputies open the barricades so they can fill the reserved space outlined by the white scar around the pavement. The entire downtown is packed with locals, old and young alike. The sea of mourners extends down every side street. They rumble in anticipation, shouting and stomping their feet as they wait for the vigil to begin. Curly and two deputies Gabriela doesn't recognize guard the foot of the makeshift platforms, outfitted in tan fatigues. Assault rifles cross their chests. Brad patrols across the street from the bakery, tipping his hat when Gabriela makes eye contact. Becky Stokes stands on the stage at the far right mic behind a podium, wearing a clean black jumpsuit with a sparkling gold belt and reviewing flashcards. Her camera operator waits in front of Antique Row where the rest of the press pool gathers under a canvas tent. Becky grabs the mic as several musicians take the stage behind her, prepping their gear.

"Good evening, ladies and gentlemen," Becky says. The crowd quiets. "Thank you for joining us tonight in what promises to be a wonderful celebration of the lives of the friends and family we lost this week."

A squeal of feedback interrupts her opening remarks. The onlookers flinch, glancing at one another and covering their ears for brief solace. A sound technician at a console in front of Gallagher's Pub makes the necessary adjustments. Above him on the roof, Gabriela spots the faint image of Darrell Mebane, bow poised, beside a clunky HVAC system.

"I can't tell you what an honor it is to represent the people of Holt County as we welcome Satyr to the stage," Becky says.

The crowd cheers while Becky twists flowing red locks around an ear. Gabriela winces at the irony of the band name. *Satyr.* The woodland companions of Dionysus that tried to rape Eurydice and caused her death. Orpheus's wife. *Satyr.* If the modern word *satire* doesn't come from it, it should. *Satira,* in Italian. Exposing people for what they really are.

"Their inspirational songs will help unite us as we try to heal from our recent suffering," Becky continues. "Ladies and gentlemen, please give it up for Crow Creek's very own rocker, Dante Rose!"

The entire street bounces as screams erupt when he takes the stage dressed in blue jeans and a Black Sabbath concert shirt. He hasn't changed much since the debut album Gabriela bought a decade ago, except that he's put on a few pounds around the midsection and looks more like the modern Vince Neil than the vibrant Kurt Cobain he once was. After strapping on an electric guitar, he snarls, curling his lip and grinning at the center mic.

"Thank you so much," he says. "You're beautiful. Thank you."

The fans holler and chant his name, drowning another dose of feedback, before Dante interrupts them. Gabriela scowls. If Cherlynne Lawrence were at console and Gabriela were calling the cues, they wouldn't be having these technical glitches.

"Thank you," Dante says. "Thank you, really. I'm so excited to be here tonight with my brand new band. Let's hear it for Satyr, ladies and gentleman. What do you say?"

The crowd screams again, this time chanting the name of the band for twenty seconds until Dante stops them with brief introductions of all the players. The streets sway under the setting sun, enthralled faces dipping in and out of brick shadows. Gabriela can't help but jump as she and Sara link elbows, caught in the fervor. As much as she doesn't understand the paradox of (or approve of) holding a concert to celebrate the dead, she can't wait to absorb the music. Heavy metal reminds her of her childhood in *Châtillon* where blossoming garage bands shook her neighborhood late every summer afternoon as the brooding sounds of Metallica and Pantera drifted over from the States before *Papà* died and harmless youthful rebellion seemed as dangerous as life could get in her mundane Italian village.

Dante clears his throat and grips the microphone. "Here's a song I wrote about three years ago, y'all. Been playing it at every gig since. Seems appropriate for tonight. Hug your loved ones. You never know what might happen or why. Here's a number called 'Lost Children.' Thank you. We're Satyr."

Dante steps away from the mic and points at his lead guitarist, who pounds three power chords in a dark tritone before the remaining bandmates sweep in with screeching rhythms and an ominous backbeat. Dante swivels his hips as he returns to the mic and launches the opening verses. By the time he gets to the chorus, he plucks the mic off the stand and aims it at the audience so they can sing with him in unison.

"Will they run? Can they see inside me?"

The band moves through the bridge and into a thunderous solo that transitions from the bass guitar into a vibrant lead. They shake their long sweaty hair and flex their wiry muscles under sleeveless novelty tees. Screaming fans charge the police barricades, but they're held out by armed deputies, leaving the cast and crew of *Bury Me in Autumn* to rally by themselves in the ringed intersection.

Crouching, Dante belts the final verse. "The blood on my hands is just a reflection of loved ones I've lost on the way. Waiting for darkness, I suffer in silence, holding hands with children who pray."

The fans rejoin the chorus as Satyr rocks through the coda and strikes the final note, elevated by delirious applause.

Dante spits and bows. "Thank you. Thank you so much. Really, y'all are amazing. We love you. Thank you."

The fans explode with shouts and stomp their feet, demanding an encore.

"I don't know." Dante shrugs, almost frowning. "What do you say, Ms. Stokes? Think we can give them one more?"

Cheers vibrate the street and shake the downtown buildings.

Becky flashes a scripted grin and raises her mic. "Of course you can."

More cheers and shouts. Gabriela catches herself stomping and clapping but can't stop. Sara smiles and thrusts devil horns above her head with both fists. Red eyes swirl a response in the empty windows above the stage across downtown. Maybe they reflect the sea of enchanted faces flooding the streets below.

"Thank you so much," Dante says. "Really, this is amazing. I love y'all. Thank you."

"No, thank *you*," Becky says. She still hasn't reset her mic.

Dante readjusts his fingers on his SM58. "Y'all ready to rock one more time?"

The fans go wild outside the barricades, along all the store fronts and down the side streets. Jumping, screaming, pushing, shoving. Even inside the ceremonial circle, the cast and crew rage, quaking to the vibe. Gabriela and Sara bump shoulders as the fever rises.

"I can't hear you," Dante says, grinning.

Another uproar louder than all the rest. Gabriela can't hear her own screams.

Dante smiles. "Here's a song we wrote especially for tonight. It's called 'See the Light'. Hope you enjoy it."

The lead guitarist races into the opening sequence of hard driving chords hounded by a thumping bass and striking beat. The musicians go airborne, flying off the stage and kicking their feet while Dante warbles through two verses about finding your way home no matter how far you roam and knowing where to go when you think you don't know. Gabriela's heart flutters, lifting with the lyrics and soaring with the rhythm. Sara leaps beside her, banging her head and tossing sweaty hair.

Dante belts the chorus. "See the light. See the light. Everybody see the light. You don't know where you're going or where you been. You can't see the world for the shape it's in. See the light. See the light. Everybody see the light. You won't be alone when all hope is gone. Follow your dreams and it won't take long. See the light. See the light. Everybody see the light."

The song ends to thunderous applause. Gabriela can't catch her breath. She sees the light. She's found her way. She's finally home. The rest of the world fades away. Her troubles. All her sorrow. This week's brutal deaths. Becky Stokes. Amanda Simmons. Ralph Delacourt. His wicked sister Peggy. They don't exist. They don't fucking exist anymore because all she has right now is this moment in the crossroads where straight and crooked lines connect. Nothing else matters. Not *Mamma*. Not *Papà*. Both distant memories in a life she never lived in *Valle D'Aosta*, a place she hasn't seen. Not even Deborah can find her here. Or Brad. The love they kindled this week wanes in comparison to the passion she feels as Satyr clears the stage and the cast and crew circle, united with the entire front office staff and volunteers, holding hands for Pastor Aken's arrival. He rises tonight in the wolf's mouth in Crow Creek. That's all Gabriela cares about.

scene 8.

"Thank you, Dante," Becky says as she crosses to the center of the stage, holding her wireless mic. "What an amazing performer, ladies and gentlemen! Simply incredible. They couldn't have done a better job if I'd asked them to, really. I know you're all warmed up now, aren't you? You're all exactly where the pastor needs you. So, why wait any longer? Haven't y'all waited long enough? Ladies and gentlemen, put your hands together and give a great big shout out for First Baptist's one and only, Ethan Aken!"

Once Becky finishes, the pastor duckwalks across the stage in his double breasted suit and sable cloak. The rim of his blood red John Bull tophat tilts down so the crow feathers point up out of the copper band. The matching ascot dangles around his neck. He does a quick shuffle in his polished Giorgio Brutini boots and snatches the center mic. He's more gorgeous than Gabriela's ever seen. How perfectly his lobeless ears frame his flowing black mane and his prominent nose accents his flawless caramel skin. She hopes her future children have those same features. She hopes Pastor Aken would bless her by fathering those children.

"How about Dante Rose?" he shouts. "Y'all believe that guy? What a band! Let's give it up one more time for Satyr, good people of Crow Creek."

The crowd gives it up. Gabriela gives it up so hard.

"He's fucking beautiful," Sara yells over the cheers.

"Right?"

"I would so fuck him right now," Sara says.

The bruise on Gabriela's wrist burns. The weight of the *cornicello* strains her neck. She doesn't care. "So would I."

"Becky could watch for all I care!"

Pastor Aken scans the downtown streets. "That's right, good people. Come closer. Let me see your eyes. You have so much to be excited about. You're giving me the power of our Lord and Savior Jesus Christ, aren't you? That's right. Closer, yes. Move in real tight. I'm so happy y'all are here tonight to join in our celebration. We were lost, but now we're found. Like Dante said, right? We see the light, don't we, y'all?"

The cast and crew huddle as the pastor prowls the stage above them. He rotates on a polished heel, pale skin flickering until bones and muscles meld under a flash of copper scales.

"We see the light," he repeats.

The stage lights dim, shifting colors from a bright wash to a muted blue. Except for the adoring faces around her, the rest of the crowd retreats. They make noise and respond on cue, but they're distant. An invisible audience. Gabriela doesn't need to hear or see them anymore. All she has is Pastor Aken now. He's who they all have.

Hands slip into hers on either side as the circle tightens. Maybe one belongs to Sara, but she's not even sure of her presence anymore. A pulse rising from beneath the pavement cushions her. She feels herself bouncing. Her head bobs and weaves. A low hum escapes her lips as she breathes the earth's heartbeat.

"Y'all ready for a miracle?" Pastor Aken says. "Do y'all believe? Well, you better because the world you know ain't never gonna be the same. Not after tonight. Not after the miracles we're all about to witness. I want y'all to take a look down at these good people right here at my feet. Can you do that for me? Y'all see what I'm seeing? These good people have lost their brothers this week. They've lost their *brothers*, do you hear me talking to you? But, you know what? It doesn't have to stay that way. Not if you believe. Not if you believe in the power of Jesus. What do you hear when I say the word *God*, good people? What do you hear? Hmm? You know what I hear? Can you feel it? That's right. When I hear the word *God*, it makes me feel so good."

Fog fills the circle as the earth rolls under Gabriela's feet. She caroms and chants, fighting to keep her eyes open. The hum invades her mind, capturing her thoughts and transcending her to a higher plane. To someplace so far away she can't be reached and doesn't want to be. The lights dim again so the intersection is almost impossible to see even while she oscillates in the center with the rest of the cast of *Bury Me in Autumn*. The world undulates now. No longer lit by the source fours hanging on the portable gridiron. Their energy glows, igniting the scar in the street that surrounds the intersection. The pavement expands and contracts beneath her boots. A brilliant light emerges in the center, glistening in the mist. Gabriela strains her eyes so they won't close, but all she wants to do is rest her head and go to sleep because it's so wonderful out here under the stars. She can hum and bounce and chant with all her friends by her side and let the Holy Spirit wash over her as it shines like God's beacon through the unending shaft of light and hypnotic song.

(see the light see the light everybody see the light)

Gabriela bites her lip and tugs Sara's hand but can't break loose.

Not the light. Not the light. Don't see the light.

(you don't know what you think you know)

Her eyelids flutter as sleep beckons. Deep beautiful sleep where Pastor Aken waits, spreading his arms so he can envelope her in his silky cloak and hold her forever. The world spins. The world but not the world. Gabriela flows with the motion as James Patterson rises within the light in the center of the circle.

(not james not james not james)

“DO YOU BELIEVE?” Pastor Aken shouts. “Do you believe what can God do?”

(not god not god not god)

Gabriela pulls her hand again but can’t free herself. Her eyes quiver. The earth sways, rocking and tilting to the rhythm of the chanting crowd. She adores the refrain. Wants nothing more than to continue. Wishes she could hum and buzz and jump and testify until the rapture because God is good. He’s so *fucking* good. Connor Simmons rises within the light and joins Mr. Patterson. The two smile and embrace.

(not connor not connor not connor)

“I’ll ask you again, good people. DO YOU BELIEVE?”

“I believe,” Gabriela whispers.

Tommy Nolan rises. All three together now. Embracing in the middle where they belong. Back from the dead like Pastor Aken promised because he works miracles, and Becky Stokes is his daughter and she works miracles, too. Sweet, beautiful miracles. The type that makes birds rejoice. Not nasty crows like the ones that watch from atop the Orpheum marquee. Fetching cardinals, red like Becky’s sultry mane. They sing *cher, cher, cher* and *wit-chew, wit-chew, wit-chew* and *purty, purty, purty*.

(not tommy not tommy not tommy)

i know it’s not tommy but i don’t care because it can’t be tommy but it doesn’t matter because tommy’s dead and this not-tommy isn’t real he’s fake because i saw him hanging from the fucking lineset when i was with brad he’s dead and BRAD BRAD BRAD please fucking help me because i’m trapped i’m a fucking zombie right now like the ones we saw down in the tunnels and OH MY GOD i can’t breathe and that’s a fucking manhole cover that’s not the holy spirit that’s a fucking sewer grating they climbed out of the fucking sewer that’s not a miracle that’s not a miracle because pull (tiri) *pull* (tiri) *pull* (tiri) *PULL* (TIRI) *PULL* (TIRI) *PULL* (TIRI) —

scene 9.

Gabriela heaves, tearing her hands free and breaking the circle. Her eyes snap open. Sara screams. The cast and crew collide, toppling like dominoes on the unsteady pavement.

"Stay calm, y'all," Pastor Aken says onstage. "Please stay calm."

"Please, everyone," Becky says, retreating to her podium. "Don't be alarmed. This is under control."

"The fuck?" Sara says.

Gabriela scans the street in front of the bakery but can't find Brad. "I don't know."

A fire truck slides across Cardinal Avenue and crashes into a storefront, spraying glass. Gabriela shields her face. The crowd roars and starts to run. Chief Riddle barks commands at his volunteer crew while they duck for cover. An emergency vehicle ricochets off the end of Antique Row before landing on its side, squishing an elderly woman unable to clear its path. More panic. The press pool abandons their slumping tent and heads for safety. Curly and the two deputies hoist their assault rifles as they rush toward the police barricades.

Peggy Delacourt, waddling down King Street, struts into view on her knotted cane. The paunchy Sheriff Osbourne creeps behind her, clutching a handkerchief to his lips. Amanda Simmons floats between the two. She rotates both hands, lightning dances, and a police cruiser lifts off the street. The car spins, under Amanda's control, and smacks a flickering street lamp. The pole teeters before crashing into a rooftop a few doors down from the bakery.

Gabriela can't see Brad or Deborah.

"Didn't think you'd start the show without us, did you?" Peggy cackles as she dips her chin below the starched collar of her polyester business suit. "We do hope we're not too late to enjoy the fun."

Matt Leath hollers for the theatre group to make a break for the Orpheum. Keeping low, they snake around the corner of the stage, clinging to the storefronts as they evacuate. Sara starts to follow and signals for Gabriela to join the line near Becky's feet while she and Pastor Aken continue to beg the crowd to stay calm.

Gabriela shakes her head. "I can't."

"Why not?"

"Brad."

"Are you fucking kidding me?"

"I can't leave him."

Sara grunts and scoots closer to Gabriela. "Fine."

An arrow whizzes down from Gallagher's Pub and catches Peggy in the left shoulder. She writhes and falls to her knees, snapping the makeshift shaft. Blood squirts from the wound. She screams. Another arrow sails, piercing her gut.

"Osbourne!" Peggy lunges forward to the pavement, vomiting blood. "You filthy bastard! Help me! Help me! I'm stuck like a Carolina pig."

Osbourne pockets his handkerchief and flounders to her side, gasping. Another arrow cuts the air and hits his right forearm. Shouting, he waves his hand and unholsters his gun, but loses his grip. The revolver slips to the street. Curly rotates on his heels, dropping to a knee, and raises his assault weapon toward Gallagher's Pub. The other two deputies dart for cover behind the capsized police cruiser, the tips of their weapons visible above the inverted bonnet as Brad sprints to the edge of the intersection.

"Gabriela!" Brad aims his pistol. "Get down. GET DOWN NOW!"

Gabriela grabs Sara's wrist and yanks her to the asphalt. Sara curses as they topple. Before Brad can squeeze the trigger, Amanda curls her fists, generating a fireball that she launches at Gallagher's. The pub explodes. Collapsing brick and broken glass shower the fleeing crowd and knock Brad into the portable sound booth. The technicians dive, bracing against the steel girders as the entire console buckles.

"Brad!" Gabriela screams, but Sara pins her near the discarded manhole cover as Amanda launches another fireball at the overturned police cruiser where two deputies spray assault rifles at her. The corner of King Street and Cardinal Avenue ignites, torching the last of the fleeing theatre members and incinerating the cloth awnings. Gabriela cranes her neck and watches Anika and Terese, the wardrobe crew, douse one another's flames. Assistant director Paula Bradley, blackened by the blast, staggers across Cardinal Avenue. She's jostled by a group of teenagers scampering away from the explosion and knocked to the ground. They stomp on her while they run until she's motionless.

Sara rolls off Gabriela. "We gotta get out of here."

"Okay." Gabriela climbs to her knees. "Okay, let's move."

"The bakery," Sara says.

Gabriela nods and swings her hips low so she can crouch while they escape. As they pass the stage apron, Becky pulls a crooked horn out from under the podium and pounces Pastor Aken. She drives him to the deck, twirling the horn and ramming the sharp edge deep into the side of his neck. Blood jets above his ascot. He claws at his throat, knocking off his tophat. Becky hitches as she shapeshifts. Her face contorts until her snout elongates. Jagged teeth split her gums, oozing thick saliva. She arches her back as thick ginger fur sprouts. She snarls and stabs again, piercing the pastor's heart before she completes the transformation. Pastor Aken slumps, the erect horn in his chest a misshapen tusk. Becky-wolf springs off her hindquarters and chomps the wounded pastor until he keels into a broadening pool of his own blood. The blood washes the stage floor and spills to the street where the pavement cracks and forms a stream to the open manhole. As soon as it flows off the edge and into the shaft, the earth shakes. The circular scar surrounding the intersection ignites like a fuse. The pavement swells into a concrete bubble before dropping. Gabriela and Sara roll toward the center as the entire crossroads sinks. Sara screams and kicks but can't stop her roll. Gabriela stretches her arm and catches Sara's hand as they slide down together. The pavement tears loose. Buildings crash above the fading horizon.

"Help!" Sara shouts.

"I won't let go."

Gabriela tucks her knees so she can roll to her back and dig her feet into the collapsing asphalt. Sara swings wide, but above, where fresh red clay covers the slopes below the fractured street as it sinks. The ground quakes again. The broken pavement rises and falls until a bright light bursts from the center. The wolf's mouth opens.

scene 10.

Maenads emerge. Becky's sisters. Large, nasty wolves with thick gray fur. They gnash their teeth, fangs dripping. Gabriela loses count after six rise, leaping out of the flattened sinkhole until they disappear on the streets above. As soon as the last wolf soars, the light vanquishes.

Where's Dionysus? Why didn't he come through?

Gabriela slips off the edge of the shaft toward the abyss. Unable to keep her footing, she strains her neck when Sara squeezes her hand, clutching a loose fragment of the street to keep them both from sliding down. A large explosion shocks the streets above where more people scream and buildings crumble.

Gabriela exhales, unable to pull herself out of the shaft where her feet dangle under the earth. "Let me fall."

"What?" Sara says.

Gabriela repeats herself but in Italian. *"Lasciami cadere."*

"Gabriela?"

"I don't belong here. I never have. Maybe there's some other world that wants me."

"Fuck that."

Sara heaves, but her hand slips so only their fingers stay hooked.

"Let me fall."

"NO!"

Sara slides off the broken pavement. They lose contact for a split second, Gabriela plummets, but Sara's able to readjust her grip and link their hands as she catches the ledge of another chunk of concrete.

"If you fall, I fall."

"You don't have to do this." Gabriela glances at the world above — the starlit circle of sky innocent of the devastation on the streets of Crow Creek. "Save yourself."

More explosions above. Growling. Screaming. Rapid shots fired.

Sara flinches and shakes her head. "You fall, I fall."

"Sara, please."

"What's it gonna be?"

A youthful face, almost grinning under his yellow helmet, appears above Sara's shoulders on the street beyond the sinkhole. "Miss Rossi?"

"Clark?"

"Uh-huh. Thought I saw you take a tumble. Need a hand?"

"Please!" Sara yells.

"Mama always says you gotta help your friends. We're friends, ain't we? Huh? I mean, I know we only met each other two times, Miss Rossi, unless you count whenever you come through my line at the Food Castle even though you don't talk to me regular. Maybe it's cause I'm married or whatnot. Your funny accent sure does tickle me, though. I work the express lane, in case y'all forgot."

"Clark!" Gabriela shouts.

"We're friends, ain't we?"

Gabriela sighs. Tears swell. "Yes, Clark. We're friends."

"Here." Clark flattens his chest and drops his arm off the serrated edge of King Street, reaching for Sara with his gloved hand. "Maybe you can tell me your name, ma'am? Since we're friends and all, and I'm about to save your life."

"Sara. I'm Sara!"

Clark pulls. Gabriela lifts herself out of the shaft until her boots scrape the splintered pavement at the bottom of the sinkhole.

"Done this once before," Clark says as they scramble upward. "Not the whole sinkhole rescue. Saved lives, though."

"That so?" Sara says.

"At the store, mmm-hmm. Took a bullet for Dante Rose once. A bunch of others, too."

Sara reaches the surface and continues pulling Gabriela until Clark clasps her free hand.

"You must be something special," Sara says.

Clark winks. "Mama always says so."

scene 11.

Gabriela slides over the last meter of red clay and scoots away from the sinkhole. Clark motions for the two of them to stay down and hustles along Cardinal Avenue to tend to a long-legged pregnant woman holding hands with a toddler. He guides them safely through the broken glass door of a real estate agency. Gabriela scans the intersection for Brad but can't find him through the isolated flames or damaged buildings.

Most of downtown has cleared. Tossed vehicles line King Street up to *Mi Despensa* at the corner of Third. Maenads devour the partial remains of Amanda's victims. Another chews on Peggy Delacourt, stretching a bloody tendon loose from her thigh before leaping to Sheriff Osbourne and ravaging his chest and throat.

Across from Antique Row, Chief Riddle swings his axe but misses a wolf that corners him against a brick façade. The wolf recoils and springs, clamping the fire chief's shoulder in her massive jaws. He loses his helmet. Blood splashes the billboard, drenching posters that advertise an upcoming Labor Day block party on Ninth Street by the railroad tracks. By where Brad must've lost his daughter. Chief Riddle flourishes his axe but can't land a blow. The wolf drives him against the building. Under the carnage, Gabriela hears a distinctive crack and shudders as the fire chief goes limp.

Gabriela spins away.

Opposite the toppled platform assembled for tonight's vigil, Curly aims his assault rifle at an approaching wolf as she prowls over a splintered police barricade. He backs away into the street, firing. The wolf shakes off the quick rounds and squats before she leaps, biting Curly's forearm. The automatic weapon swings wildly, spraying what remains of a fire engine. Sara pulls Gabriela to the sidewalk several doors down from the bakery as Curly screams. They dip beneath the leaning street lamp. The Maenad swoops. Curly's brown hair shakes loose from his black tactical cap as the wolf wrenches the powerless deputy's head off his shoulders.

"Do you see Brad?" Gabriela asks, lowering her eyes.

Sara points. "There!"

Across the street, Amanda traps Brad against a steel girder supporting the portable sound booth. She rotates her hands, but before she can launch a strike, Darrell Mebane leaps down from the sunken roof of Gallagher's Pub and lands on her back. They wrestle each other to the pavement and roll toward the sinkhole.

Gabriela slips out from under the post. She takes two steps off the curb, and Becky jumps in her path. Not Becky-wolf. Becky Stokes. Editor-in-Chief of the Crow Creek *Sentinel*. Pastor Aken's daughter. Red hair cascades in the evening breeze.

scene 12.

Sara bumps Gabriela from behind.

Becky grins. "Going so soon?"

"They need our help!" Gabriela shouts.

Becky glances toward Darrell and Amanda as they grapple on the asphalt. "Do they now?"

"Amanda," Gabriela says.

"Amanda Simmons?" Becky peaks an eyebrow. "That's Amanda? Connor's sister? She came through just now? *How?*"

Gabriela shakes her head. "Not just now, no."

"No?"

Amanda pins Darrell's arms and stops their roll, plunging sharp teeth into his collarbone as Brad tackles her. They teeter on the edge of the sinkhole.

"*Per favore!*"

"When?" Becky asks.

"This week."

"Please don't tell me." Becky scratches her chin. "Please don't tell me that's what happened under the stage last night?"

Gabriela nods. Blood gushes between Darrell's fingers as he staggers to his feet, clutching the puncture wounds and clasping the portable steel frame for support. Amanda grabs Brad's throat.

"But how?"

"Connor. He thought he could help her. Make her better. *Mossa! Sposta ora!*"

"That fool."

Becky whirls on her heels and signals the Maenads. Jowls dripping, they converge on Amanda. Nine in total. Amanda tosses Brad against an overturned ambulance. He collapses in a heap as she levitates above the sinkhole out of the reach of snapping jaws. Maenads growl, circling the intersection along where the scar ran before the street dropped. With Sara behind her, Gabriela moves to help Brad and Darrell, but Becky thrusts her hand across her chest.

"Not so fast, Miss Rossi," she says. "Let's see how this plays out."

Amanda grins and wiggles a finger. The toppled street lamp vibrates and starts to swing. Gabriela and Sara duck as it cruises by.

"Bitch!" Becky hollers and leaps over the post.

The street lamp slices the air across King Street, scattering a handful of Maenads, before it crashes into the remnants of Gallagher's Pub. The wolves snarl and gnash their teeth, reforming their positions around the circle. Two on the opposite side spring, front claws splayed. Amanda whips around in time to jab one with a closed fist, but the second scratches her shoulder, slicing open the pale flesh beneath her lazy summer dress.

Amanda screams, loses her balance in midair, and tumbles into the sinkhole. The two wolves land on top of her, chomping and scraping as all three slide toward the center. Amanda twists over a fractured portion of the pavement and kicks a Maenad in the chest. The wolf squeals and leaps over the borehole, digging savagely in the red clay with her brawny hindlegs to lift herself up to the street. Amanda grabs the remaining Maenad as they both spiral toward the center shaft. She spins over the wolf's back and slides her forearm across the shoulders, snapping its neck. The Maenad goes limp.

Becky shrieks, cueing more wolves to attack. Three jump on Amanda as she rises from the sinkhole. Two bite high on the collarbone. The third Maenad scores a direct hit on her hip. The wolves thrash while they plummet, growling and tearing her flesh, until Amanda folds her arms across her chest. With a quick jerk, she throws her hands wide, tossing the three Maenads against separate ridges of the broken street. They yelp and scramble for footing as they skid in the clay, balancing on fractured asphalt.

Amanda doesn't relent. She balls her clenched fists. Sparks ignite around her knuckles. She rotates above the open shaft, casting fireballs at each of the trapped wolves. They shriek as they burn, unable to escape the streaking flames.

Becky lets out a high-pitched whistle that makes Gabriela and Sara cover their ears. The last of the Maenads sprint around the circle as Amanda floats overhead, landing near the flattened press tent. The Maenads transform, shifting from their wolf bodies to human form. The five barefoot women wear gallant silk robes with gold sashes. Sabers, hilts laced with sculptured grape leaves, dangle off each hip. Long wavy manes, streaked white and gray, drift across their shoulders. No two have the same color eyes, each a different shade of green. Drawing their swords, they march toward Amanda as she approaches.

Becky commands her sisters to charge. The ancient gladiators thrust and slice steel. Amanda dodges, wailing as several blades hit. One of the Maenads missteps after striking and trips over a broken barricade less than five meters from where Gabriela and Sara stand off the curb. Amanda straddles the stumbling ravisher and digs sharp fingernails into her ribs as she leans over and bites her neck, draining sacred blood.

(she bit her and drank her blood she bit her and drank her blood)

Maenads strike with their swords. Lightning courses through Amanda's body as she feeds, rendering their constant blows useless. Unharmed, she tosses the desiccated Maenad aside and strides around the sinkhole.

"Enough!" Becky hollers.

The ancient priestesses withdraw, coupling behind Becky on either side as she charges Amanda full speed. They collide in front of the leveled platforms, screaming and slashing.

"We should run," Gabriela says.

"Where?" Sara says.

Gabriela tosses her chin toward Brad and Darrell, who nurse their wounds near the twisted sound booth.

"Quel modo."

They start to run. Maenads grab Sara. She screams but can't break loose.

"Sara!"

scene 13.

Pale spindly hands reach for Gabriela but miss as she tumbles into a somersault. When she springs to her feet, Wanda Butler and her deformed son Helms hobble out unscathed from behind a delivery van parked by the bakery. Sara shouts for help as Maenads wrangle her near the sinkhole, each clasping a wrist and ankle.

Wanda pokes a slinking worm under her cheek. "She's here for us."

"Eh?"

"Amanda."

"For you?"

"For all of us."

Helms grunts, solitary eye widening. "All of us."

"She knows our pain."

"Ms. Butler?" Gabriela says.

"She came to us in a dream."

Gabriela shakes her head. "You shouldn't be here, Ms. Butler."

"Life is what the dead dream of."

"No, you need to go. Get back to the library. Anywhere. Just go!"

"We can't leave," Wanda says.

"Why not?"

"We belong here."

"Che cosa?"

Wanda simpers. "You don't."

Helms jabs his crooked cane into Gabriela's gut, knocking the wind out of her. She bends over gasping as the giant cripple hooks a nailless hand under her shoulders and sweeps her off the ground. Helms flexes his arm, tightening his grip while Gabriela flops.

Maenads drag Sara to the edge of the sinkhole while Amanda and Becky exchange blows. They draw their swords. Amanda shifts her weight, driving Becky to the pavement. Becky squawks and flails her arms. She flashes, exposing bones and muscles until she transforms. Becky-wolf snarls, snapping at Amanda. Maenads raise their blades after Amanda cups her hands, gathering energy. Lightning flashes. Flames erupt, scorching Becky-wolf. She roars and leaps, snatching Amanda's hands in her jaws and dousing the fireball. They spiral into the sinkhole, thrashing and sliding down the red clay. The Maenads drop Sara and dive into the gaping pit. They swing their sabres at Amanda until she separates from Becky-wolf and pushes free, breaking her fall. She disarms a rasping Maenad and levitates out of the sinkhole, landing curbside with her back to Gabriela. Becky-wolf springs off her haunches and bounces to King Street. She morphs and faces Amanda. The other Maenads ascend to her side, eyes swirling.

scene 14.

"You shouldn't have come through," Becky says.

Amanda curls her lip. "You don't know the worlds I've seen."

"This one belongs to me."

Becky snaps her fingers. The closest Maenad tosses her a sword. Amanda recoils, clapping her palms until fire burns, but Becky moves to Sara. She lifts the blade.

"NO!" Gabriela shouts as she struggles to break free from Helms.

Brad stumbles away from the broken sound booth, raising his firearm. He gives no warning and fires, hitting Becky in her chest. She falls to her knees and drops the sword. Blood spreads across her black jumpsuit. A pitiful wheeze escapes her wrinkled lips.

"Now you'll never stop her," Becky whispers. She tilts and plummets face first toward the sinkhole, leaking a trail of blood that trickles off the edge.

Amanda rotates toward Brad as Maenads scurry to attack from all sides, swinging their blades. Amanda balls her fists and generates sparks. Brad pulls his trigger, shooting Amanda in her shoulder. She staggers. Lightning dances off her fingertips. Gabriela kicks and screams, but the bolt sizzles overhead.

Deborah steps out from behind the delivery van, brandishing a stainless steel *espresso* pot. "Never stop her? We'll see about that."

Deborah shoves Wanda Butler and cracks the pot over her son's head. Helms lunges forward, dropping Gabriela. The ground rumbles when she hits the asphalt. She rolls to her side and lifts her chin as Becky's blood circles the open shaft and drains into the earth.

He rises in the wolf's mouth and comes for her wearing flowing robes and an ivory wreath that rests upon golden tresses draping across his delicate shoulders. He comes for her into her world from across the universe holding his thyrsos, *a timber staff wrapped in grape leaves and topped with a furrowed pine cone. He comes for her from the stars where there are no stars and straight and crooked lines connect like electrical currents. He tells her don't look back. Don't look back at the world you left behind. The world you left behind will always be your past. If you look back now, you'll never escape. He takes her hands and starts to dance. His hands are soft but strong. His hands remind her of* Papà's *hands. He tells her* Papà *sees her always.* Papà *loves her always. He swings her into his arms. He swings her into his arms and thanks her for the song she sings for him. The song she sings for him* in bocca al lupo. *He tells her not to be afraid of the wolf's mouth because she doesn't settle, she conquers. She breaks legs. She breaks legs and moves forward when he comes for her so they can dance together to the song she sings for him. She spins and whirls free to embrace the world she's in. She spins and whirls because the earth drops, shifts, pauses, and skips. She only needs to move forward and push. Push through from this world to the next. Push into the wolf's mouth. Sing the song and push. Push,* mio caro. *Push (*Spingi)*! Push (*Spingi)*! PUSH (*SPINGI)*!*

Gabriela jumps to her feet and rushes forward, raising her hands.

(when the time comes you'll know)

She pushes Amanda in the chest while sword-wielding Maenads thrust their weapons. The ground trembles again. Amanda topples over the ridge and into the sinkhole. The wolf closes its mouth and swallows, chomping with long sharp teeth. Amanda disappears in the beacon of light, shrieking. The Maenads chase after her and are gone.

scene 15.

Becky staggers to her feet and runs, flickering as she transforms. She slams into the collapsed stage and changes back. She can't hold her shape. Gabriela chases after her. Brad calls for Gabriela to wait, but she hops to the stage without looking back and pulls the goat horn out of the dead pastor's chest before racing along the sidewalk.

Becky leaps over a tossed vehicle and loses her balance, hitting the pavement. She flashes, sprouting thick fur, and squeals. Her human shape returns. An arrow soars over Gabriela's shoulder and hits Becky in the hip before she crosses the street near the Orpheum. She stumbles and skids on her knees until Gabriela jumps on her back, clawing and thrusting the goat horn.

"Puttana del cazzo!" Gabriela shrieks. *"Ti ucciderò!"*

Becky bucks, tossing Gabriela before she can penetrate. She loses her grip on the horn. It slides down the street and teeters on the edge of a storm drain.

"NO!"

Gabriela crawls along the asphalt as Becky hops the curb, but Brad is right behind them and grabs the horn. He pulls Gabriela to her feet. They don't exchange words, only brushing fingertips before Gabriela seizes the horn and sprints to the theatre. Becky crouches, hindlegs extending as she crashes through the front window.

Shattered glass showers King Street.

Gabriela pushes the doors open and rushes into the lobby where Becky-wolf growls, saliva dripping off her snout in glossy tendrils. She clenches and snaps her jaws, severing Cedric Young's arm below the elbow. Blood sprays nearby cast members as they leap over the ticket counter to avoid Becky-wolf's gnashing teeth. Cedric waves his chewed stump while he screams, streaking the picture frames and artificial cherry blossoms with squirts of blood.

Becky returns and falls to her knees. Gabriela pounces, kicking and screaming as they crash through the auditorium doors and roll down the aisle. Becky cracks her head against a row of seats and swings her legs until they both come to an abrupt stop. Gabriela slips her arm under Becky's shoulders and scoots her hips. She presses the edge of the horn against Becky's exposed throat. Becky flickers. Her breasts hitch in uneven gasps. Blood from the bullet wound soaks her chest. Darrell's silver-tipped arrow flexes in her hip as she thrashes in Gabriela's arms.

"You'll never find your place," Becky hisses.

"I'm right here," Gabriela says.

Becky arches her back. "You're not."

Gabriela drives the sharp horn into her neck. Thick blood swells around the base as Becky sheds Gabriela and shifts. Becky-wolf roars, bolting over the back of the seats and reaching the unlit stage where she collapses and transforms. Her chest heaves as she spins to her back and tugs at the horn with both hands until it springs loose. Bloods spews from the gaping wound. Her eyes flutter. Gabriela stumbles to her feet and scampers down the aisle.

She climbs the steps, crosses the stage, and picks up the horn. She straddles Becky while she pants and spits.

"I crossed worlds and couldn't find you," Becky whispers.

"You didn't know where to look."

Becky shakes her head. "You're a ghost."

"Vivo nell'ombra."

I live in the shadows.

Half-grinning, Gabriela drops to her knees and raises the horn above her head. The stage lights flicker. Floorboards moan. A slight breeze pushes the drapes. They ripple and wave. This time, there is no apparition. Her *cornicello* glows. The Chi-Rho burns. Gabriela plunges the horn into Becky's chest, clasping the shaft between her outstretched fingers and lowering her weight. A solitary breath escapes Becky's thin lips. Gabriela steps off the stage and falls into Brad's open arms as he trots down the dark aisle.

scene 16.

When Gabriela and Brad return to the sinkhole, it's Darrell Mebane who cracks the first joke about the coffee pot, not Sara.

"You really beaned him."

"Very funny," Deborah says as she helps Wanda Butler to her feet.

Shrugging, Darrell relaxes the arrow he has trained on Wanda and her son. He slings his bow across his shoulder and hands Brad his sheriff's hat from off the pavement.

"We didn't mean to hurt no one," Wanda says.

"I know," Gabriela says.

Helms pulls himself up on his cane, solitary pupil dilating.

Wanda hooks her son's elbow. "We've suffered for so long."

"Maybe we all need to do a better job of accepting who we are," Brad says.

Sara dusts off her jeans. “And where we are.”

“Ain’t gonna arrest us then?” Helms asks.

Brad tilts the tip of his hat over matted hair. “For what?”

Helms waves his cane at Gabriela. “For what I done.”

“Best I can tell.” Brad bites his lip. “Y’all were trying to keep her out of harm’s way.”

“Thank you, Sheriff,” Wanda says.

“Besides . . .” Brad scans the downtown streets where fires wane in the damaged buildings. “. . . we got more pressing issues.”

“Didn’t Frank say they rebuilt his hometown after a nuclear bomb exploded?” Gabriela says.

“Nuclear bomb?” Deborah asks.

Gabriela nods. “*Sì.*”

“The one that killed JFK, remember?” Brad says, grinning.

Wanda clears her throat. “I believe it were the mafia that killed JFK.”

Brad raises an eyebrow. “Ma’am?”

“Y’all take care now.” Wanda winks and strolls down Cardinal Avenue toward the library.

Helms staggers beside her on his crooked walking stick.

“Guess I’ll go see how the bakery held up,” Deborah says, peeking around the delivery van.

Gabriela hugs her. Deborah’s hands slip down to her wrists where she traces the Chi-Rho.

“I wonder if you’ll get one yourself now,” Gabriela says.

“Me?” Deborah chuckles. “Why?”

“For saving our lives.”

Deborah shakes her head. “You did that, *mio caro*. All I did was a hit a crippled man with a coffee pot.”

Darrell grins. “And you think I’m the one telling jokes.”

"Well, if all else fails, my Elvis tattoo will keep me safe," Deborah says.

"Cugina?"

Deborah smiles and waves as she crosses the street. "Goodnight, Gaby."

Darrell gathers his shirt sleeve and mops up the last of the blood that runs from the bite marks on his collarbone. After saying goodbye, he picks up his quiver and a few homespun arrows before he disappears behind the ruins of Gallagher's Pub. Maybe he knows of another underground tunnel that leads home to Houndstooth. Hopefully one without a direct pipeline to the earth's core because no matter how far the straight and crooked lines connect, Gabriela believes he's had enough of gravity drives and magnetic fields. They all have. In this world and the rest.

Brad takes her hand. "Told you."

"Told me what?" Gabriela says.

"You'd know when."

Gabriela smirks. "How about you coming in at the last minute?"

Brad shrugs and hugs her.

"The bullet Darrell gave you must've helped."

"Sure did," he says, lips brushing her cheek.

Sara coughs into her fist. "Sheriff, if you don't kiss her, I will."

"I thought you said I wasn't your type," Gabriela says.

Sara rolls her eyes. "You never know."

"It's my accent, isn't it?"

"It's kinda sexy, yeah."

Brad laughs but doesn't kiss her. "We're taking it slow."

"That so?" Sara asks.

Brad nods.

Gabriela grabs her phone. "I should call *Mamma*."

"Now?" Brad says, raising an eyebrow.

Gabriela slides her arms around his hips. "You're correct, sir. The timing would be awful."

"You got that right."

"I don't know what I'd tell her anyhow."

"No?"

"No." Gabriela scratches her chin. "But I know what she'd say."

"Oh, really?" Brad smiles. "What's that?"

Gabriela smirks. "I'll keep that one to myself."

She unclasps the *cornicello* and hooks the gold chain around Brad's broad neck. He examines the tiny red horn.

"What's this for?"

"You're gonna need it more than I will."

"Oh, really?"

"Sì."

Flashing lights and blaring sirens permeate the night sky over Crow Creek. Maybe from as far away as Queensboro. Or even from Winter in Frank's world. Together, Gabriela and Brad walk away from the sinkhole. His strong grip might go right through her shimmering hand if he squeezes any tighter. But it doesn't. He doesn't. For now. Sara Cooper follows, laughing.

We all have our own angels.

Acknowledgments

I've wanted to write about a haunted theatre since college. Fourteen years ago, I drafted *The Last Bitter Hour*, an unpublished novel about a drama teacher whose marriage fails after the loss of a child. The seeds of this haunted theatre were first planted in that book, especially the character of Ralph Delacourt. The theatre in downtown Crow Creek is a cross between the movie theatre where I worked while attending Northern Arizona University and the Hanes Theatre where I currently work. The late Bobbette Falcone, house manager at the Orpheum in Flagstaff, is the direct inspiration for Ralph's younger sister Peggy (some of you might also remember her as Margaret Ganis in *Queensboro*). This book belongs to Bobbette as much as anyone. I love and miss you.

This novel never would've happened, however, if I hadn't met Fabiola Fassi this past summer while my wife and I vacationed in Paris to celebrate our twentieth anniversary. For years, I struggled to find an inspiration for the main character of my story, but from the moment I first saw Fabiola smiling behind the front desk at the Citadines along the Seine River, I knew she was who I was looking for. She doesn't work in theatre, but she's an Italian expatriate with all the qualities I desired in a protagonist. Bright and beautiful, she doesn't settle. And yes, she even has a short temper (watch out, Tristan!). I'm also grateful for the many questions she answered about Italian culture and language. As an American of Italian descent, the instant kinship I felt with Fabiola fuels this book.

I shared the manuscript with many readers before publishing. Alexis, Rico, Danny, Mom, and Stephanie, thanks for your feedback. Also, thanks to Frank Cammarata for his constant support. I hope he catches The Beatles reference and laughs. Thank you to Coventry Kessler for editing and Kanaxa for the amazing cover design. Thank you to all the folks at Gold Avenue Press, especially Ethan Aken, who continues to work his magic on the page.

Often, I'm asked to categorize my writing. I dabble in horror, thriller, mystery, science fiction, romance, action/adventure, and literary fiction. This is a work of speculative fiction, I suppose, because it encompasses all those genres. I hope you enjoyed reading it as much as I did writing it. Please leave reviews on my Amazon or Goodreads page. I'd love to hear from you.

About the Author

Thomas Drago is an English and drama teacher living in North Carolina. He graduated from Northern Arizona University in Flagstaff. He is married and has two children. He enjoys going to the movies, listening to rock and roll, and watching baseball. His favorite number is 29. Family legends trace his ancestry to Vlad Dracula. *Maybe.*

A member of the Horror Writers Association, American Theatre Group, and American Film Institute, Drago has published over a dozen stories in various literary magazines and anthologies. He's the author of the *Crow Creek* Trilogy, *Raised on Rock*, and *See Nike Run*, all available from Gold Avenue Press.

Visit www.tsdrago.com for more information.

Printed in Great Britain
by Amazon